Dogwood Plantation

By

Carrie Fancett Pagels

© 2020 Carrie Fancett Pagels

Ebook ISBN: 978-0-9971908-7-8

Paperback ISBN: 978-0-9971908-8-5

Cover Design by Carpe Librum

Editor: Narielle Living

Hearts Overcoming Press

Published in the United States of America

Dedication

To
My Dear Friend, Tara Mulcahey—Always a blessing, always loved

&

In Memory of
Cornelia "Neil" Brous—I looked for you all those years, Neil,
and you were already Home, dancing among the stars

Endorsements for Carrie Fancett Pagels' Books

Dogwood Plantation

"Award-winning Carrie Fancett Pagels' tender story will tug at your heart-strings. Her expert weaving of love, loss, faith, and romance is sure to draw you in and keep you turning the pages until the satisfying conclusion of this sweet historical romance."

Bestselling Author Debbie Lynne Costello

"Although not a light read, 'Dogwood Plantation' is an award-worthy, beautifully written, romantic tale for historical fiction fans everywhere! Bravo, Carrie Fancett Pagels!"

Reader/Reviewer Diana L. Flowers

My Heart Belongs on Mackinac Island

"An enchanting love story, *My Heart Belongs on Mackinac Island* is sprinkled with warmth and humor, grace and faith. A highly enjoyable read!"

Tamera Alexander, USA TodayBestselling & Christy Award-winner

"Pagels may become one of your favorite authors when you journey to Mackinac Island with her memorable, captivating characters. Maude's Mooring is a beautiful love story with an ending that will sweep you off your feet."

Romantic Times, A Top Pick

"Carrie Fancett Pagels' talent for weaving historical detail into descriptive prose will pull you in and won't let you stop. . ."

Suzanne Woods Fisher, Bestselling Author

Return to Shirley Plantation

"As a historical novelist, Carrie Fancett Pagels has a voice you can trust. Woven into the story are rich historical details and cultural nuances that enriched the story and deepened the characters."

Jocelyn Green, Christy Award-winner

"Truly rich historical research, a wonderful plot twist, and the clean and crisp pen of Carrie Fancett Pagels; a tender tale of love amidst the clash of the blue and the gray."

Julie Lessman, Award-winning & Bestselling Author

Saving the Marquise's Daughter

"With a unique European-American setting and characters inspired by a true historical couple, *Saving the Marquise's Daughter* has romance and suspense in spades. . ."

Laura Frantz, Christy Award-winning author

". . .a lovely endearing story!"

Sarah E. Ladd, Bestselling author

Mercy in a Red Cloak

"The reader will feel immersed in a rich telling of two hearts reluctant to hope for a future together, where honor, sacrifice and duty would trump notions of romantic longing."

Kathleen L. Maher, Award-winning Author

Tea Shop Folly

"*Tea Shop Folly* by Carrie Fancett Pagels is a sweet romance story that readers will thoroughly enjoy. I would recommend this story to readers that enjoy historical fiction, romance."

Singing Librarian Books

The Steeplechase

"*The Steeplechase* is a fast-paced, well-rounded love story rich in historical detail that enriches the plot, rather than overwhelms it. I cared about the characters, too."

Susanne Dietze, Award-winning & Bestselling Author

The Christy Lumber Camp Series

The Fruitcake Challenge

"The author clearly did her research on this story—the details are spot on. It is a lovely, sweet story that quickly pulled me into the culture of an 1800's lumber camp....and made me want to stay."

Serena B. Miller, Award Winning & Bestselling Author

The Lumberjacks' Ball

"Carrie Fancett Pagels has a charming way with words. Her stories are written with engaging characters, and her descriptive style of writing allows the reader to become fully immersed in the storyline."

Jen Turano, Bestselling Author

Lilacs for Juliana

"The aroma of fresh cut pines, flapjacks, and lilacs permeate the readers' senses in this heartwarming tale of a young woman's sacrifices, hopes, and dreams—and an unpretentious hero who sets those dreams in motion!"

Diana L. Flowers, Reviewer

Prologue

Dogwood Plantation, Charles City, Virginia, 1814

Cornelia trembled in the open door to the plantation owner's bedroom, a handkerchief covering her face—not much protection against yellow fever, but something. Lee Williams lay still, paler even than Pa had been at the end, in what was about to become the Dogwood Plantation owner's deathbed.

"Miss Gill?" Lee's voice rasped like a dry corn husk scraping over a tabletop.

Her knees shook harder. She daren't go any closer. She had to think of her brother Andy, too. This pestilence spread quickly. Far too fast. She'd been summoned home from her position in Richmond only two weeks earlier but it felt nigh unto an eternity with all the illness and death. "Yes?"

"Bring... Carter... home."

Her hands joined her knees in wobbling. If she made this promise, could she live with the consequences? And how would she get to Williamsburg? She couldn't go on her own.

"Promise... me." Lee struggled to lift his head and began to cough.

1

She took two steps back, ready to run. Someone grabbed her shoulders and she jumped, the handkerchief slipping from her face.

"Miss Gill, you got to go get Master Carter." Nemi, the Williams's house servant quickly released Cornelia's shoulders. "Sorry miss, but you was about to knock me plum over." The heavyset woman took two steps back and lingered in the hallway.

Cornelia covered her nose and mouth again and faced the dying man, who was only a handful of years older than herself. Lee's wife, Anne, had died only days earlier. Their passel of children were isolated in their rooms upstairs.

"I will go and get Carter." Never mind that her own father's body had just been laid in the grave, with no funeral and no words spoken over him other than what she and Andy had managed. What a terrible way to part with their beloved father.

Charles City County had never seen the likes of this outbreak of yellow fever. The epidemic struck in all classes from the wealthy, like Lee Williams and his wife, to the poor slaves in the fields. She'd pick herself up and do what she had to do.

"Nell?" Lee's light eyes pleaded. "It... wasn't me... who sent you away—"

Cornelia raised her hand, her eyes moistening at his use of her childhood nickname. "Shush, it doesn't matter now."

Lee closed his eyes.

All that pain of separation from Carter. Even with the hateful things Roger Williams had said to justify sending Cornelia to Richmond and away from Pa and Andy, this horrific yellow fever epidemic and the war had wiped away her anger at Lee and Carter's father. And anger at Carter, too, if she was honest with herself. She had to let that go. Those little boys upstairs had no one to care for them now except their Uncle Carter, and she'd not let them down.

Nemi shuffled forward. "Missy, you tell them schoonermen to take you to get Master Carter."

Yes, she could have those men who were well enough to sail take her to Williamsburg. She nodded.

"I'll take care of Master Lee." Nemi shook her head slowly. "Won't be long now, Missy."

Cornelia drew in a shuddering breath. *God, grant Lee a peaceful passage home to Glory.* "Do you think the people outside of Charles City know about the contagion? Will they even allow us in port?"

"The good Lord gonna help you bring Master Carter home, I know it in my heart." Nemi pressed a hand to her chest.

As Cornelia turned to go, she could have sworn she heard Nemi mutter, "He need to be here for you, too." Had she imagined it or had the servant spoken aloud the same words in Cornelia's own heart?

She left the house and hurried across the vast Dogwood Plantation property to her own home. She'd get her brother, Andy, and begin their journey. She didn't want to leave the grieving twelve-year-old alone.

As she approached the cabin, she spied her brother. "Oh, Andy, Mr. Lee is at the end."

Andy swiped at his tears.

"We need to go to the college and I'll need you to go into the men's dormitory for me to get Carter."

"Will you tell him, though?"

"Yes." She didn't need that duty to land on her brother's young shoulders.

They went into the cabin and gathered a few items to carry with them and headed out. An icy cloak of despair settled on Cornelia's shoulders as she and her brother hurried past the Catalpas that edged their property, the tall tree's frond-like leaves waving. The same breeze that stirred the branches should hurry them toward Williamsburg once they were aboard the schooner—and would place her face-to-face with the one man she couldn't bear to see again.

Chapter One

Williamsburg, Virginia

How did one plan a future when their world was crumbling around them? Carter Williams tapped his fingers on the long wooden table that served as his and his peers' desk, trying to focus his attention on his law professor. The College of William & Mary Law School had been his original plan—but that plan had included Cornelia Gill at his side. Since he'd spied her in Richmond several weeks earlier, her visage preoccupied his reveries.

He exhaled a slow breath. Instead of daydreaming of what he'd lost, he should spend time praying for his former crewmates still at sea.

Beside him, Ethan Randolph whispered, "Have you heard that Bonaparte might soon be defeated?"

Carter nodded in what he hoped was an imperceptible manner. He didn't need their professor shouting at him today.

Randolph, like Carter, had mustered out of the Navy with injuries. "More British ships will thus be directed toward America."

He dipped his chin slightly. He was tempted to pray about that, but God didn't seem to listen anymore. Carter rubbed his painful leg, a daily reminder of his own fragile humanity. Twenty-six years old and now disabled from serving his country. The ornamental sword they'd awarded him for bravery had done nothing to erase his injury.

Professor Danner's robes brushed Carter's arm as he strode down the aisle and paused at the next row. "Here at the second oldest institution of learning in our country, we expect law students to remain awake." A loud thwack echoed in Carter's ears. His classmate, John Bradley, awoke and jerked upright.

A sharp rap on the wooden dais startled him. "Mr. Williams, what think you of the act proposed to reexamine the Kentucky and Virginia borders?"

An image of Daniel Scott dragging Nell across the Virginia line and into Kentucky surged through Carter's mind. Sweat beaded on his forehead. "I believe it shall go forward and the Indians will be stripped of their rights." 'Twas Professor Danner's own position. If Carter were to become an elected official, how would he persuade his constituents that such a move was morally wrong?

"An intelligent fellow you are, Mr. Williams." The professor's bushy eyebrows rose as he sought other quarry. "Mr. Randolph, could you elaborate on why Mr. Williams might be correct?"

What was Daniel Scott's position on the matter? He'd left long ago and was rumored to practice law in Kentucky. What an irony that would be if the miscreant was now involved in politics. Carter unclenched the fists that he hadn't realized he had made. Daniel no longer posed a threat to himself or to Nell. Yellow fever was the Williams's enemy, not Daniel. Thankfully, his brother and sister-in-law wrote that they were taking appropriate precautions to protect themselves from the scourge.

Professor Danner pointed his stick at Bradley who seemed quite alert now. "Give us some air in here."

Bradley rose and opened the mullioned windows on the far wall, allowing a crisp breeze to enter. As a gust filled the first-floor room, students smacked their hands down on their papers, securing them to their desks. Carter spied a dray lurching down Richmond Road adjacent to the building. He stiffened, certain he recognized the wagon as his family's own, kept at the Williamsburg wharf. He struggled to stand, hoping to secure a better look.

Yellow-blonde curls—like corn silk—identified the driver as Cornelia Gill. A boy sat beside Nell—her brother, Andrew. His heart beat the staccato sound of a drumbeat readying for war. *Oh Lord, please no.*

5

Someone in Carter's family must have died. He could fathom no other reason for her arrival. She wouldn't have sailed down from Charles City were it not for some grave purpose.

His legs trembling, he clutched the desktop and lowered himself into his seat.

"Mr. Williams? Are you unwell?' Professor Danner held his Elmwood pointer high.

"'Tis my family's conveyance on the road." Carter loosened his collar and dabbed at the perspiration on his forehead. "I must beg your leave, sir."

"Indeed, you may have it." Professor Danner gestured to the door.

"Thank you, sir." Carter steadied his cane beneath him and grabbed his haversack before easing down the aisle and out the door. *God, if you have given me another burden to bear, I shan't speak to you at all. Ever.*

Cornelia sat erect, the reins in her hands, as she and her brother, Andy, drove past the institution of higher learning. Students strolled across the campus, some toting books. They seemed to have no cares in the world other than their studies. No knowledge of the devastation taking place only twenty-five miles away.

Andy's eyes widened as he took in the fine brick structures, the wide windows, and the College of William and Mary's manicured green lawns. "I sure wish I could go to college someday."

If only Andy could pursue a gentleman's education. "Well, I suppose if God wants you here, He'll make a way." Only a miracle would place her brother in school on this campus, or in any other school. She wanted to remind him of how lucky he was to be alive, how fortunate they both were, but she bit her tongue. They'd lost his mother too soon and now their father, too.

Thank God she had learned to drive a dray around the Williams's property when she was younger. Those rusty skills came back when this was all she was offered at the wharf. The Williams's carriage was at the college already. Cornelia turned the wagon into the roundabout then took the road leading to Carter's lodgings on Jamestown Road.

"That's the place." Andy pointed to a tall brick building near the road.

She spied a turnout for carriages nearby. "I'll pull in over there." Cornelia maneuvered the wagon up the lane. "When I tie off, I'll manage the horses' care."

"Yes'm."

She pulled next to the curb and the hitching post. Gathering her skirts around her, Cornelia lowered herself to the mucky ground. If only she had a pair of pattens attached to her shoe bottoms that would spare her boots.

"Andy, the manager at the carriage stables said Carter's room is on the bottom floor, the first door to the right. The college placed him in a room closest to the entrance because of his leg injury."

Andy jumped down. "Yes'm." Before she could give further instructions, Andy ran across the lawn to the building.

Well-dressed students walked by, a few casting quick glances her way. In a short while, she'd be physically closer to Carter than she'd been in years. He'd been so much of her life at Dogwood Plantation that being separated from him had been like having half of her body ripped off. He'd been her best friend and she—his. That was until his father had decided that Cornelia, as his plantation manager's daughter, was far beneath his son's station. Roger Williams sent her off to school in Richmond when she was fifteen, convincing Pa that she'd get schooling that would help her one day if she was to become a governess or some other such vocation which Mr. Williams had deemed "appropriate" for her. She'd foolishly wished that the education she'd received would make her more worthy of Carter and that Mr. Williams was really trying to help her. But all he wanted was for her to be far away from Dogwood Plantation. Tears threatened.

Before long, she spied her brother heading toward the dray. Andy led a contingent of young men, arms full of trunks and crates. Andy's head was bent, his eyes red. How terrible it was that he had been tasked with explaining why they'd come to bring Carter home. And no doubt he'd explained their own loss. She blinked back tears—she would not break down.

At the queue's end, a dark-haired figure hobbled, tugging on his waistcoat periodically as it crept up with his awkward gait. Her heart leapt—ached—as she yearned for what could have been. If only God would remove the love she still harbored for him. His buff breeches immaculate, his coat superfine wool, Carter cut quite a figure, even with his pronounced limp.

"Right here, miss?" The first young man, a stocky fellow, paused with a leather chest filling his arms. When she nodded, he hoisted Carter's trunk into the wagon-bed.

A redheaded student with a navy and yellow waistcoat hopped up on their conveyance and stared at Cornelia. "I say, aren't you that renowned horse-breeder Davis's wife?"

No, she was not her Cousin Hayes' wife. Heat suffused her cheeks. She ignored the impertinent young man and pointed to where the trunks and crates should be stacked. He and the other young men followed suit.

"Cornelia?" She jumped when Carter's fingers gently squeezed her shoulder. Warmth flooded through her as she turned to look into his deep brown eyes. Sadness flickered there, chilling her response.

"Nell, please tell me Andy is wrong." His low voice begged her to lie. "Surely Lee isn't dead and Anne, too?"

This close to him, having his distraught face only inches from her own, Cornelia fought her tears. "I'm so sorry, Carter."

"And your father, as well?" Tenderness rolled over every word.

Like an overripe melon dropped in the field and bursting, all the pent-up emotion Cornelia had been holding back released. Carter wrapped his arm around her, the other supporting him on his cane. He patted her back, his hand firm. This was right, this was where she belonged, this man was supposed to have been her world. Still was, if she trusted her heart.

Warm breath grazed her ear. "No one told me, or I would've been there for you."

Would he have? She sniffed and pulled away, wiping her tears. Since he'd returned from the war, he'd not even sent her a letter and yet here she was accepting his embrace. Over his shoulder, Cornelia saw a slender lady dressed in a high-waisted Empire-style blue dress. The dark-haired beauty's refined features knit together as though Cornelia had gotten the pick of the litter while she'd been given naught.

Casting a disdainful look, the woman opened her lacy parasol and stepped into the sun. Carter pivoted to see whom Cornelia was gawking at. "Sally?"

"What is going on here, Carter?" Ice dripped from her carefully enunciated words. Clearly, she believed she had rights to Carter's affections.

Cornelia cringed, embarrassment heating her cheeks.

Her old friend pulled himself up to his full height, a hand's width taller than the last time they'd stood so close.

Andy moved toward the young lady, his arms akimbo as though assessing her. "His brother died, Miss, and his sister-in-law, too. He's coming home with us."

Sally's gaze slowly raked over Andy from head to toe. A muscle twitched near her pert nose.

A tall fellow passed between her brother and the young lady, heading toward Cornelia and Carter. He fixed his gaze first on the mass of blond hair blowing about her face. From his starched cravat to his expensive polished boots, the young man reeked of old money. Why wasn't he at war? Had he paid someone else to take his place? Likely many of these young bucks had done so.

"Surely you remember me?" The blond stranger stepped closer to her and audaciously squeezed her hand.

"No." She jerked her hand free, knocking elbows with Carter.

"Are you not Miss Gill? The daughter of Dogwood Plantation's manager?"

"My father died." But she wasn't wearing any kind of mourning gown—how could anyone have known? She'd need to make up some mourning clothes soon for both herself and Andy. "And Lee Williams died today."

Cornelia heard the young man's intake of breath. "Please accept my condolences. Both of you. I'm sorry Carter, I..."

She kept her eyes downcast as Carter stepped away to join the brunette.

Carter's voice carried the short distance. "Sally, I planned to send you word."

Glancing up, she spied Carter grasping Sally's hands. Cornelia's heart compressed and she averted her gaze again.

The blond gentleman shifted uneasily before Cornelia. "Pardon me. Obviously, you don't remember me—I'm Chase Scott."

9

Daniel's brother? Cornelia jerked her head up, giving her a momentary sensation of spinning.

"Forgive me if I've alarmed you." Something in his dark eyes belied the apology.

She needed to sit down as dizziness threatened to topple her.

"Come sit." Chase guided her to a bench, seating himself next to her closer than was proper.

The redheaded fellow joined the two, staring down at them. "Do you know each other?"

Cornelia scooted a bit away.

One corner of Chase's wide mouth turned up, as he gazed fixedly on Carter and Sally. "My brother offered to wed Miss Gill and take her to Kentucky with him." His cool words chilled her. "But she refused him."

"I was not yet fifteen." *And in love with Carter.*

"You're not fifteen anymore." Dark eyes roamed over her. "And he's home. Who knows what might happen."

Home? Daniel Scott had returned? Daniel's intensity had always frightened her, reminding her of a fiddle whose too-tight strings were bound to snap.

Chase pointed to Carter and Sally. "Those two look pretty cozy. Perhaps Miss Sally doesn't realize that Carter's father left him out of his will—because of you, I believe." The man's even white teeth flashed in the sunlight.

Because of me? "You are mistaken."

"I think not. I intern with the Williams's attorney."

"I cannot believe you have the audacity to speak of such things when Lee has just passed and yellow fever is ravaging the very countryside where you grew up." Cornelia scowled at him. Chase was wrong about Carter being disinherited. He had to be.

Sally nodded curtly at Carter and then turned on her heel and left him.

His bad leg dragging, Carter rejoined them. "I see you and Chase have reacquainted yourselves."

Daniel's brother stood. "Please accept my sincere regret for the loss of your brother. He was a good man and for your sister-in-law, she was gentility itself. And Miss Gill, for the loss of your father." He bent and pressed cool lips to her hand. Her stomach churned in protest.

10

Carter allowed his gaze to follow Chase Scott's retreating form. An ache formed behind his temples. The man examined Nell as though she were a novelty in the campus food hall—perhaps apple cobbler or an old-fashioned Shrewsbury cake instead of their standard pie. He had resisted the urge to slap Chase's face, not wanting to upset Nell any further. Though not as bad or as rough around the edges as Daniel, Chase was another example of someone with boorish behavior.

Nell's face remained flushed. Perhaps he should have done something about Chase Scott.

"Carter, I'll drive us to the dock."

He eyed the bench seat and then Nell. Could he squeeze in next to her, and if he did, dare she protest? This wagon belonged to his family, not hers.

Nell sighed and tilted her head at her brother. "Hop into the back, Andy, would you?"

Andrew screwed his face up at her. "It's bumpy back there."

Carter gestured to the wide seat. "Come now, we can all sit together. Plenty of room." He assisted Andrew up and then Nell, the wagon rocking beneath them.

As he settled next to her, Nell anchored her arms to her sides, as though afraid of his touch. Soon Nell had maneuvered the wagon onto the side street.

"Sissy, you have to turn the other way to get to Richmond Road."

She glanced left and right in confusion, scanning Jamestown Road. Carter held out his hands. "Give me the reins, Nell."

Perfect pink lips narrowed into a frown. After a moment's hesitation, he grasped the reins, feeling the warmth left behind from her hands.

"I'm so sorry, Carter." Nell's periwinkle eyes searched his face. The desire to throw his arm around her and pull her closer tempted him. What could he offer her? His father ensured that he possessed nothing—at least, that was what he'd been told.

"My brother, Anne, your father… can it be that they are truly gone?" Carter shook his head. God was cruel. "But the boys have been spared?"

Andrew leaned across his sister's lap. "They're awful upset."

"As would be expected." Nell patted her brother's arm.

And what about these two—parentless now, like himself? "And yourself, Andrew, how are you doing?"

The boy straightened. "Plum tuckered out from all the work of caring for Pa. And wore out from all the cryin' and the carryin' on. I feel like someone plucked my heart right outta my chest while it was still beatin'."

Carter's own chest squeezed in reaction. This was the child the boys' tutor had called unteachable? "Eloquently said."

Carter shifted his hips, bumping into her skirts. "Sorry, Nell, but with my bad leg, I…"

"Tell me if you need me to move." Granted if she moved further over she might fall off the dray.

He took a shaky breath. "Tell me—did Lee suffer much?" His voice held a tremor.

"No. I was there with him at the end."

Andrew reached behind Nell and tapped Carter. "I'm sorry about your brother."

"It is I who should be comforting you, for your greater loss of a father."

The boy hung his head. "It don't seem real."

"Andrew, be assured, I will lend you and your sister whatever support is within my power."

The sound of wheels rolling on the packed dirt road echoed the noises in Cornelia's mind—the churning of loss, disappointment, and encroaching poverty crushed together. The perfume of the flowers, blooming all around them in the cultured gardens of Williamsburg and the faint essence of Bergamot from Carter's spicy cologne stirred the scent of hope, though.

If Carter were to run Dogwood Plantation, then he'd have a say in who worked as manager. Cornelia cleared her throat. "Do you remember all the talks we used to have about the running of a plantation?" She cringed. Even to her own ears, she sounded desperate, needy. But wasn't she? She couldn't return to work at the school, not with needing to care for her younger brother. With Carter so close beside her, all those feelings from years ago rose inside of her, yearnings to be a permanent part of his life.

"I recollect more the sharing we did—about my father and your grandmother in particular."

She laughed. "You showed up in my hidey-hole one day."

"*Your* hiding place?" Carter reached his arm around behind her, resting it on the back support. "As I recall, you hid under our front steps."

"That might be, but I considered it mine."

"According to your grandmother, all of Dogwood Plantation was hers."

Cornelia drew in a deep breath. "True." And if grandmama's husband of over twenty years hadn't gambled away her inheritance, then at least the land would have remained in the family.

A carriage approached them and rolled past, the driver dipping his chin, his tricorn hat showing its age as sunlight burst through the clouds. They'd almost reached the wharf, and they still had their trip upriver on the schooner ahead.

She could perform the plantation manager's job, she was sure. If only she weren't a woman. She badly wanted to ask Carter if she might take her father's place.

If she didn't secure a position for herself somewhere, immediately, she and Andy would have nothing to sustain them.

She had to trust in God. And she'd also have to seek Hayes's help, her only living kin—yet recalling how others believed they might marry gave her pause. Surely Hayes didn't entertain such notions, did he?

Cornelia fixed her gaze on Carter. "I know this isn't a good time, but since you offered your assistance—would you consider making me the plantation manager?"

"Of Dogwood?"

Of course she meant the plantation position that her father had held for so many years.

His shocked expression spoke the words that his mouth didn't form—the position was the one thing he couldn't give her.

13

Chapter Two

The sun dared to rise over their cabin yet again this cool morning despite Carter's denial—Cornelia could not step in as plantation manager despite her skills.

"He said 'no'," she whispered to herself. Wanting to scream and shout, she instead swept the cabin clean with a vengeance, surprised that her brother hadn't stirred. He needed his rest.

This was Lee's remembrance day, though, at the church, and she had much to do before she helped Carter get his nephews ready for the service and the burial.

She settled on a sturdy chair that Pa had built and scooted closer to the table. She caught a few short breaths before she faced her cold corn pone. She'd toted in the firewood and hauled up the fresh water. Collected eggs. Fed the dogs that Pa had raised for Hayes to sell so that they'd all have a little extra food on the table. She'd stoked the fire. Milked the cow. Selling the cow would give her one less thing to do. But what would she do about milk for Andy, cheese for the two of them, and buttermilk for the dogs?

Dear Lord, for what I am about to partake of, may I truly be grateful. And not the miserable insufferable wretch I feel right now. Amen

Quite the prayer wasn't it? Mrs. Skidmore, at the academy in Richmond, would have laughed but then chastised her had she dared utter aloud such a sentiment. But the headmistress had been so good to Cornelia. She blinked back a tear. She missed everyone.

Cornelia exhaled loudly. Andy still hadn't stirred. With each day's passing since Pa had died, he drew more within himself. "You've got to start getting up, Andy."

"Hmmm." In the bed, against the west wall, Andy moved beneath the covers.

She brushed a strand of hair from her face. She'd longed for her locks to turn a burnished mahogany like Anne Williams's glorious hair had been. But Anne was gone forever, now.

"You're getting to the age where those concerns are so much pure vanity that it's a sin," her father's advice echoed in her mind. *"Take caution lest you become like the heathen—all frippery and flounce and no substance."* The headmistress at the academy had likewise offered cautionary advice. Who would guide her now?

Thank you, Lord that you never leave me.

God was sufficient. She could cast her cares upon Him. Jesus could carry her through today.

"Andrew Gill, I've got cornbread and buttermilk here for breakfast."

Cornelia crumbled the cornbread onto the dish. She poured the buttermilk remains onto her plate and let the pone sop it up. Time to churn more butter. What she'd give for a teaspoon of molasses. But their sweet, dark liquid was long gone, as was the coffee. Instead, she drank weak tea.

Making do. Doing without. She'd lived in such a fashion until she'd been sent off to school. There, she'd been given new clothing and had been fed well. She'd been supplied with books, too, and taught bookkeeping skills. The school's owner had kept her on as an employee after she'd finished her studies—a true blessing. Before she'd gone off to school, Daniel Scott planned to take her from her home when she too young to be wed—and carry her to Kentucky where he promised her a "land of plenty". She closed her eyes, recalling Carter chasing Daniel off. But soon after, she'd been sent to Richmond. Not much later, Carter left school and joined the Navy, off to war, with nary a word to her.

She rapped her short fingernails on the old wood table. It was a fine piece of furniture. Visitors often commented on how out-of-place her cherry and mahogany table and sideboard were with the few sturdy oak

15

pieces her father had made, but Cornelia knew they represented both her mother and her father. Her mother had always hoped that her father would do well for himself and recover some of what Cornelia's grandfather had gambled away. But that had never happened. A temperate and deeply religious man, Pa had always said God intended for him to be right where he was—managing the neighbors' plantation operations.

Andy drew aside his bed's privacy curtain. "Sissy, are you gonna press my good pants for the funeral?"

"Let me put the iron by the fire." She got up from the table and brought Ma's iron closer to the heat.

Andy threw off his scrap quilt. "I'm hungry."

Cornelia cut a piece of cornpone, set it into Andy's bowl, and poured buttermilk over it. "Here, have some."

"All right." His gold-green eyes had lost their sparkle. Normally her visits home were happy times.

"I know things are hard, but I'm so glad we have each other." Pa would have wanted them to count their blessings, and Andy was the biggest blessing she had.

With the yellow fever outbreak barely contained, Carter didn't expect more than a handful of mourners at his brother's service. Lee's casket had already been taken to the graveyard. Carter led his nephews toward the church. He removed his hat as he crossed the threshold into the small Episcopal church. *So simple, yet so beautiful.* The early colonial church's familiarity comforted him. He needed to get through the day. As the boys' next-of-kin, save for their flighty maternal aunt, Carter would no doubt assume responsibility for raising them.

He turned to his nephews. "Stay with me." The words tripped on his tongue. The boys had used the same phrase with him earlier, issuing a collective, "Stay with us, Uncle Carter." *Lee, oh my brother, how can I have lost you?*

Unlike a normal funeral, no parish members clustered at the double doors to greet him and the boys warmly as they entered. He spied only a few familiar faces inside. This epidemic had everyone, himself included, frightened by its ferocity.

Despite his initial reluctance to accept Nell's assistance with the boys, he wasn't sure how he would have managed without her today. Behind him, her blonde curls bouncing, Nell carried Albert, the youngest of Lee's children.

"Let's get them settled." She inclined her head toward the front pew.

Of all the boys, little Albert most resembled Carter's brother.

"Let me have him for a moment." Carter extended his arms, took hold of the boy, and pulled him close. Albert wrapped his tiny fingers in Carter's hair and yanked.

Nell extricated the boy's hand, several dark, wavy strands of hair dangling from his fist. She took him back into her arms and pointed with her free hand. "Andy, sit next to Eddie, here in the middle." As disparate in quality as their clothing was, clearly both older lads had grown and required new attire. In Williamsburg, society may have frowned upon the two boys' association. Not here. The priest wouldn't have allowed such snobbery.

Carter held Charles' and Lloyd's hands. "Come with me, boys, down here." The two middle siblings slid into the pew.

Nell took Albert around the pew to enter from the window side.

Carter glanced at the priest, shifting his weight from his aching leg.

For the briefest moment, Carter looked for his elder brother. *Lee's gone. He'll never sit with me again.* How many times had they sat beside one another on this very pew? He blinked back the moisture in his eyes. Carter hadn't deigned to show himself inside this church since he'd returned home from the war the previous year—injured and too embarrassed by his own failure.

The day had taken on a completely unreal sensation. At any moment he expected Lee to come through a side door and embrace him. To ask about his studies. What had either of them been thinking—that Carter could simply attend William and Mary, come home an attorney, and then run for political office?

His eldest nephew, Edward, stared ahead, glassy-eyed. Carter's chest ached for the lad, for all of his nephews. He remembered sitting in this very pew and grieving the loss of his mother. And a few years later, his father. At least he'd had the luxury of a separation of years—not days—in their deaths. Carter lay his hand atop Lloyd's. The small hand's clamminess proclaimed his nephew's distress.

Andrew Gill rubbed his eyes with his fists. Surely he was grieving the loss of his own father.

Mr. Maynard, a church deacon, tapped Carter's shoulder. "Carter, there's a woman here claiming to be the boys' aunt. Shall I seat her with you?"

Swiveling in his seat, but careful not to stare too openly, Carter caught sight of Mariah Wenham dressed in riding clothes. From where had she come so quickly? He didn't realize he gazed at her open-mouthed until he returned his attention to Mr. Maynard. "Yes, please."

Nell turned and half-rose to give up her seat as the deacon led Mariah around. But when Mariah reached her, she pressed her small, gloved hand on Nell's shoulder and slid into the pew behind them. Mariah raised her hand in acquiescence toward both Nell and Carter.

"I am fine back here."

Relieved by her speedy arrival, Carter surveyed his nephews' faces. They had taken no note of her. Unease crept through him. While he preferred to not uproot them—might this woman, who had shown no interest in children, challenge Lee's wishes for the boys to remain here in Charles City?

The priest arranged his Book of Common Prayer on the podium and began the service. His tenor voice comforted Carter. Whenever Albert squirmed, Nell invented a distraction—whether moving her fingers in a silly fashion that didn't draw the priest's attention or whispering softly in the toddler's ear.

Mariah's eyes widened every time Carter glanced behind at her. She appeared terrified. But of what? Perhaps she was afraid to take on the boys. Did she not know his brother's directives—that the children should be cared for by him? She and Carter were the boys' next of kin. However, with Mariah established elsewhere and himself in college, she may be the more stable caregiver. Yet might not his old friend, at the aisle's end, be the best caretaker of all?

Capable, strong Nell. He couldn't help but compare her to Sally... Unconcerned with appearance and social convention and with a natural beauty requiring no embellishment to make her shine, Nell was one of a

18

kind. Sally, or Sarah Elizabeth when she was being formal, was all spit and polish and boarding school refinement.

Carter should have been paying attention—Reverend Henry gestured for them to rise for the benediction. Dismissed by the priest, Carter turned. Several old friends and neighbors looked at him, most with expectant, yet sad, gazes. He rose and signaled Mariah to join him, but she shook her head and averted her gaze. He and Nell had agreed that the two youngest boys should be taken outside while he greeted those few who might be in attendance, to accept their condolences.

Nell bent to take five-year-old Lloyd's hand. "Come on, little men." She led him and Albert from the building. She gifted Carter with a shy smile, so reminiscent of those they'd shared as grief-numbed youths. Then she and the younger boys disappeared to the grassy field nearby.

"Here, Edward." Carter positioned his oldest nephew beside himself. He plucked a sprig of dogwood blossoms from his dark coat and tucked some in Edward's mourning coat.

Before Carter could explain procedures for the small greeting line to eight-year-old Charles, the boy's older brother Edward spoke up. "Charles, right here beside me. Just repeat what I say or add a little. Or nod. All right?"

When had Edward become so self-assured? He held the air of someone who had a load settled upon his shoulders and was steadying to walk forward under it. A smile accompanied his pride in seeing his nephew handle himself so well. His midshipmen could have taken cues from this boy.

Stomach churning, Cornelia scanned the crowd of mourners. *Did I imagine Daniel Scott seating himself in the last row as the service began?* What would have prompted him to have done so? When she glanced over her shoulder earlier, the glimpse of a tall, dark-haired man had frozen her senses. She'd turned back around, praying it wasn't so. But she didn't see him outside where they now gathered.

Mariah Wenham edged closer to Cornelia.

Cornelia stopped Lloyd before he jammed a stick at Mariah's leg. "Don't hurt your auntie."

A kind of choked laughter gurgled up from Mariah as she raised a hand to her throat. "I don't know a thing about raising children." A decade or more older than Cornelia, Mariah appeared younger, despite her old-fashioned riding clothing. Did the styles in South Carolina lag behind those of Tidewater Virginia?

Laying a gloved hand on Cornelia's arm, Mariah leaned in closer to whisper. "Do you know the Scott family?"

"Why do you ask?" Her heart clutched in her chest.

Perspiration dotted her forehead. "I'm sorry. I expected them to be in attendance. I saw a man who resembled Daniel."

Cornelia opened her mouth, unable to get the words out. Had it indeed been Daniel? Surely he'd altered in appearance over the years.

Albert wrapped his chubby fingers in Cornelia's skirt and pulled. She bent to loosen the child's hands.

Mariah pulled out a fan. "I cannot believe Lee is gone."

"I can't believe it either. And he didn't want you to have to be responsible for your nephews. He told Hayes." But apparently not Carter, who'd mentioned he wasn't sure if Mariah would want to take the boys to South Carolina.

"Hayes Davis, the horse breeder?" Color bloomed in Mariah's cheeks.

Cornelia lifted Albert into her arms. "Yes, he's...he was a close friend of Lee's and also..."

Mariah moved closer to Cornelia. "Is Mr. Davis *at* the plantation?" Her husky voice sounded breathless.

"No. Do you know him?"

Fine eyebrows arched and then lowered before Mariah's face settled into an unreadable mask. "Not really. But his character is well known."

"For?" *For what? His horses? For being the president's friend?* But Mariah hid behind her fan and didn't answer.

Mariah waved her fan, refreshing Cornelia as well. "I think my brother-in-law was right. Carter would make the consummate politician."

"This is his brother's funeral. I believe he's just being polite." Cornelia jostled Albert on her hip.

Who was going to care for the children? The southern belle admitted she knew little about children and Carter wanted to return to school.

"Mariah, do you have a governess in mind, if the children go to South Carolina with you?"

The color again drained from the woman's beautiful face, and she furiously fanned herself, scattering dust from her traveling clothes. "I wouldn't dream of taking the boys from their home."

Cornelia set Albert down and he ran to Andy, who took his hand and accompanied him to the copse of magnolias nearby. "Did you know your sister was unable to keep a governess?"

"Lee mentioned that a house servant acts as nurse." Mariah's lips formed a pretty pout. "They've always been darling boys when I visited. No more active than others, I think."

"Eddie said his mother threatened to tan their hides if they misbehaved while you visited." Though Anne wouldn't have actually carried out her threat.

Mariah raised her eyebrows. "I see."

It wasn't Cornelia's business, but curiosity drove her to voice her question. "How did you arrive so quickly?"

Mariah batted her eyelashes furiously. "I happened to be in Richmond when I heard of my sister's death. I was visiting with another family member." The last few words were barely audible.

"Oh." Cornelia knew of no Wenham relatives in Virginia.

"I confess I took a public coach to Charles City. Then rented a horse to get here."

Mariah Wenham renting a horse from the local stable defied reason. *Let Carter figure it out.* It wasn't Cornelia's concern.

Carter finally headed in their direction with Eddie and Charles trailing behind him.

Cornelia needed to throw off the chains of resentment she'd carried around like shackles. He'd gone off to the Navy and left her. He'd never sent her any letters at the school in Richmond. . She'd never had the chance to correct Carter's misconceptions that she hadn't encouraged Daniel's ungentlemanly behavior. It was as if she no longer existed.

Perhaps she should go with Hayes to his farm in Orange County. Then she wouldn't have to see Carter every day.

As her old friend, her love, neared them, her heart quickened. *He's come home to Charles City, like me. Will he stay? Can I stay?*

21

Chapter Three

Carter hoisted Lloyd into the carriage, where his aunt received him. He needed time with Nell, time to think.

"Mariah?" He pointed to Andrew. "Young Gill shall ride the horse to the stables at the Cross Roads for you to return it."

Andrew headed to his sister. "Can I?"

"I am sure you can." Nell cast him a cautionary glance. "And yes, you *may*."

Carter closed the carriage doors.

The horses pulled forward, carrying his nephews home. A pang of guilt settled in his chest. He needed a moment alone to free his mind of that which overwhelmed. Somehow, he was to manage a plantation and raise four boys who were grieving the loss of both parents. *I need you, Lee.*

Carter crossed to where Nell stood and took hold of her arm. "I'll drive you."

Her snug jacket strained as Nell took a deep breath but she smiled and walked toward the wagon. "Alone?"

Three tails wagged as her dogs rose up to greet them. Trying to make light of her question, he patted each dog's head. "We shan't be alone. Your valuable animals shall guard you." When Lee had shared the price to purchase a trained hound, one suitable for family farm life, Carter had been surprised.

A blush tinged her cheeks, but she allowed him to assist her into the carriage. "You'll send someone for Andy, then, after we return?"

Carter took a breath, wincing from the pain in his leg. "Indeed." He pulled himself up into the wagon.

They rode in companionable silence, as though they had never parted. He couldn't resist glancing at her beautiful profile. If only she could be happy. Instead of turning toward home, he continued south.

"You're not going to see the Scotts, are you?" Nell's fingers crept up to her throat.

He frowned. "If the retired rector was unable to come to the funeral, why would I seek him out? Why do you ask such a thing?"

"Daniel." She swiveled toward him. "He's coming home."

Guilt grabbed him by the neck and shook him hard. If he'd paid better attention to Daniel's unwanted attention to Nell when they were younger, he may have prevented the man from pressing his suit upon her.

"What brings him home?"

Nell squashed her tiny reticule like a cook working a lump of dough. "His grandfather says he seeks a wife."

A wife? Hadn't Daniel insisted Nell agree to be his wife and go to Kentucky? A decade had passed. At almost five and twenty, she became a mother to her brother, despite having never been a wife to any man. Nell would do whatever it took to take care of herself and Andrew. Even become the plantation manager, which he'd denied her. But by refusing, had he placed Nell in a position where she might return to Richmond?

"Would the Academy allow you to return to work?"

"Indeed, if I didn't have Andy with me."

"Oh?"

"They provide me with a room." She stared down at her lap. "But no males are allowed at the academy."

"I see."

"I must find a way to support myself and Andy."

Carter rubbed his knuckles against his thigh. He'd broken his middle knuckle when he'd protected Cornelia. Daniel departed for Kentucky shortly thereafter—he along with many Virginians seeking the Promised Land far beyond the blue mountains.

Nell grazed his enlarged knuckle with her index finger. *She remembers.*

"I need a position where both Andy and I are safe."

"Is anyplace safe during this war? During these outbreaks of yellow fever?"

"I don't know." She chewed her lower lip as she gazed at the approaching woods.

Carter diverted the horses down the old trail to a narrow side road. He loved riding back here.

As the carriage rocked, she clutched his arm. "What are you doing?"

"I'm taking you to the place where my father forbid me to go." He breathed in the forest's earthy scent as they rolled onto the sheltered lane. "It's a peaceful place."

Evergreens stretched up over the ancient path, wide enough only for a narrow wagon.

"Do you still play dulcimer?" He missed the soul-soothing music.

"Sometimes. Not lately. The headmistress considers it an unsuitable form of music for the girls."

"Probably thinks it too low-born for her wealthy plantation owners' daughters."

"So only the piano for the girls."

The organ music at the church had put him in such a melancholy mood. He had to shake it and master his emotions if he was going to be of any use to his nephews.

Even with Nell beside him in his special place, Carter couldn't escape his recollections. As the woods rolled by, Carter recalled every young man under his command who had died. "I lost many men, many friends during my time at sea. This truly has been a second war for independence. This war must end."

"It's frightening that the soldiers are coming ashore and harming innocent civilians."

"The British need to cease thinking they can do whatever they wish to our people."

24

"It's shameful, Carter. The British are impressing young men—boys even—into service. Grabbing them and taking them where they have no desire to go." Was she talking about the British or Daniel Scott now?

In the back, the dogs' low snuffling sounds were periodically interrupted by a yip or low growl.

Nell chuckled. "I think the dogs are dreaming."

"Even then, I don't escape the terror of this world."

"Oh, Carter." Nell's voice held something rich, something deep—the remnant of love.

He didn't want to ruin this moment by saying anything to break the spell of being here, beside Nell. Tree limbs scratched the sides of the wagon as it creaked along, almost as if warning him that he was trespassing into territory where he didn't belong.

"I know you wanted to serve your country."

He caught the narrowing of those magnificent eyes of hers, the ones he'd always lost himself in, like the purest ocean.

"And I want to protect the lives of those in our commonwealth. The College of William and Mary has been a good place for my legal studies." Expressing the words helped clarify his goals. "I want to do more." His heart ached for those families whose sons had been taken and had yet to be returned by the British navy. "Weak-willed politicians contributed to those abductions."

"You hope to enter politics, then?"

He had imagined that his relationship with his professor, a prominent man in the community as well as on the campus, might assist him. "I have an excellent teacher who has encouraged me."

Perhaps with Danner's lovely daughter Sally on Carter's arm, his own infirmity would be overlooked. But it wouldn't erase the pain he felt with every step.

"Your family hosted so many prominent politicians at your own home. Surely you learned from them?"

"Do you think Jefferson pushed for the congress to fully fund our navy? Our army?" He snorted. "Madison is scrambling now to overcome those mistakes."

On the seas and in the fields, politicians cost the nation lives during this war. But with Nell beside him, it felt as though his equilibrium was being restored. How freeing to be able to express anything to her, like when they were younger.

Ahead, frothy white flowers escaped their dark-green captors.

Nell shifted position, moving away from him. "Sally, the girl at school… is she your sweetheart?"

He felt her eyes on him. Perhaps there were some things they could not freely discuss. He weighed his words. "She has been very kind. We have attended many social functions together." And Sally had pursued him as relentlessly as a nineteen-year-old girl could.

"I see."

Did she discern that his selfish thoughts commandeered the helm and a mutiny would be needed before he reached home?

"Nell, do you remember the time our fathers sat on the porch talking about our futures, not knowing we were under those stairs?"

"My pa knew." Nell's tight voice held defensiveness.

He rubbed his thumb across the backs of his fingers. "He did?"

"He wanted me to know what was planned for you."

"I'd already told you."

"You did." Her voice cracked. "I didn't know your father agreed with you. About the navy. I…"

"Father decided. Lee would inherit the plantation. I was to…" Find his own way. If he intended to marry their manager's daughter.

"How do you feel about returning now? And Lee's sudden passing?"

Dark rings beneath her eyes tugged at his heart. Always thinking of others, Nell hadn't paused to begin grieving her own father.

Fighting the urge to pull Nell close and kiss the golden strands that clung to her forehead, he grasped the leads. He'd never had to stifle such an impulse with Sally. She didn't call forth the feelings that ran rampant when he was with Nell. The woman so close to him marshaled all her forces, commanding his attention.

A bump in the road shot agony through his leg, but Carter restrained his moan. Sometimes he welcomed the pain that gripped him. It was so different from the shock he'd experienced during naval battles and the deaths of his men.

"Are you all right?" Nell's hand covered his own.

He breathed slowly, willing his body to calm.

26

"Carter, are you in pain?"

Perspiration covered his brow. "I'll be all right."

"I'm so sorry... about your leg."

Nell had to caretake her invalid mother for many years before Mrs. Gill died. That sad tone of voice she expressed about him was the same she'd used when speaking of caring for her mother. He'd vowed as a boy that he'd grow up and take care of Nell so that she'd never have to shoulder such responsibility again. His heart sank at the knowledge of the burden he'd be if he changed his plans.

He squared his shoulders. Sally didn't pity him. She considered him a war hero first and foremost and a worthy candidate for her father to sponsor in a political career. "I'll be all right in a moment, Nell. Do not trouble yourself over me."

From the corner of his eye he observed her frown as she, too, sat straighter.

"There's so much trouble in our world, Carter, I do not think we can escape it."

A muscle pulsed in his jaw. There was truth in her words.

The bower opened overhead and the evergreens retreated. Dogwoods lined the roadway, a perfect double column of pinkish-white blossoms as far as the eye could see.

He heard Nell's sharp intake of breath. "I've never seen anything so lovely." Something stirred in him. A sureness, a promise. He searched the cerulean sky for some sign; for it was as though that message had come from One who long ago abandoned him. There would be an end to the trials and tribulations eventually.

Carter slowed the horses, wanting to savor the moment, to share this quiet beauty with Nell. He swallowed. "This path emerges soon." He pointed to a gentle curve.

"Oh." Her sigh held pent-up disappointment. How could he return joy to her countenance?

"The path runs closer to the river there." He slipped his hand into hers and squeezed. "It's beautiful, too, you'll see."

"This part looks very familiar." Nell breathed in deeply, her elbow pressing against his arm. She felt right. Truer than anything had in a long time. Despite the difficulty of what he was about to face as he determined how he could help his nephews while continuing his own training.

Head tipped back, Nell may have been praying but she whispered, "It's so familiar, as if I should remember it yet I don't recall being here."

He should have brought her but his father had already warned him off the land, which wasn't theirs. "It is adjacent to your property. Have you ever explored back here?"

She shook her head. "Grandmama Lucia and my parents forbade me to go anywhere beyond what had been cleared. I can't exactly recollect why, but I assumed it was because it belonged to someone else, and we shouldn't trespass."

"It's not ours. Maybe it belongs to the Scotts. They own the next property."

The two sat in companionable silence.

Nell's features tugged in confusion. "How could I have passed by all this beauty and not realized it was here?"

Sad for his old friend and longing to rectify his own contribution, Carter drank deeply of the pink-tinged ivory blossoms' fragile fragrance. "We miss loveliness because we are so intent on our goal that we miss God's beauty and His creation." Had those words come from his own lips?

Nearby birds warbled, as if in agreement. "Shall we move on?"

"Yes." Nell squeezed his arm and he slapped the reins.

"Here we go." The horses quick-stepped around the bend and into full view of the river.

"There it is. Look—the James River." Tears shimmered in her eyes. Her pretty face made radiant in her appreciation of the glittering river meandering alongside the overgrown carriage path.

A pristine beach and clear blue water beckoned before them.

Nell stared straight ahead, her body jostling into his. "Should we be here?" Her voice was a whisper. The floral scent he inhaled was hers, not the flowering trees that edged the trail on the right, pops of white and pink peeking from the treeline.

"If only I could live here in such beauty." Her voice so low he wasn't quite sure he'd heard her, and Carter didn't want to ruin the moment by asking her to repeat herself. He gazed down at her perfect features, focused so intently on their surroundings. Even the dogs were silent. Only the sounds of wind, waves, and birdsong accompanied them over the flat terrain. Reason cautioned him in the hushed environs. It would be so easy to pick up where they had left off. But it would be wrong. Sally may have expectations of him. He may have led her to believe that they were courting. She certainly acted as though they were despite him never having given voice to the request.

Carter wouldn't hurt Nell again for the world. He'd been surprised she hadn't found someone to settle down with. A good man, perhaps a farmer with a large plantation from an old Virginian family like she was. Like they both were. What a shame that her grandfather chose to gamble his inheritance away.

And his brother Lee created a scandal when he'd married the younger rather than the older Carolina belle after a long courtship. Despite that affront, Mariah Wenham, Anne's sister, visited Dogwood Plantation yearly. No animosity was noted. And Mariah, might she take in the boys? She'd inherited a large estate in South Carolina.

Songbirds warbled nearby and the breeze picked up. Young cardinals darted amongst the dogwoods. Carter needed to return to school if possible and Nell would go on with her own life.

A headache gathered a legion of troops at his temples. "The boys— did they express any preference to you about where they wished to reside?"

"I heard your brother appointed *you* guardian." Nell's eyes narrowed as they eased closer to the river.

"Edward's inheritance will require safekeeping. I know nothing of managing children." Much less a plantation. He'd never been interesting in farming. And he certainly didn't approve of enslaving people, as his father well knew.

"You'll learn." Nell's voice turned as sulky as little Albert's when Carter denied him an extra biscuit that morning.

Mariah Wenham on the other hand, a spinster aunt and heiress… "Wouldn't their aunt desire a family since she's never had her own?"

"I don't rightly know."

At over thirty years of age, Mariah would likely not marry. Perhaps Lee had ruined her taste for marriage. His brother stated he owed his sister-in-law a favor and carried guilt that Mariah never married.

29

Remorse settled on Carter's shoulders as Nell's radiant face took in the beauty of this special sanctuary. He'd never brought her here. Hadn't shared this place with a soul.

Cornelia inhaled the fresh river breeze. Cherry trees blossomed bright against the stone ruins of what must have once been a substantial two-story home as the cart rolled on.

"Whose home was that?" Her voice sounded tremulous to her own ears.

"I don't know."

"It seems familiar." Unbidden memories came to her of someone with a dry, thin hand holding her own. "It's so sad. Someone lived in that house and now it's vacant."

"It is peaceful here, though."

But the recollection of standing before this very house, possibly with her grandmother, was unsettling. The drive thus far had been so beautiful, she didn't want to ruin it now. Carter was the one needing comfort today.

She inclined her head toward him and pointed to the sapphire river winding at the drive's termination. "Do you miss the sea at all? Does the river remind you of what you can't have any more?"

Carter pulled the horses to a stop again and the dogs yipped. "Is that what you think? That I miss Navy life?"

"I didn't mean to offend you." Movement alongside the road caught her eye.

Carter bent and unsheathed a knife from inside his boot. "Not much good if the trespasser possesses a gun," he muttered.

All three dogs bayed. Carter stretched his arm across Cornelia, presumably to protect her.

From the thinning cherry grove, a man emerged—hair in a queue, an older, more muscular version of Daniel Scott. He placed his fists on buckskinned hips.

"Carter Williams with Cornelia Gill?" The frontiersman rubbed his chin. "My brother said you're courting his professor's daughter, Carter. Wouldn't she be upset to see this?"

Nell's jaw dropped open. "What are you doing here, Daniel?"

The ferocity of her question surprised her. Although the Bible encouraged forgiveness and to love one another, something akin to hate dripped from her words. That, and fear. She clamped her teeth over her bottom lip.

Daniel laughed. "I was about to ask the same thing. This property adjoins that of my grandfather's."

The dogs continued to whine.

Carter still clutched his knife. "A fact of which I'm aware."

"I sometimes stray here." Daniel swung the dead rabbit that hung over his shoulder.

Carter sat straighter. "This property doesn't belong to you."

"Nor to you, Carter." Daniel spat into the grass and crossed in front of them. "Now as for whether it belongs to you, Cornelia, I can't say."

Tremors coursed up Cornelia's arms as Daniel departed. Her dogs finally settled in the wagon bed. "Daniel Scott is as nasty as ever." The sight of him reminded her of how he'd grabbed her and kissed her so forcefully beneath the cherry trees at Scott's Hundred those many years ago. She cast a quick look at Carter.

He wrapped his arm around her. "Are you all right?"

"I don't know." She didn't. And she should remove his arm but she couldn't. When he did and urged the horses forward, she felt bereft at the absence of his touch.

"What do you really think he's doing in Virginia?"

"I…" Nothing about Daniel made sense to her. Because she hadn't hit him nor fought him when he'd shocked her with his kisses, he had presumed she'd agreed to run off with him to Kentucky those many years ago. And he had shown up at her home to claim her.

"We don't need Daniel's presence in Charles City at this time. Not with all the other things we must deal with."

We? The word sent hope spiraling through her. But perhaps he meant himself and his nephews. "If only my father and your brother had lived."

Mixed emotions flickered through Carter's eyes. Beyond the next curve, a long lane ahead, lined with crushed oyster shells. "Here's the river approach. We're nearly home."

Home. A place with no parents and where she must care for a brother who had little to eat. She had to try again. "Carter?"

31

His dark brows knit together.

"How are you going to manage the plantation? Are you sure you won't need help?"

Reestablished in his former bedchamber, Carter removed his dress clothing article by article, grateful that the burial in the family plot had proceeded undisturbed. Niggling guilt urged him to confess he'd spent much of the brief ceremony watching Nell's curls bob in the breeze. How would they manage the plantation? He couldn't put Nell in charge. It simply wasn't right to have a woman in such a position. He'd find something for her. Perhaps she'd be willing to help Mariah care for his nephews. They liked Nell and even minded her. And if Mariah removed them to South Carolina then Nell would be far from Daniel Scott. Even if Daniel's visit to Virginia was transient, Carter wouldn't rest well knowing he was but one plantation away.

Carter placed his clothing inside the wardrobe and succumbed to the fatigue and sadness that drained him. He lay on his bed, candlelight flickering on the plaster ceiling. The funeral had somehow been a peaceful experience. With Nell at his side, he'd felt surrounded by fellowship, in Christian love, despite the few people who had been able to attend.

Nell. Love. Why did those two words always seem to be together in his mind? Despite the paucity of those present at the church, during this yellow fever outbreak, the broader love always present in the Charles City community was evident. Similar to Nell's youthful blanket of acceptance—no stipulations whatsoever. 'Twas what he'd missed while absent with the military. That sense of belonging. Even with naval friendships and camaraderie, the acceptance and understanding of who he was had been missing.

But if he didn't return to school, failed to complete his education, could he ever represent the people of Charles City in the commonwealth's government? Or were the few men present today correct—that he should come home, and if he chose to run for office in the future, he as a planter could receive their support. But this was Edward's plantation. Carter had nothing… other than a permanent limp and a host of responsibilities.

Chapter Four

Carter forced open his eyes. Filtered light from behind his drapes shone on his mantle clock's face. "Past nine o'clock? Blast." He threw off his bedclothes and in a short time made himself ready and descended to the main floor. He hesitated at the staircase's base, grasping the curved finial. Was pain tightening his chest or the notion of entering the office? *Father's office. Lee's.*

He must review the accounts. He grasped his cane and stepped to the left, pausing before the tall door. He turned the heavy brass knob. The door swung in. Instead of heavily draped windows gathering dust, he entered a sunny room.

He'd expected the office to be in disarray, as Father had kept it. Wood floors lay bare—absent carpets that required weekly beatings. Oriental ceramic decorations once atop the desk and on the mantel piece—missing. Lee had a mind for business and kept order. But hadn't Carter possessed a keen mind for the military? All of his superiors had claimed so. Limping toward the desk, each painful step reminded him of what his pursuits in the Navy had accomplished for him.

A rap at the door interrupted him as he pulled the chair away from the desk. Bronze hair, mostly covered by a scarf, announced the house servant, Macy. "Master Carter?"

Brought with Anne from South Carolina, the girl had grown into a beautiful young woman. She should have been sent away from this place, and freed—something Lee apparently had been unwilling to do.

"Yes, Macy?"

She kept her green eyes downcast. On the streets of any city, dressed in fine clothing, would anyone ever identify this light-skinned woman as a house slave?

"That lawyer be here. He say you sent for him, sir."

"I did—a week ago." The man had sent no word. "So he's arrived? Please show him in."

"Yes, sir." Macy pulled at her apron.

Had Lee put a provision into his will for her to be freed? Their father, although having gifted each of his children with slaves, had given specific instructions about how he wished them to be treated. And orders as to what should be done when they, the owners, had died.

Jackson Forrester strode in and surveyed the room. He gazed over his pince-nez eyeglasses. "Carter Williams?"

Why did the man always act as though he couldn't remember who Carter was? "Glad you could make it, Mr. Forrester."

"Took me a while to get everything in order. Next meeting needs to be in town. In Richmond." The brusque tone left little doubt that the man was put out at having had to travel to the countryside.

Carter nodded. "I appreciate you making the trip. Include a fee for appropriate compensation in your bill."

Forrester eyed a side chair.

"Have a seat, Mr. Forrester." Carter settled into the dark stained Windsor chair behind the massive desk. He felt five-years-old again, swooping into his father's office, interrupting him to see if he might accompany him on a ride. Jackson Forrester's hair had grayed during that time. His face was a little more lined, but he'd always worn a pinched face.

"I imagine you wish to hear what your brother wanted done with this estate." The man's voice held a slight mockery. He displayed two documents. Carter had advised Lee on provisions in the will, a copy of which was sent to him at William and Mary earlier in the school year. Had his brother incorporated any of his suggestions? An ache surged through him—he'd never imagined needing a will so quickly.

Why two sets of papers? "What do you have there?"

"Ah, I have one you are expecting to see and other papers. Perhaps intended for the hearth fire." Forrester's crooked teeth flashed.

What was the man talking about? Carter needed to clear his head. He rang the serving bell. "I'll request tea be brought in. You can elucidate."

"Five of us know about this second codicil but two are in the grave."

"My brother and sister-in-law?" Carter inhaled slowly.

"Yes. I doubt the *boy* knows anything about this document unless his *mother* told him."

"What boy do you refer to and what woman?"

The door creaked open and Macy stepped into the pool of light streaming through the mullioned windows. When she spotted Forrester, her cheeks reddened and she turned toward Carter. "What might you gentlemen be needin', sir?"

Forrester cleared his throat. "I'm parched after such a long trip. I'd like a tall glass of cool tea with some sugar, plenty of sugar. I like it *real* sweet."

The man's tone wheedled as his eyes freely roamed the girl from behind. Carter's blood chilled. If Forrester remained the night, in the South Flanker, Macy needed to remain at the Great House, clear of the miscreant.

"Macy, have Lucinda bring cool tea from the ice house and a tray of lemon tarts."

"Yes, Master Williams." She curtsied.

He cringed. Later he would instruct her to never address him as 'Master' again.

Forrester ogled Macy. "Lee promised her to me if you had to sell any property."

Liar. Carter clenched his jaw. The door clicked shut. His brother never would have promised Forrester such a thing. They'd always agreed that none of their slaves would be sold to other estates. Lee spoke of sending Macy up North but hadn't done so before his death. And Father's letter had clearly stipulated his wishes.

When Carter said nothing, the lawyer continued, "I'm supposed to have first rights to purchase your cook, Mama Jo, and the big fella who does the figuring."

"Isaac?"

"He's the one."

Why would his brother promise Isaac? The man was indispensable, yet he, too, had succumbed to the illness. Carter could only hope that somehow he could make some sense of his brother's record keeping. This was not his strong suit. He huffed out a breath. Lord help him, he might have to give in to Nell's desire to manage the books. "Wish I still had access to Isaac. Alas, he died."

Forrester's mouth flopped open like a trout waiting for a worm. "Dead?"

Carter nodded. Laughter and squeals rang out nearby. Outside his window, the boys played a game of chase. Nell's brother, Andrew, didn't seem to be keeping up with them as well today, stopping and bending over to cough. Carter rose from his desk and went to the window. "Thank God those boys made it."

"Yes, well, as I am sure you imagined, the will names you as guardian for your nephew until Edward reaches maturity. After that he will be sole heir to the estate."

Carter frowned. "Nothing for my other nephews?"

"Customary to leave something. We'll discuss it when you come to Richmond."

His heart weighed heavy. His own father had denied him. Roger Williams promised to change his will when he'd heard of Carter's plans to marry Nell—an offer Carter never made. On what would he have supported her? Carter rubbed his jaw. He'd slipped back into his habit of grinding his teeth.

The door swung open and an elderly woman waddled in, hips swaying as she brought fragrant tea and a tray laden with lemon bars and pecan tarts. Carter went to the tea table, his finger tracing the light dust that covered it. He pulled the vertical piecrust-shaped cherrywood upward and locked it into place in the horizontal position. No one had touched it since his brother died. Unease filled the pit of his stomach.

Lucinda's shiny, dark face remained fixed on the task before her. "There you be, Master Williams." She set the tray down. "You be wantin' me to pour?"

Despite the pain in his leg, he'd do as much as he could. "No, thank you, I'll take care of it."

Lucinda attempted a bob.

"Please instruct the servants we aren't to be disturbed."

The woman left, the floor creaking as she crossed to the door and gently closed it behind her.

"You thank your slaves?" Forrester laughed. "What will you do next—free them?"

If only he could. If only all people would. "Perhaps." Carter turned from the man. He clenched his teeth and poured a tall glass from the crystal decanter, moisture beading on the vessel's exterior and making it slippery.

Forrester cleared his throat. "Just remember me when your cook and little house slave need to be sold to pay your debts."

Carter set the tumbler of tea down heavily on the tray. What would this man know of Lee's debts? Carter himself hadn't yet reviewed the ledgers. And his implication, an outright lie, that Lee would have promised him anything, made Carter want to take the man by the collar and throw him out. Deliberately stilling himself, he once again sensed tugging in his heart to call on a power higher than his own. To call out to the One who had once ruled his actions so long ago.

I am here. God spoke to his heart.

"I know you're there," Carter spoke the words aloud.

"Indeed, you'd do well to remember that I'm here." The man's voice grated like wood creaking on an ocean-tossed vessel. "Recall me when you start selling off bits and pieces here and there like your brother did. A shame that woman couldn't manage her own affairs."

With great care, Carter lifted the tea and the small plate of desserts and limped toward Forrester. The man held out his hands, eyes wide, saving Carter at least two awkward steps. "What woman would that be, sir?"

Someone banged on the door. "Let me in at once, Carter."

The attorney jerked backward, almost tipping his chair. "Mariah Wenham is in this house?"

Carter sighed as he hobbled to the door. "Always stays with us when she visits."

"Outrageous." Jackson Forrester rose. "I'll take my leave."

"I presumed you'd stay in the South Flanker."

"No, Mr. Williams, I shan't. I shall stay with my kin at Rose Hill. I bid you good day."

Full sun evaporated the morning dew as Cornelia surveyed Pa's garden behind the log cabin. She pushed her straw hat lower over her eyes and bent to forage for greens to cook with ham for their dinner. She knelt and first checked whether any root vegetables would resist her gentle tug. From a distance, a tall man lumbered toward her. His almost-bowed legs identified her cousin, Hayes Davis—her only living relation. Andy and she had not seen much of him until his mother, Cornelia's great-aunt, passed away.

Cornelia rose from her row of turnips, an underdeveloped vegetable in her hand. She chewed her lip, considering—did she have enough victuals to feed Andy, Hayes, and herself? As he neared, it was clear her relative was in dire need of a haircut and a good beard trimming.

She called out to him in surprise, "You've come to Dogwood Plantation." His home in Orange County was over five days ride on horseback. Pa said Hayes came about twice a year, always bringing a pup for Pa and Andy to raise and train. He'd befriended Carter's father by selling him prime horseflesh—but Hayes had not revealed to him that he was the nephew of Roger Williams's foe, Cornelia's grandmother. She'd gone on to Glory by that time but old Mr. Williams still held onto his resentment.

An expression of relief flitted over Hayes' strong features. "Sweet thing, of course I came once I heard."

Dressed in tan and ochre, the horse breeder almost blended with the farmland. When he reached her, Hayes bent to kiss her cheek, smelling of spearmint and licorice root. Would he offer to haul Andy away from the only home he'd ever known so that Cornelia could return to Richmond to work at the school? Or would he ask her to come with them?

"I'm so sorry about your Pa. He was a good man." He pulled her in for a quick hug.

She touched his wool sleeve. "It's good to have family here."

Sorrow darkened his hazel eyes. "I'm sorry I couldn't get here sooner." He pulled away and surveyed her head to foot like he would one of his horses, assessing for health. "I came as soon as I got word."

A tight smile sliced through his long beard. He wasn't an unattractive man. But at only thirty and a few years, gray streaks flowed through his shaggy beard. Hayes and Ma were first cousins, so he was a second cousin to Andy and Cornelia. The horse breeder was a hardy, good-natured man. And wealthy.

"What a long way you've come. Let me get you some tea. Come on in and sit a spell."

"Yes'm, I'll do that. Thank you, Nelly." Hayes yanked his hat off and rolled it between his big hands.

They rounded the corner to the cabin and almost ran smack into Carter Williams. "Nell—I see Mr. Davis found his way."

He laughed. "And why shouldn't I be able to find my little Nelly's cabin? Been comin' round here for a long time."

"Indeed?" Carter's voice held skepticism.

"Ya didn't see me 'cause you were gone off to war, then at college." His gaze lingered on Carter's injured leg. "Your pa and brother filled over a quarter of your stable with prime horses from my farm during that time."

If Carter's mouth were pressed together any tighter his lips might disappear. "I see."

Hayes wrapped his arm around her shoulder, almost possessively. Cornelia cast him a sharp glance but he ignored her. When she looked at Carter, pink spotted his cheekbones.

He thinks we have been courting!

"It's not like that, Carter."

"Like what, Nelly?" Her cousin glanced between the two of them. His arm weighed heavy as a yoke on which hung heavy buckets of water, and she ducked to release herself from him.

39

Hayes cast her an odd look before addressing Carter, "Your nephew did the proper thing by writin' to me. I stopped at the house to thank him."

Carter took a step rearward, planting himself on his good leg and supported himself with his cane. "Edward sent word?"

Hayes tucked a plug of tobacco in his cheek. "Yup. Sure didn't know 'bout Lee's passing. Hard to believe a young fella like Eddie put quill-pen to paper so quickly after his father's death."

A shadow passed over Carter's face.

"I'd have been here sooner, had I heard about your father passing, Nelly." Eyes glittering, her older cousin pulled at his beard. She'd need to trim it for him.

"We were waiting to send word once we were sure there were no more yellow fever outbreaks."

Carter stamped his cane. "Mercifully, this pestilence seems to have run its course."

"Met your pretty little Miss Wenham, too."

Cornelia stepped closer to Carter, who was frowning. She touched his arm.

She lifted her gaze to meet Hayes's. "The boys need all the family around them right now, don't you think?"

Her cousin's bushy eyebrows lowered and his eyelids twitched. She hoped he'd not inhale his chaw and choke.

Levi, a field hand, paused by the cabin. He removed his low-slung hat.

"Levi, I'm sorry…" Carter's soothing voice broke, "about your brother's death from the fever. He was a good man." What a pity that was the only way Isaac could obtain freedom.

"Yessir, he was. Mr. Williams and Mr. Gill good men too." Levi swiped at his nose.

Cornelia blinked then wiped away the tears that fell.

Taking the man by his elbow, Carter pulled him away for a moment, before Levi continued on to the slave quarters.

Hayes moved close and rested his chin atop her head. She wished it was Carter so near.

When Carter returned to her side, Hayes stepped away. Carter glanced between the pair. "We welcome you. Plenty of room in the North Flanker

Guest House, Mr. Davis. Miss Wenham is staying upstairs in the Great House."

Her relative narrowed his hazel eyes as if challenging Carter. "If ya don't mind, I'll stay right here with Cornelia and Andy."

What was her cousin thinking? Hayes Davis aimed to make Carter bristle. Instead, Carter coughed. Hayes moved toward him and slapped him on the back.

When the fit passed, Carter scowled. "Sir, you cannot stay in her cabin. It would look, well…"

Neck stiffening, Cornelia stifled the desire to protest. *Since when does he think he can tell me what to do?*

The big man's lips twitched. "I don't see why not."

He was trying to irritate. Hayes normally stayed in the North Flanker at Dogwood Plantation, Pa had said. But then again, he'd normally come on business whereas this was for a family visit.

"This is my land." She rocked her blistered feet in her infernal stiff boots, the kind she'd worn while growing up here. "And my home." Bending down so the two couldn't see her crimson face, she untied her leather footwear and tossed one half boot toward the porch, then the other. Wiping her hands, she stood, wiggling her bare toes. Wouldn't Mrs. Skidmore, at the Academy, be shocked if she could see Cornelia now?

Hayes grinned. "Feels a might better, don't it, Sweetness?"

Sweetness? Since when had he tagged that pet name on her? She'd certainly not granted permission for such allowances.

Carter sighed loudly. "Miss Gill, you mightn't care about appearances. But for Andrew's sake, Mr. Davis should stay in the North Flanker Guest House."

Shoulders relaxing, she nodded. "They'll treat you well."

Carter eased his rigid stance. "It's settled. Mr. Davis, I shall get you situated." Half-lowered eyes met hers in gratitude. Or was that resignation?

Soon the two men had left and Cornelia returned to her chores. She grabbed the cornhusk broom and swept around the hearth. What had grandmother seen when she peered out this glass window? She must have been proud to have glass in the opening. Cornelia touched the log walls. A memory of cold, hard rock rolled beneath tiny fingertips flitted past before she could claim recognition. She pulled her hand back and rubbed it. Since she and Carter had ridden by the beautiful property and the abandoned stone house, memories were returning.

Grandmama Lucia used to gaze across the field and rant about the beautiful home her husband planned to build there. But Grandfather, thought to be killed in the Revolution, never returned from the war. When a stranger, Mr. Williams, had shown up one day with a deed of sale, Grandmama said she fainted dead away.

Some years later, Carter's grandfather told Grandmama that her husband lived up North with a new wife. *He'd gambled and lost this property.* And once Mr. Williams built that fine home, every day Grandmama Lucia would rock on the porch and look upon it. Sometimes crying. Occasionally, she wandered up to the Dogwood Plantation property, and Ma would have to retrieve her.

Cornelia brushed the wide planks so vigorously that she hadn't heard the five pairs of feet shuffling across the doorstep. She pivoted and teasingly aimed the small dirt pile at the boys.

"Stop, please, Miss Gill." Eddie, the oldest of the Williams boys, grabbed the handle.

"What are you doing?" Lloyd's blue eyes widened.

She slapped a hand on her aproned hip. "More like—what are you all doing here?"

Andy cocked his head at her. "Ain't it lesson time?"

She narrowed her eyes at her brother. "Don't you mean 'isn't it lesson time?'"

The smallest Williams boy, Albert, reached his arms up to her. Cornelia exhaled loudly. Although she was attired in his mother's dress, since her friend Macy had been directed by Carter to give Anne's garments to her, Cornelia was not Albert's new ma. But she bent and lifted the tiny boy. "You need more meat on your bones, Al-boy."

He giggled. "Al-boy."

Eddie sat in a chair by the table, his eyes dancing. "Did you have a nickname for my uncle?"

Cornelia laughed, long and loud. "Some names I gave him weren't very nice."

"Father called him old stick-in-the-mud." Eddie's grin dashed across his face, then disappeared.

Albert poked her cheek. "Father gone."

The child could have poked her heart with that sharp finger. She wrapped her hand around it and kissed the tip. "You'll see him again one day."

"In heaven." Andy stood at the window as though searching the sky for the boys' father.

"What else did your father say about his brother?" Why did the boys give him so much trouble?

Eddie sat next to Andy, rested his elbows on the table, and formed his fingers into a steeple in front of his face. "Someone too noble for his own good."

"Gonna get a setdown, Father always used to say." Charles volunteered this information. "And he did—he's a cripple."

Cornelia snapped her towel. "Charles, don't say such things."

The gray-eyed boy shrugged. "Well, it's true."

"Your words were very unkind. I never want to hear you speak of your uncle like that again, do you hear me?" Cornelia shook with anger. Waiting, she fully expected the boys to get up and leave because of the sharp tone she'd used.

"Yes'm," a tiny voice chirped.

"Oh, I'm sorry, little one. I yelled in your ear." She rubbed Albert's silky head and then carried him to the rocking chair. By the way he was yawning, he'd be asleep soon. She settled into Grandmama Lucia's rocking chair as the boys clustered around the table.

Eddie brought his fingers together like a tent. "Miss Gill, could you explain to me about star patterns and indications for planting season?"

And so the lesson began. "I'll get out the Farmer's Almanac." She answered their questions and discussed plantation management until the sun kissed the tops of the southern pines and Albert had awoken from his nap.

She stretched. "Even if you follow planting advice, and do all you can, it is still up to God whether the crops are good."

"I don't see why my uncle can't let you manage this plantation." Eddie stood and motioned for his brothers to join him. "You know more about numbers and crops than anybody I have ever met."

He was such a serious boy. Fatherless and facing uncertain times, the boy was trying to be a little man. Surely Carter could relieve him of some of that responsibility. "What I've learned has come from listening to my father all those years of growing up here."

Someone rapped on the door. It was too even, too rhythmic to be her cousin. "Come in."

Albert woke and stretched an arm toward the rafters, where herbs and vegetables dried.

Carter entered through the doorway. He held a woven basket she recognized from the kitchen at the Great House—a seagrass container from Charleston. Mariah had brought it on one of her visits. From within wafted tempting odors of chicken, potatoes, gravy and yeast bread.

Carter thrust the basket forward. "I brought this for you."

Andy accepted the food. "It's just like we prayed for last night. A miracle."

Her cheeks heated with embarrassment.

The smile slid off Carter's handsome face. "A hot meal. Nothing miraculous."

"Sure is to my stomach." Andy set the food on the table. "Thank you kindly."

Mortified, Cornelia crossed her hands over her growling stomach.

A bushy brown head appeared behind Carter's smooth dark one. "I see yer playin' little mama, aren't ya? Mighty nice of ya, Nelly, considering yer being an orphan yerself and no ma to guide you."

All eyes, wide, turned upon the big man.

"What did I say?" Hayes tilted his head. "And why aren't you dressed for dinner?"

Carter gestured the boys toward the door. When Albert ran to him, he scooped the little boy into his arms.

Cornelia stood to her full height, not quite eye level with Carter's dark gaze before meeting Hayes' hazel eyes, so like her mother's. "We haven't been invited to partake."

"Of course you have. Ain't that right, Carter?"

She bit her lip.

When Carter said nothing, Eddie fixed a cold stare on him. "I am owner of this plantation. And if you don't invite this kind lady, I shall demand satisfaction."

Hayes snorted, then chuckled when uncle and nephew continued to face off. "So you gonna use pistols then? Or will it be swords?"

Eddie strode out the door, past his uncle, pausing only long enough to grab his baby brother. "His choice."

"Do ya need a second, son?" Hayes cocked one eyebrow.

Carter's lips formed a narrow line. "So that's how it is, then, eh?"

Pressing the toes of her work-boots close to Carter's bad foot, Cornelia was tempted to stomp. How dare he imply by his tone that she had put Eddie up to the request?

"Mister Williams…" She drew his surname out. "You may infer whatever your silly head wants to think. But if you'll excuse me, we'll partake of the repast your cook so kindly sent us."

His lips twitched. "I assembled that basket."

She swallowed some of her bitter pride. "Thank you." She caught her cousin's eye. "You're welcome to join us, Hayes, but we won't be put out a bit if you want to sup at the big house."

"I'll stay here with you, little angel—catchin' up on things." Hayes winked at Carter. "But have no fear, I'll retire to the Guest House this evenin'."

Eyelids at half mast, Carter nodded then exited, like a ship launching into deep seas, leaving a large wake behind him.

The bluster seemingly gone out of him, Hayes came and knelt by Cornelia, taking her hands in his. "You may not have money, but you're from a good blood line. Don't ever forget that, cousin Nelly."

She sighed. He sounded like she was a mare from some good breeding stock. At her work in Richmond, she'd been a valued employee. If only there was some way to bring Andy back to Richmond with her. But where could she place him? And how would she be able to afford lodgings away from the school, which didn't allow boys? Mayhaps they could make an exception for her since he was her brother.

Chapter Five

"Unh-uh, no. I ain't goin' up to no Richmond girl's school." Andy's words from the night before still echoed in Cornelia's ears as the sun rose pink over the jagged pine treeline behind the fenced kennels. A long "ow-ou" greeted Cornelia, and she smiled. A lone shadow shifted near the kennels. A tall figure bent and tossed something inside. Fear skittered through her. Had Daniel Scott snuck onto their land?

As her eyes adjusted, Cornelia moved closer to her dogs. The man stood.

Hayes. Cornelia released the breath stuck in her chest.

"Nelly, darlin', these dogs are the best yet." Hayes' smile spread across his face, his white teeth shining even in the low light.

"Pa was happy with the training he and Andy had done with them." Hayes had been right to begin bringing pups to Pa. He'd been a natural at training them. To Andy, they'd been the perfect distraction when their mother died. And now he, too, was adept at managing the hounds.

Insects buzzed in the low brush near them. "More mosquitoes gonna be hatchin' soon with all that rain. Make sure Andy and you have nettin' up in the cabin at night, ya hear? Might even put some over these kennels."

Cornelia surveyed the long row. Several dogs nursed their new pups. Slowly, she scanned the fenced yard. "I'm glad the dogs have a safe place." But would she be able to keep feeding them? Little had been sent down from Mama Jo of late.

"These pups have an excellent lineage. I know your pa trained them well, with Andy's help."

"Yes." She wiped a tear from her eye.

"I'd be glad to help you get the pups sold to good families again this year."

"That would be much appreciated." As would the income from the sales. Pa used the funds to pay for taxes on their land, which seemed mighty high to her for their land and cabin.

Hayes tugged at his earlobe. "And I reckon we best talk about Grandma Pleasant's—"

"Good morning," Carter called out curtly.

Cornelia pivoted to see him leaning on his cane. Was he spying on them?

Hayes squared his shoulders. "No offense Carter, but this here is a private conversation."

Irritation etched Carter's fine features. "I apologize for my intrusion."

The two men glared at each other but neither retreated.

The man raised a hand. "I think Carter needs his gal, Sally, here, to keep him in line." The glimmer in his eyes when he glanced between Cornelia and Carter told her that Hayes was up to something. Carter's scowl could have put frost on the new growth in the fields.

Hayes turned his back on Carter, bent and ran his hand over Lex's hind quarters. "Nelly, there's a little hot spot back here. Come feel."

Glancing anxiously from Carter to Hayes and the dog, Cornelia went to Lex and knelt beside him, Hayes warm shoulder rubbing against her own. A small spot near her Pa's best dog's right hip burned with heat. "You're right."

"Go get some liniment, baby doll."

Cornelia pointed to the crockery pot not inches from where Carter stood. "There's some right there."

"I want the... special... ointment, sweet thing." He drew out each word in a voice he'd never used with her before. The muscles in her shoulders tensed—her mother, his cousin, used such a tactic when she was

47

mighty serious. Hayes meant for her to go to the cabin—no nonsense about it either.

"I see." Would it be like this from now on? If she was dependent upon the mercy of others, was she also to forebear their whims? "I'll get the salve."

And if she married a man like Hayes, would all his sweetness change to vinegar? She must speak with Carter about her options if she remained on her farm. Surely he'd listen to reason—a trait in which he excelled, until he'd decided to join the Navy.

Dear Lord, I pray that some of his reasonableness has remained. And if not, please work Your will in him. In Jesus's name, amen.

Carter knew he shouldn't be antagonizing their visitor, but strong winds of fury filled his sails. "What do you mean by bossing her around like that?"

Hayes blew out a breath. "Pah!"

He moved his body trying to find comfort but it wasn't to be had. "Obviously you wish to speak with me in private."

Hayes shoved his hands into his coat pockets. "I love Nelly, and I want the best for her and Andy."

This horse breeder, this friend of his brother's, loved Nell. Those words did something to Carter's senses even though he knew they shouldn't. He should be grateful that his childhood friend had a protector. Instead, anger and resentment rose in him like a huge cresting wave on the sea, one that was going to slam down hard in a moment or two and pull him to the depths.

"She's been on her own for a long time and now with Andy to raise, I figure they belong with me."

Carter couldn't manage a response.

Hayes whistled and called a dog to him, then began taking him through his paces. This pup was vigilant to the point of nervousness, like a midshipman after his first battle. "Andy does fine with these hounds, but he'll need help."

Between hand motions, a word or two command, and rewards with treats from his pocket, Hayes had the dog performing exactly what he requested. Would Hayes accomplish the same with Nell? *Heaven forbid.*

A pup in the next kennel whined and Hayes shushed him. "This one—he's gonna bring top dollar for his pedigree."

Had he lost his friend to this domineering man? Was this what she wanted? Someone to order her around, give her a job to do, keep her at her tasks?

"When she marches down the aisle, she'll have a pocketful of money from selling these dogs." Hayes's chuckle and self-satisfied smile irked Carter, but he restrained himself.

"So, despite Andy having lived all his life here, you wish to take him away?"

"Correct." The man glowered again.

"Does Nell understand that you expect to sell the pups to fund her, um, trousseau?"

"Her wedding things? No, I'd give her all that. Send her to Richmond to get whatever she needs before she marries." Hayes narrowed his eyes. "Do you take me for a skinflint, son?"

"No, I've heard you're a generous man." But it wasn't proper for a man to be purchasing clothing, certainly not intimate attire, for his betrothed. He imagined suggesting such a thing to Sally. Perhaps, for once, he'd get a reaction out of her. Did Miss Sally Danner possess any true feelings or thoughts of her own? And Nell—when hadn't she given her opinion? Just now, when Hayes Davis ordered her to her cabin, albeit in couched terms, Nell had been utterly compliant. The man knew better how to manage her than Carter did. Perhaps he needed to learn how to request, nay order her to do something, yet save her feelings while doing so. Make it appear that she was choosing to do what he asked. No, that was manipulation.

Hayes relaxed his shoulders. "I wanted to mention that if'n you don't feel up to going through with the Puppy Day planned for here at Dogwood then I understand."

"Do you think people will still expect the event to occur?"

"I could hold it up in Orange County, on my farm—no sickness up there."

"Charles City is now safe." Safe enough—no outbreaks presently.

"People are nervous about the possibility of another one." Hayes scratched at his face through his beard. "I could bring Nelly and Andy up

49

for that and give them a chance to rub elbows with my neighbors. You know President and Mrs. Madison own the plantation adjacent my land."

Carter wouldn't give Hayes the satisfaction of thinking he was impressed. The Williamses, too, traveled in high circles. "When is this event planned?" And did Hayes intend for Nell and Andrew to live with him before they married? Hayes Davis's notion was getting worse and worse.

"Soon. Maybe within the month." Hayes smiled. "I can get my place all gussied up before then."

"No." The word came out more harshly than he intended. Carter cleared his throat. "I believe it should be canceled since we are in mourning here."

"Something occurs to me. I don't know how things are in these parts, but if'n the invites or announcements were already sent out then you may find people on your doorstep regardless."

The man was right. He sighed. "We'll go forward with the event if my nephews and Nell and Andy agree."

Eddie Williams appeared in Cornelia's doorway, no brothers trailing behind him, as they had done in the days since their father's death. "Miss Gill..."

Seated at the table, Andy finished his breakfast. He waved at Eddie, who grinned.

She shook her hands, wet from washing morning dishes. "Just 'Nell' when you're here."

"Perhaps 'Miss Cornelia'?" The boy beamed, his handsome little face so much like a young Carter.

She dipped her chin.

Eddie closed the door, keeping out some sunlight but also the flies. "I want you to manage my plantation."

Her heart dropped into her stomach. Had Carter agreed? "Is that so?" She flicked both of her damp wrists against the scratchy material of her apron. If she did the job, she wouldn't have to accept her cousin's charity nor a possible proposal. *That would be a relief.*

Andy ducked around her, his mouth full of cornbread. Crumbs fell from his mouth, and she put a hand up to stop him. But he wasn't a puppy to be trained and she let her hand fall. "Andy, it's not polite to eat in front of others."

He smiled at Eddie. "I like Mama Jo's cornbread better'n Sissy's."

"Andy, that's unkind." She resisted the temptation to swat him.

The two boys giggled and she did, too. "Sit down, Eddie. Do you want some cornbread?"

"No, thank you. I need to ask for your help." Eddie pulled a wooden horse from his pocket—one her father had whittled. "The new overseer is upsetting everyone."

Yesterday the man's rants carried to her garden, where she worked, two fields away from where he was bellowing. Such a man wouldn't take time to carve tiny animals for children. "I know what my father would have said about such an overseer. But you'll need to ask your uncle."

Jaw muscles twitched in Eddie's otherwise immobile face. "Mr. Frye threatened to whip Macy yesterday."

She flinched. Her friend, one of the Williams's house slaves, had never been whipped. Cold, smoldering anger brewed with fear and dread. "Macy? What was she doing out there?"

"I don't know, but we can't abide such punishment here. Grandfather and father wouldn't..." The boy's eyes welled with tears.

His stiff posture forbade her to hug him, as she wished to do. "I'll talk to Uncle Carter. Talk some sense into him about my plan."

He sounded more like a little general than a ten-year-old boy.

"You do that, Eddie." Dogwood Plantation's future owner departed.

Andy handed Cornelia his plate. "We could stay here then, right—if you managed the place?"

She exhaled through puffed lips. "It depends upon what Carter says."

With a snort, Andy trod to his bed and smoothed his quilt. "I don't want to move to Orange County."

Neither did she. She washed and rinsed their few dishes and considered what life might be like at Hayes's place. Servants would do such work as this. The notion of being separated from Carter, again, was too much to contemplate. She had to be honest with herself. But to remain here, to see him daily and know there was no future for them—would that not be even harder to bear?

Chapter Six

Cornelia didn't want to ask Carter for anything—including a ride to church. She waved flies away as she and Andy trekked to Westover Episcopal Church. If Hayes had remained one more day, she could have asked him for a ride. Swamp oaks rose on either side of the road, providing shade but harboring varied pests.

Andy's chin jutted out. "We shoulda rode with someone."

Her infernal pride. "Only a bit further." She should have asked Carter and set aside her pride and anger. She clenched her fists. Not after again he had emphatically denied Eddie's request for her to take her father's place. Sighing, she considered his alternative offer—care for his nephews. Considering that she already had the boys at her cabin many hours each day, she found his offer offensive. She knew what a pittance a governess made and she'd never be able to support herself and Andy and pay the taxes on their property much less any upkeep. Her options were limited, especially with fear of yellow fever.

Her brother kicked up dirt in the road. "Why didn't we use the wagon? Carter never said we couldn't."

She blotted her forehead with her handkerchief. "No, he hasn't. You're right." Nor had he said they could. So like Carter—to withhold announcement of something he'd already decided upon. Had he done that with the sailors on his ship?

"I am?" Andy's eyes grew wide. "I'm right?"

Was she so ornery he expected her to issue an instant denial? She crinkled her mouth. Of late, she'd been irritable. Since Pa died, then Anne, and Lee and many others. This yellow fever scourge had laid Charles City—and her—low.

The steeple pierced the skies beyond the bower of pines. They'd be the first to arrive, other than the preacher and deacon. She didn't expect many would attend, not with the recent outbreak. Her feet ached in her town pumps. Pride, infernal pride.

Andy threw a pebble down the road. "Can we sit with Eddie?"

"I don't think he's coming." He and his brothers had been keeping late hours up at the Great House, with their Aunt Mariah failing to issue a curfew. Carter wandered around the plantation like a lost soul—looking over the plants, checking on field workers, asking why so many had gotten sick and died. If she became plantation manager, she could help with all that.

Finally, they arrived. Cornelia lifted her skirts, hurried up the steps into the sanctuary, and led Andy to the church's left side. Sunlight broke through the windows. The past several weeks felt more like months. Keeping her eyes downcast, she and her brother slipped into the pew.

From here she could gaze out at the copse of trees, including the apple orchard, where pink blossoms danced about like ladies in silk gowns. Like the delicate creature she'd never be. "You're too outspoken, Cornelia," her father had always said. Cornelia flexed her long fingers, her nails trimmed to the quick as they had been when she'd grown up here. No gloves on these hardworking hands, not even on the Sabbath—she'd forgotten that she'd possessed any.

She went to the window and opened it to welcome the fresh breeze. From outside, the creak of wheels and the snorts of horses carried.

Footsteps behind her preceded a soft tap on her shoulder. She turned.

"Miss Gill?" Old Reverend Scott's benign smile and presence should have pleased her—the frail gentleman was well enough to be at the service. But when Daniel strode through the doors, all pleasure vanished.

She focused her attention on the retired priest. "Father Scott, good to see you." *If only you'd left your grandson at home.*

Her heart hammered in her chest. Cornelia returned to their pew and gestured for Andy to kneel. Thank God for the parish ladies who had covered the kneelers with velvet cushions.

"Come on." She and Andy knelt and prayed. *God, if you deem fit, give me a position on the plantation—one that is true, and good, and right. And keep me safe from Daniel Scott. Amen.*

She looked up. Carter's elegantly tailored cutaway coat clung to his shoulders as he closed the church window shut.

He turned and pointedly looked at her. "Don't want to let the bees inside."

Outside, honeybees had swarmed the camellia bushes. Her cheeks warmed. She'd rather be chased by bees than by Daniel.

Earlier she'd paid no heed to the nectar lovers. Soon they'd produce honey in the hive. She clutched her handkerchief. No sweet clover honey for her and Andy this year—not with Pa no longer a Williams' employee.

Carter set aside his cane and lowered himself into the pew ahead of her. Scrunching forward, he rubbed his leg.

"All rise!" The Episcopal priest entered, then ascended the curving stairs to his dais. Andy latched onto her arm. When they sat again, he'd probably fall asleep, exhausted from taking on Pa's chores.

Cornelia's entire body could have been strafed with a stiff horse brush as she sat in the pew, so aware was she of Daniel behind her. She tried to shake off the sensation, but failed.

Daniel Scott sat planted three rows behind Nell and her brother. The brute surely noticed that she had grown into the most beautiful creature in the county. Her appearance hadn't factored into Nell's earlier appeal to Carter—the reason he'd told Father that he *would* marry her. It had been the connection between them, the understanding they had of one another. And it persisted now despite their differences in social class, which no longer seemed as wide as the ocean. Her time at school in Richmond and her work there had altered her into a confident woman with poise.

Still, Nell was stubborn, which must be why she'd not accepted his offer of a carriage ride this morning. He glanced over his shoulder. She was angry with him. But he couldn't risk her roaming the fields, especially when families of slaves he'd never seen before now inhabited the plantation. The temporary overseer claimed the new slaves used a South Carolina Gullah dialect he couldn't understand. Lee had never discussed the management of the plantation with him.

When the service ended, he reached for his cane.

"Wake up, Andy, time to go," Nell urged her brother.

Carter stifled a chuckle.

"Andy, come on. We've got a long walk home," Nell entreated.

Carter rose and moved out of his pew.

"Can't we ride with Carter?" The whine in Andy's voice was one Carter now regularly experienced with his nephews.

Daniel moved forward, toward the other end of Nell's pew.

"Brother—go out the other way." Nell pointed toward where Carter had positioned himself.

"Care for a ride home?"

Nell's beautiful eyes reflected gratitude. "Yes, thank you." She pushed Andy toward the side aisle and exited.

Carter braced himself as Daniel had the audacity to move to join them and placed his black walking stick between Daniel and Nell. Would the barbarian assault her even in church?

Daniel dipped his chin. "Good day to you, Miss Gill. Mr. Williams."

Nell ignored their old neighbor while Andrew eyed him warily.

Did Carter wish him a good day? No. And he wouldn't lie, not in God's house. He wished repentance for Daniel. And a good thrashing.

Carter hoped his voice would hold the threat he intended. "'Tisn't the place for any conversation between you, me, and Miss Gill. Leave us be and good day to you."

Reverend Scott, lips tugging downward, tapped Daniel's shoulder. Daniel turned from them. Carter exhaled as the Kentuckian assisted his elderly grandfather from the sanctuary.

From beneath dark silky lashes, blue eyes shyly peeked up at him. "Thank you." He resisted the urge to pull Nell's arm through his.

"Let's go." Andrew pulled at his sister's hand.

As Carter hobbled toward the church exit, pity flashed across an elderly parishioner's face. From the intense chewing Nell gave her lower lip, she was yet angry about his refusal for her to manage Dogwood

Plantation. Something about Nell's gesture comforted him. He wanted to grab her shoulders and demand, "You don't feel sorry for me one bit, do you?"

He stifled a laugh. He could love a woman like that. One who never let him give in to his own sorrows. Who never allowed him such a luxury. If only Sally were the same way. Instead, she doted on him, waiting on him hand and foot as though he was an invalid. He wasn't.

"Could you take me out to the fields after lunch and show me the blight you mentioned to Edward?"

Her head snapped up. "I'd be happy to."

Light returned to her eyes. Standing this close, he could smell the light floral fragrance, delicate as the periwinkles her eyes brought to mind. But he'd never met a stronger woman.

"Andy and I would be most grateful for a ride home in your carriage, if you don't mind."

How could he ever mind being close to her again?

Cornelia twisted her mother's handkerchief in her hands, unsure of the best way to get into the carriage. *What am I do with all these blasted skirts and petticoats?* She'd walked everyplace on foot in Richmond.

Andy bounded up into the carriage. Good. He'd sit between them. 'Twas more proper.

Without warning, strong arms elevated her into the open carriage, Carter's shoulder leveraged against its side for support. Daniel Scott strode by, large white teeth flashing in his tanned face, his smile mocking. She averted her eyes.

"Oh," she gasped. "And without so much as a by-your-leave, Mr. Williams." Her cheeks flamed as the elderly Randolph sisters passed by, arm-in-arm, staring up at her.

Carter climbed in, settling so close that her skirts scrunched up next to his leg. "Your brother needs room to sit, Nell." His brow crinkled as sweat broke out on it.

Was he in pain from lifting her?

He pulled out a handkerchief and patted his forehead.

Andy leaned forward. "I don't like that man—Reverend Scott's grandson or not."

"Neither do I." A muscle in Carter's jaw jumped as he flicked the reins. "Let me know if you ever see him anywhere on your property or mine."

"Yes, sir."

"We men need to take care when we deal with delicate flowers such as your sister."

Carter sounded serious, but Andy snorted. "She ain't delicate—she's been out in them fields lookin' at the blight and shakin' her head."

Cornelia cringed. She didn't want Carter knowing what she'd been doing. "I was curious. I'd wondered about the current hot spell and its effect upon the crops. According to Pa's Almanac, the weather was more consistent and temperate during the previous year's growing season." She'd also wondered about the health of slaves, because Andy indicated their rations would be cut if the plantation didn't produce enough of their own crops to feed everyone.

"Ah, so you thought you'd help me out in the fields, even though I'd asked you, for your own safety, to remain on your own land." Carter's tone of voice, although holding an edge, also suggested he found her behavior humorous.

"You do know me well, Carter, so draw your own conclusions."

"All right. And what recommendations do you have for me? I'm sure you're simply bursting to share some."

"Consult the agrarian in Charles City as soon as possible. From what Eddie and I have observed in the fields we'll need his advice—assuming he's recovered from yellow fever."

"I have received my commander's orders and shall carry them out forthwith." He grinned and nudged his leg closer to her.

She grabbed her fan from her reticule. This was going to be a long ride home. And from the flushed feel of her skin, a hot one.

Chapter Seven

Already late spring, and there should be good crop growth but such was not the case. As Carter neared the fields, the early morning light revealed striated stripes of yellow woven through each new green leaf—just as Nell had said. Leaning on his cane, he bent and lifted the fledgling leaves of a corn plant. Blight that dotted immature leaves two weeks earlier had worsened.

Lee's records indicated that over a third of the income last year came from this crop's yield. They had to do something. He'd send word to learn whether the county agrarian could come out.

He wiped the coarse homespun sleeve of his brother's work shirt across his brow. How did the field workers tolerate its stiffness? Who had woven the fabric and sewn together this clothing? It certainly wasn't of the quality Father had provided for the workers.

He glanced over his shoulder toward a slave cabin, where he had spied a loom. Had a servant woven the cloth? Had money become so dear that they couldn't afford to purchase such a basic commodity?

Movement caught Carter's peripheral view, like a swift sloop approaching on the seas. Edward surged across the field, passing close by but not seeing Carter bent low over the corn plants.

The boy sneezed. The fields this time of year had been Carter's undoing as well—one reason he'd never bothered to learn about agriculture, planting, nor management of a farm. He'd always dreamed of sailing on the ocean. Although he'd relished the smell of the earth and of growing things, the vegetation at the plantation had made him cough and sneeze every spring and fall. His sensitivities, alone, hadn't propelled him to the Navy. Many prominent visitors to Dogwood Plantation agreed with their father that the military needed to be developed and in particular the Navy. All the politicians who spent time at their home had encouraged his interest.

By joining the Navy, had he been trying to please his father? Or had the reason been more personal—to earn a living so that he might support himself and Nell. Breathing in deeply, he realized his leg pain had lessened since returning to home—near her. And thankfully, the vegetation didn't bother him physically now.

If only my past mistakes didn't bring me so much pain.

As she stacked the dry dishes atop the table, someone pounded on the door. Cornelia jumped, releasing Andy's cleaned and dried plate with a clang atop her dish. The door swung in, a big man filling the frame.

"Hayes, what are you doing back already?"

"Well, I've got an open invitation. Plus, I've had business in the region. Some for my friend, the President." A brief expression of dread flickered over his face. She'd seen that look before when others spoke of the war.

"Are you mustering up more troops?"

"Somethin' like that Nelly, but don't you worry none about it." His features softened into what looked like a forced mask of contentment.

First Carter and now her cousin? She drew in a slow breath. "Please tell me you're not enlisting."

He placed his broad hand over his heart. "I'm not enlisting."

"Good."

He cocked his head at her. "Are you glad to see your cousin again?"

"Of course, come in."

He gazed down at her, stroking his beard. "Ya still willin' to trim my beard up for me, Sunshine?"

The good-hearted relative was willing to take her and Andy into his home. She swallowed. "Yes, of course."

Hazel eyes searched her face "So yer still willin'?"

She sucked in a deep breath. Her cousin's repeated question teemed with other queries. Willing or not, soon she'd be doing many things she'd never considered before. Cornelia shivered. Better get used to this man's needs and his customs if she might become his wife. He hadn't asked her yet, though. Hadn't even mentioned it directly.

Hayes stepped outside. "I'll wait out here."

She retrieved sheers and a razor from the hutch. "Andy, go fill that bowl with water."

Her brother popped the last of his corn muffin into his mouth. He seemed to take an eternity as he slowly chewed and swallowed. He tossed back the last of his cider.

"I'm waitin' patiently." The emphasis on Hayes' final word contradicted his melodious voice.

She chuckled. One thing was sure—Hayes would bring some sorely needed humor into her life, like rain after a long dry spell. But her thoughts immediately jumped to Carter—quieter, like a soaking summer rain that went on and on, drowning all other sounds. Then water drops touched all creation until the downpour ceased and the birds emerged in droves—singing.

Carter hunkered near the corn plantings close to Nell's cabin so he could watch Hayes. *Unbelievable—Davis thinks he can stay with Nell and her brother.* He'd not even bothered to stop up at the Great House.

Nell emerged from the cabin, scissors in her palm and a cloth tossed over her shoulder. A few yellow curls escaped her chignon. She bent low over Hayes. Her day-dress buttoned to her throat, although the top two buttons were undone.

Hayes cackled about something. The man had the most annoying laugh. *That isn't true.* Carter might like the man if he wasn't loitering around Nell.

A small hand pinched his shoulder, startling him. "Edward, you startled me. What have I told you about sneaking up on people?"

His nephew frowned. "What are you doing—spying on Miss Cornelia?"

"I'm not…"

The boy crossed his arms. "What do you call it then? Reconnoitering? Espionage?"

Carter shook the kinks out of his back and rubbed his leg. "Where did you learn those words?" The boys had driven off their very expensive tutor, if the books were correct, the previous spring. It was unlikely that his eldest nephew had been part of that effort, however.

Edward grinned. "Miss Cornelia teaches us new vocabulary every afternoon before the little boys nap. She's much better than Mr. Tate ever was."

"You don't say."

"I do say. Just did." His nephew grinned.

Carter wiped his brow. "Well, what is it you want?"

"Miss Cornelia needs to take over her father's spot. She needs to act as manager." Edward's face was set as though carved in marble, like the headstones of his two parents would be.

Sorrow for his brother and sister-in-law settled on him like sail blown free, wrapping damp and clammy around his soul. Edward reminded him so much of Lee. His mannerisms were even the same. But he possessed Anne's large, wide-set eyes. She'd been the most intelligent woman he'd ever met. And Edward was following suit. His tutors had described the ten-year-old as an academic prodigy—but he'd prefer to be out in the fields rather than sitting somewhere studying.

Did the boy discern something that Lee and he had not? Nell as manager versus departing with Hayes Davis? Irritation shot through him at the idea of her wed and gone. Weighing the options and finding them wholly unequal, Carter clapped Edward on his back.

"Capitol idea, nephew."

The boy blinked. "It is?"

"Indeed. Solves a multitude of problems." *With the mess the books are in, I'm almost undone.*

"But you didn't think so last week when I asked."

"You've shown persistence and initiative, two traits I admire."

Edward frowned in the direction of Nell's cabin. "What's she doing? Why is Miss Cornelia standing so close to Father's rough-mannered friend?"

Not ill-behaved—unrefined. "Humph! He's the wealthiest horse breeder in the commonwealth." Carter followed the boy's gaze. Nell stood between the man's spread legs, her old-fashioned skirt billowing as she leaned in.

"Uncle Carter?" Concern wavered his voice.

Edward didn't need to say another word. They took off as fast as Carter's injured leg and his cane allowed.

If Nell leans any closer to that man she'll be pressing against his chest.

Her laughter carried across the distance. "Hayes, you're a handsome man after all." She clucked her tongue.

Cornelia pressed her right foot on Hayes' outstretched boot. "Stop moving. You're like Pa—can't sit still for a minute."

"Aw, come on, Nelly. If'n you don't finish up I'm not gonna be able to catch up with that sweet little gal from South Carolina." He grinned up at her. "She wants to talk horses with me."

Did he mean Mariah Wenham? She sighed. "Cousin Hayes, if you knew what was good for you…" Rumor was that the only thing Mariah knew about horses was how to place a wager for a race. At the sound of feet clomping toward them, she whirled around.

Half-running and half-hitching his bad leg along, Carter headed toward them like a bull loose from his pen, charging directly at her. What did he take offense at now?

"Woah there, son, what's steamin' your kettle up?" While Hayes's voice held fear, he had only to stand and grab the former Navy lieutenant to halt him. "What'd she tell ya?"

Carter, face flushed, halted.

Eddie stepped forward, between them. "You're our new manager, Miss Cornelia!"

Carter nodded, confirming her appointment.

Relief flowed like warm honey from the top of head to her toes. "Thank you."

Andy came alongside her. She hugged him. "Tell Mr. Carter and Mr. Edward thank you!"

Her brother held a handful of Hayes's hair clippings that he had strewn on their plants to keep the deer away. "Thanky kindly! I didn't want to move to no old horse farm."

She glanced in her cousin's direction. Hazel eyes darkened and his smile disappeared. *I don't want to hurt him, but I don't want to leave either.*

Cornelia pinched his shoulder. "Andy, apologize at once."

"Sorry," Andy mumbled and returned to his task.

Carter squared his shoulders. "What do you mean by your question, Mr. Davis—about what some female might have said?"

Her cousin stroked his clipped beard. Cornelia slapped his hands away from his face and took a soft brush to his jawline. "You look years younger. And very handsome."

Turning to gauge Carter's reaction, Cornelia froze. Anger creased his eyebrows together, the indentation between his nose and lips rolled together, his nostrils flared, the cleft in his chin a chasm.

Hayes pushed Cornelia's hands away. She hadn't realized she'd left them on his broad shoulders. "Excuse me, Nelly." He stood, a head taller than her and a half head above Carter.

Shifting his hip and leaning against the cabin, Carter demanded, "What did *who* tell me?"

Full lips formed a circle inside Hayes's now-trimmed beard. "Did the boys' aunt say somethin' to ya' this morning?"

"Mariah? No. Why would she?" The spit-and-fire left Carter, with few coals burning feebly as his face contorted, then relaxed.

"She wants the boys to each have a new pony. I said I'd talk it over with you, first."

Carter settled into Lee's chair in Father's old office and stared at the numbers before him. *Ponies? Unless I can decipher these accounts and*

discover more money somewhere, we'll need to look at selling off parcels of land.

The door creaked open and Lee's friend entered the room, unasked. *Sometimes he acts like he owns the place.* Carter gazed at Hayes Davis over the desk, covered in logs and receipts. He motioned to a chair.

Davis tugged at his trousers, lowered himself into the seat in a lumbering fashion that recalled backwoodsmen. However, Hayes was no frontiersman but rather the most respected horse breeder in all of Virginia. Why then, couldn't Carter manage to make himself more agreeable to the man?

Rubbing his close-cropped beard, Davis pulled the chair closer and leaned forward, then stood and went to the window. "If Nelly and Andy came home with me, I could care for them." Laughter and boys' voices carried through the raised window.

"Unnecessary." That retort burst out like a rebuke from an officer to an enlisted man. Carter squared his shoulders.

Hayes turned, his bushy eyebrows raised. "Do you believe her Pa, or yours for that matter, would want her working here managin' things?"

Pain squeezed his leg as he rose to hopefully chase Hayes from the room. Carter collapsed back into his chair. He'd overdone it by walking too much of the property the previous day.

"You all right?" Hayes poured a glass of water from a carafe into a crystal glass and offered it to Carter.

Reluctantly, he accepted it. "Thank you."

"Listen here, surely you know your nephews need the consistency, the continuity of family and friends."

"I do."

"Then you must understand why I'm concerned about Nelly and Andy. This arrangement you've got is untenable—and yes, I do know a few big words, by the way. The way things are ain't gonna last."

Carter's neck grew warm and he tugged at his starched collar.

Hayes narrowed his eyes. "Don't you intend to return to the college?"

"It is not your concern what I do." He locked eyes with the man and refused to give ground.

65

Averting his gaze, the horse breeder picked up a wooden model of a pony from the walnut secretary's top shelf. Mr. Gill had whittled the toy when Edward was born. The year when so many other things went awry.

"Then I reckon you oughta feel the same way about what I do. They're my concern, not yours."

What did that mean? Irritated, Carter closed his eyes. Opening them again, he caught fleeting anger on the older man's face.

"You're not growin' sweet on my Nelly, are you now, Carter? Are you simply tryin' to keep her with you?" Unlike his normal slow, melodic speech, Davis enunciated every word as though holding a threat.

Hackles rising, in instinct, Carter felt for the third drawer. The pistol. His breath caught. *Calm yourself—he's only asked a question.*

"As you may recall, I have been... calling on a young woman in Williamsburg." Had he? Rather, Sally Danner had pursued him.

"Reckon I remember. The question is—do you?"

Chapter Eight

So much had changed in one day that Cornelia couldn't help but wonder what was next. She'd finished examining the planting record and the yields the previous night. Her concerns and Carter's aligned—which was good. Today would be bittersweet, for she'd no longer be instructing the Williams boys as she had for the previous weeks.

Cornelia hung Andy's washed and rinsed trousers over the rail behind the house. The sun would dry them in no time. She dumped the wash water over Ma's rose bushes, in sore need of moisture. The three younger Williams boys rounded the corner of the cabin. "We're here."

Charles took the tub from her and hung it from a peg hammered into the rear wall.

"I'm tickled that you want your last day's lesson, boys, but Andy and I have got to tend to the hounds before we do anything." Tomorrow she'd have to figure out a new schedule. *I hate to take this time from them.*

Lloyd squashed his hat down further over his chestnut curls. *He needs a haircut.* "We'll come with you."

She swung little Albert up into her arms, noting that his hair, too, required attention. "Where's Eddie?"

Charles' gray eyes darkened. "In the fields."

"He's walking with Macy. She's scared of that man out there, old Frye. Uncle Carter sent for him—he's being replaced."

"Yes, I'd recommended that he be sent on his way."

"And Macy brought a basket to the workers." Lloyd lifted the napkin from atop the small box he carried. The scent of corn muffins wafted up, and her mouth watered.

She brushed caramel-colored hair from Albert's eyes. "I hungy." The toddler reached out, and his brother handed him a muffin.

Cornelia set him down, her stomach growling. "Should we all eat a little while we walk? Before we work the dogs?"

Albert took a large bite in agreement as the other two tore into the container's contents. Charles brought a honey-infused baked good to her.

"Here, Miss Cornelia."

Warm, buttery goodness filled her mouth. These were not the dried-out creations she produced. Did Hayes's horse farm have a well-appointed kitchen? Did he have cooks and servants who would take care of all those chores for her? They'd never traveled to the Orange County farm, which was a far spell away. Their great-aunt, Grandmama's sister, had never visited them, either.

"Come on." She led them from the yard, and they followed like ducklings after a mama duck. She nibbled on Mama Jo's treat as they made their way. When she finished, tiny fingers tugged at her skirt. She lifted Albert up, and he blessed her with an angelic smile.

Charles stepped forward alongside them. "When we get our ponies, we can ride all over the property."

As if to emphasize, Albert pointed his index finger east toward the farthest fields.

She kissed his forehead and then wiped the tiny boy's face with a handkerchief. *I'll miss these afternoons together.* Unbidden, moisture formed in her eyes. After every one of Mariah's visits when Cornelia had lived at home, Macy had told her of Mariah's boasts about her estate. Why was she gifting the boys so extravagantly? Was she trying to bribe Carter so she could take them back to South Carolina with her?

"You are definitely getting ponies?" She and Carter had agreed that with the costs of feed and seed as well as contracting with a physician for their worker's care, the boys would need to wait. But apparently Mariah had other ideas.

"Mr. Davis is bringing them when he returns for Puppy Day."

68

The dogs, having caught her scent, began to bay. Their lonesome howling corresponded to her inner reaction. "Mr. Davis? Puppy Day?" *What is he up to?*

Albert jabbed his finger at her cheek. "Pony."

"Auntie Mariah wants us to have a pony." Lloyd pulled his brother's finger from Cornelia's face.

She set Albert down, taking his hand. "Perhaps she meant in South Carolina."

"No. For here. And Mr. Davis said he had four he could bring down with him."

They made no sense. She rubbed her head. "We're not having the Puppy Show because..." Good gracious, did they really believe that with the scourge of yellow fever, the war, and the deaths of their parents and her and Andy's father that the event would proceed? Maybe she misunderstood what Carter had said. Disappointment washed every sweet feature in the three upturned faces.

Charles shrugged. "Uncle Carter said people may still show up because it looks like Father sent invitations out before..." The child's eyes filled with tears. He crossed his arms and turned away from her.

The barking grew louder. The dogs ran loose. *How had they gotten out?*

"Halt!" Andy's voice rang out.

The tan, white, and black hounds paused, some with tails still twitching. Heart pounding, Cornelia put her hands on her hips then drew in a slow breath. She didn't know whether to praise her brother or scold him.

Lloyd and Albert clapped. Charles swiped at his face and then did the same.

A slow grin crossed over Andy's face. "Should I put on a demonstration, Sissy?"

The trio jumped up and down and she nodded her head in assent and lowered herself onto the grass. She held Albert on her lap and motioned for Charles to sit beside her. These boys did indeed need someone looking after them. Charles's tears had broken something loose in her heart and tears streamed down her face as her younger brother displayed his competency with his dogs.

Carter hurried as fast as his leg allowed him. When he heard the dogs baying as though they'd cornered a fox, he increased his pace. He'd been told that these were not dogs bred for such inhumane activity but rather as family hunting dogs and pets. But once a hound that trait must continue, he presumed. He'd found no one at the Gill cabin but spied the tracks of small feet heading toward the kennels. Earlier, Hayes mentioned his suspicion of someone tampering with the kennels. If those tracks belonged to his nephews and a stranger lurked, the dogs could be barking a warning. But the hounds suddenly ceased their noise.

Rounding the corner past an ancient barn, Carter spied Andrew taking the dogs through their paces. Nell's mouth brushed the top of Albert's head, and pleasure flowed through him. He could almost feel those soft lips on his own, imagined her holding a child of her own. Of their own. His face heated at the thought. He moved toward the small group.

Albert waved at him wildly as he neared.

"What do you say, boys? Would you approve of Puppy Day going forward?"

"Yes."

"Hurrah!"

"Then I shan't turn folks away who show up here on the planned date."

Macy hadn't ventured out into the fields since the former overseer had left and the new one had begun, but she arrived now. The young woman held out a buff-colored envelope, stifling a giggle as she released it into Cornelia's hand. Elegant script, so unlike the earthy man, denoted the letter as one from Hayes.

Macy surveyed the workers bent over sickly looking plants and pulling up weeds. "You gonna keep doin' this?"

A tiny square—a miniature portrait of a handsome man fell to the ground. Macy lifted it, wiped specks of dirt off, and handed it to Cornelia.

Soft, wavy hair framed an expressive face. Medium-dark eyes were large but the focal point was the man's sensual lips, beneath which a firm chin, marked by a cleft, suggested a determined nature. The nose was even and somewhat large, but proportional to his features. High cheekbones framed a face perfectly in balance.

"That be Mr. Davis."

"Perhaps." Who would know with all the hair that covered the man? Cornelia opened the letter.

Macy brushed at her apron. "Do you think Mr. Davis be a good man?"

"Of course I do."

The servant lowered her head as two workers passed behind her, both making bold to look the house slave over.

"Do you men need something?" Cornelia hoped her firm voice carried a warning.

"Gettin' some water."

Neither man looked familiar, nor was the anger that filled their dark eyes. She stood taller, her spine stiffening.

Eddie ducked out from beneath the shed's overhang, nearby. "Your closest water is over where you were working."

The two men glanced back at Macy and her. Then the men turned and headed out.

"It ain't right you bein' out here, Missy." Macy squeezed her hand. "And with Miss Mariah headed off for Charleston today, what is Mister Carter gonna do about tendin' to those boys?"

"I'll help as best I can." Cornelia opened the letter to see what her cousin had to say.

> *My Dearest Cornelia,*
>
> *Please pray about my offer. I'd delight in you and Andy joining me here at Pleasanton. It is my fondest desire that you be happy and cared for. Should you wish to keep any or all of the beautiful hounds, I have kennels at the ready. When I return, I shall make my intentions clear and ascertain your wishes. I fear you are living with the faintest of tendrils holding you in your present circumstances. I will always be here should that fragile thread break free. God's word is quite clear on my responsibilities to you and Andy.*

71

May I be so plain as to say that I feel your brother shall not benefit from this choice you have made to step into your father's shoes? Your father and I spoke of this possibility and never would he have considered that you should subject yourself nor your brother to the demands you are now both under. I shall not shirk my obligations should you reconsider and come to Pleasanton posthaste.

With Love,

Hayes

While the missive was completely unlike her cousin's usual manner of speech, she knew him to be an educated man. Was this a proposal? Did he have to shame her into the effect her decisions might have upon Andy? She peered down at her work clothes, dirty from her forays into the stables and the fields, suddenly embarrassed. In Richmond, she'd been attired plainly but had always been clean and tidy.

Macy cleared her throat. "I been thinkin'."

Cornelia straightened. "What is it?"

"I was wonderin'…" Macy's lovely green eyes met Cornelia's with longing. "Ya look so fine in Miss Anne's clothes." Tears brimmed in Macy's eyes. "Would a man find me appealin' if I was to wear a fancy dress? A decent man?"

This young woman caught the attention of men while dressed in slave's clothing—sometimes in ways that required Pa's intervention. If Cornelia could, she would reach out and hug Macy and tell her how beautiful she was, in finery or rags. "Macy, come to my cabin tonight, and I'll give you one of those dresses and you'll see."

Her broad pearly smile was the best thank you Cornelia could have received. They'd been friends since childhood. Every time Cornelia returned to Richmond, after brief holidays in Charles City, they'd always told each other how much they'd miss the other while parted. But truth be told, if Cornelia could set her friend free, she'd be happy for her to go far away to where she could make a life for herself as a freed woman. If only she could do so.

After dinner, Cornelia selected the shortest of the three dresses she'd been given. *This should fit Macy perfectly.*

72

"Andy, go give the dogs their meat. Spend some extra time with them tonight."

Her brother scraped his chair away from the table. "Thank you, Sissy."

Thank God he loved those dogs, for they surely brought him comfort.

As he left, Macy stepped in, tugging her wrap around her. "Are you sure about this, Missy?"

"I am. Come in." Cornelia handed the olive-green dress to Macy, whose hands trembled. "Why don't you dress in Andy's space? Pull the blanket across for privacy."

Macy eased in behind the old wool blanket. "Never had any trouble figurin' out a man's intentions before."

"I'm certain your mama made sure of that."

"She did. And other than that nasty overseer scarin' me, I've never had a true problem—your pa always straightened it out. Until now." Macy's garments fell to the wood floor with a soft swish of fabric.

"So you don't know what this man wants?" Cornelia tapped her hip, the paper of Haye's letter in her pocket crinkling in response.

"Think I do, but I's not sure." The sound of thick folds of skirt being arranged carried through the blanket.

"You must think he has honorable intentions to be so concerned." And to go to this trouble.

"No man look..." Macy sighed. "Feels like he look right into my soul."

Cornelia stifled a snort. The only man she'd ever felt that way about was Daniel Scott. Prickles of premonition ran up her arms to her shoulders. "Does he say he loves you?"

"Yes, but I don't hardly know him like a sweetheart."

Acid poured into her stomach. "Has he, I mean..." How should she ask this?

"He be a gentleman—treat me like a lady."

The fear eased from her in a cold wave. "He's respectful?" But Daniel had been, too. At least at first. "Don't give him any allowances for improper behavior, Macy."

Shame niggled at her. What if she had put a stop to Daniel's advances right from the beginning? But she hadn't known what he was trying to do.

73

She'd make sure Macy understood how devious men could be when they were trying to get their way with a woman.

A few moments later the blanket was pushed aside, and Macy stepped forward. The olive gown brightened her green eyes and made the natural pink in her cheeks more prominent. Cornelia raised a hand to her chest.

"Oh, Macy, you're so lovely."

If they pulled her hair up, she'd be more beautiful than the pictures Miss Anne used to receive from Paris. Drawings of models wearing the newest styles. She took her friend's hands and pulled her to the old mirror. Then she took it from the wall and held it for her so she could see herself.

Macy commenced crying. Cornelia placed the mirror on the table and pulled the younger woman into her arms. "Listen, sit down. I am going to try to help you. Teach you what I know about how some men behave and how to figure out if this one really is a gentleman."

She pulled away and stared into the girl's wide eyes. "Or if he's not."

They settled at the table and she tried to think of any and every thing that she could have done differently to not have encouraged Daniel's wrong inferences as to what her behavior meant. "First of all—don't let him think he can touch you. Not even what might seem innocent."

"Not at all?"

"No. And make sure you say something immediately if he does." What if she had slapped at Daniel's hands when he had grazed her cheek with his hand? Or told him not to rest his arm on her shoulder?

By the time Andy returned, Cornelia had exhausted her store of painful memories. *If I can spare her the upset I endured then I will have done my duty.*

Her brother went to the cabinet and grabbed a biscuit. "You want one, Sissy? Macy?"

The young woman rose. "I best be goin'."

"Aren't you gonna change out of those fancy duds?" The boy sank his teeth into the biscuit.

Macy's heart-shaped face reddened. "I'm gonna meet up with…"

Cornelia held her breath. Who was the man? Had it been a field hand? Or was it Gabe, the freedman recently hired for the stables?

Gently curved lips formed a pretty pout. "I best not say his name." She gathered her clothing and came to Cornelia, squeezing her hands. "Thank you."

"Be careful."

"I will."

Cornelia put her hands in her pockets, crumpling the letter again.

"What you got in your pocket?" Andy pulled the letter out, and she snatched it away.

Her brother wasn't a good reader but he could read well enough. He didn't need to see this missive. "It's from Hayes. He says he really wants us to come live with him." And had laid a load of guilt at her feet. Was she really doing the right thing for her and Andy?

"Already knew that."

But did he know what that would mean? The ease both she and Andy would have at Pleasanton? She'd not weighed what such a move could mean for her brother's education and welfare.

"He wrote that he loves us." She had always sensed the love and concern of their cousin.

"Of course he does. And we love him."

"Yes." But could she love him as a wife loved a husband? Not when her heart already belonged to someone else.

Chapter Nine

Red-tinged skies above the James River portended an ill day ahead as Cornelia strode toward the plantation's brick buildings. A few people had sent word that they would be coming out to purchase a dog as a pet for their children during these difficult times. But Carter had been unable to locate the list of those invited. As she passed the smokehouse, the storehouse for grain, and the dovecote, she tried to shake off the foreboding. The time until Puppy Day had flown by. She didn't blame the guests reticent to travel to Charles City. The yellow fever outbreak had ended, but people's nerves were still taut at the notion that the dread disease might reach their communities.

"Good morning, Miss Gill," the stablemaster called out as he brushed one of the Williams's horses. The tall beast munched on a carrot and flicked his tail casually, but the little quivers in his flanks suggested he was aware of the goings on around him.

She stepped onto the Queen Anne forecourt that divided the two flanking sets of buildings. All manner of servants crisscrossed the lawn.

Workers, their arms stacked high with linens, trailed into the Flankers. Soon Hayes and those guests who decided to attend, despite the situation, would be pulling up the driveway. Her cousin's latest missive hinted that he was concerned about someone's salvation and that he would "appeal to that person's spiritual nature" during this visit. Did he mean Carter?

Cornelia paused near the laundry. Today would be another long day, one that included time inventorying the stables and barns, after she started with a review of Lee's ledgers. But what if they were successful in their sales? She and Andy would have more options. Cornelia shrugged away the memory of Daniel telling her that he was her only choice for a better life.

Levi trotted by her, his wheelbarrow piled high with early vegetables. "Mornin' Missy Gill."

"Good morning."

Her stomach roiled. *Oh God, please help me.* Her mind was in a muddle, her previous night's dreams filled with images of Carter, Daniel, and Hayes pulling at her three arms, one having grown from where her heart was.

A breeze stirred the air, carrying with it the rich scent of earth and new growth. She took a slow, deep inhalation.

"Missy Gill, you be lost?" A laundry worker teased as Cornelia walked by the building. Pungent lye soap assailed her nostrils. She scowled at the girl, who covered her mouth and giggled.

Crossing the forecourt, Cornelia dodged carts rolled by workers along the pathways as she made her way to the kitchen. Lured by the smell of ham and something savory, she raised her skirts and was up the steps in a thrice.

The smell of Mama Jo's good cooking encompassed Cornelia in the large kitchen, but when she entered the older woman was nowhere in sight. Wide planked tables were covered with bowls and implements for cutting, grating, and chopping food. Several younger women continued their work but Macy ceased stirring a massive pot of stock. "Lucinda, keep an eye on that pot for me, will ya?"

"Sho' thing."

Macy set the ladle down on a plate and joined Cornelia, grabbing her hands and tugging her into the hallway. "So much commotion be goin' on around here."

Inside, her nerves were all atwitter. Outside, something metal clattered onto the bricked pathway, and Cornelia jumped.

Macy pulled Cornelia to a corner as men carried crates of produce inside. "My beau be comin' by tonight." Emerald eyes danced in delight.

So he didn't live at Dogwood Plantation. "Your beau?"

"He tell me to call him that." Her friend's face glowed. "He want to marry me."

Marry her? Cornelia swallowed. How would Carter take that news? Why should anyone be able to own another person? Why was Macy considered someone's "property"?

"I done what you told me." Macy's lips pressed together. "But I have to slap him once."

Cornelia drew in a breath. "And?"

"He 'pologize somethin' fierce. Say he never disrespect me again." A glint in her eyes preceded a giggle. "He try to kiss me but I pull away. Like you told me."

Someone cleared their throat behind them. Carter, dressed in riding clothes, stood framed in the doorway. Warmth flowed through her—he was able to get up on horseback again.

"Macy, I believe you are needed in the kitchen." Carter's lips compressed.

The servant curtsied.

"Nell, I suspect your assistance is unwanted here." Dark eyes challenged hers.

This wasn't why she'd come looking for him. Carter was supposed to bring her some measure of peace—of comfort. Like when they were young.

He took her arm and led her to the brick stairs and outside. She tried to shake free. "That was uncalled for."

"As is giving romantic advice to the servants." His tone was as cold as the ice beneath sawdust in the Ice House.

"You're correct." She scowled at him. "I should be advising you." *Like telling you that the professor's daughter is not right for you.*

He squeezed her elbow and led her into the green's center, between the buildings. "You gave Macy Anne's dress, didn't you?"

Cornelia stared at the line forming between his dark brows, the sign of a coming explosion. "Yes."

"Why?"

She turned away from his unblinking stare. "Because I wanted to help her feel…" Beautiful, valued, special—a lady. Exactly as Cornelia wanted someone to make her feel.

Carter was so close she felt his breath on her cheek as he exhaled. "Some fellow has been meeting with her. Cook told me."

Meeting his gaze again, she discerned worry. "Who?"

"No one knows."

Was he blaming her for the man taking an interest in her beautiful friend? She shrugged and averted her gaze. "Doesn't Macy have a right to be happy?"

"Are you still so naïve—don't you understand?"

He thought her innocent, not wanton? Some tight thread of twine uncoiled from her heart. She'd never been sure if he blamed her for Daniel and his attentions.

His grip tightened. "It's dangerous meeting alone. She's yet a slave." She could hear rage below the surface of his carefully modulated voice.

"What about you, Carter? Do you know so much about meeting unchaperoned with young women?"

He released her elbow and took a step away. "I'm not proud of my behavior while in our country's service, if that's your meaning."

Her pulse quickened. "How so?"

Guilt flickered across his face, chased by pain shuddering through him. He grabbed the back of the bench nearby and took a few short breaths.

"Let's just say that the young ladies of Annapolis were treated to a grand display of my many latent charms." His self-mocking laugh was accompanied by sadness in his eyes.

Carter had acted the cad? She'd never have imagined.

"Shocked? Perhaps you should be."

"Why, Carter?" She didn't care what he said. Carter Nelson Williams wouldn't have dishonored a woman.

"Oh, nothing too terrible or devious." His lowered himself onto the bench.

"But you misled young women into thinking you cared for them?" His voice and expression suggested Carter was laughing at whatever romantic attempts he had made.

79

"They had their share of kisses." He met her eyes. "But I never lied nor took advantage."

Had Daniel believed he spoke the truth, too?

Carter's face hardened into a mask. "What have I to offer anyone?"

"That's the most ridiculous thing I have ever heard."

Eyebrows raised, he grabbed her hand and pulled her toward the bench. "Sit down. You're making me nervous."

"I like that idea." But she didn't really. She'd come here hoping they could draw some strength and comfort from each other. But it wasn't to be. She sat, arranging her skirts around her. "Such a nuisance. Pa didn't make me wear these when I lived at home."

"That's not true and you know it." He covered her hand with his. She tried to pull free but he clutched tighter. "Your father required proper attire when you had company. And we may well indeed have many more guests than who have sent their responses." Perspiration beaded on his brow.

His firm hold on her loosened and she freed her hand. "Hayes is coming soon." Her words came out in a whisper.

"Do you love him?" Was that a slight tremor she heard in his voice?

"Of course I do." Her second cousin was a dear.

"Then why did you want to take over the manager's position and stay here?" His plaintive voice urged her to explain.

"I wanted to help." But the work was hard. Although she could follow Pa's notes, she was having difficulty with Lee's ledger sheets. Lately, concerns over the work had given her sleepless nights, begging God to show her what to do.

"If you wanted to help, you could have cared for the boys."

She'd thought their aunt might wish to help raise them. "Mariah..."

"Mariah be hanged. If you love Hayes Davis, why not accept his proposal and go?"

Was he reading her letters? "Do I go up to your house and ask to see the letters from your sweetheart?" She slapped his leg, shocked by the sting from the well-muscled surface. She withdrew her hand and rubbed it, embarrassed by her action.

"Of course not."

"Do I ask you why you haven't returned to college? Sent these boys on with their aunt? No." She was yelling now but she didn't care who heard.

Geese squawking overhead competed for attention. Cornelia tried to get up but Carter grasped her arm and stayed her.

"Hayes is a wealthy man."

Carter wants to be rid of me.

"He's prominent with powerful friends in government. You'd never lack for anything you or Andrew ever needed."

All movement around them suspended. The servants walking by, his nephews chasing one another, the birds flying overhead. Cornelia took several slow breaths. Was her stubborn independence and pride going to cause her brother to suffer? When both could be well provided for at Pleasanton? *Lord, I don't know what to say. What to do.*

"And Miss Danner? Could we say the same for her?" She rose and faced him, planting her hands on her hips. "Can she give you everything you've ever wanted? An educated young lady, from a fine family, dressed and cleaned up like a porcelain doll. Why aren't you with Miss Sally, Carter?"

Cornelia smoothed her skirt and headed toward the Great House's first-floor office and entered. Inside, the paneled wall's lower half gleamed a serene French blue. Neat stacks of papers filled wooden trays atop the desk. Behind, between the two tall windows, the lateral filing cabinet contained papers from bottom to top, all visible through the glass doors. How unlike pa's office in the South Flanker, where she would work most days. That office was much more like her workplace in Richmond. However, unlike that utilitarian place, her new Dogwood Plantation office possessed tall windows that looked out over the lawn and was larger, albeit almost as sparsely furnished.

She padded across the soft wool carpet that Nemi and Lucinda brought down from Anne and Lee's room for Carter. Hard to imagine him spending much time in this office, and he'd confessed he hadn't. She slid behind the desk that smelled vaguely of beeswax. Pulling the heavy chair back, she settled in, finding it more comfortable than she'd imagined.

Lee. So young to die, to have never known Christ's presence in his life on earth. Until the end. If she had anything to say about it, his children would hear of God's true riches. But would Sally Danner share the news of salvation with their children if she married Carter?

Securing a quill pen, Cornelia dipped it and tapped, releasing the extra ink back into the bottle. She scanned the columns of figures. Amount diverted - $1.75. The same amount weekly until month's end, when it increased tenfold to $17.50. She tallied her total.

The only notation was CWM. Was this an abbreviation for Clayton Williams, the Williams' cousin? A notorious blackguard, Clay had been around on any number of occasions sniffing out any extra money Lee had.

But Clayton hadn't even come to the funeral. From what she knew of relations like that, they'd show up at the funeral, yellow fever contagion or not, and claim that someone promised something dear to them. He'd have at the least contacted them soon after the burials. *No, not Clay.*

For the next few hours Cornelia poured over every notation, every jot and tittle, until her head ached. Eddie drifted into the room, clothes dirty from the fields. He casually draped his hat over a carved foxhound head on the chair's arm rests.

One day this would be Eddie's domain, if the plantation wasn't in as much debt as Carter feared the records showed. The boy trod to the exterior wall and paused before a Sheraton gaming table above which hung a narrow shelf. He ran a small finger along the outline of a ship, carved of a light-colored wood. "Uncle Carter can't tolerate being in here."

"What about you?"

"I like it. This feels most like Father, of any room in the house." His mouth tilted up but his eyes drooped.

"I believe it would be a wonderful place to get work done." She ran her hands around the leather-trimmed blotter on the desktop. It was elegant, the furnishing bespeaking a wealth that she would never know. *Unless God so willed it.*

Eddie pointed to the sheets of sums before her. "What are you finding so far?"

"It's a bit of a mystery." Cornelia rolled her lips together, then reached for the glass of cider, savoring the tangy apple drink. "Do you know if your father had any dealings with a family member with the first initial C—besides Carter, of course?"

Eddie peered over her shoulder. He pointed to the transferred numbers from the other sheet and their notations. "CWM—is that why you ask?"

"Yes. If he owed a family member money, though, it seems to me someone would have come forward by now. It's been several months since this has been paid."

"Father always abbreviated Williams as Wms. 'Twas what he said."

What else had his father told him? "Eddie, sit next to me, please."

"Certainly." He pulled a hardwood chair to her side of the desk.

What a good pupil he'd likely been. "Do you miss your tutor?"

He shrugged. "I miss my parents most of all." His words pierced her heart.

She slid a hand over his. "I miss mine, too." If Sally Danner lured Carter from Dogwood, how much more lonely would she feel?

The two sat for a moment, both silent. She refused to cry. But her eyes disobeyed her mind. She accepted Eddie's handkerchief and dabbed at her face. *Pa, I miss you so much.*

Re-reading Hayes's letters in the privacy of her home, Cornelia wondered if she had deciphered his meaning correctly. She stared at the miniature portrait of the dashing man. Surely this was Hayes, and what a handsome figure he was. But he was still her cousin—a second cousin but her only relation.

What had Carter meant when he said he had nothing to offer Sally? Was he so disturbed by his injury that he didn't feel like a man anymore?

Determination rose up in her. If she chose to marry Hayes, she was going to help Carter feel better about himself before she did so. He would be her project. She would get his books in better order than Lee had left them, and she'd finish the plan that Pa had set out for future plantings. She'd help Eddie and Carter find a suitable overseer. If only their workers were there by free choice instead of enslaved and forced to work the soil. Her conscience had objected to living amongst people who continued the barbaric tradition. Hayes was the one who had first planted the notion in her mind that there were other options to running a successful farming operation than making slaves work the land. He employed only freedmen and women at his horse farm. So if she married her cousin, at least then she'd not be part of something she deplored.

Dogwood Plantation belonged to Eddie, not Carter. But Carter was tasked with helping the heir and his brothers. Eddie possessed a natural talent for managing people, including the new workers. He could get anyone to do almost anything by asking a few short questions. If only she had that talent. What would she do? She'd get Carter to see that despite his injury he would make a wonderful husband and Sally would be a fortunate woman to have him. That would make him happy—wouldn't it?

Crossing the fields, Cornelia wilted along with the crops. Now at day's end she stood in the farthest section from her cabin. Poor planning, but she had accomplished all she'd set out to do this day.

The bell clanged and workers headed off to their own long row of cabins at the property's edge.

Cornelia pulled off her straw hat and wiped a hand across her forehead. She'd been in an office, at the stables, and in the barn earlier. How must the field slaves feel? Likely every muscle ached from walking the rows, from bending to examine the plants, and from long hours on their feet.

A rider with a broad hat slung low headed toward her, the horse kicking up dust. Her heart kept rhythm with the animal's trot.

She blocked the sun with her hand but didn't recognize Carter until he slowed the horse and drew close to her.

"I'd like to speak to you." His lips were tight and twitched as though he would brook no argument from her.

"I'm sorry, Carter. I didn't mean to yell at you earlier."

He leaned over and reached for her, hooking his arm around her waist.

"What are you doing?"

With a vise-like grip, he lifted her up onto the horse and settled her in front of him. Although she felt the heat of his chest and the sweat seeping through his shirt it didn't bother her. He smelled good, like cedar and spice and of his own masculine scent. At first she tensed but in a moment she relaxed into him.

"I'm sorry, too." His voice was husky. She felt his strong thighs squeeze as he urged the horse forward. "We need to talk."

About what? Cornelia tried to not rock against his body as they rode forward but she couldn't prevent herself from pressing against him. "Someone might see us."

"Let them," he whispered in her ear and urged the horse into a canter.

Her pulse quickened. This wasn't the Carter she knew. And loved. Was this the young naval officer who kissed whoever he wished and then left them be? She stiffened and tried to hold herself away from him but the attempt was futile. How could he behave in such an intimate way with her when only this morning he'd urged her to run off with Hayes?

He wrapped his arm around her more firmly. "You cannot continue on like this, Cornelia."

No, she couldn't continue imagining what it would be like to go to sleep in his arms and wake up beside Carter each day. She closed her eyes and allowed herself to revel in the sensation of being held against him. Something that might never happen again.

"Hayes is here."

He had to ruin it. She resisted the urge to poke an elbow into his ribs.

"When he sees how exhausted you are from your work, he may thrash me for not forcing you to stop."

The horse slowed and Carter directed him toward a copse of tamaracks.

"Where are you going?"

"I want to talk with you somewhere in private." He released his arm from her waist, and she wished he hadn't. She leaned into him. Would he try to kiss her? Was this a ruse?

"Carter, I can't marry Hayes." Not if she compared him to another man all the rest of her life. "It wouldn't be fair to him."

"He loves Andrew—won't mind taking care of him. Delightful boy, no trouble at all."

What if Hayes wanted to marry her but didn't wish to raise Andy? "Of course."

"And I cannot ask Sally to wed."

85

"You won't?" That sounded like a croak. "Carter, you shouldn't feel unworthy because of your leg."

Was that what she believed? That his leg made him feel lesser? Didn't it? Anger welled up in him—at himself.

The fear of not knowing if the British might yet win this infernal war. And what would happen to Dogwood Plantation and his nephews should that happen? Might there be reprisals for their uncle having served against the foe?

He pressed his forehead against Nell. Her slim body was softer and more curved than when she was younger. And his reaction to her stronger. Carter inhaled sharply and moved the horse from the woods.

"I need to get you to your cabin, Miss Gill." Needed to put some distance between them, to cool these feelings before he behaved in a most ungentlemanly way. In the way she apparently was cautioning Macy in managing in a man. Might Nell heed her own advice?

"Will I be Miss Gill for this upcoming event then?"

He felt her shoulders brace. She strained forward but he pulled her close against his chest, nuzzling her silken curls. What would it be like to hold this woman in his arms, to claim her as his, for the rest of their lives?

"Because if I'm going to be Miss Gill then I will surely address you as Mr. Williams." Nell stated this threat as though a terrible epithet.

He chuckled. Life with Nell would be full of teasing.

Using his seat, he urged the horse on. As they passed closer to the carriageway, he spied Hayes Davis's carriage through the tree break. Had Nell seen him? More importantly, had the man spied them, and if so, what might he do? The man had a temper. And Carter wouldn't have blamed him in the least if he called him out over this improper behavior.

He slowed the horse. "I'm sorry, Nell. I never should have done this." They were almost to the Gill cabin.

"Set me down here, Carter. I'll walk the rest."

Stopping, he didn't argue. She was right.

Nell kissed his cheek, her soft lips moist against his warm skin. She slipped to the ground and ran. Taking his heart with her.

Chapter Ten

Why did I kiss Carter? After she'd advised Macy to never do such things prior to marriage. Cornelia ran a finger over her lips as she ran to her home. Outside the door, she untied her boots and kicked them off. She entered the cabin, where Andy was preparing supper.

He grinned at her. "Sissy, I saw Hayes's buggy go by, did you see it?"

Her heart pounded in her ears. Had Hayes seen her and Carter? She'd been so enthralled with the feel of Carter's arms around her that she'd considered nothing else. Wonderful scents carried from the hearth.

"Good thing he couldn't smell the good fixings I made for supper or he'd be here now." Pointing to her dulcimer in the corner, he grinned. "Wish you'd play tonight."

"Maybe I will."

Soon she sat at the table, set with ham, biscuits, and sweet potatoes. As Andy said grace, she wiggled her toes. How much longer could she continue trying to fill Pa's shoes? After supper, she washed the dishes.

Andy went outside and called the dogs to offer them their scraps. "Tonnie, Lafe, Lex—come."

As she finished cleaning, she heard Andy playing with the dogs and laughing.

"Hey, Sissy, someone's coming."

Cornelia stepped out and spied the two men in the dusk—one figure limped while the other lumbered alongside.

Why were both coming out here? Hopefully Hayes hadn't seen them earlier on horseback.

"Here I am, just like I said." Her cousin removed his hat, revealing a haircut since his last visit. She perused him carefully. His hair appeared as it was in the miniature portrait.

Andy ran past and threw himself into Hayes's arms. Some of Cornelia's tension left. Her brother was beginning to get over the shock of Pa's death. This was how Pa said Andy used to greet their cousin when he'd visited them often after Ma's death.

Hayes briefly embraced her before wrapping his arm around her, too. As though claiming them as his family. Which they were.

Carter caught up with Hayes, joining them.

"What brings you here, Carter?" Especially after having just spent such close contact time with him. She wished the arm clutching her was his.

Carter cleared his throat. "Hayes brought some beautiful ponies with him. Might Andy join the boys in looking them over?" Sweat dotted his brow as he grabbed the back of a chair.

Cornelia ducked and shook free from Hayes's arm. "Are you ill?" She stepped toward him to place a hand on his forehead. Warm hands prevented her touch as fingers wrapped around her bare forearms. Her breath caught in her throat at the contact on her skin, reminding her of their earlier encounter.

A broad hand squeezed her shoulder and pulled her away. "Now don't you worry none about him, sweet thing. His little miss is up at the house waitin' to see him."

She swallowed hard. "At the house?"

"That's right. The professor's girl will look after him."

Sally Danner was among the guests? She gaped at Carter, but then forced her mouth closed again. Carter's forehead furrowed.

A thin smile crossed Hayes face. "You didn't know? Arrived about the time I did."

88

"Indeed, more guests are arriving than we presumed would, considering our situation." Carter's flat tone didn't reveal his feelings about Sally's arrival.

Hayes swiveled toward Carter. "You don't have to worry about entertainin' me. I'll be down here a lot."

"Hooray, Sissy said she'd play the dulcimer tonight." Andy clapped his hands. "And you can sing."

If Hayes wanted to ask her to marry him, this wasn't the time. No need to make a spectacle. She wished she could tell him yes, but it wouldn't be right. She elbowed him. "Don't pass up this opportunity to mingle with your friends and potential customers."

A shadow crossed his face and he rubbed his whiskered jaw. "Could save me time with some other business—"

"Hey, where'd ya get the ponies?" Andy rocked back and forth on his heels.

"From a farm down in Yorktown."

"Yorktown?" Carter and Cornelia asked in unison.

Carter covered his mouth with his fist and coughed.

"I saw them hitched to a rail at the shipyard there."

"The shipyard?" Carter cocked his head at her cousin.

Hayes nodded. "Need to talk with you later 'bout some goin's on. Could use your help."

"Certainly."

Cornelia couldn't stifle a sudden yawn as fatigue hit her. "I'm awfully tired tonight, Hayes." She felt Carter's eyes search her face.

"Aw, that's no fair." Andy huffed a sigh.

"How about you all go to see the ponies." She made a circle with her index finger to indicate the three. "Tomorrow, Hayes will visit us for a spell."

"Andy, I reckon I've found the prettiest bay mare for you in all of Virginia. Stands a might tall, but if ya keep growin' like you are then you'll need a sixteen-hand horse before long."

"Really? You'd get her for me?"

"Already made an offer."

"Thank you!" Her brother rushed into her cousin's arms.

Was that a bribe?

Ponies for his nephews and the offer of prime horseflesh for Andy—how was Carter supposed to compete with that? But what he dreaded right now was dealing with this unexpected visit from the Danners.

He'd just taken one step away from the Gills' cabin when Sally's high-pitched voice called out. What in the world was she doing way out here? He watched, aghast, as Sally Danner, skirts lifted, stepped over cow patties to get to him. Dressed in a gauzy cream confection, she minced toward them in satin-covered shoes.

"Father said I shouldn't come out here."

"He was, indeed, correct." Carter stared at her in astonishment that she'd go to such lengths.

With Hayes blocking her view, Sally couldn't have seen Nell, who now peeked from behind her hulking cousin.

Carter frowned. "What are you doing here, Miss Danner?"

"You invited us, don't you remember?" Her pert nose crinkled. "Any time, you said. And we'd heard of a few of our friends coming out for Puppy Day, so we presumed the invitation still stood, despite…" Her look of sympathy seemed feigned. Perhaps because her eyes didn't draw down at the corners as her mouth had.

He cleared his throat. "Unfortunately, we had no way of knowing who had been invited given all that has transpired. We agreed it best to let the sales bids for the puppies go forward. For consistency for my nephews and—"

Sally interrupted his explanation. "For Miss Gill's sake?" Her lips pressed together in disapproval. "I heard she has quite a reputation."

He exhaled, wondering if she had seen him with Nell on horseback earlier. He didn't wish to upset her. "She's been educated in Richmond and employed by a top-notch school. Be careful in what you say."

"Well, she's not there anymore, is she?"

"Her father died." Would it be best for Nell to return to her work? What about Andrew, though?

She fanned herself. "Chase shared a bit about her background."

What had he said? Carter had the urge to pound Chase Scott if he came across him any time soon. He shifted his weight onto his bad leg, trying to block her view.

"Whatever is that girl doing, Carter?" She pursed her lips, the words coming out like a stage whisper.

Pivoting, he tried to see. "What girl?"

"Her." She pointed one kid-gloved hand past him and to Nell who stood, hands on her hips, wiggling her bare toes in the grass in a very unladylike manner.

He pushed her hand down. "Miss Danner, please don't point at Nell like that."

"I see. Now I'm Miss Danner? After you have called me by my Christian name for months?" She glared up at him from beneath starry eyelashes, her mouth in a firm pout. "And yet that woman is called by her given name."

Exhaling he lowered his head. He did owe her social courtesy. "Sally, please come to the house."

Her smile wobbled. He didn't want to deceive her. No future existed for them. Not ever. He took her arm and turned her toward the Great House.

"Let's go up and get you settled."

"We're not staying here." She pulled her arm away. "We came by early to tell you we'd attend the festivities tomorrow."

"I see. Where will you be?"

His professor's daughter turned one more time to glare at Nell and Hayes, who were laughing over something. "Papa wanted to visit his old friend, Reverend Scott."

"You're staying at Scott's Hundred?"

"Yes. We'll be quite comfortable there." She tilted her head and batted her eyelashes. "Their grandson, an attorney from Kentucky, is so very entertaining."

"Daniel?"

"Yes. He's almost as charming as Chase." Sally's cheeks pinked. "Or you."

He should be jealous. Or angry. But the only irritation Carter felt was that Daniel could be anywhere near Nell again.

91

An interminable amount of time passed before Sally finally departed. Thankfully, Hayes Davis had joined him after the boys had their fill of the ponies. He was the one man who could give Nell and Andy the security they deserved. If only Carter had been able to do the same and hadn't lost his living. If he returned to college then perhaps one day he could support a wife.

Bacon sizzled and popped somewhere in the cabin, rousing Cornelia from sleep. From her bed, she inhaled the smoky sweet scent. "Andy?"

"Hey, Sissy, I let ya sleep in since ya don't have to work today."

The previous evening, Macy brought word that over a dozen guests had arrived and a large dinner would be served that night at the Great House. Cornelia was issued an invite, too.

"I fed the dogs, got wood chopped, and our breakfast is almost ready."

"What time is it?" She needed a bath, had to wash her hair, go over the books again, and do a dozen other things before the dinner later that evening. Throwing the quilt off, she stretched, muscles aching.

"You needed a good sleep in, Sissy. Even the field workers got a break today."

A series of staccato raps sounded on the door. "The boys are comin'!"

Sitting up, she reached for her wrap. "What are they doing here?"

She drew the curtain aside and entered the main room.

"I asked 'em when I was up at the kitchen earlier. Oh, and Mama Jo sent lots of good scraps for my pups—and bacon to cook for us, which I'm doin'."

She didn't want to know what those boys were doing in the kitchen, which was supposed to be off-limits to them. "Andy—"

"They're gonna help me haul water for your bath."

Andy threw open the door. All four boys piled inside, filling the small space with their presence. She went to the fire and removed the bacon just as it was beginning to smoke. As she took care to remove the portions, the boys sat at the table.

"So you'll all be my helpers today?"

"Yes, ma'am." Eddie rapped his knuckles on the tabletop. "We're good workers, as well you know."

She did know about his hard work. The boy accompanied her almost everywhere while she worked. His knowledge was invaluable, filling in gaps since she'd left Charles City. "Your efforts are much appreciated."

Hours later, her hair washed, rinsed, her body bathed, Cornelia thanked God for the efforts of each small child, including Albert, who napped on Andy's cot, his angelic face a reminder of God's goodness.

Hayes and Andy were working the dogs. Eddie had gone up to retrieve one of his mother's gowns that he assured her was "exactly right for this occasion." Charles and Lloyd had weeded her garden, hauled and dumped buckets of water, and entertained their baby brother with wild antics.

Now she sat in the sun, winding rags through her hair as Albert snoozed. It would be nice to have some curls to pin up. At work in Richmond, she'd been forced to keep her hair severely confined.

She spied house servant, Nemi, trudging toward the cabin. When she neared the boys, who had a good deal of dirt attached to their bodies, Nemi shook her head. "They be needin' to get their own self cleaned up good."

The scold in the slave's voice dampened Cornelia's good humor.

"Massah Davis be here soon to fetch you, Missy."

"For what?"

"He don't say and I don't be askin'."

"Tell that man to turn himself right on around and don't come back till right before dinner time."

Nemi fixed her gaze on Cornelia for a moment, then she tipped her head back and guffawed.

"What's so funny?"

"Now I sees the Missy Gill I knows—and I hear her good, too." She turned around and walked away, still laughing to herself.

Hours later, Cornelia was finally almost prepared when Hayes arrived. Flummoxed by her efforts to tie her bow into a presentable appearance, she gave it one last try. Yanking, pulling, and having no success with properly tying her satin sash into a bow, Cornelia peered into her cousin's hazel eyes. "I'm not going up there for dinner. I have no

93

reason to go. You're handling the business end of things, and Andy's managing the dogs tomorrow."

"Course you do. You're a Pleasant on your Ma's side—just as good as any of those folks up there."

As though that made their poverty disappear. But a quick glance around assured her that her ancestral connections hadn't altered her circumstances one whit. "Maybe if Grandmama Lucia hadn't married a gambler then we'd be the ones hosting this dinner."

Her cousin's eyes widened. "You sound just like her right now—at least from what my ma said about her."

It was true. Grandmama often ranted about how it should be her up at the Great House. "Yes, I apologize for my sour apples."

Hayes indicated for her to turn around, and she complied. He passed the wide satin band around her waist then tightened it with a jerk. She sucked in her breath. He tied the sash snug, as though cinching a horse. Hard heels thumped on the wood floor twice as he stepped away from her.

"I'm tyin' a big bow." Strong fingers pulled the material to-and-fro.

If Carter had performed such a maneuver, she'd have fainted by now with the ecstasy of having him so near. But with Hayes, it was more like being with Pa.

"From solid stock. Ain't nobody up there at the Big House with a better pedigree. We helped found this county all those years ago."

And only a cabin and a bit of land to show for it. "I know, Grandmama told me all those stories when I was a young girl."

"Come on up and visit a spell."

With all those rich planters' daughters. And sons home from the war against the British for a bit. Others who'd never gone. Yet. When would this war end?

"We're gonna meet and talk to 'em all." He spun her around to face him.

"Thank you for fixing the sash but I shouldn't go." Cornelia wrung her hands. "I'm no good at this kind of thing."

"Nelly, we're all American." Hayes rubbed his beard. "Leastwise, this country's ours for now if we keep the British from stealin' it."

If the British invaded America, would she live under conditions so oppressive she'd have no chance to influence her own destiny?

94

A gentle smile accompanied Hayes' words. "You could make good money if we sell all the trained young pups. With this war still goin' on, families want a fine, faithful pet in their home—and one that can help hunt for game is even more valuable."

Substantial money could be made if the event went well, even with the small number of guests.

"Ya might even be able to stay right here in the little old cabin you love so much and take care of Andy."

The knot between her shoulders loosened. It wasn't love of this cabin, though the memories made here and connectedness to the people staked her here—to Carter.

She drew in a shaky breath. "Yes, I'd like to stay and care for Andy here." Even though it also meant giving up her notion of returning to Richmond to resume her work.

"If you change your mind, sweet pea..." Hazel eyes darkened. "My offer is there. Like I wrote in those letters."

Cornelia moved closer to the table and fingered the fraying tablecloth her mother made so long ago. "It's the only home I've ever known."

Relief fought with sadness as his forehead bunched, then relaxed. Perhaps his offer was due to pity and familial responsibility. He'd never shown any interest in her as a woman, not even now. Leave it to responsible Hayes to consider himself a Boaz to her Ruth, coming to her rescue.

"Well then, Sugar—home is where your family is."

Andy carried in a basket, and the scent of biscuits, fried chicken, and sweet potato pie drifted in. Mama Jo's plenteous good cooking enticed Cornelia to stay and eat with him.

"Hey Sis, hey Hayes." After he set his dinner down, he hugged Cornelia tight.

She kissed the top of his head. He smelled of clean boy scent and good cooking.

"Go ahead and eat, boy." Hayes went to the door as though to close it. He stood, looking out.

She could see past him, where overhead geese squawked as they made their way home to the North from the southern climes. A chill went through her. As children, she and Carter had talked of how if they could they'd free all the slaves on the plantation and bring them north if they wished. Then she and he would somehow start a new life there. If only that could be so.

Hayes waved. "Carter? What you doin' here?"

Cornelia released her brother and tried to get past Hayes, who blocked the door. She elbowed him and he blinked down at her before stepping aside.

Dressed in an azure waistcoat beneath his navy cutaway, the former naval officer made a striking image with his brilliant white shirt. With a swish, Carter displayed a swath of filmy fabric. "I neglected to send this with Edward earlier."

Layers of skirt fabric and petticoats weighed her down as she stepped into the cool night air. "We have mosquito netting in the cabin, but thank you kindly."

Chuckling, her cousin came onto the stoop. He swiped the cloth from Carter, shook it, twirled the sheer strip then poufed it together and settled it around her shoulders.

"Like that, I believe, Nelly."

The weightless wrap, wound by such a substantial man, encased her. Cornelia wriggled her shoulders and backed away from him toward Carter.

Warm hands grasped her shoulders and Carter's breath was hot on her neck. "I'd say you were quite proficient at dressing a lady, Mr. Davis." He almost growled his words.

Cornelia squirmed, uncomfortable with the look Hayes shot her friend. In a minute, fists could be flying. She moved between the two and stood sideways. She dare not look up into Carter's eyes. She'd seen the fire flickering there a moment before, when he'd first viewed her in her finery.

Embarrassed, she tugged at the low sleeves on her gown, beneath the scratchy wrap. "I can't keep these shoulder straps where they belong."

"I believe that's the fashion." Carter's low voice was accompanied by a finger gently touching the band. Heat seared her flesh.

"What good are they if they can't help hold the gown up?" Cornelia glared at him.

Carter chuckled and crossed his arms. Had he felt it too? That strange spark between them? "It's not I who constructed your garment, so don't blame me."

"Lil darlin', that bodice is so tight there ain't no chance of it fallin' down." Hayes tucked some chaw in his cheek. "Don't know why you ladies put up with these dressmakers' notions."

Pulling hard, Cornelia stopped when the seams began to give. "Didn't think you paid much attention to that type of thing, Mr. Davis."

"I attend to a great many things besides breedin' horses, Nelly. I'm not the ignorant buffoon you might think me to be."

Chapter Eleven

As Cornelia, Carter, and Hayes strolled toward Dogwood Plantation's brick structures, she furtively cast glances at her cousin to ensure he wasn't still offended with her. When he smiled warmly at her, she relaxed. Both she, and Hayes, kept a pace Carter could manage. Lamps illuminated the Flankers and the Great House. Musicians practiced their tunes nearby, violins both giddy in tempo yet melancholy in tone. Was that *The Last Rose of Summer* she heard them practicing? The song had been a popular one for the girls at the academy in Richmond.

Hayes scratched his whiskers. "Gonna stop at my room. I feel the need for some time in reflection and prayer. Miss Wenham'll be travelin' back, and I want to ask God for her protection."

When her cousin lifted her hand to his lips, a touch not unpleasant, her breath caught. "Of course." A godly man, kind, who wanted hers and Andy's best, and who would be fine to look upon once she rid him of his beard. What more could she ask for? *Someone I could love as a husband.*

He turned and left Cornelia and Carter to make their way to the Great House, the scent of night-blooming jasmine wafting up. "I didn't take him for a religious man."

"Hayes? Oh yes. He even trained to become a Baptist preacher." The warmth of his kiss lingered on her hand, and she rubbed the spot. *I don't want to love him like that—it isn't right.* He was her closest kin.

Carter looped Cornelia's arm through his, her bare hands glaring at her.

"I forgot my gloves." She withdrew her sun-darkened and scratched arm. *I need to look like a lady tonight.* She needed to cloak her hands so they didn't betray her new "place". Between the ink stains she couldn't quite scrub out of her hands and her sun-browned arms from walks through the fields, she'd surely be spotted as an outsider to this event.

Carter halted and appraised her, his dark eyes settling on her exposed flesh. A whiffle of breeze stirred and intensified the jasmine's perfume. Carter draped the net wrapping lower, grazing her skin with his warm fingers, effectively baring her shoulders but covering most of her arms.

She squeezed her hands together to stop their trembling. When Carter touched her, no logic could control her reaction to him.

His thumb loosened her fingers. "Here. If you grasp the bottom of each end, your wrap should provide sufficient cover for the sun's effect upon your arms."

Hands now resting atop her wrists, standing this close to her, Cornelia could imagine Carter taking one more step toward her. Kissing her. His eyes turned almost black and the rim of brown almost disappeared. She was holding her breath, slightly dizzy. *If only he would...*

"Williams, there you are. Glad we found you." A distinguished-looking man called out as he emerged from the North Flanker.

Carter stepped away from Cornelia, warm air hanging between them. "Professor Danner? Your daughter said you're staying at Scotts' Hundred."

"Yes, they've been very cordial."

"Very thoughtful of them to invite you."

The older man's upper lip quirked as he stepped toward her. "Who might this lovely young woman be?"

Sally emerged from the building arm-in-arm with Daniel Scott. Cornelia's breath caught. Surely he was not attending the dinner. If Eddie had issued that invitation, she most definitely would disagree. Frozen to the spot, the sounds of insects buzzing, birds chirping, and breeze blowing mixed to a dull roar in her head.

Carter took a step closer to her. "Professor Danner, this is Miss Gill, whose father was our plantation manager."

He didn't mention that she'd now assumed Pa's position.

"Enchanted." The man bowed. "I heard you were a beauty but now I see that is an understatement. You resemble an exquisite rendering of Venus in your gown."

Heat seared her cheeks and she couldn't utter a word. As he approached, Daniel's hooded eyes raked her from head to toe and then lingered on her low bodice. Sally stood stiffly beside him.

"More like the huntress, Diana," Daniel murmured.

Sally's lips pinched. All Cornelia could manage was to stare. Like a statue.

Pain washed Carter's face.

Sally took his arm. "Do you need to sit down?"

Cornelia glanced about. "Where is your cane?"

"Trying to do without that infernal stick." He took a couple of gasps of air. "The pain will pass. Just a spasm."

Mr. Danner drew Carter over to a bench. "This happened frequently at college. I hoped country walking would improve the strength in your leg."

There was much she didn't know about Carter's life while they'd been apart. As Daniel took two steps closer, she wished Carter's cane was handy—she had another use for it.

Daniel's dark eyebrows knit together. "You were injured, Williams? In this infernal war?"

Carter shot a look of disgust at the Kentuckian.

"My brother Chase said naught about it, only that you were attending the college again."

If she hadn't known Daniel, Cornelia would have thought the man genuinely cared. But he'd never been a good actor before—just someone who did what he wanted, when and how he wished, without regard for others. Yet his face reflected empathy.

Sally patted Daniel's arm. "Do you think this war will be over soon?"

"I certainly hope so. My fool brother intends to enlist before he misses out."

As others stared at him, the frontiersman shrugged off his gaffe. "Didn't mean to offend you, Carter. Just speaking my mind."

Same old Daniel. Not thinking of how others might feel.

100

A grim smile worked its way across Carter's face. "I believe Miss Gill phrased my enlistment in exactly the same way."

Had she? Embarrassed by the recollection, she turned away, clutching her arms.

The clock chimed eight, and Carter hadn't once been able to speak to Nell. At least they'd bid Daniel adieu, and the uninvited guest left of his own accord. From across the room, Nell's blonde beauty shimmered, though she appeared skittish as a cat who'd had its tail pulled by one of his nephews. He couldn't get near her for anything despite this being his family home. And Sally had attached herself to him as though he were one of her newest porcelain treasures in her hope chest.

Sally Danner, in his mind, had unarguably been the most polished young belle in the room. But Nell's palpable presence shone like the family's silver—glistening in the candlelight.

When Sally pressed her slim body close against his side, Carter shrugged away. Such forward behavior wouldn't be overlooked in the county. He couldn't imagine Nell engaging in such antics. Near the fireplace, a cluster of young men pressed in on her. She edged away from them and moved to a group of married couples chatting by the punch bowl.

Carter tried to free himself but the professor's daughter tugged at his lapel. "Daddy, don't you think Carter looks splendid in his Navy frock coat?"

Her father raised a shaggy white eyebrow at her, one hand resting inside the buttoned opening of his vest. "Wonderful meal, Carter. Afraid I overindulged. Think I better take some fresh air outside."

Nell's golden curls bobbed as yet another country gentleman pushed through the small crowd expanding around her. Her hands flew around her as she spoke, causing the bit of fluff around her shoulders to dip and swell like ocean foam.

Pouting, Sally tapped on his arm, reeling his attention toward her. "You seem preoccupied this evening. Why don't we join Father outside?"

"Yes. Let's do." As Jack Hastings pushed through the guests toward Nell, Carter halted. If that barbarian so much as... He caught him in the pantry earlier, when Macy had appeared frightened half out of her mind. Jack claimed he'd overheard Macy saying that a heavy tureen needed to be carried out and thought to help. He was trying to help, all right—help himself to the servant.

Sally squeezed his arm hard. "I need a change of scenery, too."

When he didn't move, her pretty face twisted most unbecomingly, her irritation etching every feature. Was this what she would become in time? Even when Nell was furious with him, she was still so pretty that he wanted to kiss her.

His professor's daughter stomped off in the direction her father had gone, onto the covered porch that wrapped around the side of the house. She likely carried Carter's political ambitions off with her. He sighed.

Jack reached his long arm around Nell and adjusted the gossamer wrap around her milky shoulders. *If that loudmouth perceives the whiteness of her neck and brown skin on her arms, might he remark? And embarrass her?*

Striding across the room like a ship under full sail, Carter's leg stung as though a hundred bees attacked him but he pressed on through his guests. He snatched a tart from atop a platter to fortify himself, in case… In case what? Would he call the man out right here and for what purpose? Just laying eyes on Daniel earlier that night had launched him into a foul mood.

Where was Hayes? For someone planning to wed Nell, the man was conspicuously absent. When Hastings bent and whispered in Nell's ear and another guest moved away from the couple, Carter got a clear view of her scarlet cheeks and the mortification tarring her face.

Elbowing in between Hastings and Nell, he spied the salacious grin fixed on the brute's face. "Bothering this lady, are you, Hastings?"

"I don't think so. Am I, ma'am?" His slimy inflection of ma'am indicated he'd intended no respect.

A servant passed by with a fresh platter of sweets. Jack swiped three from the silver tray and displayed the delicacies in his upturned palm.

Eyes blazing, Nell said nothing. Rarely had she lost her wits, so whatever the fiend said must have been shocking indeed. Carter slapped his hand against his thigh, somehow expecting to feel a sword there.

Nell pulled herself up. "He… Mr. Hastings wished special privileges, which I have no intent of granting him."

Sucking in his breath, Carter prepared to call Jack Hastings out at dawn. *Two pistols. I'll demand that Hayes Davis be my back-up man.* He'd put a hole through Hastings. Carter could almost smell the pistol smoke.

Hayes joined them, frowning at Hastings with a not much softer look for Carter. "What's goin' on over here?"

Nell rolled her pink lips together. Carter's heartbeat sped up. It mattered not that she was a beautiful woman whose father's death left her adrift. *For Hastings to attempt to compromise her was beyond the pale.*

"This man…" She pointed at Hastings, her voice rising. Nell was about to make a scene in the ballroom at Dogwood Plantation, and it would be a tremendous one. She stomped one foot down on the red wool carpet. *At dawn, pistols drawn, and Hayes would be his second.* But he wouldn't need him. Carter might be lame but his shot was true.

"Hastings believed he could have *first pick* of the newest litter." Nell's voice carried to all the guests clustered around them. Silver clinked as forks dropped against blue and white china plates.

What? He wants the favor of first pick of a dog? That's all? Carter wanted to laugh but his head and leg pained him. Nell was going to be the death of him.

Behind him, Peter Smythe whirled, jabbing an elbow into Carter's back. "What say, Hastings, how dare you? She's agreed to a lottery."

"That's right." A woman no taller than Edward, rapped Hastings arm with her closed fan. "You'll get your chance just like the rest of us, you heathen."

Hayes shook his head. Carter and he exchanged glances before he said, "Angel face, don't you be lettin' no good lookin' fellow sweet talk you into givin' any special favors."

Lit by the hundreds of candles, Nell's golden hair glowed like the portraits of angels Carter had viewed when he'd taken his tour of Europe.

"What you gapin' at, Mr. Williams?" Hayes clapped a hand on his shoulder. The others slowly drifted away from them, murmuring their disapproval over Hastings' behavior. "Why, here comes your sweetheart. Or is she goin'?" Hayes cackled.

103

Carter turned to view Sally almost pushing her father out through the entryway to the room.

Chapter Twelve

"Sissy, get up." Andy's plea broke through Cornelia's exhaustion.

Sun streamed through the side window. *Oh no—I overslept.*

"It's late—we gotta get down to the dogs. It's Puppy Day, and I could use a little help."

After getting free from the bedcovers, she straightened her sleeping gown. No time to unbraid her hair and change right now. She had to help Andy review the dogs before the event. Cornelia shoved her feet into an old pair of slippers and headed out the door into the full sun.

Andy called from the cabin, "I'll be down in a few moments, Sissy."

Within a short time, she arrived at the kennels. Movement at the building's end startled her. She shaded her eyes as a man unfolded himself and stood.

Daniel stood there as if he owned the pups.

Her heart hammered in her chest beneath her lightweight nightdress. As in previous encounters with this man, her body betrayed her, affixing her to the spot as tremors began.

"Did you wear that down here especially for me?" Although the words taunted, his face appeared innocent enough, and he even turned slightly and raised a hand as though to shield him from looking at her.

She found her voice. "What are you doing here?"

He dropped his hand. "Guarding your dogs from thieves."

His even features betrayed no lie. Daniel appeared serious. Doubt began to subtly repaint her memories of him.

"Why would you do that?"

"Because I care about you, Cornelia. That should be no surprise."

Her hounds were unperturbed by his presence. Had he come to the kennels before, since returning? Were those his boot tracks she'd found and not Hayes'?

"Miss Gill, as a Christian, I have forgiven you for misleading me." He removed his tan leather frontiersman's hat and clutched it to his chest. "You broke my heart but I have moved on in my life. But it doesn't seem you have. You're still a spinster."

He may call himself a Christian, but she doubted he'd ever given himself over into the Lord's hands. "Mr. Scott, I will thank you to take your leave." She turned and began to run to the cabin, ashamed that he had seen her in her nightclothes.

"I will leave as soon as your brother comes down here."

She halted. Did he know their schedules? Cold chills ran down the back of her arm as she hurried home. Carter was right. She and Andy might not be safe there by themselves any more.

The neat wardrobe contents, save for one small section, and the scent of sandalwood and cedar almost undid Carter as he searched his brother's wardrobe. *Lee—how could you have left me?* Having filled out in the upper body since returning home, Carter chose one of his brother's more subdued country gentleman jackets for the day. Pants that coordinated were inexplicably missing. Carter brought the coat and a white shirt to his room where he was able to match the jacket quite well with a pair of butter-soft buckskin pants. He dressed himself, having grown accustomed to serving as his own valet.

As he reached into the top drawer of his bureau in search of a pin, his hands brushed against a wood frame. He pulled the painting free, the sight of a golden-haired angel purchased in Paris arresting his attention. His father had sent it to him years earlier, but Carter had been so angry with him he had shoved it in amongst his handkerchiefs and neckcloths. The beautiful angel reminded him of Nell. Had Father believed so? Carter dabbed a dash of lavender water around his collar. He wanted a moment alone with Nell. He peered into the oval mirror above the low Chippendale chest. His face was still the same. But as he headed out to the stairs, he required no reminders that his body had altered.

As he'd requested, Nemi had left a mug of buttermilk and an apple muffin atop Lee's desk in the office. Carter spent the morning's remainder reviewing the books while their guests slept off their late night revelry. Several hours and one large headache later he arrived at the same conclusion he'd reached during previous perusals of the records—the plantation required cash income soon. Exiting through the back, he set off for the field.

A handful of tables, covered with linen tablecloths, were arrayed with assorted comestibles. Hayes had spared no expense for this event even though attendees were far fewer than normal. Now Carter was about to join those wishing to purchase the puppies sired by the best hounds in the region with the best temperaments for families. And he couldn't afford to buy one for himself. He tugged at his brother's cravat.

Their guests, including some newcomers this morning, slowly streamed into the green field. At the far end, closer to the Gills' land, two rows of chairs had been set up. He spied several elderly ladies and tapped a servant's arm. "Please be sure to seat those with infirmities first, Levi."

"Yessir. But I'm thinkin' those ladies be better off with a lapdog." The tall slave's dark eyes darted to Carter's leg. Thus far today, his infernal leg had not pained him. Not as much as Levi's pitying look did.

Turning, he mentally tallied the number of people heading from the carriages to the grounds. The number had swelled to over two dozen. Last year, Lee had told him they'd stopped counting attendees at one hundred.

Bonaparte had been defeated, the British likely rallying their navy and sending more warships their way—yet here these Virginians were. His father would turn in his grave. Father and his friend now-President Madison's heated arguments had centered on the country's lack of military preparedness. Doves versus hawks and the peace-lovers had prevailed, endangering the fledgling country. Carter had done his duty to protect his country. With the change in world events, would he be summoned forth again, despite his disability? Today, he'd merely socialize.

Evie and Sylvia Randolph, a contrast of silver hair and heavy gold jewelry, greeted him. "Thank you for inviting us, Carter."

These two early guests had known his family long before he had been born. "Very glad you could make it, Miss Randolph." What should he call the other one? He raised the first sister's gloved hand to his lips to cover his embarrassment.

Sylvia and Evie tittered. He took the other sister's hand. "Miss Randolph." Again, he pressed his lips to the cotton glove.

The two, faces pink, headed toward the damask-cloth-covered table. Punch, sandwiches, tarts, and petits fours would cover every inch. Silver serving items had been in the family for generations. If he had to sell the family silver to support his nephews, what kind of money could he expect to receive during these uncertain war times? Far less than what they were once worth.

Edward ran toward the tent, set up mid-lawn. Once he got there, he bent over, panting. "She's back, Uncle Carter."

The two spinsters turned and frowned at his nephew's outburst.

Carter compressed his lips. "Who?"

"Aunt Mariah, sir. She's here."

Scanning the river entrance to the house, from where Edward had run, he sighted only strolling clusters of visitors. "Surely not this quickly." A round trip excursion to South Carolina should have taken weeks.

"She's brought enough belongings to keep her here a year or more, sir."

At this declaration, Carter excused himself and followed Edward toward the house. He'd miss the first showing if he got tied up with Mariah. Of all the timing. "Edward, you boys were supposed to go to her when she returned. Why did you not tell me she had sent word ahead of her arrival?" Blast, his leg began to pain him something fierce, and now he was lambasting his nephew.

"She didn't send word." Edward turned and pinned him with his sharp gaze. "She's not a cadet on a ship, sir, to take orders, and neither am I."

"No, I'm sorry, I..." But the boy ran ahead to the house, leaving Carter straggling behind him.

Lloyd jumped from the last step at the house's rear exit. "Uncle Carter, Auntie Mariah says do your business." He made a silly face.

108

"Cousin Hayes is helping her." The boy turned on his heel and hurried up the rear stairs.

Cousin Hayes, indeed? So that was where he was—still up at the house. How had the man ingratiated himself with his nephews so quickly? *He was Lee's friend.* It was his brother who had arranged this event with Hayes to begin with, primarily to get good horse stock for himself and for Hayes to maintain his contacts near Charles City.

As Carter walked into the crowds, forming into clusters, he recalled Mariah Wenham, the Charleston belle. She'd never married, inhabited a mansion on the Ashley River, and likely counted her money all afternoon while slaves attended to her every need. She'd get a rude awakening staying now that she was encamped with them. A more worrisome woman he'd never met. He turned to look, expecting her to prance out to the event.

A rakish but effeminate man wove toward the crowd gathered around the punch bowl. His wide-brimmed hat was pulled so low that Carter couldn't make out the young man's features, but his smooth jawline betrayed him as a youth.

As he neared, the strong scent of lavender cloaked him. The clothing pulled at a memory. Nell had earlier sent a message up to the house to be on the watch for possible dog thieves. The young man was attired in Lee's vest, breeches and leggings. The very ones that matched Carter's coat.

"You there!"

The youth disappeared into the crowd before Carter could catch him. Stopping near Sally and her father, he caught his breath. They chatted with Hugh Martin, a wealthy merchant and attorney Forrester's wealthiest client. A widower, women from Baltimore to Norfolk pursued Martin. Each cool look from Sally fanned the flames of the man's interest. He edged ever closer to her.

"Don't you agree, Miss Danner—Richmond is more cosmopolitan than Williamsburg?"

Sally sniffed.

Professor Danner reached into his interior coat pocket for a handkerchief and wiped his brow. "Norfolk is the busiest city. With this war continuing, who in their right mind would allow their daughter to visit that city? It's filled with Navy personnel."

The disdain in Danner's last two words irked Carter. He searched the man's patrician face and his daughter's perfect features. Chase Scott once confided, 'Your lady friend has some errant beliefs about you, Williams. Believes you're the primary heir to your father's fortunes.' Working as an intern for Forrester, had Chase read his will?

"My uncle served in the Navy." Edward pulled on his sleeve. "Uncle Carter. Might I introduce myself?"

Sally extended a gloved arm to his nephew. "How nice that your boarding school allowed you to attend." The tone of her voice suggested otherwise.

"Oh no, Miss. I'm Edward Williams." Edward straightened and looked her straight in the eye. "I own this estate. No boarding school for me."

His wide eyes questioned Carter. "At present."

Sally covered the giggle escaping her mouth.

Professor Danner shook Edward's hand. "You mean you live here at Dogwood Plantation. But your uncle owns this, does he not?" He looked askance at the boy.

Martin nodded at Edward. "Good seeing you, young Williams. I'm sure your uncle will do his best to keep up this plantation for you until you come of age. Right, Carter?"

Carter half-closed his eyes, not wanting to see the open-mouthed astonishment on Sally Danner's face and the disappointment on her father's.

Even now, he was sure she was re-baiting her hook. And Mr. Martin was the new catch. Carter had to admire that kind of determination. Wasn't that how she'd pulled Carter out of his shell? He'd been the one student who had ignored her at her father's socials, when he'd sat to the side nursing his painful leg. She'd done the chasing. He nodded toward Professor Danner, took a step away, and surveyed the crowd. Visitors tamped down their usual raucous good humor. Many expressed their condolences. He exhaled in relief that none had berated him for allowing this event to go forward. People had been kind.

Taking two steps toward the dessert table, Carter chose a large almond tart. A sleeve brushed his arm.

"Pardons, sir. Wanted to ask 'bout that pretty gal whose brother's selling them good dogs." The scratchy voice had the oddest timbre.

The young "man" wore Lee's clothes. Mortification shot through him. Surely not, surely no—yet he recalled her pulling a stunt as a young girl. "Nell? How could you?"

"Just checkin' on Andy's customers." A dimple formed in each cheek.

He caught himself before he sought to squeeze her hand. That wouldn't look proper. "Have you lost your mind completely?"

She shrugged. "I'm so nervous. Couldn't bear standing around while Andy shows the hounds. I wanted to see."

"You shall be the death of me." He sighed. "Afterwards, please dress for dinner."

Fair eyebrows raised high. "I'm invited?"

Exhaling, he considered. "I truly don't want you stirring up trouble again tonight."

"What trouble?"

She appeared genuinely perplexed. Did she not realize the effect she was having on the men? It was as though an aphrodisiac had been sprayed over all those dog-loving men who desired the best pup. She was pretty. Beautiful even.

"Do you know there are two gentlemen who want to wed you to get your family's dogs?"

Silence frosted him. Did Nell, like Sally, enjoy the power of her femininity? Gloating inside? Happy to lord it over any man who succumbed to her charms. And that of her pups.

"Is that why Hayes pursues you?"

Nell's face contorted. "Is that what you think?"

"Giving you a better chase than those pups will give a stag when full grown." Hadn't that been what Hayes Davis had done—waited until Nell matured to give chase?

"You... of all the..." Nell sputtered. "You might remember that those pups are meant to be family dogs, too, not just hunters."

Ten feet away, Sally fixed her light eyes on them. Martin used that opportunity to snake a hand around the young woman's slender waist.

111

Sally wriggled free but not before Carter caught the smile of victory that leapt across her lovely face. *Ah yes, she's having her own sport today.*

Nell's hand smacked him hard and so fast that Carter had no chance to react. She stomped away.

Martin strolled toward him, leaving Sally with her father. "Williams, did that fellow just challenge you?" He pointed at Nell as she faded into the crowd.

Nell, always a challenge. "You could say that."

Cornelia strode onward through the crowd of guests awaiting the next group of puppies to be brought out. None of the men who'd flirted with her the previous night paid the slightest notice. She wove through the maze of potential buyers as well. Funny how people having been locked up to avoid the contagion had now come out to socialize. The women's gowns were lovely, most enhanced with fine ribbons of velvet and satin. Hesitating to examine the intricate lace spanning the back of one lady's gown, she spied Chase Scott. What was he doing here? Although he was one of Carter's law school classmates, she'd not imagined Carter asked him to the event.

"My internship has been... quite enlightening so far." Chase bestowed a dazzling smile upon an elegant young lady. Here was a young man whose attentions could be far more dangerous than Daniel's.

"Do say?" Miss Taylor, the daughter of the owners of Glendale Plantation, fluttered her eyelashes at the tall man.

Chase's low laugh was deep and masculine. "Doubt you'd find it as interesting as I do, Miss Taylor."

Cornelia caught the ripple of unease that clouded his face before he once again grinned. "Ah, there's a dog I recognize." The dog came to Chase, tail wagging.

For a moment, Cornelia was sure Lafe was coming to her, and she'd begun to signal him to stop.

Chase patted Lafe's head. "His great-great-grand sire was brought by Lafayette from France. He was presented to my grandfather."

What was Lafe doing there? He should have been kenneled.

"Indeed?" The young woman's thin eyebrows lifted.

"My older brother gave our only whelp away." Jealousy tinged Chase's words.

Miss Taylor opened a lustrous mauve fan that matched her gown's bodice. "My father insists I win a bid on a pup. He wants his pack to include new blood from the Dogwood Plantation line but Carter Williams wouldn't even speak with me last night."

"From Dogwood Plantation?" Chase's disdain showed in every word. "The hounds don't belong to the Williams family."

"They don't?"

"No. For some reason that wealthy horse-breeder, Hayes Davis, has been supplying the Gills with stock each year for some time now."

Since his mother's death and as a kindness.

"You don't say." Miss Taylor's fan and head moved as she searched the gathering of guests.

Chase stroked Lafe's head. "I'm hoping Miss Gill is employing her charms upon Carter Williams."

"Why do you say that?"

Why did he? Cornelia pulled her hat lower, watching for a cluster of three men to pass by. She'd slip in among them.

"I have my reasons." Chase's low voice irritated her ears. He was not as charming as his smile suggested.

The beauty's creamy satin skirts swayed to the side as the men neared. "Haven't seen Miss Gill this afternoon. Such a pity about that unfashionable blonde hair she has."

Cornelia prayed her curls remained tucked up inside the hat. Perspiration broke out under its wide band as she awaited her opportunity.

"Carter Williams puts on more airs than the British he fought against." Chase practically spat out his words.

Cornelia stiffened at Chase's remark. She searched out a gap in the pack of the young gentlemen passing by.

Miss Taylor's voice rose. "Miss Gill seems to be treated as family."

"What a fletch."

Cornelia didn't understand the slang expression.

"How do you mean?"

"Old man Williams never accepted her, nor did Lee—certainly not as a family member. And Roger Williams ensured that she'd never be."

113

He might has well have stabbed her heart. The truth stung. Cornelia matched the group members' strides.

The young bucks paused and pointed as Albert walked past, alone save for the tiniest of the new puppies, Minnie, clutched to his chest. Where was Macy? She was supposed to be watching him.

The man adjacent elbowed her. Chase stared at her. As his eyes narrowed, Cornelia swooped Albert and the puppy into her arms and ran. The toddler giggled and pressed Minnie against her chest, releasing the squirming pup between them. Albert patted her cheeks.

"Nell. Nell." The little fellow wasn't fooled by her get-up.

Wetness suddenly soaked the waistcoat.

Albert gazed up at her with wide eyes. "Uh oh. I wet."

Chapter Thirteen

All but the last stragglers had left the plantation after a substantial breakfast served earlier in the day. It was now past two and her cousin had failed to arrive at the cabin. So Nell determined to go looking for him at the North Flanker house. She entered the building and stood, inhaling the sweet scent of tea and pastries that awaited beyond the entrance to the parlor. Cornelia listened as Mariah's delicate laugh echoed Hayes' booming one.

Here he sits, and he hasn't taken care of our wood for us yet he departs tomorrow. Was this what married life would have be like if something compelled her to change her mind and accept his offer?

She stepped into the room. Mariah Wenham, perched atop a velvet pillow on the window banquette, presided over tea—the round table before her covered with a lace-edged cloth. Miss Wenham fluttered her eyelashes at the few male stragglers who'd not yet departed, and at her cousin. Hayes leaned in, eyes wide. He hadn't withdrawn his offer to bring Andy and her to Orange County, presumably as his bride. Would he really expect her to put up with him flirting with other women if they married?

Temptation to take ahold of Hayes' ear and pull it hard overcame her but she resisted. Clearing her throat, Cornelia tapped her booted toe. Mariah's lips tipped upward, but pique flickered in the woman's eyes. She raised her gold-rimmed teacup.

Hayes stared almost gape-mouthed at the Carolina belle. Irritation skittered through Cornelia. "Hayes, you promised to help me with a chore."

Color crept up into her cousin's cheeks, now more easily visible with his beard trimmed close. Two younger men shot him a pitying look and laughed. "Didn't realize you had such a stern taskmaster, did you, Mr. Davis?"

Sable waves covering Hayes' broad forehead moved as his forehead furrowed. "I'll come down in a bit. Soon as I finish my tea with the little lady here." He smiled at Mariah.

Ebony curls bobbed around her ivory face as she averted her gaze.

"I'll expect you." Cornelia's words sounded snappish even to her own ears. She turned on her heel and exited the room.

Eddie appeared at the base of the stairs. "Miss Cornelia, are you all right?"

She nodded stiffly as he held the mahogany door open for her. She stepped out onto the front portico and crossed her arms over her chest. She had to get her temper under control.

From beneath the tool shed's musty overhang, Carter appraised Nell. Thunderous anger danced across her features. He'd taken refuge in their old play area, desiring a moment's peace after all the activities at the house with the guests' departures. If she hadn't appeared so agitated, he would have remained in the shadows.

He stepped out as Edward and Nell neared. "What's troubling you?"

"Hayes Davis." She spat out the name.

The twosome must have a tempestuous relationship. "Has he offended you?"

She shoved her hands into her pockets. "He's a man who can't keep his word. I despise a man like that." Nell turned to Edward and patted his shoulders. "You won't grow up to be a difficult man, will you, Eddie?"

"No, Ma'am." Edward narrowed his eyes at Carter.

How had Carter failed to keep a promise—as the boy's eyes seemed to accuse him of? "I agree, Nell."

She spun around and put her hands on her skirted hips. "Humph, you aren't the easiest of men, either."

"I'm difficult?" Apparently his words didn't meet her approval for she pivoted around, almost elbowing Edward in the process.

Memories of their ride across the fields tormented him the past two nights. He'd kissed her many years ago in this shed. And she'd returned his kiss. He almost could feel the warmth of that firm kiss.

Nell stopped. "Men who make promises and don't keep them are wicked and weak." Although she addressed Edward, Carter knew her jibe was intended for his ears.

Edward made a choking sound as though gagging on his own spit. Carter walked as quickly as his sore leg allowed. He patted the boy's back.

Now was not the time to clarify her former understanding with him. "Nell, this boy gave his word that he would speak to me on your behalf, and he did." Accusations like this diatribe were unfair. And he had honored his nephew's request for this ridiculous proposition that she serve as manager.

Blue eyes widened.

Carter geared up for his lecture. In his mind's eye, he was walking in front of his crew, his leg perfectly whole. "Edward sought me out, explained his position clearly, and then intervened for you. He's an exceptional sailor."

"Sailor?" Nell and Edward spoke in unison.

A low deep chuckle started, sounding as though it began in her belly and then moved its way up into her throat. "Carter, maybe you were in the Navy too long."

He caught Edward's eye. "Son...nephew... You know what I mean." Loss of sleep and the recent difficulties mangled his speech.

The yearning on Edward's young face twisted Carter's gut in a knot. Lee could legitimately have called the boy, "Son." Carter could never replace his brother.

"You were saying, Nell, that you were peeved with Hayes."

Edward shook his head slightly. "Mr. Davis was to have hauled wood up to their cabin."

"Pa used to do it and the nights are still cool." Nell raised her strong chin. "I won't make Andy do that. It would take too long. Our woodpile is low but I have a tree down on our property."

Their property adjoined this land. And Nell's family once possessed all of this acreage. What must that be like to know it had all been lost from a wager, from gambling and losing all? His brother's books—would the accounting show he'd misjudged or miscalculated the plantation's finances?

"Sir, I told her a field hand could do it instead—"

"Indeed. Excellent idea. But why not ask Mr. Davis to honor his promise? Couldn't you have reminded him instead of pouting?" What kind of marriage would those two have if they couldn't communicate the simplest of needs? Yet look at all that he and Nell left unsaid between them.

"He's been told." Nell's voice could have frosted the flowering quince nearby.

Edward's lips curled as though he sucked on a lemon. "Mr. Davis is Aunt Mariah's new lapdog."

Perhaps Nell wasn't angry but jealous. Carter's fists knotted. For someone who had aspired to serve the Lord, Davis's behavior suggested otherwise. Mariah's questionable reputation was what had ended Lee's betrothal to her. The woman had disappeared for almost a year after Lee married Anne.

"Hayes is her new pet?" Nell's fair eyebrows lifted.

"Yes, I believe so."

"Hayes leaves tomorrow."

"No, Miss Cornelia, he's staying an extra day."

All was silent except for the caw of a crow flying overhead.

Perhaps Carter should talk to Mariah. While part of him wanted nothing more than for his old friend, his love, to be cared for by a wealthy and well-connected man, another aspect couldn't wait to see Hayes ensnared by Mariah and taken from Nell. And saved for him. Selfish. And unkind. He'd talk to Mariah and warn her off.

Inside the office, Carter settled into his brother's chair. He pulled up a low stool on which to rest his leg, and awaited Mr. Davis. If Carter pressed Hayes to make his intentions known would he risk pushing Nell toward him? It was intolerable watching the horse breeder fawn over Anne's sister. Mariah was so unlike the boys' mother. A void had been left in the house that neither he nor Mariah could fill. And while Lee had been a quiet man, he knew his nephews missed their father, whose emotions were mostly shown through those intense moments when he had special talks with each boy in the office. How well Carter knew, and missed their conversations where his brother's love shone through his gray eyes, so like their mother's.

The door swung in and banged against the wall. "Sorry about that." Carter shot him an annoyed expression.

"I guess I should have knocked first."

"Come in, have a seat."

Macy arrived almost on Hayes's heels, and he stepped aside to allow her passage. The big man cleared his throat. "Macy, who was that man you were talking with down by the kennels last night?"

The serving tray rattled as the young woman released it onto the table. "You be mistaken, sir." She kept her eyes downcast as a blush spread across her high cheekbones.

"Oh no, I wouldn't confuse a face as fine as yours." The man shook his head.

If Macy were freed, and sent up North, would she choose to blend in and forget her past? Could she even? Where could she go where she'd not encounter Virginians who'd visited Dogwood Plantation and had noticed her? "What brings you here now?"

"Many of those pups are bought and paid for already." Hayes patted his coat pocket. "And I don't want anything happening to them before their owners bring them home."

Macy's shoulders trembled. Surely she wasn't seeking to free the hounds or send them off with someone. *Sometimes I think that man deliberately strives to annoy me and usurp my command.* "We'll speak later, Macy."

She bobbed a curtsy, the soles of her shoes swishing against the floor as she fled the room.

119

Hayes went to the window and rubbed his beard. "Somethin' odd is goin' on there, Carter."

"Perhaps, but let me sort that out." This man elicited the same feelings Carter had experienced as an officer with his enlisted men.

Hayes whirled around. "Those hounds belong to the Gills, which makes them my responsibility." Hayes's tone removed all doubt that he claimed Nell as his own. "And they were on Nelly's property. Macy and some young white man, in case you care, were loitering near the kennels."

"Did you recognize him?"

"No."

Who then? Carter sunk into the chair. "I'll check into it."

"See that you do." He laid a stack of bills on the desktop. "This is for anything my little darlin' needs for her or her brother before I return for a longer visit."

"Why give this to me? For safekeeping?"

"It's her money but she wanted to repay me for my expenses. Paid her taxes by herself, too." With a snort, he turned and went to the tea cart and set baked goods on a small china plate and poured a cup of tea. "Acts like she doesn't want to be indebted to me—of all the fool notions."

Perhaps Nell was making distance between them. Mayhap she wouldn't marry the man after all. He stifled a laugh at the notion that Nell wanted the wealthiest bachelor in Virginia, President Madison's friend, to keep money from the puppy sales. A stubborn and independent woman.

"When I come back, I hope Nelly and Andy will be ready to move up with me. Will stay long enough to get them used to the idea." A grin spread across the man's face.

Dressed in a gauzy yellow gown, Mariah entered the room as though taking over the helm. She went straight to where Hayes sat and jabbed a finger into his shoulder. "Were you going to leave and not allow me to wish you a proper farewell, Hayes?"

Rising, the man towered over Mariah. He could have lifted her and moved her out of his way in a thrice. Instead, Hayes raised one of her dainty hands to his lips and bowed. "When I come back, my dear, we shall have a serious conversation."

Mariah collapsed into Hayes's arms, to Carter's utter astonishment. Davis bore her to the sofa, nestled against the far wall.

"Send Eddie to get Nelly up here," Hayes barked at him. "Or get the servant. Probably those darn corset strings are pulled too tight."

And how exactly did he know of this?

As though reading his mind, Hayes gazed over at him. "My wife had a penchant for such nonsense."

Wife? He'd deal with that information later.

Mariah groaned and attempted to sit up.

Bending over her slight frame, Hayes lifted her and headed toward the door. "If you're not gonna help me then call for that servant girl, Macy. I'll bring Miss Wenham up to her room myself and help her."

In three long strides, Hayes carried Mariah from the office. Carter followed them into the hallway and spotted Macy making her way down the hallway, a tray in her arms, stacked high with food.

He cleared his throat. "What are you doing?"

"I be takin' this upstairs, like Miss Mariah told me."

Hayes, holding Mariah, stopped on the landing where Carter's nephew, Charles, stood. "Show me where your aunt's room is."

Carter caught the servant's eye. "Macy, will you please go—"

"Yessir." She cut him off with an odd fleeting smile and marched up the steps, china cups rattling against saucers as she went.

Chapter Fourteen

A sharp rap of Carter's Wellington beaver hat against his thigh cleared the dust from it. He awaited the buggy carrying him to Richmond for his medical appointment. The carriage pulled in front of the stable and his driver, Squires, gestured him toward it, a footman jumping down to assist him inside. According to Mariah, Hayes had departed earlier, after being assured she was well. Their guest left without bidding Carter farewell. *Just as well.*

So Hayes was a widower, and he might be more anxious to finally bring Nell home after years of doing without a wife. Carter's chest ached as he pictured Nell in the office, head bent over her notes, assuming her father's job.

An hour later, they arrived in the commonwealth's capital. While his driver secured the buggy and horses, Carter stretched his limbs, stiff after the long ride. He ambled to the coffeehouse, lured by the scents of rich chocolate, spicy cinnamon buns, and fresh-ground coffee scents.

He entered the cozy establishment and inhaled. Nothing like the sea air, salt pork, unwashed sailors, and canon fire smoke aboard a naval vessel.

A woman of middling age ushered him to a minuscule table by a window. "What shall it be today?"

"Small pot of chocolate, please." Carter rubbed his jaw, realizing he'd forgotten to shave that morning. "And a roll." He pointed to a tray of fresh cinnamon buns, heaps of butter melting atop them.

Giving him a wink, she set a mug on the table. "I'll grab the biggest one."

Carter chuckled. He must be a quick read. Hadn't Nell said that was something she'd always liked about him? His needs announced themselves upon his countenance before he'd given them voice.

A newspaper, left behind on the window sill, displayed *British Ramping Up Efforts* on the front-page headline. If he could get aboard a ship again, would his experience be of some use to a crew?

Hunger and thirst satisfactorily appeased, but conscience pricked by the article, Carter paid his bill, slipping an extra coin to the server as he left. He stepped out onto the brick walkway. A pain shot up from his ankle, into his calf, and then tightened above his knee cap. He grimaced. *Curse this blasted leg.*

Across the street, he spied the sign for his former ship's physician. Dr. Quinlain had been discharged from service and set up practice in a building on the newer boundary of Richmond. Dodging a carriage and a youth atop a brown gelding, Carter reached the plain oak door at street level. He opened it, entered a small entryway, and confronted the steep flight of stairs. The odor of fresh white-wash surrounded him.

A silver-haired man descended the steps, the soles of his shoes tapping with sureness of purpose.

Would that I were so agile, even now.

Each laborious step up the staircase eased the embarrassment Carter had about seeking help with his infirmity.

Now waiting in a hard-backed wooden chair, Carter questioned his real reason for coming to this examination. If he improved his gait, might doors open to him? Or did he wish for Lawrence to bar him from even considering that option. He stood, cool breeze rising up from the stairs nearby, as someone opened the door on the lower level.

Standing and stretching his leg out didn't help, rather made his appendage stiffen further. He snapped open his watch's cover and noted the time. It had been some time since his last appointment. The surgeon, Dr. Lawrence Quinlain, served with him. Carter respected no other physician more. Dr. Quinlain had saved his leg, working tirelessly to keep the wound clean and Carter from taking fever.

The paneled door finally opened. A bent woman, about eighty years of age, appeared. Garbed in the old-fashioned way, her clothing was still fine, the wool not moth-eaten or frayed.

"Good to see you, Mrs. Middleton, and take care on those stairs," a cheerful man's voice called out. Behind her emerged his old shipmate, the doctor ruddy-cheeked.

"Carter Williams. Look at you—I don't even see a walking stick."

"Doing a tad better." Some days.

Lawrence's broad smile extended across his face. He waved a broad hand forward. "Come in. How's your family?"

Carter's chest constricted. His leg dragging, Carter lifted his hip to give the knee assistance. "You mustn't have heard—Lee died in the epidemic. Lost his manager and a quarter of the field hands, too."

Gentle eyes met his. "I'm very sorry. I know you and your brother were close."

He'd cried out for Lee and for Nell after his injury aboard ship. *Not for Father.* Both men remained silent for a moment.

"I haven't kept up with our local happenings, I'm afraid. With Bonaparte defeated, I've followed our military news, mindful of my own situation." The surgeon grimaced. After the shipwreck, Mrs. Quinlain's influential father made sure that Lawrence returned home to her and their seven children.

Dr. Quinlain went to his desk at the rear of the room. "We had no outbreak here in the city."

"Would that we hadn't at Dogwood, but I am now guardian of my four nephews." Carter took a deep breath.

"That's a big responsibility but no greater than commanding a ship."

The older man gestured to a chair but Carter shook his head. "I've been sitting long enough." He braced himself against a chair. "Their aunt may relieve me of duty if she transports them down to South Carolina."

Dr. Quinlain pulled open the center drawer of his desk. "Is it Mariah Wenham you mean?"

"Yes. I didn't realize you knew her." Had Carter mentioned her to Lawrence while they served together? He didn't believe so.

Lawrence held his gaze, a frown working between his eyes. He shoved the drawer shut. "I'm the new physician for the boys' school nearby."

The good doctor never had been good at maintaining his focus.

"Good for you, Lawrence, congratulations." Carter rubbed his face. "Concerning Miss Wenham, how did you make her acquaintance?"

"Oh that..." Dr. Quinlain shrugged. "You were talking about your nephews. Whether you should move them to South Carolina with her. Best keep them where everything is familiar, if you can. Do you have a governess?"

"Not yet." Because they'd never been able to keep help for the boys. Yet Nell seemed to manage them fine. "If I can't salvage our crops and figure out what my brother did..." Carter sensed his face beginning to flush. *I shouldn't have said anything.*

His friend came around and perched at the end of his desk. "As bad as all that, is it?" He gestured to a chair.

Carter remained standing. "If I sit, I won't be able to walk out of here again."

"It's a miracle you still possess that leg." The physician shook his dark head. "God spared you, Carter."

Had the Lord done so? For what purpose? "I wanted to be an attorney, perhaps a politician someday. But now I've had to leave the College of William and Mary."

"You can always return."

Carter wiped his damp forehead. The pain in his knee burned. It felt like being anchored without a hint of a breeze, under an unrelenting sun in the Chesapeake Bay.

Dr. Quinlain moved toward him and squatted, pulling up his pant leg. "Scar looks good, very smooth."

Jagged mutilated skin, much like the lightening that caused it, extended down his leg. "I bet you told your last patient, the elderly woman, that she appeared to be of courting age, too, didn't you?"

His former associate laughed. "No, but speaking of courtship, have you a sweetheart?"

Carter gasped as his friend probed his injury site. "I did. A professor's daughter. But I fear..." No, he didn't fear, rather he experienced something akin to relief. *Was Sally betrothed to Richmond's wealthiest man? While a golden-haired martinet now directed Carter's thoughts and actions like an admiral of the fleet?* "Ouch!"

The doctor stopped prodding. "Hurt?"

"Like the devil. Should be glad I don't call you out for that." Carter bent over to rub the spot on his knee that had been squeezed.

"Simply doing my job." His lips flattened in disapproval. "Getting soft on us, lieutenant?"

Biting back a retort, Carter considered. "Yes, and I intend to take up hoop embroidery posthaste."

His friend pointed to the chair. "Sit for a moment and let me check the mechanics of that leg."

Carter glared at the man as he lowered himself, first clutching the sturdy chair's arms and sinking into it, a disabled vessel unable to launch.

Dr. Quinlain placed a wide hand under Carter's knee and raised it. "Let it dangle."

"No." It had hung, dead, for weeks after the injury. Sweat broke out on his brow.

"Lieutenant, you've obviously recovered the leg's usage. Release your control over it. You shan't be unmanned—nor were you so altered in the accident." Dr. Quinlain grinned. "You can still marry, become a father."

That comment didn't merit a response. Carter wiped the perspiration above his lip, bracing himself. Dr. Quinlain reached one hand to Carter's ankle and extended the dead weight up before gently lowering the leg.

"Now do what I did." The physician frowned at him. "By yourself."

Had Lawrence lost his senses? But by the beady look in his eyes, sighted upon him, there would be a blast from those cannons if Carter didn't comply. He squared his shoulders and breathed in slowly. The first two motions, while difficult, were achieved. He smiled up in victory.

Dr. Quinlain pointed his index finger. "Now the other movement."

Concentrating hard, Carter extended his leg. When it was halfway up, it dropped to the floor, the glass orb on the doctor's desk raising then clattering down with a thump before rolling to the edge where his friend caught it. "You need to keep exercising your leg but I think you are doing remarkably well."

Well? Would he ever run after a child? Or dance again? He pictured a blonde woman clutched tightly in his arms, one whose throaty laugh bubbled up from deep within her. And his body recalled the feel of her back pressed against his chest as they rode across the field together. His cheeks scorched.

"How much more use might I recover?" It had been almost a year now.

His eyes crinkled as he set his mouth. "Only God can say, Carter. You do the work and He'll do the rest. There's damage but I have no way of assessing other than watching your recovery over time."

Carter hung his head. God hadn't been saying much of anything to him for some time now. But hadn't He? Through Nell, through the clergyman of his home parish, and when he'd deigned to open his nephews' Bible to read to them at night. Carter's own King James Bible lay at the bottom of the Atlantic.

"Thank you."

"Tis my pleasure."

And his livelihood. "Lawrence, what can I do for you? You wouldn't take payment last time."

His former ship's surgeon stood and adjusted his lapels. "I was hoping you might ask." His narrow lips twitched. "Am I correct—do you still have the Gills living nearby? The ones whose pups are so prized? I believe the daughter works at the girl's academy here in Richmond."

Odd prickles crept down Carter's arms. Yet another man asking about Nell? "Yes. She had but she's returned to Charles City. Her father was our manager and one of those who passed away from the yellow fever outbreak." Poor Nell. He cleared his throat. He'd sounded like a bullfrog.

"I'm sorry to hear that." Lawrence appeared sheepish. "Miss Gill mentioned her family's hounds to my wife when they both worked on a church bazaar together."

Little Nell Gill would never have imagined she'd rub shoulders with doctor's wives at church bazaars in Richmond. Father's plan for evil had brought about good. Wasn't that what the Bible said also—that God could bring good from bad situations?

Lawrence cocked his head. "True what they say?"

"What might that be?" That Nell was opinionated and determined? Beautiful, feisty, intelligent? He grabbed his handkerchief and wadded it into a ball.

"Well, everyone in these parts is talking." A calculated grin settled on his old shipmate's face.

Planting one leg firmly on the carpet, Carter jutted his hip to secure his position, waiting.

"They say her family's pups are the very best. My eldest son, Bartholomew, would love to have a dog. And I would love to have one well-trained and sweet-natured as the Gills' are purported to be."

He flexed his bad foot. "Even I shan't promise one of those—they are so dear."

Happiness fled his friend's face. "I'd hoped to distract him with a puppy if I am yet recalled to service."

This war wasn't over yet. The military needed men like Lawrence, but there would be a cost. "What about your practice, the hospital?"

Dr. Quinlain shrugged. "I'd have a colleague come in and help while I'm gone."

"Miss Gill took bids on all but three. Let me see what I can do."

His words brought a glow to his old friend's eyes. "Bart will be the happiest boy in Richmond." They shook hands and Carter left the office, passing a dark-haired boy who sat earnestly reading the Bible as he waited.

Lawrence glanced between him and the youth not once but twice. *Odd.*

"Well, I'm off."

"God be with you."

Oh, God, are you here? Can you not make yourself known?

As the door closed behind the two, Carter could have sworn he'd heard the boy's plaintive voice asking, "Is that my father's…"

The door had closed with finality or Carter might have reentered the office. Carter froze midway down the stairs as a sudden chill descended upon him. No, he didn't know the boy. Had he known the boy's father? Had the father been in his crew? He'd ask on his return.

He resumed his descent, his leg spasming and his stomach sinking the closer he got to the bottom.

128

Now to talk to Nell about this little agreement. As independent as Nell was, and as much as she needed the money from the hounds—what had he been thinking?

She'd be furious.

Chapter Fifteen

Living again amidst enslaved people, albeit fairly well-treated by the new overseer, had begun to disturb Cornelia's sleep, stirring up dreams of faceless field hands crying out. Pa, too, had been bothered by the slaves' plight. And now she was responsible for the office work that supported their continued enslavement. A quarter of the Williams's workers had died. A full quarter. The number was unthinkable. Far more had passed away than those amongst the gentry. She had to find the funds to support the hiring of a physician to help those who'd remained. One thing she could do something about immediately was replacing the workers' clothing, which was in shreds.

She rose from her bed, ready to begin her new routine. Andy had taken over most of Pa's duties with the dogs. He also cleaned and cooked for the two of them. The work as manager was harder than her work at the school. She returned home each evening almost too fatigued to even cook a pan of journey cake ahead for their breakfast.

"Andy, time to get up." The sun had already risen and she needed to get up to the South Flanker.

"I don't feel good." His cough was deeper than the previous day. "Need to stay in bed today."

Cornelia opened the window to stir the air in the cabin. "I need your assistance if we're to remain here."

"Should've had a smarter brother. One who could really help." His muffled words revealed that he was crying.

Her brother knew right where to get her—he'd put a pain in the center of her heart. She went to his side. "Andy, you are intelligent. You show it in ways other than choring and reading and writing. Look how well you put those puppies through their paces at the show." She sniffed away her tears.

He closed his eyes. "My head hurts bad."

She grazed his forehead with the back of her hand. "You're hot." *Dear God, not another terrible illness.*

"I told you."

She pulled Grandmama Lucia's quilt around his shoulders. Perhaps they should have gone with Hayes. Too late. She poured water from a pitcher into a crockery mug and set it on the floor beside him. "I'll return as soon as I can, but I have to let someone know."

"I'll be okay for a while. Gonna sleep."

"Do you want me to open the door? Let some more heat out?" She pushed away the dark blond locks of hair that lay on his forehead, her heartbeat ratcheting up.

"No. Just leave the window open." He shivered. "Can I have my drawing pad, though?"

Grabbing his paper and pencil, she held them for a moment before releasing them to him.

"Thank you, Sissy."

Trudging across the fields, she chastised herself. *I should have taken Hayes offer. I am one pigheaded fool. God, did I hear you right? Didn't you tell me to stay? I was sure that was you speaking to my soul.*

Jemma, a field hand, waved her scarf at Cornelia. "Can you come looky?" The broad-shouldered woman gestured to several rows of beans. Fungus covered all the new growth.

"There's a concoction Pa used." She cogitated till the ingredients came to her and she quickly explained it to the young woman. "You'll have to keep hauling buckets of water and mix those ingredients into the water and then pour it over the plants."

"Yes'm, we'll do it."

131

Cornelia hurried toward the Great House. If it rained, then all of Jemma and the others' efforts will be for naught. Carter would have to call in the agrarian from Charles City, again, to help them.

Cornelia spied Eddie up ahead. "Eddie, Andy has a fever. Could you go up and get Carter for me?"

The boy squared his shoulders. "I'd be happy to assist." *Such a grown-up acting boy.* She hoped he didn't lose his childhood like she and Carter had.

Cornelia lifted her skirts and rushed back to the cabin. Pushing the door open, she spied Andy's ashen face and heard each rattling breath he wheezed.

Lord God—no.

It sounded much like the others had just before they passed, but he hadn't had their symptoms. She couldn't lose her brother.

God help us both.

Cornelia ran to him, her breath as ragged as his.

Already this morning, Carter had hobbled around the field's perimeter. His leg throbbed, a continuous reminder of the ship's disaster. Lightning, not a cannon, had terminated his services as a naval officer. God's wrath?

Per Dr. Quinlain's instructions, he made extra walking a goal for himself. He admired the brick buildings that flanked each other like partners lining the common green. Magnolias, centered in the U-shaped drive that led to the house, glistened with dew, their conical flower buds promising brilliant white blossoms. He'd passed the flanking kitchen and laundry buildings, turned at the cylindrical brick dovecote, and then looped behind the stables. A groomsman curried a horse. Nearby, brass on the boys' new pony trap was being polished as a stout man supervised.

"Good morning to you, Mr. Williams." Avery Hicks had managed the stables and carriage house for as long as Carter could remember.

"How's that new rig doing?"

"Fine, no problems at all."

Other than paying for it, which Carter wasn't sure Lee had done. Reviewing the records that Nell had carefully earmarked was more painfully slow than his strides. Several notations in the records still eluded

132

them both. In addition to the already plenteous plantation expenses, Mariah had begun asking for a trip into Richmond, presumably to spend money she apparently didn't have and he certainly couldn't lend her.

"Very good." He tipped his hat and returned to the crushed oyster shell walkway. Then he strolled in between the fields and the Gill cabin, hoping to check on Nell.

Carter scanned the fields, populated with workers. He willed his leg to cooperate as he headed toward the Gills' cabin. As he approached, a feminine arm slipped a red handkerchief in between the doorframe and the ancient door before jerking it shut. Their sign for trouble.

His heart rate increased. If only he could run. *Lord I haven't asked for much. I know I cannot do this thing, but if by your will I might, enable me to do so.*

Carter drew in a long breath, steeling himself for pain and for possibly falling as he forced himself into a slow run. He moved faster when he held his knee straight when he came down on it. In a moment he was at the cabin door, bent over, hands propped on his thighs as he panted.

From inside, he could hear Nell's urgent prayers. "Lord, help me, help my brother."

He knocked and then opened the door, not wanting to wait another minute. Andrew was covered up to his neck with a mountain of patchwork quilts, all askew. The scent of cold ashes assaulted his nose. No fire glowed in the grate. Andrew shivered on his narrow bed.

Half-hopping, Carter went to the boy. "When did this happen?"

Red-rimmed eyes, underscored by dark circles, revealed Nell's sleepless nights. Why hadn't he noticed her fatigue earlier?

"He's had a cough." She patted at her gray skirt. "But not like this. It worsened this morning with the fever."

Carter tried to shake off the images of young men dying in their hammocks of some contagion they'd picked up in port. "We have to get him to a doctor."

Tears washed Nell's cheeks. "I gave him honey and tea at night and that helped some."

He wanted to pull Nell into his arms, to comfort her. Instead he gave her his handkerchief.

"Thank you." She sniffed. "Did Eddie send you, or Mariah?"

133

"No, I haven't been up at the house." He went to the bed and pulled away the top coverings, keeping the bottom one to wrap around the boy. If he took a deep breath, and if God helped him, he could get Andrew up. He'd carry the boy until they came across a field hand who could run to the stable and ask for the carriage. He hoisted the boy up, surprised by Andrew's slight weight. Carter's leg held as he took a step.

"Mariah was here only a little while ago. She said she would send for Hayes."

Carter stumbled then caught himself. "Mariah, here?" Unfathomable that she'd stoop to visiting at the Gills' cabin. "And what does she think Hayes shall do from up in Orange County?" Or was he yet out conducting business along the James River?

Fresh tears flowed from Nell's eyes. "I don't know."

"We need to care for Andrew right now." Blasted interfering woman. He'd tell Mariah his opinion of her meddling when they returned.

"Yes."

"My physician is a fair spell from here but I trust him utterly."

"Anything, I'd give him whatever he asks if he can save Andy." Nell shuddered as another round of tears spilled from her eyes. "He's all I've got."

It took his entire composure to not set her brother down and go to her and reassure her. "Nell that's not true."

She choked back her tears. "I'll come with you."

"No, it would be quicker if I take him alone. I'm taking him myself right now. Is anyone else ill like this?"

"No one."

"Go check with Edward later. If necessary, quarantine the workers and those at the house. Don't hesitate—please."

He'd given her orders. Would that help her regroup, if she had a mission to complete?

Nell wiped her face with the back of her hand. "When will you return?"

"Perhaps tonight, tomorrow if the weather turns, as it might. Only God knows." He hadn't been able to stop those last words.

Blue eyes searched his face.

"Nell, if Dr. Quinlain must keep Andrew at his hospital, I'll send word, but I will stay with him. I know you'd do the same for my nephews if they needed it."

He'd never seen her so vulnerable looking. So young. Appeared no older than the girl he'd shared his woes with years earlier. "You've still got me."

Carter resettled Andrew in his arms and made his way over the threshold and off the step, mindful of keeping his balance. He wanted to go before his friend detected the moisture glistening in his own eyes.

Elijah dashed up. "Let me carry the boy, sir."

Having gotten underway, it was best for Carter to continue on. "Run up to the carriage house and tell Mr. Hicks to ready the pony trap immediately."

Dear God, spare this boy. Heal him from whatever ails him. Amen.

From the walkway, Mariah waved her lacy handkerchief like a signal flag. If he understood her correctly, Carter was supposed to come to the home port. Unlike Nell and Andrew, she had no true need of assistance. He clenched his jaw and circled the carriage to where Mariah waited.

Andrew groaned as they stopped.

"I'm coming with you." She clutched a reticule the size of a portmanteau.

Carter shook his head, pointing to Andrew. "He's very ill—could be contagious and we don't have room for baggage."

"I am going with you. There's room on the floor for this."

"Can't you see how ill this boy is?" Pressing his eyes closed, Carter wished that she would disappear. When he reopened them, she hadn't. Instead, Mariah came to the buggy's side.

"Mariah, I insist you remain behind."

He startled as with a jounce she got in. Carter stared at her. "How did you manage that by yourself in such attire?"

"Practice." She gave him a slow appraisal. "Something you'd do well to imitate."

He'd gotten up by himself, if that was what she meant, but he wasn't going to argue anymore. He had to get Andrew to Richmond.

"All right, we're off." Carter glared at her. "But don't blame me if you become ill."

"I shan't" She sighed heavily and waved at Avery Hicks as they rode by. "Such a kind man."

"Indeed." Why had she any dealings with him?

Mariah rearranged the covers around Andrew, surprising Carter. "What a hard life he has had, Carter. And what a rock his sister has been."

"I agree." What was she getting at?

"It doesn't seem fair."

"No, it does not." He chewed his lower lip.

Mariah's sigh cut through the air. "I forgive your rude behavior. Your concern is very evident. When we're afraid, we become angry."

"Perhaps I'm afraid a lot then."

She laughed. "If you mean you are irritable, cross, and difficult then I must agree—you must be terrified of your situation." Mariah patted his arm with a gloved hand.

"What about you? Do you ever get so worried that you act as wickedly as I apparently do?"

"I didn't say you or I were wicked now, did I?" She gazed out across the fields, full of cash crops if they grew.

He urged the ponies into a quicker pace as the trap rolled out onto the main road. "My behavior in the past has been rather sinful."

A bank of clouds overhead momentarily blocked the sun, casting a shadow over Mariah's even features. "Who among us is without sin?"

Carter glanced at Andrew, who was attempting to snuggle closer to Mariah. "Didn't take you for being especially religious."

"Trust me, I have done some very foolish things. Sinful things." She pressed her hand to Andrew's cheek. "But one day there will be an accounting. And I fear my day will come very soon."

She turned toward the drive they passed, one leading to Berkeley Plantation. "Who lives there?"

"A fine family." For once, on these latest visits to Dogwood Plantation, Mariah had not bragged about the Wenham home in Charleston.

"What?"

"Probably full of sinners, Mariah."

136

She giggled. Her dark mood passed as soon as it began and "You're a tease, Carter Williams."

"As you said, I need practice in some things." He exhaled. "Blaming God for our past mistakes won't help us."

"No." Her voice was a bare whisper.

"And it won't get this child to the doctor any quicker."

Andrew snored softly as he nestled against Mariah's shoulder.

A lone rider approached them, slowing as he passed. He nodded to Carter and winked at Mariah.

"A fine-looking young man." Mariah awkwardly opened her fan. "But dirt-poor."

How would she know?

"Didn't take you for a snob."

"I'm not." She snapped the fan closed. "I'm broke, Carter. Ran my family's estate into the ground."

Chapter Sixteen

The bulwark Carter hastily built around the panic rising within him, threatened failure. One more family member to support— an adult accustomed to spending freely. Until he completed his accounting, Carter wouldn't divulge their own financial woes. He trusted Nell to likewise keep their dire straits a secret.

"You know my first obligation is to my nephews." Mariah was to have been one of his options of rescuing the boys if need be. A blockade hindered that route now. "However, I shall assist as I can."

Mariah had just sunk his alternate plan faster than his ship had gone down. If he groveled to the admiralty to return to service, and it was granted, then he'd at least have more income.

Encouraging the horses to pick up their pace, Carter wished he could put some space between himself and Anne's sister.

Mariah raised her voice over the increased noise from the road, "You're the only one I could ask."

The two rode at a pace that prohibited normal conversation. His plan hadn't been feasible with or without Mariah's pronouncement.

Andrew groaned periodically. Mariah continually wiped his brow and adjusted his covering.

The commonwealth's capital would provide a welcome reprieve from Mariah and the new load of tonnage she'd added to his worries. Richmond never looked lovelier.

"We've arrived." Carter stopped at the livery stable, newly constructed and fresher smelling than any such establishment he'd ever visited.

Mariah exited by herself. "I've urgent business to attend to." She disappeared before he could request her help with Andrew.

Carter touched the boy's arm. "Andrew, I'll return in a moment."

He made arrangements for the horses and left a deposit for the cost of their care with a young man who couldn't have been much older than the sick child in the carriage.

He returned to the wagon, where Andrew lay, and took him into his arms. After sitting so long he wasn't sure he could carry Nell's brother the entire distance. He stopped every ten paces, needing to adapt to the stabbing pain in his leg. The stairs to the medical building were another matter. He could manage only one at a time without pausing.

By the time he got to the stairs' top, his muscles spasmed. He settled Andrew in a chair outside his friend's office and rapped on the door. In a moment it opened.

"Back already?" Lawrence Quinlain's thick hair was mussed as though he had been napping. "You happened to catch me in. This is normally my study day at home."

Andrew slumped over, his head in his hands. So young. So helpless. *God save him.*

Cornelia allowed herself to cry like a baby. Not like a woman—like a frilly, noodle-headed girl.

Hadn't Jesus wept, too? That made her feel sorrier than ever. "Lord, I know you wept for your friend. But I'm supposed to be strong."

Stronger than me? God seemed to whisper to her soul.

She sniffed. "Maybe not."

Was there anyone greater than God was? "No. I'm sorry, Lord."

Won't you trust me?

"I'm afraid to."

A fresh round of tears flooded down her cheeks. Cornelia patted them with Carter's handkerchief. It smelled like him—of leather, cedar, and something musky. She held it to her nose then pulled it away, feeling the embroidery thread that was raised up on the corner. His mother's initials. What would it be like to have a Hope Chest filled with beautiful things? With linens embroidered with her initials on them—CRG for Cornelia Rose Gill. Or would it be CRW, Cornelia Rose Williams? That was how she'd imagined her name reading when she was a child. She'd fancied she'd marry Lee, Carter's older brother. They'd spy on him with his sweethearts and watch them kiss behind the barn. Lee, of course, had never noticed she was alive, and was much older than her. Perhaps the same age as Hayes. If he didn't have that gray hair in his beard would Hayes look younger?

When he returned, she'd ask if he'd get a shave. She'd volunteer to do it for him having shaved Pa often enough. She swallowed. Would it be so bad being married to her kinsman? It didn't seem right. But her options were limited. If Andy died... He couldn't. If he did, though, she couldn't stay here. *She wouldn't.*

Hayes could marry her and take her to Orange County. Errant thoughts wandered to Carter's warm arms pinning her hard against his chest as they rode across the fields. She trembled.

Cornelia got on her knees on the hard wood floor. "Lord, not my will but Thine."

The sudden rap at the door startled her. "Who is it?"

"Nemi. Macy say you be needed," she called through the door.

Her back stiffened. *Oh no.* She stood and threw the door open. "Are the boys sick?" Not them, too.

"Well, Missy Gill, you could say." The servant's voice held that whiny tone that grated on Cornelia's frayed nerves.

"How?"

The ashy-skinned young woman rubbed the toe of one shabby shoe against the other, staring at them as though they might repair themselves if only she kept at it long enough. "They will be ill if a body don't stop 'em."

When Cornelia arrived in the Great House formal dining room, tea cakes, lady fingers, and trays of biscuits were spread out on the shiny mahogany table. Dark fingerprints tracked up the blue silk drapes.

140

"Oh, Miss Cornelia, I believe I ate too much." Eddie's next younger brother, Charles, ran to the window and threw up the sash.

"Me, too." Lloyd set down a cake plate covered with crumbs and rubbed his bulging stomach.

Albert waved chocolate and whipped cream-covered hands. She bent over the toddler. "Where did you get this, Albert?" He beamed up at her and wiped his hands across her face. The slimy concoction slithered down her neck.

Retching ensued from the window.

"Unka say." Albert plopped onto the carpet, dragging tiny fingers over the woven leaf pattern.

Cornelia grabbed a napkin from the table, wiped at her neck and face then grasped the youngster's flailing hands, wiping them clean before he could lay hold of her skirt, too. Then she patted at her face again for good measure.

Pale-faced Charles slumped into a Queen Anne chair. "Uncle Carter promised we could have our fill of what was left over in the pantry, including extra sweets from the Puppy Day event."

"Surely you cannot believe he meant like this."

After poking, prodding, and making Andrew cough, Dr. Quinlain raised his eyebrows. "Can you leave him here at the hospital?"

What his friend termed a "hospital" was a private building, the upper level filled with beds for patients. "You are referring to your own establishment, yes? Not the public hospital here."

"No, I'd like to keep him here if I can. There's room."

How were his nephews faring at home? Macy had been tasked by Mariah to watch over them but the house servant had her own chores to complete. And Nell, how would she react? Would she rail at him when he didn't return with Andrew?

Carter shifted his stance to ease his hips. "It's that bad?"

"A deep lung infection."

"Perhaps it's a family weakness."

"Why?"

"The same malady had claimed Mrs. Gill."

"Could be a familial link, but we can't say." Dr. Quinlain returned his instruments to his bag. "I want you to check his room at home."

"His bedchamber?" The boy had only a low curtained bed on the cabin's west wall—not far from the fireplace, just beyond the table that was used for all purposes.

"Yes. Often something is overlooked that can cause these reactions."

"Such as?" The sailors he'd dealt with had brought much of their illnesses upon themselves with drinking, too much tobacco, and frolicking with willing young women while in port. Carter hadn't much experience with natural causes of sickness other than his own difficulties with hay, which wasn't growing yet.

"Is it kept clean?"

"His sister would sweep out every last grain of sand were she able."

"Perhaps moisture seepage—mold for instance."

There was a musty, almost mildew, smell when he'd entered the cabin on days when it had been closed up, such as recently. "Perhaps."

"How old is the structure?"

Carter laughed. "I believe it's the oldest building in Charles City. Originally built in the late seventeen century—cedar."

"You don't say. Andy said he lived in a log cabin."

"This boy's ancestors were among the earliest English settlers. If the Pleasants could survive those attacks by the Natives, perhaps he can get past this malady." But even to his own ears, it didn't seem right that a log cabin could have kept out such attacks nor have lasted so long. A niggling doubt formed in his mind. One involving a stone building settled amidst a row of dogwood trees.

"One can hope."

"And pray." Those words came more frequently of late.

The last of what Cornelia now termed the Terrible Trio was washed, dried, clothed in fresh bedclothes and put to bed. She slumped into a padded armless chair nestled in an alcove between the two bedrooms.

Now Cornelia knew why Carter couldn't keep staff for the boys. How on earth had Mariah Wenham managed them? Raising a small oil lamp she intended to douse, she inferred what had transpired—nothing. The woman had made these children do little. Their toys were strewn like chicken feed about their room. The house slaves had hung their clean clothing but their dirty outfits were thrown on the floor near their beds.

Of course the youngest couldn't care for himself. Cornelia had been outraged when she realized no one had even recently bathed Albert. The boys admitted that Miss Wenham had asked Macy to perform the task, but she claimed she hadn't been able to maintain a sufficient hold on the squirming toddler to get him clean.

Eddie had shared all about his brothers when he'd joined them an hour earlier. Now he took his dinner in peace downstairs. "Miss Cornelia, I tried to help, but I'm their brother. They won't listen to me." He'd grinned then. "You know my brothers are a tough lot when I'd prefer to be in the fields with the workers instead of chasing them down to make them behave—which wasn't happening, regardless."

Pushing away a stray strand of hair, bone-weariness overtook her. These normal, healthy, intelligent boys had given her more trouble in one day than her brother, with all his difficulties in learning, had given her in the previous year.

God, I need to be more loving to Andy, less worried about what he cannot do and more full of praise for how you have blessed him with a sweet and loving spirit, and a special talent for diagramming and for remembering things. How was her brother? Was he perhaps even now coming home with a remedy?

In silence, she trod across the thick wool rug and extinguished first one lamp and repeated the procedure with the others. Hearing movement in the house, downstairs, she strained to listen in the alcove's velvet darkness. In a moment, her eyes adjusted to the dark. She grasped the doorknob. With a soft creak, the door opened in toward her—a sliver of lamplight spilling a pool of yellow on the floor.

"Carter?" Her heart beat faster, surprised that he'd returned.

Elation surged through her as she waited to hear news of her brother.

He adjusted the wick of his lamp and a wider circle of light revealed concern in his eyes. His mouth, clenched in a thin line, and his silence doused her joy and increased her foreboding.

"How is Andy?" she whispered. Her old friend motioned for her to follow him out. He held the door for her as she exited the "den of

143

iniquity." Soon, the room would be renamed as the boys were brought into line.

When Carter gave no reply, Cornelia examined his face, deep hollows shadowing his eyes, giving him an eerie appearance. She grasped his free hand. "Tell me, what is it?" *Lord, no, you can't have let him die. No!* A wave of dizziness threatened and she wobbled but Carter pulled her toward a nearby chair, setting the lamp on a small table.

Hysteria rose within her. This was a replication of her father's behavior when Ma had died. Perspiration broke out on her chest. "Where is he?"

"He didn't make it back ..." was all she heard as her breath left her. The light faded and she crumpled into Carter's arms.

Chapter Seventeen

"Andrew is at the hospital, Nell." He arranged her on his lap, supporting her with one arm behind her shoulders and the other beneath her knees. "We had to leave him there."

She was warm, soft, and almost limp in his arms, slumped fully against him, pressing his spine to the wall. While he didn't like her being upset, the sensation of her on his lap was undeniably pleasant.

Should have told her what I promised Lawrence.

He'd hesitated immediately telling Nell about the hospital because he wasn't up to managing her worry about the hospital's cost. Pure selfishness. He'd wanted neither negotiations, nor an argument, this evening. Nor to explain about the promise of one of her puppies as payment.

"I'm sorry."

Nell still didn't reply.

What if Mariah came up those stairs and encountered them like this? Would she believe that he'd sought to compromise Nell? He recalled her trimming Hayes's beard outside her cabin, just as nonchalant as if she were peeling potatoes. He exhaled.

Nell snuggled against him and sighed. He held himself still, aware of his own reactions. He hadn't held a woman like this since before his injury, not even Sally. Not difficult to find willing arms before then. That was before he and God has a serious talk about his behavior. Then he'd been injured. Had God punished him?

No. God didn't work that way.

"Nell," he whispered into her ear, her thick sweet-smelling hair brushing against his nose. "Andrew is in the hospital, a private establishment."

She shook her head and struggled to sit up but then relaxed into his arms. He hadn't meant to give her a shock. But if Andrew didn't conquer this lung disorder, then what?

Her brother was alive. In a hospital in Richmond.

Cornelia had tried to move, to release herself from Carter's hold, but those strong arms supporting her could have been Neptune's mighty arms lifting her from the sea. Her lack of resistance to his charms commanded her. She kept her eyes sealed shut, not wanting him to know she was alert.

As she opened her eyes she wondered if she was steady enough to stand.

It's not right to continue this close contact. It could jeopardize his relationship with that girl—the professor's daughter. But hadn't Sally sauntered off on the arm of Hugh Martin, perhaps in pursuit of a heftier money bag?

"What did the doctor think?"

"Hmm?" He rubbed between her sore shoulder blades. It felt so good. "About Andy?"

"Yes."

"Dr. Quinlain wondered if something in your cabin was causing the cough." He continued massaging the tension that had built up from her worry over her brother.

"The cabin?" Her neck muscles tightened but Carter's expert maneuvers soon released the knots.

"He suggested we check and make sure nothing has moldered—"

"I keep that house clean as does Andy." Still, she had to admit that every time she'd returned home, she'd noticed the dank odor.

"Yes, 'tis more to do with the house's age—possible seepage or such." His voice soothed as did the motions of his fingers.

146

"You should stop."

He splayed his hand wide across her back, his fingers working in slow circles. It felt heavenly.

"Yes, I should." His voice was husky. "But you don't want me to, do you?"

She believed in honesty. "No, I don't. But it isn't proper."

"Didn't know you cared about that." His fingers moved up to her neck, massaging deep into the tender skin beneath her curls.

"I do care about Andy getting home." Her head lolled back as she relaxed into those probing wonderful motions.

"He made no promises as to how soon that would be but your brother is in good hands."

As am I. "You better let me up." Her mind urged her upward but her body begged her to remain right where she was.

"I don't think you mean what you're saying."

Daniel's words echoed in her mind, and she recollected her wits. "I don't want any tongues wagging about you." But she couldn't seem to move away from him, not fearing he would ever overstep. "With all you have going on, it wouldn't be right."

He snorted. "When did you start caring about my reputation?"

It wasn't Carter she feared would cross the line. Cornelia sighed, fighting the urge to press herself against him and kiss him until he begged to be released. He was right in his assessment. "About two minutes ago."

Laughing, he patted her shoulder then eased her upright. "All right, up you go, Miss Gill."

Recognizing she was no longer wanted in that comfortable sanctuary, Cornelia unfolded her body and sat up. She hesitated a moment, sitting on his knees, struck by a notion. Springing up, she turned. "Stick out your leg for me."

The lamplight made the pinched circle of his mouth look even rounder. Carter threw out his good leg. Cornelia pushed it down. "Not that one, the other one."

His eyes became slits but he complied, assisting it with his hands as he straightened out his injured leg. "Nell, what are you about here? This is what Dr. Quinlain harassed me into trying."

147

"Just do what I say." She ran her tongue over her dry lips. "Let go of it now."

"I can't." Carter tipped his head up but she diverted her gaze. "It will fall."

"You can." She pressed a hand against his shoulder. "Try harder."

Grunting, Carter released his hands from beneath his leg and then groaned as he held the trembling limb up. "Are you satisfied?"

Cornelia clasped her hands together. "No, hold it up longer. You can do it."

In the light, beads of sweat made an irregular pattern across his wide brow, one dark curl dipping into the middle. "Easy for you to say."

Excitement welled up. She envisioned babies being raised and lowered on that knee. Bounced as he played the part of the pony and the children the riders. "I want you to do that for a count of ten, then keep building up. Do it a few times every hour."

"Hourly?" Carter chuckled as he dropped his leg down. "So shall I get up during the sermon on Sunday and announce, 'Excuse me, Reverend Henry but I am under strict orders to comply with maneuvers involving my leg'?"

"Well, that's not such a bad idea. Be discreet. Raise your leg up a little from the floor and hold it there. No one would notice."

Carter fell silent. Light flickering in his dark eyes made it difficult to discern his emotions. "Why are you encouraging me? Why would you spend time trying to cure me?"

Heat singed her cheeks. She loved him. "I care. You're my… friend. You always have been, since we were children."

He squeezed her hand but released it at the sound of hard heels clicking up the stairs, a candelabra held high. Across Mariah's unguarded face a host of emotions flew—shame, despair, anger, and an intense longing. For what?

One hand crushing the fabric of her skirt, Mariah paused. "The aggravating girl was skulking around near the livery stables." She sighed. "She was supposed to be minding the boys."

Carter gave her a slight push and Cornelia drew in her breath. She'd been so startled she hadn't thought to get up. "Don't worry, the boys have been bathed and put to bed."

"Good. Thank you."

As Cornelia got her feet beneath her, her mouth worked before she censored her words. "I could keep helping with them."

"Excellent idea." The tiny woman stepped forward, rose up on tiptoe and kissed her cheek. A whiff of French perfume combined with fruity sweetness.

As the woman walked away, Cornelia pressing a hand to her cheek, touching something sticky. *Jam. What in heavens?*

Mariah turned, light skittering over her features. "Carter, you must insist Cornelia stays here. Until her brother returns."

"I can't." Who would watch over the pups? "My clothes and things…"

"Mariah is right." She sensed the heat from Carter's body as he rose behind her. "'Twas bad enough before. With your brother gone, you cannot stay alone."

Bad enough? Had he been concerned for her? Still, she bristled at the idea of him telling her what to do. "I'll be fine." But what if Daniel had been watching them?

Footsteps continued down the hall. "Let me get one of my sister's sleeping gowns for you."

A warm hand squeezed her shoulder. "There—'tis all settled."

Unease stirred in her belly. "And where would I sleep?" Carter's room was on this floor, wasn't it? Stiffening, she stood still.

She heard his intake of breath and then felt the warmth as he exhaled near her neck. "In with the boys. That little alcove by the door."

So that was her place now. A servant's bed near the door. She stiffened. *I should never have let him touch me like that.* Another wave of dizziness overcame her and she leaned against Carter.

"For tonight. We can talk about things more tomorrow."

A tiny finger poked at Cornelia's cheek. Little Albert plunked down. "I wet." She promptly lifted him from the covers and took care of his needs, bustling through the boys' bedchamber to find what she required.

How did I get myself into this?

A rap on the door was followed by Carter's dark head visible in the low light within the room. "I'm going to the fields, Nell, to look at the fungus you mentioned."

Standing in her nightgown, she searched for something to cover herself with. Spying nothing, she pulled Albert in front of her and sank onto the boy's bed. "Thank you. Stay there. I'm not dressed." And how was she to manage that with the children all around? She'd have to send them down with Macy, when she arrived.

"I'm going to ask Elijah to take a message to the agrarian if it's as bad as you said."

Clutching Albert closer, she took a deep breath. "Yes, that would be best."

"I'll send Macy up." The door closed behind him and then reopened. "Might you speak with her?"

She knew exactly what he meant—about what Hayes said. "I will." Macy had been the closest thing to a friend she had. But she could be awfully ornery if someone called her to task. Especially if her beau were involved.

"Thank you."

When Macy still hadn't arrived after an hour, Cornelia played "the dressing game" with the boys. Each had to turn their backs to each other and put their clothes on and could not turn around until the last one had announced "done." And if anyone cheated then they got no dessert that day. All but Albert managed well. He ran to her and tugged at Anne's dress, one Mariah had brought to her.

"That's Mama's." He tilted his head to stare up at her.

"Yes, it is, Al-boy." She secured the last button on her overblouse and lifted him into her arms. He put his hands on the curls that were free around her face.

"Want Mama."

Tears pricked her eyes as the child's overflowed.

Charles joined them, still buttoning his pants. "I miss my father."

"Me, too. Both of them." Lloyd stopped struggling with one of his shoes and stomped his foot on the floor. "It's not fair."

Cornelia placed a hand on Albert's head and pressed him to her shoulder. "I know."

Eddie knocked on the open door. "Mr. Davis told us that God would never leave us. He'd never forsake us."

Cornelia waved him in and Eddie complied, his eyes darting around the room. "Is Andy here?"

"No."

"He's not in your cabin, either."

"Andy had to stay at the hospital."

"But he'll be all right, won't he?"

A dull ache started in her chest. "I don't know."

Chapter Eighteen

Light breeze from the James River tickled Carter's neck—what a blessed relief to do without a cravat and all its interminable knots. Carter paced before the two-story brick kitchen out-building. Inside, he twisted with decisions he must make, such as what he was going to do about Macy. His father and Lee should have freed her upon their deaths, yet they'd left it to the next generation.

Time to keep promises. Still, he required help with the children. And he had a right to know what was distracting the house servant from her duties. As for himself, thoughts of Nell prevented all but a few hours' sleep, leaving him ragged as the field workers' clothing.

Macy emerged from the laundry building that faced the kitchen across the forecourt, her arms stacked high with linens. No, those appeared to be articles of clothing.

"What have you there, Macy?"

She stopped and a bundle fell from the top.

When she said nothing, he grabbed up the garments. Workers' clothes. "What are you doing?"

"I been to the laundry."

"Why?" They had other workers there.

"So I can get the mending done."

"Mending?" He examined the shirts. "These are not from the house servants."

"No sir." Even white teeth chewed her full lower lip as she stared at the floor.

He held up the top one. Small holes pock-marked the garment. Grabbing another, he found the same, and the final one had cloth so thin that it would shred if he was to pull on it.

"Aren't these to be made into rags?"

"No sir, I been stitching them up."

Feet clattered up the brick stairs. Carter turned to see Nell and the boys enter the hallway. He sighed. "You're needed at the house, Macy."

The servant's chin tipped up. "I'm trying to keep clothes on your peoples' backs."

Shame washed over him.

Nell ushered the boys into the large kitchen where Mama Jo was busy baking bread for supper. "You go watch, boys, and don't touch anything."

Carter was sure he'd heard Macy snort but her countenance revealed nothing.

Nell pulled a pair of pants free from Macy's arms. "You've been putting the buttons on again?"

"I have."

"Good." Fair eyebrows rose. "No new clothes were given at Christmas, were there?"

Were things as bad as that? He'd stayed in Williamsburg for all but Christmas Eve and Christmas day.

Macy's green eyes could have bored right through his. "Nothing."

Carter took a step rearward, almost stumbling. "No shoes, no stockings, no clothing of any kind?"

"No, sir."

Nell frowned. "Would it help if I reviewed Lee's books from right before Christmas, again, and see what happened?"

The number of household servants had almost doubled. Why?

"Pa said an unexpected expense happened near Christmas."

He'd reviewed every column and still hadn't made sense of some notations. "Yes. You might be able to help with a section. I'll set it atop the desk. You can review it when you have an opportunity."

153

Macy smiled at Nell. The two had always gotten along well, even when the girl was young, sent with Anne as a wedding "gift" from the Wenham's plantation. His lip curled at the notion of giving one's daughter another human being. Yet it was done often enough.

"Missy, I bring the boys their breakfast oncst I put this stitchin' away." The girl's smile vanished when she nodded curtly at him. "Mister Williams?"

"You may take your leave. Thank you."

A line formed between her eyebrows and then softened. Anne had often acted agitated in Macy's presence. Lee had ignored Macy. Carter's brother kept his eyes fixed upon his wife, as though to gaze upon any other woman was too much temptation.

Cool air entered from the hallway as Cornelia opened her eyes, roused from a dream of Carter holding her close, kissing her tenderly. Blast him, he was invading her sleep now. A house slave exited, the door softly clicking closed. Overhead, dim light illuminated the frescoed ceiling in the nurse's alcove.

Cornelia lay the outfit from the pastor's wife on the quilt-covered bed. Serviceable and feminine, more importantly the garment wasn't Anne's. She touched the shiny skirt's fabric, gathered at the sides with a bow. The chestnut color would set off her hair. Pulling a few curls loose from the mass she'd pinned atop her head, she patted her upswept coils in satisfaction. She'd be almost as tall as Carter with this style and a pair of pumps.

Carter had asked her to come join him in the North Flanker's dining room for an early breakfast. Cornelia secured the last hairpin. A tap on the door announced Macy.

"Don't you be lookin' pretty?" Macy smiled appreciatively. "I'll get the boys up. They be dressed and ate their breakfast before you get back."

She squeezed Macy's hand then Cornelia swished into the hall and down the staircase, the stiff material scratching against the wall. Pausing, she glanced up. The staircase appeared suspended in the air. Like her heart had been ever since Carter had held her close in this very house.

After exiting the wide paneled entry hall, she closed the door behind her. Stepping into the warm morning air, she caught sight of a black and gold phaeton continuing up the long drive through the mist. She headed out to the carriageway.

When the driver pulled the horses to a stop before her, a youngish man, perhaps late twenties or early thirties in age, attired in a gentleman's day suit, emerged. He waved away help from the footman. As she stepped toward the drive, she could make out the dimples on the man's clean-shaven face. His handsome visage was familiar. She responded to his warm toothy smile by returning a tentative one of her own. "Hayes?"

Carter looked out the Flanker's dining room windows, awaiting Nell. The coachman, atop an expensive carriage top, pulled his team to a stop. A well-dressed gentleman disembarked, tall beaver hat in hand, and stepped onto the walkway adjacent the drive. Nearby, a young lady dressed in serviceable daywear clutched her bare hands. Sun pierced the overhead clouds, illuminating golden tresses beneath her bonnet. Nell—dressed in a garment he didn't recognize.

The man, a dandy by his fine appearance, opened his arms and Nell rushed to him. Carter's gut took an emotional hit as the tall man lifted and twirled her around in the air as though she were but a sack of goose down. Taking one step closer to the window, the glass fogged from his breath. Nell stroked the man's jawline and then kissed his cheek. Squinting, he examined the phaeton for markings as the horses pulled around the drive. "D" for Davis.

So it was done. The two were meant for each other as this happy reunion announced. He shoved his hand through his hair as though that would bring to mind some solution. But Hayes was Nell's answer, not he.

"Well, well." Mariah's dry voice snapped him to attention. "Looks like my Mr. Davis has someone else's arms wrapped around him."

Concern coiled around Carter's heart. "*Your* Mr. Davis?"

She tilted her head at him. "Good morning, Carter. Sleep well?"

No, truth be told. Visions of a golden-haired angel enticing him to kiss her had woken him several times in the night. "Can't say that I did."

"Have anything to do with your Miss Gill?"

"She's not my Miss Gill." Was she? He inhaled deeply, catching a whiff of his shaving soap.

Mariah linked her arm through his. The clean-shaven Hayes and serviceably attired Nell strolled, arm-in-arm, toward the building. She gave a shuddering breath "All I saw was his money. I'd say I was overlooking hidden treasure."

"I can see that women might find him appealing in his current state."

Mariah gave a curt laugh. "Honey, I found him attractive before—the president's friend and the richest bachelor in Virginia. Now…" She pointed to Nell. "I think I can take care of that situation for you."

"What do you mean?"

Outside Hayes leaned to whisper something in Nell's ear that caused her to tilt her head back and laugh. She was beyond beautiful when she was happy like that. Could he ever fill her with joy? He had nothing to offer. His name and connection were all Sally would have gotten. Now Miss Danner had both the possibility of a prestigious name, money, and position if the man she now pursued succumbed to her charms. Carter didn't care. His fisted hands spoke a different response toward Hayes. The horse breeder wasn't going to take Nell from Dogwood Plantation. Away from him.

"I had Mr. Davis wrapped around my little finger before he left here." Mariah's narrowed eyes followed the couple's every movement as they approached the door. "I have charms that girl has never even imagined, much less tried on a man."

Carter sensed his eyebrows rising to his hairline. "Goodness, Mariah, I had no idea you were so… talented."

She laughed. "Indeed. Never underestimate a Carolina belle."

Carter rubbed his jaw and deliberately unclenched his teeth. The door closed and Nell stood clutching their guest's arm. When Hayes's eyes alighted upon Mariah, he carefully removed Nell's hand, brought it to his mouth for a quick kiss and released it. Was Hayes a snake dressed up in a new silk suit? Had he just shed his old skin?

"Thanky kindly, Miss Mariah, for sendin' me that note." Hayes crossed the room, leaving Nell lingering at the door. "I'll do whatever I can to help Andy."

Carter took a step toward Nell but then she tucked her chin in resolutely and came to him. Her gown swished as she walked, and the marble tile echoed every footstep.

Hayes turned and chortled. "Ya sound like a chicken scratchin' when you walk in that getup."

Mariah squeezed his arm. "Now, Hayes, that was unkind. Apologize."

"It's the truth."

The dark-haired beauty peered up at Hayes from beneath half-lowered eyelids. "Say you're sorry."

"Sorry, Nelly," Hayes called over his shoulder. Nell frowned at him.

Gesturing to a chair at the wrought-iron table, Carter pulled it free. He helped Nell settle her skirts within the chair's confines, its arms curlicued, trapping her clothing.

"Can you believe the difference?" Nell's voice held awe and admiration. "He's so handsome." Her whispered voice offended his ears.

Mariah cocked her head at Hayes. "I think I liked you better before."

Hayes's shoulders flexed. "Ya did?"

"You appeared more mature. Like the man you are. A man of property and means."

"Is that what ya think of me?" He cackled. "Why, I'll have to have ya come up and visit at my home. And I promise ya, little sugar, I'll grow my beard back."

Straining away from Carter, Nell shook her finger at the two. "No, don't you dare. You've never looked so..." She raised her fingers to her mouth. Her gaze turned to Carter, warm eyes darting over his features, her pink lips parted. She swallowed then stared down at the tea cup in front of her.

Hayes's smile faded. He cleared his throat as Mariah glared at Carter, silently willing him to do something.

Carter reached for the peach compote. "Miss Wenham and I plan to visit Andrew today. Come join us for breakfast before we go." It would be best if he were to visit with Mariah. Spending time with Nell bordered on dangerous.

"That so?" Hayes rubbed his big hands together. "I had hoped to visit, but I'll just spend time with Nelly. We have a lot to catch up on. Plans we need to make."

Nell stared at Hayes Davis, as though seeing the man for the first time. Was she a lovesick female? Satisfaction warmed Carter though, realizing she had just given him a similar appraisal. Was she trying to choose between himself and Hayes? Did she know she had a choice?

Mariah fluttered her fan. "Perhaps Cornelia and Carter could go and we could catch up on our last conversation, Mr. Davis. About whether American foxhunts shall proceed come fall or whether we shall all be fleeing the British."

"We should pray about what each of us might do for our country— how we might make a sacrifice or contribute in some way." Hayes's voice sounded different to Carter's ears. Then the man grinned. "But I'm expectin' our forces to whoop some English—"

"Ladies present!" Mariah's tinkling laugh was followed by an expression of mock horror.

Carter didn't trust himself alone with Nell. "You desired a respite from my nephews, Mariah. Wasn't that why you wished to go?"

Next to him, Nell gagged on her mouthful of tea. He patted her on the back.

Hayes made an effort to rise but Mariah patted his arm. "Carter will help her."

"Carter, stop it. You're going to break my ribs." Cornelia fixed him with what she hoped was an icy stare. She wouldn't have his warm hands on her. Not anywhere. She shivered.

"I'm sorry. Are you all right?" He sounded hurt. And he kept knocking his knee into her skirts, bumping her leg.

She reached for the tray of pastries just as Hayes did. Heat seared her cheeks as he caught her eye. His face was almost as handsome as Carter's.

"Ladies first." He held up the assortment for her to choose, giving her an opportunity to look away. *Lord have mercy, that cousin of mine cleans up good.* If she did have to accept a proposal of marriage from him, she'd insist he keep that graying beard shaved off. She exhaled, looking up into his comforting gaze.

He was still her same old cousin Hayes, her only kin. She wasn't going to sacrifice that relationship for anything. Across the table, Mariah's eyes glittered. She smiled only in the bottom half of her face, the upper half full of suspicion and resentment—*like I'd wager mine appears when I'd been a selfish child and took the last biscuit instead of saving it for my brother.*

"You like Hayes." That popped out of Cornelia's mouth so fast she didn't have time to stop it. Pink spots formed under Mariah's wide eyes.

The woman reached for her fan and flicked it open so fast it practically blurred. "Of course I do. Doesn't everybody just love Mr. Davis? He's so kind."

Her cousin stared at the boys' aunt even as he held the creamware dish out for her. She plucked one tiny muffin from the platter.

Mariah pointed to the windows. "Oh, such lovely hummingbirds."

They turned, but try as she might, Cornelia couldn't make any out. But they were so small and fast, she could have missed them. When she swiveled around, Miss Wenham's fan was atop the table and her bodice dipped lower than it had been. Cornelia blinked. She must have imagined that Mariah had deliberately pulled her neckline down.

Hayes laid a hand atop Mariah's tiny one, rings circling all her dainty fingers except her thumb. He blinked. "Didn't see nothin', sweat pea."

"Why, you probably weren't looking hard enough."

Cornelia nibbled on her biscuit. Carter's elbow jostled her sleeve. Heat at being so close to him moved up her chest. "Move over, will you? I need a little room here."

She set the biscuit on the china plate. As she bent to retrieve her reticule, she saw Carter hadn't moved an inch. She sat up and released the latch on her sandalwood fan.

As she gazed over the top, she caught Mariah Wenham winking at Carter, as her mouth twitched in a most unusual manner. *She wants to laugh at me!*

"Might you share your private jest, Miss Wenham?" Cornelia readied for a fight.

"You two remind me of Carter's parents."

Cornelia opened her mouth, but Carter squeezed her free hand. "I agree, Mariah. Father would scoot up next to Mother and the next thing you knew she'd be trying to get him to leave her be." He laughed.

159

So he had deliberately pressed against her then. Heat seared her cheeks.

Shrugging, Mariah peered up at Hayes. "Then Mr. Roger would just sit there, planted like an oak."

Carter's knee squashed against her again. She angled her hips slightly away.

Hayes draped his arm over Mariah's shoulder. "Darlin' I've been alone too long. Wouldn't let my wife *just be*, either. I'd be thankin' God every day that I had her. And makin' her darn sure she felt appreciated." Sorrow flickered across his face.

Both she and Mariah blinked rapidly at Hayes. Cornelia was sure her face was as flushed as Miss Wenham's. It was as though Hayes had read her mind. Yes, she wanted to be treasured. But when she turned to Carter, his cold eyes announced his opinion. She swallowed her disappointment as he scraped his chair away from her.

What a silly goose she was. Imagining Carter still had feelings for her. He'd merely been trying to comfort her the other night.

How much longer would Nell stay here? With the enraptured look she gave Hayes, she'd return with the man to his horse farm within the week—unless Anne's sister intervened, which Mariah appeared determined to do.

Mariah poured Hayes more tea, then plunked two lumps of sugar in it, not even bothering to use the silver tongs.

"How'd ya know that's how I like it?" Hayes grinned like an idiot at Mariah.

She patted his hand. "Because I observe everything about you, Hayes."

Oh, she had him now. Carter spied the line of red forming around the man's starched collar. "Do ya now?"

"Indeed I do."

By all appearances, Nell appeared to have partaken Doc's special tonic for the gut and was about to spew it forth. Jealous?

The boys' aunt gazed in rapt attention at their visitor. Little minx—she'd dropped her sleeves off her shoulders and now fussed with them.

160

Hayes reached out to help Mariah. Carter rolled his eyes. He forced back a chuckle at Mariah's antics. She must want to pull this fish in badly.

"Hayes, are you too tired to drive any more today?"

"Not for you, darlin'."

Any more false sweetness from Mariah, and Carter might be ill, but Hayes appeared to fall for it. Mariah kept her gaze affixed on the big man. "Why don't we go check on Andrew today?"

Beside him, Nell became rigid. He was about to object—what might Dr. Quinlain say about their payment arrangement? If Hayes discovered that Carter agreed to one of Nell's pups as Quinlain's payment, he might raise Cain.

Hayes slapped his hand on the table. "Sure enough, I'll do it. Want to see if Andy's ready to live on a horse farm."

Irritation galloped over Mariah's face. She cut her eyes between Nell and Hayes. "You can tell me all about your home on our way to and from Richmond."

Nell sat up straight. "Just one moment—"

Carter interrupted her. "Hopefully, they'll bring Andy home. If not, we'll go up to either visit him or bring him home ourselves."

Standing outside, Cornelia bit her lower lip as she and Carter waved goodbye to her cousin and the children's aunt as the carriage rolled away. Cornelia had to face those boys. Would rather take on a loose bull. But she gave her word. How could they be so well behaved at her cabin for lessons, yet so unruly at their own home? But she couldn't help loving them, they were so sweet, each in his own way.

A chill breeze came from the direction in which the couple had departed—east to the main road before turning north to Richmond. A flash of sapphire caught her eye as a bluebird flew overhead. Was it looking for its mate? The nests were beginning to fill throughout the property.

Carter inclined his head toward the departing conveyance. "Those two seem so unmatched a pair, yet…"

Snorting, Cornelia swatted at his shoulder. "He's a man of faith and her only belief is in Mariah."

Carter blinked rapidly. "God save her."

161

"He can if she'll allow Him." Frivolity fled. "Hayes and I have that in common—our deep belief in God and our salvation through Jesus."

When his jaw muscled clenched, Cornelia pinched him. "Don't worry. Hayes would never yoke up with an unbeliever."

Carter kicked at the dirt with the toe of his polished boot. Cornelia tried to poke him but he grabbed her hand.

She pulled away. "You're gonna get those dirty. Stop."

"Let's be clear—you and Hayes are both strong Christians."

"You know I am. Hayes doesn't believe in foisting religion on anyone. Says it's all a relationship with the Lord—one must come freely without coercion."

"Can't say I know anyone not influenced by someone."

Her hackles went up. "I didn't say we aren't to share our faith in hopes of bringing others to salvation. I plan to encourage my own children to follow the Lord."

His cheeks reddened. Carter's gaze from beneath hooded eyes sent a shiver through her. "And with whom will you be having those children—Hayes Davis?"

His dark eyes pierced hers, and she looked away. This topic must be brought into line. She swallowed and tried again, ignoring his question.

Carter positioned himself in front of her and took her hands in his, his features tight, set. "Nell, I believe you are being naïve. About Hayes. And about Mariah."

"I…" She tried to pull her hands away. He held them tight and took one more step closer.

"Listen. Mariah could come onboard a naval vessel and control every man there within the hour." He laughed. "She'd have them taking down rigging that should be sent up and hauling up a keel that should be lowered. The sailors would all say *'thank you, ma'am, for your advice.'*"

Cornelia stopped tugging. "Hayes has a strong character. He'd never succumb to her feminine wiles."

"And you trust him?"

"Of course. What kind of ridiculous question is that? He wouldn't compromise Mariah." While she'd never considered Carter a threat to her virtue, he wasn't the same young man she once knew. More worldly. Who knew what all he had done while in the Navy.

162

"Don't you care that he chose to go with her and not stay with you?"

"I told him I had the boys to watch today." She tried to pull her hands free but he slacked his hip and grinned at her, holding fast.

She sighed. "Remember? I gave my word to you. Something Hayes and I have in common. We keep our word no matter what."

"Like the chopped wood, I suppose?" He cocked one eyebrow at her.

She sucked in a breath. He had her there. "Hayes could fall in love with her, I didn't say that. And he's a man. He's got eyes in his head." And those eyes had been firmly locked on Mariah. "But he'd never marry her."

Carter stepped in so close that she could smell his spicy shaving soap. "Because why? Mariah attends church regularly. Has all her life."

Was he the one who was naïve? She fought the urge to step away from him. "And that means what? That she can warm a bench?" She tilted her head, exasperated. "Please, Hayes is smarter than that. He can discern falseness."

Carter's dark face, so close that she could see flecks of amber in his dark eyes, grew ruddy. What about him? Had he only held the pew spot?

She took one step away, his hand restraining her. "You used to talk with me about God. Why don't you anymore?"

He tipped his head down. "Perhaps I'm like Mariah. My parents brought me to and from church, read the daily office, and repeated rote prayers every night. Maybe she and I ignored their instruction."

She squeezed his fingers. "Did you ever ask Jesus to be Lord of your life, Carter? Remember, like we discussed right over there?" She pointed to the laundry building, where several slaves hauled dirty linens from the house, their dark faces shiny from the heat.

When he didn't respond, Cornelia felt a pang in her heart. Was he a lost soul? *Dear Lord, don't let Carter tune you out. Let him hear from You.*

She released his hand and stepped back. "Hayes helped me to reach your brother."

Dark eyes widened. "Lee?"

She swallowed and nodded. "I couldn't bear Lee dying without knowing the Lord. So I spoke with him about receiving the Lord as Savior." Blast it, those tears wanted to fall.

Carter's face remained stony. "Sounds like you and Hayes have much in common."

"Of course we do. He's my closest kin. Other than Andy, of course."

Chapter Nineteen

"Closest kin? Hayes Davis?" In relief, the excess cargo weighing down his soul heaved itself overboard.

"He's our cousin."

A strong wave splashed his thoughts. While prohibited by canon law, Hayes was not Episcopalian. Did the Baptists have such rules? Flotsam and jetsam washed aboard, making a mess of his thinking. Her tone made him rethink every notion he'd had about Hayes' and Nell's relationship.

Lloyd rushed across the crushed oyster shell walkway. "Miss Cornelia, Albert poured the syrup on the table, and Nemi says she ain't cleaning it up."

"Isn't." Nell and Carter's voices merged.

"No, she said 'ain't.' I heard her." Lloyd took a deep breath. "And she says she ain't gonna watch us bad boys no more and you better get in there." His nephew imitated the high-strung woman's voice.

Carter would bring this all under control. "Let's go up and investigate. I'm sure it's not so dreadful."

Giving a snort, Nell grabbed Lloyd's hand. "I'm sure you're wrong."

"It's everywhere, Miss Cornelia. 'Tween the cracks in Mama's table. 'Twas all soaked through."

The youngster craned his neck upward. "Nemi tried to sop up the mess and it ruined Mama's tablecloth."

Anne had prized her Irish linens, but when Carter inquired about the everyday tablecloths none could be found. "When did all this hap—"

"Since Auntie got here. She don't mind what we do."

"Doesn't mind." Nell shook her head. "That's God's truth. Mariah doesn't seem to give a fig what these children do."

Nell narrowed her eyes. "Why isn't Nemi or Macy watching—"

"Nemi says she has cleaning to do and Macy says *I do for your Auntie Mariah and she do for me.*"

What was that supposed to mean?

Exasperated, Carter looked the boy over. "So Mariah is supposed to be watching you boys for Macy but she isn't?"

The boy's little face scrunched in irritation.

"And don't interrupt me again—not if you know what's good for you."

They continued up the walkway, Lloyd fuming. So be it. Carter had been nice. And understanding. Now these little boys would need to be brought under control. His command. Order would be restored in this home post-haste.

Cornelia exhaled loudly as she scanned the bed chamber's detritus. *Disaster.* "Three nights since the boys' room was cleaned."

Her brother would never have made such a mess. Andy was such a help. He probably had the hospital ward organized. He'd have told them where to place everything for maximum efficiency. She smiled. *Not here, though.*

Leaning against the doorjamb, Carter's cheek muscled jumped. "Your father would never have allowed this behavior and neither shall I. Henceforth, I shall conduct inspections. Morning and evening there shall be reports from your Aunt Mariah."

Charles waved his hand.

Carter sputtered, "What is it?"

"Auntie Mariah said we'll go live with Uncle Hayes."

Crossing to where the boy sat perched on his bed, Cornelia placed a finger under his chin. "Charles, you shouldn't tell falsehoods." That was one behavior she couldn't abide.

After he joined them, Carter pressed his fingers against her shoulders. Penetrating warmth spread across her back. He dropped his hand. Grabbing the wooden post at the end of the bed, he steadied himself and knelt by the boy.

"Is it true, Uncle Carter?"

"What, Charles?"

"You don't want us."

Color washed over Carter's strong features. "No, that's not true."

She cleared her throat. "And boys, Mr. Davis is not your uncle."

"He's Andy's uncle. If you marry Uncle Carter then he'll be our uncle." The child stuck a finger in his mouth.

Cornelia stumbled for words, sure that her own face mirrored Carter's perplexed expression. "Mr. Davis isn't Andy's uncle."

"Miss Gill and Mr. Hayes are…" A frown crowded between Carter's eyebrows.

A small form wriggled beneath a counterpane cover. *Albert.*

She tromped to the toddler's bed and heaved the blankets free. Pink cheeks bulged with something. Bending, she caught the sweet smell of candy and her breath caught. He could choke. *Die.*

"Albert—sit up." When he hesitated, she carefully pulled his slight weight upward, her heart beating hard despite the minor exertion.

The heavy thump of Carter's good leg echoed in the room. "Spit that in my hand!"

Wide eyes gauged Carter's intent.

Dear Lord don't let him swallow that entire wad of candy. Albert's cheeks stopped moving but his throat muscles wobbled.

Dampness in her eyes caused Cornelia to blink. "Please Al-boy, spit it out. You can have some later. When you are sitting up downstairs. After a meal. But never, ever again in your bed. I won't have you dying on me." Her own throat constricted and she stifled a sob. Another link broke free on her restraint.

The boy spit a slimy glob of pastilles, licorices, and cherries into his uncle's hand. Carter's aristocratic nose furrowed. "Thank you, Al-boy."

He fished a handkerchief from his waistcoat to house the contents. When Cornelia caught his eye, they both exhaled in relief.

167

Charles plopped onto Albert's bed. "Aunt Mariah says when you say things at the same time, it means you're gonna get married."

"Going to get married," they corrected in unison.

Oh no, that came out wrong. He cringed. Carter didn't need his nephews passing such information to Hayes. "Tis South Carolinian nonsense so don't repeat it."

Nell dropped to her knees to look beneath Albert's bed.

"Aha." She retrieved a stack of wooden trays and two bowls of moldering cornmeal muffins.

Golden curls bobbed as Nell held the dishes from her body. She carried them to the window and tossed the container's contents away from the house.

"Wondered what that smell was." Charles's dry voice triggered an attack of giggles from his brothers.

"Thought it was your feet." Lloyd plopped on his bed.

Charles tossed a pillow at his younger brother. "Smelled like yours."

"Enough." Carter shifted his weight, his leg throbbing. "I'm issuing a cease and desist order."

"What's that mean?" Charles relieved Nell of the kitchen articles.

"Something about a sister?" Lloyd giggled.

Carter tweaked the boy's nose. "No. Cease and desist means to stop something."

Charles headed for the door. "Stop laughing?"

"No, stop spreading rumors and repeating nonsense about the adult members of this household. Is that clear?" He enunciated the last three words carefully.

"But it's the truth. Aunt Mariah says she's marrying Mr. Hayes." Lloyd glared at him, his little fists balled like Carter's did when he was angry.

Mariah *had* implied something similar to him. "Was that precisely what she said?"

"What's presizing?"

Nell brushed Lloyd's hair from his face. "You need your hair trimmed. And precisely means exactly. Did your aunt say those same words?"

"Yes," the three boys agreed.

Carter averted his gaze from Nell, not wishing to witness the hurt and anger he expected to see there. How could the man be so bold as to propose marriage to two women simultaneously? But had he? He was her cousin. Perhaps not. He allowed his glance to wander to Nell's pretty face, her features gathered in worry. Perhaps so.

"Proper ladies, such as Mariah, don't do the asking, do they Miss Gill?" Carter made a show of winking at Nell.

Eyes wide, Nell's well-formed lips pursed into a sour expression. Gads, she appeared as though she'd sucked on a lime to hold off scurvy.

Lloyd took her hand. "I'm a gent-man, and if Miss Cornelia was my lady, I'd ask her."

With a laugh, she planted a kiss atop his head.

"Correct." Carter needed to get those boys off this topic and have them tidy their room. "A gentleman does the asking." Like he should be doing had he any income with which to support her.

"Auntie Mariah says Mr. Hayes isn't a gentleman." Charles smirked up at him. "But he has a bigger spread than Dogwood."

Lloyd spread his arms wide. "Like a lord's."

"Horsies." Albert pointed to a nearby painting of Lee mounted atop a chestnut stallion.

"Mr. Hayes will take care of us." Lloyd glanced from one brother to the other.

I have not. I have failed them.

"He said Auntie's the most purtiest woman he ever laid eyes on." All three nodded, even the little one, his fair eyebrows raised high.

"I'll have a talk with your aunt when she and Mr. Davis return. We can straighten this all out. But until then you will not repeat this to anyone. Do you understand?"

"Shhhh." Albert raised a tiny finger to his mouth.

"That's right. Shush, don't tell a soul."

And his own soul. He needed to do something about that. "We're going to get this room cleaned up ship-shape and then work on Edward's."

169

Nell crossed her arms. "His is fine."

"How do you know?"

"I checked in on him. And his is always neat—unless Charles gets in there to play with Eddie's collection of soldiers."

"He's gonna give them to me soon." Charles' crossed arms brooked no argument.

Carter's head squeezed as if crushed between two giant masts. "Let's work together."

Nell saluted him. "Are you our admiral?"

A pillow flew across the room and Carter caught it. "I've gotten a promotion if I am." He chuckled.

"Orders?" She beamed at him.

What are her options, if what they say is true? She could have married a wealthy man and lived a life of ease. Something Carter could never give her. Unless he returned to school and finished his studies and began his living in law and then politics. Sweat trickled under his collar, and he ran a finger beneath his neckcloth.

Should he seek to rejoin the Navy, with this war not yet ended?

The rest of the day, they'd all walked the dogs, retrieved Nell's dulcimer so she could play for him and the boys, and caught up on the lost years. He'd laughed more than he had in all the years since their parting.

Macy finally caught up with them by the stables, where the boys took turns riding the ponies. "I been looking all over for you."

Carter cast her a sideways glance. "Were you now?"

"Yessir." She averted her gaze. "Mama Jo say bring them up for dinner."

He nodded his assent and Macy rounded up the boys and headed off.

"Are you hungry?"

Nell shook her head.

The sun dipped lower in the sky, and Hayes and Mariah hadn't yet returned. "Let's go to the office. It possesses the best view of arrivals."

Once inside, they peered out the office window. Soon, from where he sat, Carter spied the carriage circling the drive.

Nell jumped up and down like an excited child. "They're back."

"Indeed. And there's no man for the door, so let's go and let them in." Carter rose and Nell followed him.

170

"I pray she has good news." Nell's breathless voice held fear.

He longed to kiss her worries away but trod onward and unlocked the door. Thin light from the setting sun cast Mariah's face in a rosy glow. Not only that, but her eyes were bright.

"Thank you." She lifted her skirts and entered.

Nell appeared to be holding her breath.

"Andrew sends his love and Dr. Quinlain says he improves every day."

"Thank God." Tears flowed down Nell's face.

To his surprise, Mariah enfolded the taller woman in her arms and patted Nell's back. "There, there. All will be well."

Carter fervently hoped so. He'd promised his men such things and had been wrong.

Chapter Twenty

Cornelia slipped out early to work with the dogs and puppies. The three boys were asleep as she put the pups through their paces.

"Follow Lafe, pups."

Tonnie kept nuzzling her leg, between commands. "Andy is fine, Tonnie." She needed her brother to be well. Unfortunately, the demands of the plantation and the boys' care kept her from visiting.

The pack made progress daily. Pleased, she returned across the fields to the Great House. Upon reentering, she spotted a cream-colored envelope unopened on the hall tray. Spidery handwriting addressed the missive to Carter. Cornelia turned it. Sealed. With no one else present in the receiving room, she raised it to her nose and sniffed. Carnation. She sneezed, and released the letter as though it were contaminated.

The professor's daughter must have sent the perfumed letter. Was she tempting Carter to return to college? Cornelia could do naught about it. Except pray.

Eddie descended the marvelous floating stairs and joined her. "How are you today?"

"I'm well, thank you."

"Macy says she'll watch the boys and you can do your office work."

"Lovely, then you can come see if you can help me with a mystery I can't solve. Let's go to. . ." She still thought of the space as Roger Williams' domain or Lee's.

"To where Carter does his work or to your father's office, Miss Cornelia?"

Obviously Eddie was struggling with the same distinctions. "Carter's office."

The boy followed her and soon they were bent over the desk, examining the odd ledgers.

She pointed to the area where she had not been able to discern what the abbreviations meant. "Do those initials mean anything to you?"

"You mean here?" He touched his finger on the column of large disbursements.

"Yes."

Withdrawing his hand, Eddie examined the numbers. He pointed further down the page of figures. "There—see that?"

She focused on the letters—CNW CWM.

"I know what that means. It's Carter Nelson Williams." The boy nodded. "Yes. That's it."

"That's a lot of money to be diverted from the plantation to your uncle." Excessive. Enough for two or three people. Besides which, Carter had his own money from his years in the Navy and from funds his father allotted him. Didn't he? And if he didn't, Lee had his own family to care for and a plantation to run. The amount could have paid for clothing the field workers desperately needed. She would go to Richmond herself and see if she couldn't at least procure the fabric for new clothes.

Eddie rubbed his chin. "That seems a great deal of money for college, though."

Did Lee perhaps have a mistress somewhere and used his brother's initials as a cover? No. He may not have been a religious man but she was sure he was faithful to his wife. And Cornelia certainly was not asking his son about that. She poured both Eddie and herself cider from the crystal decanter on the desk and then took a long drink.

A brisk rap on the study door preceded Carter, his face pained. Was his leg bothering him terribly? "I drank that foul tea you prescribed, Doctor Gill."

She almost choked on her mouthful of cider. Doctor? She wasn't especially fond of doctors. People died when doctors got ahold of them. Still, she prayed that Dr. Quinlain would help cure Andy. "Don't call me that."

"Why not? You've given me a routine to strengthen my gimp leg and recommended three foul tinctures I'm to partake of each day." He scratched his chin. "Perhaps Torturer Gill might be a better title."

Eddie laughed. "Uncle—I've just solved a riddle."

"Good. Do tell. You know I love puzzles."

"Not that kind. We think we know about the missing money."

Carter quirked a dark eyebrow and stepped forward. His face was dangerously handsome when he smiled that way, with one side of his mouth tipped upward.

"Father had a list of funds marked as CWM and Miss Gill presumed 'twas for a family member."

Drawing closer, he detected the total figure. "Yes, this now-undiverted amount is paying for animal feed and seed and supplies."

"I think that is your college fees, Uncle." Eddie's smile disappeared as lines around Carter's eyes furrowed. "And perhaps a stipend?"

When he said nothing, she was aghast that he would accept such a large amount from his brother, who evidently was struggling to pay his own expenses. "Was it really so much?"

Carter's mouth worked and his brow furrowed as though he were trying to cipher. "I'm not sure I wish my nephew to hear this."

Her heart dropped into her stomach. She'd suspected Carter might have gotten himself into trouble after his release from the Navy. Gambling or carousing or perhaps something involving a young lady. She'd heard he was "half out of his mind" after he'd almost lost his leg and his livelihood. The Navy was all he'd ever wanted. Had he a child to support? Would Lee have hushed such a scandal?

"Uncle, I don't need to leave." Eddie went to him and slapped him on the back. "I know what that stands for."

Carter glanced up at the boy. "You do?" His voice was hoarse.

"Father sent that to the College of William and Mary, and some to you, each week and monthly, for your expenses, did he not?"

His mouth working like a fish preparing to take the hook, Carter grimaced.

Macy tapped at the door. "Would ya'll like some apple butter? Last batch we got. Best get some before I offer it to your other nephews." The scent of warm apples, butter, and bread wafted across the room.

Cornelia's mouth watered. Other than the cider, she had nothing since early morning. The brass clock showed ten past two. "Thank you, Macy."

Her lovely friend set the small platter down on a tilt-table. Today she wore the blue cotton dress that Cornelia and she had made over into a work dress. This garment accommodated her curves far better than the rags she'd been wearing.

"None for me." Carter took the bread, spread with apple butter, set it atop a floral china plate and presented it. "Nell?"

Eddie grabbed two slices, sliding one heavily covered with the spicy fruit spread onto the other plate. When Macy frowned at him, he shrugged. "Uncle Carter didn't want his and there's no use wasting this good food."

What had the slaves been eating? She'd not asked. Guilt took a place at the desk with her. After Macy exited, she closed the door behind her.

Carter squeezed Eddie's elbow. "I'd like to talk with Miss Gill. Please check on your brothers."

Saluting, the boy smiled. "Yes, sir, anything you wish for me to convey to Aunt Mariah?"

"Dinner is at seven o'clock sharp. Dress is simple, family only, and Mariah needn't spend an hour applying cosmetics."

Cornelia raised her eyebrows. "You mustn't dictate how she's to present herself at dinner. It isn't right."

Eddie snickered as he departed.

Rising, Carter turned to look out the window. "What isn't right is a brother forced to become father to his own sibling."

"Lee?" She frowned. "You saw him that way?"

"When one brother squanders his money and then cannot pay his own way in life, yes, I would say my brother became a father. And myself the profligate son."

"I see." A stone settled in her gut as she removed the sheet from the figures. Lee paid for Carter to finish his education. Why? To keep Carter from coming home? Prevent him from getting near her again? She found

175

anger at the dead man rising in her gullet. "So that was how you were attending school? Not from your earnings as an officer?"

"That's correct, although I do have a small stipend now that I could use..."

Could use for what? To go back to the College of William and Mary? Back to Sally Danner, whose missive lay in the hall atop one of his family's heirloom silver trays? A knot tied itself around the bread in her stomach. "You plan to return to college?"

When he didn't reply, she brought her fist down atop the papers, the inkwell spewing a blob of ink that spread across the top page. She blotted it quickly then rose. "I've spent all day trying to track down where money has been siphoned from these boys' inheritance. From their father's earnings and you sit there and tell me you would return to college and not repay them?"

"It's not like that." Carter raised his hands. "Let me explain."

She wadded up the crumpled sheet and threw it at him. "Get out."

He opened his mouth then pulled his features into a scowl. "This is my home—my office."

"Fine." Cornelia pushed the chair back with her derriere and rose, unwrapping the encumbering skirts around her.

She strode from the room then stopped by the front door and grabbed her hat from its peg. Squashing it on her head, Cornelia stared at the letter, yearning to open it. Instead, she snatched up the copy of the *Virginia Gazette* that Carter had brought back with him from Williamsburg.

She opened the back door then descended the curved stairs to the yard. She didn't have to look behind her to know who had reopened the door and was standing atop the stairs. She wasn't Carter's friend. Not anymore. And she owed him nothing. Certainly not his newspaper, which she intended to read. She would savor every word.

Nell hadn't given him a chance to explain. If he finished his law studies, he could provide a stable income not dependent upon such things as weather, animals devouring the crops, blight, and pests. Should the plantation's finances prove untenable, if the boys lost their home, he could provide for them once their debts were settled. But no, Nell acted as though this decision were about him frivolously pursuing academic pursuits.

Closing the heavy door behind him, he turned, noticing the envelope. Sally's handwriting. Was it a wedding invitation? Shoving it into his pocket, he decided he'd read it later.

Cornelia slumped onto the bench outside the cabin, a modicum of peace returning. She ignored the tears that slipped down her cheeks and flicked open the *Virginia Gazette*. She scanned the columns. Rewards for the return of runaway slaves. Advertisements for "neat sewing" and carriages. She flipped back a page.

The Social page was peppered with the usual names. Charity Pendleton married to Mr. Hugh Martin? He was the man Sally had flirted with so outrageously at Puppy Day. Cornelia smoothed the paper and read. She had assumed that Sally and Hugh had begun courting. The details in the column revealed the groom was indeed the wealthy widower. Not much of a gentleman, if he had led Sally to believe he was free to pursue her. Cornelia set the paper down.

So that was why Miss Danner had written to Carter. The chase was on again, and Carter was the fox. Anger heated her chest and she opened her top button. She shouldn't have brought the paper from the house. *Forgive me Lord. But since I have it here, I might as well read it all.* Cornelia stretched out her legs and leaned back against the log cabin then resumed her reading.

Turning to the legal notices, Daniel Scott's name riveted her attention mid-page. *Daniel Scott, Esquire, seeks to know of any who would give claim to being the father of Coleman Nathan Williams, age eleven, and of anyone having documentation claiming said child as being heir to Dogwood Plantation.* The paper fell from her hands to the dirt.

Finally having located the bill from William and Mary, Carter compared the sums. The amount wasn't the same as indicated in the ledger. He'd gone over the figures for an hour. Outside the window, his nephews cavorted on the lawn with a passel of pups. This past week, Nell's care for the boys eased his mind considerably.

Steeling himself to step on his painful leg, he took a deep breath and returned to the desk for a final review. As he turned to sit, Sally's envelope dug into his ribs.

Lowering himself into his brother's chair, he slapped the letter down atop the desk and opened it. As he scanned the missive, irritation rose with every sentence. He closed his eyes and then re-read, focusing on the true meaning.

What a silly creature—every word, every exclamation point, was meant to distract from the actual message. She wanted to ascertain if it was true that he had no inheritance. But it was her last line that gave him pause. *Have you heard the rumor that there is another heir to Dogwood?*

How could that be? And if it were true, then who could that be? Mentally reviewing the past several months, Carter tried to recall the attorney's words. Would he and the boys be set out to sea with nothing? It couldn't be. But if it were true, then what?

Chapter Twenty-One

Cornelia lay prone on the cabin's wood floor, the mustiness causing her to sneeze. *Lord, what am I to do?* In her spirit, she felt that nudge to return. She didn't want to.

Wind gently blew outside the cabin, knocking small bits of debris against the window. She flinched. *What about this message in the paper? And am I supposed to go with Hayes? Is that what you are trying to tell me?*

Mariah was the one meant for him, wasn't she? Chills ran through her as she slid her hips back. What was she supposed to do about that woman?

God's Word said to love her.

Mariah loved only herself, and she only wanted Hayes for his money. "Love her? Really?" She got up from the floor and dusted her skirt off. Part of her wanted to run to Hayes, tell him that she would marry him, and could he take her far from Dogwood Plantation.

Cornelia sniffed back her tears, grabbed the paper up and hastened to the Great House, the fields and the workers a blur as she passed. She had to speak with Mariah Wenham before she dealt with this notice in the paper. Had to find out if the woman had any idea of the commotion she was causing her cousin—and herself. Surely God wasn't speaking to her heart that Mariah and Hayes belonged together.

On the lawn, Charles threw a large bone for Max, the strongest pup, while Lloyd and Albert chased the others. Mariah was nowhere in sight, although she'd promised to watch over them. Perhaps from her bedchamber window? Glancing up, a figure stood silhouetted behind the mullioned windows. Cornelia would find out. She strode past, waving to the boys.

Hayes and Mariah? Beautiful, willful, and charming with her cap set for someone who acted like a country bumpkin. Cornelia swept the notion aside and replace it with the clean-shaven and handsome, tall, strong, and intelligent Hayes. Most of all a man of a rock-solid faith. How could he consider a woman so shallow?

Was Mariah so wicked she considered only his money? And I'm supposed to love her, too? Cornelia shook her curls.

She scampered up the back stairs and went inside, stopping at the post table to slide the newspaper back beneath the silver tray, the envelope now absent. She stomped upstairs and continued past the boys' room before pausing at Mariah's paneled door.

She knocked lightly, straining to hear a reply.

"Who is it?"

Cornelia opened the door, stained in contrasting dark and light tones. A woman, dressed only in under-garments, perched on a vanity stool before the window, her nose close to an open book raised before her. Cornelia froze and cringed. Had she mistaken the room? Sparse brown hair hung lank down the woman's bony back. Thin as a rail, with no flesh on her, the chair must have been most uncomfortable for this stranger. Carter must have had an unexpected arrival. Cornelia eased backward, mortified.

Sun streaming through the windows illuminated a black wig atop a bronze stand, set on the bureau. Cornelia raised her hand to her mouth. The woman turned just enough to reveal Mariah's beautiful profile. When fully clothed, she possessed an enviable bosom, but this shadow had little.

Cornelia leaned against the door, shaking. The hair loss must be from starvation. No wonder her waist appeared so impossibly thin. And her womanly curves were all from padding. While Cornelia wanted to protest Mariah's deception of her cousin, the rational part of her, nay the spiritual, longed to kneel at her feet and ask her what had happened. What brought

180

her to this state? Cornelia had thought Mariah's corsets were laced too tightly.

The emaciated woman closed her book and rose. She turned, her hand grasping the wig.

"Mariah?"

Startled, the woman knocked the stand and wig to the floor. Birdlike hands flew to her mouth before touching her hair. "Please, don't…"

Pivoting, Cornelia turned the key in the lock. "Do you want to start at the beginning?" She faced her again. "And tell me what happened?"

"What do you mean?" Mariah sat upon the stool, clutching the wig.

"You haven't eaten regular in a long time, have you?"

Mariah's small hand went to the side of her face. "I look dreadful. I know." Tears ran in rivulets down her splotchy face.

Cornelia walked to the bedside and sat on its counterpane cover. "When the boys said you had no home in Charleston, they meant none at all, didn't they?"

Mariah's pale pink lips quivered as she fought back a sob. "Not for some time." She grabbed a handkerchief and blew her nose rather undaintily.

"That's why you were able to get here so quickly with your belongings? Where were you staying?"

"In a boarding house in Richmond."

"For how long?"

A sob escaped. "I was en route before my sister died. I knew she'd take me in. I wouldn't have to explain anything. But then, she died."

Sodden blankets of grief settled around Cornelia's shoulders. "Does Carter know?"

Mariah nodded. She choked back a laugh perched upon a sob. "I told him. I was afraid he'd find out from someone when he went to visit Andrew."

"I see."

"Friends in Charleston have some of my belongings. Things I couldn't bear to sell."

What did Cornelia, herself, have that she couldn't bear to part with? Quilts, some figurines passed down, and her land. Perhaps more than Mariah now possessed.

181

"And Lee sent me money every month for a while."

Might that be one of the ledger's notations? Cornelia's brain was too overburdened to do the figuring.

Mariah blinked back more tears. "I've been a fool—a woman getting up in years who threw away her inheritance on parties, gambling, and horses."

"I'm sorry."

Mariah shook her head, hair flopping about at her shoulders. "Not so much as I." She fingered the thin strands. "And the loss of what scripture calls a woman's crown of glory—this was one of God's cruelest punishments."

"A man who values only appearance will never be a suitable spouse." Cornelia covered her mouth. Had the Lord meant for her to share these words with the boys' aunt?

Wide eyes blinked at her. "I just read a similar passage in my Bible." She tapped the book on the table, a smile playing at her lips. "How remarkable."

The two sat in silence for a moment. Was God speaking through her to this woman? To someone she secretly had scorned but now pitied?

"I've asked God repeatedly to forgive me. Turned to a book I used to scoff at, in order to find answers. But I feel so…" A flood of tears overcame the woman and she bent her head over her lap, wrapping her arms under her knees.

Cornelia scooted closer. *What to say, Lord?* "You don't feel like you deserve forgiveness, do you?"

"No."

Cornelia patted her back, feeling every rib. "No one does, Mariah." Her voice was strained to her own ears.

She'd never forgiven Carter for running off to the Navy. For never writing her—not once. For coming back and never visiting her. Tears pricked her eyes. As though she'd never existed. For almost dying and causing her to mourn him, crying her eyes out for days, only to find he had survived—that was the most cruel of all. "That's why it is called grace."

The wall she'd built around her own heart gave way, crumbling into ashes. She needed to talk to Carter. She had to talk with him about the newspaper. And she had to discuss Mariah with Hayes.

Mariah sniffed. "You have no idea of my wickedness." She blew her nose into a handkerchief. "Of my deceit. Or you wouldn't speak of God's forgiveness."

If anyone could help, it was her cousin. "Tell Hayes. Tell him everything."

Frowning, Mariah leaned back. "I can't."

"You shall. I'll go with you if you want." Cornelia closed her eyes for a moment. Her cousin was a good man. "He studied to be a minister. I'm sure he'll hear you out."

Cornelia pushed the office door open as slowly as she could and viewed Carter seated at the desk. She took a deep breath. Grandmother's words echoed through her mind. *Never marry a gambling man, Cornelia, he'll squander all your dreams away.* But her aspirations had always included Carter. But perhaps Sally had snagged his attention, again. She exhaled slowly, determined to ask about Daniel Scott's post.

Carter clutched the desk's edge, but she motioned him to remain seated. "Did you read Daniel's newspaper post?"

Carter shook his head, as though trying to clear it. "I don't know what he's up to, but I can guarantee you there is no heir other than Eddie." His dark eyes pierced hers but his voice held a quaver.

"You're not telling me something."

Carter rolled his shoulders forward then rocked back and forth in the chair. "I cannot imagine my brother fathering a child out of wedlock. Lee never so much as glanced at another woman."

"Wasn't he supposed to marry Mariah?"

"He'd never made it official. And he stopped courting her when rumors of her..." Carter's lips compressed. "...behavior traveled from South Carolina all the way to Virginia."

"But isn't it possible?"

Carter snorted. "My brother wouldn't have."

She'd have asserted the same of Carter. Yet by his own admission he'd gambled and caroused, and who knew what else he had done in the Atlantic seaports. She examined the floral pattern on the rug.

"My brother, or Anne, sent money to Mariah, which is an ongoing substantial expense I finally resolved just now."

"She told me about her situation, Carter."

"I see." Squeals of laughter rang outside. He turned to face the window.

"What is Daniel up to, though?"

"Do you think somehow he means to steal Dogwood Plantation?"

"It's very strange, and we need to find out."

Someone cleared their throat. Fully-dressed, Mariah stepped in, head bowed. "Carter, I must get to Richmond tomorrow. I have urgent business. Could the driver take me?"

Cornelia felt the woman's shame in having to beg for accommodation.

How much had Mariah overheard of their conversation? Cornelia longed to see her brother returned home. "Carter, please ask Dr. Quinlain to send Andy home." She was dreadfully ill at ease sleeping in the cabin by herself.

"Ladies, I shall grant your request on one condition."

Cornelia cocked her head at him.

"Miss Gill, who *shall be* sleeping in the boys' room tonight, will watch over my nephews tomorrow."

Cornelia tapped her toes. "As long as you understand we'll be exercising the puppies most of today." She intended to kill two birds with one stone—wear out the boys so they wouldn't get into mischief and make sure that Andy's young pups got exercise and training.

A muscle twitched in Carter's jaw. "As long as you don't sleep in the cabin."

"All right— but tomorrow night, when you bring Andy home, that's where I'm going."

"We'll see."

Chapter Twenty-Two

Dawn broke in golden hues as Carter awaited the carriage master to pull the team to a halt at the forecourt's crest. The footman assisted Mariah and Carter into their largest coach. Thankfully, Mariah kept silent, looking out the window.

Now halfway to Richmond, Mariah's quietness, while initially welcome, unnerved Carter. She stared out the window and fidgeted with an ornate silver bracelet.

A bump in the road jostled them and Mariah's heavy satchel slid toward Carter.

"That was quite a jolt." He returned her reticule.

"Thank you. I pray we have no more like it."

"Indeed."

Now was the opportunity to ask a question. "When Daniel Scott attended the College of Charleston..."

Twin light-colored orbs narrowed and fixed on him. "Yes?"

"Your plantation was like a second home to him, was it not?"

"Our mothers were old friends." She clasped her hands in her lap. "He visited some weekends and on shorter holidays."

Not wishing to make her suspicious, he measured his words. "Did he strike you as a trouble-maker?"

Her dark eyebrows rose. "Heavens, no. Quite the opposite—always trying to please everyone."

Carter suppressed a snort. Daniel was the neighbor who'd never fit in, asking the strangest questions. "He is a bit of a mystery to me, I confess."

Mariah tugged at the drawstrings on her cloth pouch. "Daniel was always riled up about some cause."

Carter shook his head. "He came home cocky."

"He was always kind to me. I fear I did not treat him with equal charity." Mariah's brow furrowed.

Unease rippled through him.

"My father was extremely happy to entertain Daniel." A single tear rolled down her pale cheek.

He hadn't meant to upset her.   "I'm sorry I brought it up."

Giving a curt laugh, she wiped her cheek. "My father should have had sons. I believe Daniel reminded him of himself at that age."

"I fear what your father may have been like then, in his youth." He was wading into water over his head—he'd not push this any further. Instead, Carter would find out what his brother's attorney might know.

Mariah gave a curt laugh. "Perhaps best not to speak ill of the dead."

"Indeed, I apologize."

She waved her hand. "Don't concern yourself, I spoke too freely. But let's speak of other things. I intend to run several errands in Richmond so please don't fret if I'm gone for a while."

"I, too, have my own tasks today." With the lawyer Forrester's earlier allusion to a second will, who else could have spread the gossip Daniel was perpetrating? Carter swallowed the bile rising in his throat. *I will control my temper. If I assault the miscreant and am thrown in jail, it is my nephews who will suffer.*

Mariah turned toward him. "I want to talk with Dr. Quinlain, first, before I tend to my own errands, if you don't mind."

"I don't mean to be rude, Mariah, but I first wish to first check on Andy. Then I'll pursue my other missions."

She shrugged. "Meet you afterward at the coffee house around two. Is that sufficient time?" Without waiting for a response, she turned to rest her head against the far window.

Forrester's office was first on his agenda, after Andy then the land sales office. His gut churned. If a document naming another heir existed, what would it matter? At this rate, even if no claim was made against the estate, they'd have to sell off portions to support his nephews.

The coachman stopped at the hospital. Carter disembarked and assisted Mariah, who averted her eyes. Once inside the building, Mariah took an exceptionally long time in ascending the stairs. While she had her skirts to contend with, her ennui seemed born of some concern not of the physical realm. At the landing, her cheeks grew florid.

Whatever was troubling Mariah would have to be addressed later. He rapped on the door.

"Come in," Lawrence called out.

The physician's office smelled of a fresh treatment of lemon oil to the dark furniture as Carter led Mariah in to meet his old shipmate. Affixed to the wall, a hand-drawn map of Virginia's mid-section was new. While quite specific, with roadways, rivers, and geographical features, the execution of it appeared rudimentary and included childish indications of horses, deer, and houses.

Dr. Quinlain looked up from behind his desk. "Ah, here to check on young Mr. Gill? He's doing well."

"Excellent." Relief coursed through him.

Rising, the doctor peered at Mariah over the top of his spectacles. "Lawrence, you said you were acquainted with Miss Wenham?"

Dr. Quinlain's lips twitched. "We're acquainted."

"Indeed, Dr. Quinlain has treated a family member of mine." Mariah's eyes bored a hole through the former ship's physician.

Lawrence's mouth slackened and hung open as though he was trying to decide whether to speak or not. "The lad is assisting in the infirmary today."

Irritation skittered over Mariah's face, her brow creasing dangerously. "I see."

Carter cleared his throat, hoping to ease the growing tension in the room. "Might I see Andrew?"

"Certainly. I believe Captain Sehler has engaged him in a chess match."

187

Their captain was here at the hospital? Joy reverberated through him. "Surely you jest."

Quinlain pointed to the hospital ward's direction. "Ascertain for yourself." The physician lowered his voice. "Sehler lost his son recently and came home. He's consoled himself by visiting in the ward."

"I'm sorry." The wind left Carter's sails. A few weeks earlier, he would have railed at God. Lately, as he'd begun to crack open his old Bible, he'd found himself less angry with his Maker and more aware of how short life was.

As Carter headed to the door, Mariah touched his sleeve. "I want to speak to Dr. Quinlain privately before I leave."

He nodded at her and she smiled, a tremulous controlled movement. At least she wouldn't be at the mercantile asking for credit where they no longer had any.

Carter crossed the windowed corridor then made his way to the hospital wing, the smell of strong antiseptic solution burning his nostrils. He knocked on the door. Metal clanked and churned before a burly man opened it. His appearance reminded Carter of a crew member from one of the many privateer ships. In contrast to their small navy, the commercial vessels that had switched to privateering, were plentiful, thank God. The country was indebted to them for their assistance with the war effort.

"I'm here to see Andrew Gill."

Hoots of laughter and a roar of a man's approval greeted Carter as he made his way past several beds and to a round wood table with four chairs. A compact red-haired man was hunched over a fine wooden chess set. Andrew was the captain's opponent while a dark-haired youth observed. It was the boy Carter had seen on this previous visit, waiting for Quinlain outside his office.

"Captain Sehler?"

Sad sea-blue eyes met his own as the naval officer rose and extended a hand. "Lieutenant Williams."

Andrew smiled up, a blanket wrapped around his shoulders. "He's my chess teacher. And I'm doin' good. Ain't I, Captain?"

"Quite a strategist."

Carter quirked an eyebrow at the boy, who grinned with pleasure. The other youth rose. Unnerved by something familiar in the lad's appearance, he noted the lad appeared in excellent health with good color in his cheeks. What was he doing at the hospital?

Sehler gestured to a chair. "Sit down with us, Lieutenant."

"Gladly." Carter seated himself in a Chippendale chair. "Please accept my condolences, Captain."

Sehler bent his head. "Tis an awful thing to lose someone so young."

Andrew reached across the table and set a tanned hand atop one even more bronzed. "You'll see your boy in heaven." Tears glistened in the boy's eyes. "Ya got to believe that, Captain."

The older man cleared his throat. "I do. 'Tis my hope."

The dark-haired youth cleared his throat. "Myself as well."

What hope did Andrew Gill have?

There is always My hope.

Carter blinked, startled by the assurance he'd received. "I... your sister wants you home as soon as is possible."

The boy's face lit up. "Did you hear that Cole?"

"Wonderful news, but I shall miss you." The boy's cultured voice, while low, was so pleasant that Carter was startled anew. Cole's enunciation bore the faint echo of someone else's dulcet tones.

"Cole helps out here—cheers us all." Andrew grinned and the other boy glanced down at the table.

The lad was of too few years to be employed in a hospital. While this wasn't Carter's concern, something in the child's voice affected his heart, imploring him to care. He didn't want to—had enough on his plate. But the sensation wouldn't leave him.

Captain Sehler waggled a rust-colored eyebrow at Andrew. "Why don't you show the lieutenant your artwork, boy?"

"My drawings?"

Andrew stepped to a bed nearby and reached beneath the mattress, pulling out a rectangle of heavy paper, marked with circles, lines, squares, and crosses. He set the paper before Carter.

"Did you make the map in Dr. Quinlain's office?"

"Yup." He slid into his seat. "Made a map for Captain Sehler to show him where the foxhunts are and where Pa took me. Would like to travel when I grow up."

Forming a tent with his joined fingertips before his saturnine face, Sehler leaned over the sheet. "A battle plan. The boy's mind is brilliant, Carter, absolutely stellar. I've never seen anything like it. A genius for strategy."

Carter relaxed into his chair. No need to sit straight as though at attention. Nell's brother a military tactician? He cast his skeptical eyes on the drawings laid before him.

Spreading the papers flat, the captain pointed at the center. "That's your ship during your last battle. And our supply boat." He tapped a beefy hand on a square. "Here are known enemy craft." Three different swoops of color washed the sheet.

Sehler pointed to the first one. "If the supplies failed to make it to our vessel, this is the exit. If the support, our flanking ships, are taken out, this is where you'd move the craft."

Carter had missed his captain's clipped tones. His superior's confident voice had calmed him during that bashing when all went awry.

"And this scenario, if all went as planned, shows where you would face the opposing British ships, aim your canons, and take the other vessels down."

Carter stared at Andrew's diagram, running the scenario through his mind. Brilliant. He patted Andy's shoulder. "Well executed."

Sehler shook his head. "The boy didn't even have to cogitate. He pointed and told me like this—boom, boom, boom..." He tapped the diagram and grinned. "Like repeated cannon fire. By thunder, what I wouldn't have given to have had him onboard!"

The brawny man at the door waggled a finger at Cole.

The boy dipped his chin. "Excuse me, I must resume my duties." Tall and broad-shouldered for his age, the boy moved with a muscular determination that recalled someone else.

"Good to meet you, Cole." Carter's smile was returned with a wary look before the boy followed the attendant away.

"A good boy, that one." Captain Sehler's voice trembled. "A shame he must be put out to work at such a young age."

Andrew shrugged. "He don't work all the time. Cole's in school a lot. But it's summer so he can help Dr. Quinlain more."

Carter rubbed the side of his face as he turned to look at the departing youth. The door-key creaked in the door's lock as the attendant shut them back in. "Does the lad wish to be a physician someday?"

With his eyebrows raised and lips drawn in, Carter's former captain conveyed that he oughtn't pursue that topic. "I don't know about young Coleman…"

Carter's concentration faltered. Cole. Coleman. 'Twas like the name Daniel Scott listed in the paper. Could this be the same boy?

"…but Andy has a future in the military or leading others into the wilderness. Like Lewis and Clark."

Andrew's eyes lit with excitement. "Doc says if I cough less tomorrow, I can go with Captain and Mrs. Sehler to their home for dinner."

Carter itched to race after Cole, yet remained frozen in place. "I see." He'd find out more about Coleman.

Sehler directed his gaze at Carter. "Is all well?"

Exhaling, he forced a smile. "Not if Andrew doesn't come home soon. His sister wishes his return to home port."

Grinning, Andrew removed his sketch and slid it beneath his bed. Time for Carter to take his leave.

"Miss Gill wouldn't begrudge her brother a visit to an old salt's home, would she?" His former superior ran his hand along his jawline.

"No. But Andrew shall have difficulty calming himself when he returns home. Henceforth, he'll dream of life at sea." Like Carter had. Nell wasn't going to like it. Not one bit.

"Then I've done my duty." The captain grinned. "I have a future recruit."

Anxious to speak with Cole Wenham, Carter rose. Yet he didn't wish to give Andrew short shrift.

The boy threw an arm around Carter's shoulder, surprising him. He brushed the boy's sandy hair from his forehead. The boy had matured. As a toddler, he'd followed Carter and Nell around, as Albert did now. A rush of affection misted his eyes. He wanted to tell Andrew that he loved him. Loved his sister, too. Wished he could give them a future together.

Carter sat where Forrester's foppish law clerk pointed. The oak bench, designed in the previous century's fashion, made his back ache. Spartanly furnished with white unpainted plaster walls, a simple rectangular desk awaited the clerk. With no pictures to brighten the walls, Jackson Forrester's license wasn't even displayed. How unlike Dogwood, where portraits of ancestors and landscapes covered every wall. Never mind that Nell's grandmother had insisted the pictures had been purchased somewhere or likely won by his grandfather through gambling.

The clerk, attired in elegant clothes, straightened some papers atop his desk. He met Carter's gaze. "I've an errand to run for Mr. Forrester."

"Feel free to take your leave." Carter shrugged.

From behind the attorney's closed doors, a woman's voice rose. "How dare you? You broke confidence and shared information you had no business doing so!"

Mariah? Carter rose and edged closer to the flimsy door that separated inner and outer offices. This was not her normal mellifluous voice. He couldn't make out the attorney's response.

"Cole is not, was not, Lee's son."

His leg giving way, Carter leaned against the clerk's desk. Mariah was the mother of the boy at the hospital? The soft Carolinian accent, the smooth tones of the boy's voice—they were hers. "I don't care if you do have a will. This isn't true."

Forrester's low voice could barely be heard. "Doesn't matter."

"What should have been private business has now become a public affair because of you. You have brought disgrace upon a respectable family, for which I say shame on you."

Carter stared down at the wood-planked floor as he strained to hear Forrester's reply.

Forrester's voice rose. "Lee's wishes are here. I've done some checking. You'd benefit by agreeing with his stipulations. I'd see to that."

"You dare to bribe me?" Her voice crescendoed. "I shall have your license, sir. Depend upon it."

"I don't ask much, only enough to set up household for myself as a respectable man in town. The cook, a manservant, and that pretty girl—the house slave."

Something crashed to the floor and Carter jerked in reaction.

"That girl happens to be my half-sister, and if you think for one moment I would convince anyone to turn Macy over to the likes of you…"

Something else hit the floor and Carter moved closer to the door.

"You shall never be a respectable man. And to use what knowledge you had, sir, is despicable."

The door to the office flew open and Mariah charged toward him, fury etching every feature as tears spilled down her cheeks.

Carter pulled her to his side, as Forrester charged out behind her, something shiny glistening in his hand. The lawyer slipped the object into his pocket. Shifting the woman behind him to shield her, Carter raised one arm out, palm up.

"What's going on here?"

Beady eyes darted about in the man's feral face. "I suggest you ask Miss Wenham."

"I've come to demand satisfaction about the notice Daniel Scott placed in the Gazette."

The man's sharp features twisted. "Again, I suspect Miss Wenham may be able to enlighten you as to her imaginings."

The door to the building opened, and Carter turned to see the clerk, his arms piled with paper.

"Samuels, will you see these two out?"

"Yes, sir." The clerk set his stack upon the desk.

"And lock the door behind them."

Mariah held her head erect as Carter tucked her arm through his and escorted her across the street.

She glanced at him. "You're walking better."

His gait had indeed improved. "Yes. Thank you."

Once they reached the walkway, she squeezed his arm. "I shall explain on the way home. About my suspicions. And about Cole."

"Mariah…" Carter bit back his impatience. Better let her sort this out first. Calm his riotous thoughts. "Agreed." He released her.

"You can leave me here." She tugged at her gloves. "I've business down the street."

His destination was in the opposite direction. "The coffee shop at two?"

"Yes, and I promise I shan't scream at this next poor man, for he's been nothing but a saint."

"Indeed?"

"Truly kind. But there are limits to charitable behavior, and I shan't test his any further." She took a deep breath, her velvet pelisse rippling around her shoulders as she exhaled.

They parted company. Carter threaded past the school, the mercantile, and the church before entering the building he'd hoped to avoid. Would they tell him anything? Carter shivered as the breeze picked up, blowing bits of debris through the air.

Who would advise him as to the best choices for all?

I can ask the Lord—I need guidance.

Chapter Twenty-Three

The sun had barely begun its descent when Cornelia was finally free to check on Andy's hounds. A tall figure within the fenced yard threw scraps of meat to the pups. Despite similar height and wide shoulders, her heart told her that Hayes hadn't returned. The pups yipped and the man turned.

White teeth gleamed in Daniel's sun-darkened face. "These new pups are coming along."

"What are you doing here?" Cornelia glanced around, but Andy and Carter were both gone. Her stomach clenched.

"I told you I'd watch over you." He knelt beside Max and stroked his side. "And I have."

Shivers ran up her spine. *Lord, please send me some real help. You alone assure my safety.* Daniel slowly surveyed her from booted feet up to her hair, swept up beneath Pa's work hat.

"You can set my blood to boiling even now." His lips twitched in satisfaction.

She had to distract him. "What do you mean by placing that advertisement in the *Gazette*?"

He unfolded his lanky frame and wiped his hands together. "Personal business I need to take care of before we go home."

What did he mean by *we*? "What's this nonsense about another heir to Dogwood Plantation?"

Daniel cocked his head. "The boy isn't Lee's heir."

"Why'd you put that in the paper?"

"I'm trying to flush out some money-grubbing liars." All the smirk fled his face. Present was the boy who used to hunt the woods, who roamed the land, who first told her he loved her.

"A strange way to do it."

Daniel's broad shoulders slumped. "Probably so, but I need to get back to Kentucky." A broad smile chased the sad expression from his face. "I have a home overlooking the Ohio River."

"I'm glad for you."

He reached for her. "Please come with me."

"You need to go, Daniel."

"Promise me you'll give me a chance. An opportunity to make things up to you."

A loud crack sounded behind her and she flinched. She steeled herself before she turned around. Hayes tapped a brown whip against his hand.

"Got a new whip for the corral." His gaze fixed on Daniel. "Nelly might like to try it."

Shock registered on Daniel's face, and he paled. "I'll leave you two to your practice."

Hayes smacked the whip handle against his palm. "That's right, Mr. Scott. Be gone."

Daniel emitted a shrill whistle. In moments, a chestnut mare appeared. He mounted the horse, glanced meaningfully at Cornelia, and left.

Chuckling, Hayes threw the whip on the ground and went to Cornelia. He pulled her into his arms. "Sweet cousin, this here is what I want to protect ya from. I want to take you and Andy with us."

"Us?" Cornelia inhaled Hayes scent of soap, hair tonic, and a woman's cologne.

"Mariah, if she accepts our Savior as her own." His face beamed in hope. "She wrote me that she's studyin' the Word."

Unsteady, Cornelia gripped his arms.

"Nelly, if we sell our property…"

Our property? This was hers and Andy's property. Not his. Anger and resentment sprouted. *No, Lord, let me behave like a lady.*

196

"Let's take a ride through the old settlement today. Talk about what we might do. I'm mighty concerned about the blight and what people are gonna do hereabouts. Why don't we let the Williams family put in some fall plants on Grandma Pleasant's property? Open that up to them."

What was he talking about? She shook her head.

"I know your pa didn't like you goin' down there, 'specially after your ma died, but it's just flat-out foolishness not to use the land. Been fallow so long, the agrarian told me it'd be perfect for late crops."

Grandmama Lucia's voice echoed from the deepest recesses in her mind. "Daughter—don't go where the old folk's home was. No need upsettin' yourself." Of Grandmama pointing out the property by the river to her. "Cornelia Rose—stay far from the ghosts down there."

She needed confirmation. "Hayes, what land are you talking about?"

"By the old stone house—down to the river."

Where apple and plum trees as well as azaleas and dogwoods welcomed Carter home on their drive together. *The beautiful place.* Pleasure washed through her. The land that occupied her dreams—one including a home there. "And you and I own this?"

"Yes, darlin', of course. That swath of land wasn't part of the parcel your granddaddy gambled away."

This exquisite land by the river had always been theirs. But they hadn't been allowed to possess it.

Tears trickled down her cheeks. God had blessed her. Given her a way when there seemed no way. Would she have to give it up? She sniffed.

"Pray with me about Mariah, too. Been awful lonesome since my wife died. One selfish reason I wanted you and Andy to come live with me." His handsome features softened. "I didn't want God givin' me another wife to love and lose. Ashamed to admit this, but I figured if you needed me to marry you, I'd 'a done so. But you really wouldn't have been my wife. Not like my Edythe."

Hayes's wife had been a sickly woman and died in childbirth, along with the baby. Her father had remarked that it must be difficult for Hayes—being a widower and living a bachelor life afterward. He'd commented that once a man had a wife and had been of one flesh it was difficult to be alone in the world. Her cheeks burned as she realized what her father had meant.

"Prayers avail much, sweet girl. Plum wore out my knees resistin' Mariah's charms. But she's makin' progress on renewin' her faith in Jesus."

On the return carriage ride, Mariah explained to Carter about her son's early beginnings. "I gave birth to Coleman in North Carolina while staying with a family that I trusted. They'd cared for my boy until I moved him to a school in Norfolk when he was five."

"Only five-years-old?" Lee had always insisted that his boys would not be sent off to boarding school.

"Yes, and I would visit with him when I could."

Carter nodded, scarcely able to believe his ears. Poor Cole. "But now?"

"I brought Coleman to Richmond when money was running out."

"And Lee found out about Coleman?"

Mariah blinked her thick dark lashes. "I'm not proud of giving his name to my son, but at the time it seemed the thing to do."

Carter ran his hand along his jaw. "But you never, I mean Lee didn't..."

"I fed him a lot of wine one night. I was desperate. Then next day I told him we'd..."

He raised a hand to stop her.

He couldn't form a coherent thought. "Cole is not my brother's son?"

"No."

"Yet Lee believed so." How terrible for his oh-so-proper brother to think he'd become drunk and sired a child. It was clear now why Lee ceased drinking wine at dinner when he'd returned from South Carolina.

"Yes, but..."

"And you allowed him to continue to think so?" Had poor Anne heard the story?

"It's not so simple..."

Was it not?

She squeezed Carter's hands between her own slender ones. "Coleman must come to Dogwood immediately. I'm afraid of what Daniel might do."

If Carter provided the boy a home, a judge may infer Coleman was indeed a Williams. "No. I cannot. Not for my nephews' sakes."

"But you don't understand."

"I do." He despised being put on the spot like this. Temper rising, he needed time to think things through. "For once in your life, Mariah, you need to be accountable for your actions. And to consider someone besides yourself."

"Daniel will take him. I know it." Her tears resumed. "And he has no right."

He waited in silence as she wiped her face dry then composed herself. He couldn't bring himself to ask the obvious question—if somehow Daniel had fathered Cole.

"If you refuse then I'll go elsewhere. Someone more generous will take us both in and claim my son as his own."

"Hayes?" Had she plotted this entire time to take Nell's suitor from her? Mariah was yet a conniving woman. "You needn't be rash, Mariah. The board is paid through the month."

He reached inside his waistcoat and patted his wallet, containing money from a secondary bank account he'd discovered in Richmond. Incoming payments from previous sales had continued to flow into the account. *Praise God for that.*

God. Would He judge Mariah so harshly?

"Who is the father of your child?"

"I…" Mariah sniffed loudly. "I cannot say with certainty." Sobs shook her shoulders.

Cornelia's heart hammered out a dulcimer beat of joy in her chest. *The beautiful land is my own.* Before her the trees, some fruit-bearing, beckoned as did the sparkling river. She wanted to stay there forever and soak in its majesty.

Hayes kept chuckling at her.

"It isn't funny, cousin." She raised a hand to her chest. "I never knew."

He pointed to the beach. "Grandma Pleasant told my mother of the family stories how Bacon's rebels slipped in and attacked them. Beat one of our ancestors badly—though she was great with child."

Such wickedness in a place of beauty.

He urged the horses around the curve and to the river approach into Dogwood Plantation, past the fields. "I figured wrong. Thought ya were stubborn, like your Ma, and wouldn't sell this land even if it meant going hungry. Your pa had no way to improve the land nor build on it."

"I think the loss of the Dogwood land made Grandmama so miserable that Ma didn't want me to get any notions." Was it more than that?

"I heard Aunt Lucia was a might touched in the head when it came to the property. And your Ma..." Hayes clamped his lips tight. "Your pa tried to convince her to sell it so you children could go to school—to improve your prospects. But your Ma wouldn't discuss it."

How had this property become such a contentious subject that all had been forbidden to discuss it much less visit the land?

"Sure would be nice if you and Andy could have a snug house built there, once this infernal war ends. If you decide to sell, you'd still get a good price for the land."

She couldn't give it up. Not yet. Not when she'd only just discovered the glorious land. "Let's call the farm Pleasant Shore, in honor of our grandparents."

He shrugged. "Don't know if Granddaddy, who abandoned his wife and child, then sold most of her land out from under her, was very honorable."

"Poor Grandmama."

"She gave Roger Williams fits. I'll never forget the story about the night you were born."

"I know she went up to the manor house and Pa had to bring her home."

Hayes snorted. "Drag her home is more like it. Told Mr. Roger and anyone who'd listen that her granddaughter would be living in their house and they should get out."

"Oh, my." Prickles of embarrassment scourged her scalp. "I am so glad I didn't know." She couldn't have faced Carter and his family had she heard what Grandmama Lucia had done.

"We can offer acreage to Carter—for cold weather crops."

"Needs a lot of tilling. I'd send Mariah's families here to do that. Truth be told, I have prayed about freeing the rest of the Wenham slaves, like I did the families. I want to wait till things are settled here for Lee's boys—then I wish to free the other Wenham slaves and offer them freedmen positions at my farm, if they wish."

"That's very good of you, cousin. I struggle with my deep revulsion to slavery. Sometimes I even consider moving up North, where more people believe as I do."

Hayes eyes darkened. "Terrible times are ahead if we don't rid ourselves of this evil institution."

"I agree."

"In the meanwhile, Nelly, we can accomplish what good we can right now."

Both fell quiet. Wind rustled through the corn fields of Dogwood as they rode past. The plants were withering, dying on the stalks. Field workers spread manure into the soil, heat rising from it in waves. The soil amendment would do no good. If plantation funds were low, how would Carter feed his family and workers? Cornelia released a long exhalation.

Soon they stopped by the carriage house. Mr. Squires took the reins from Hayes.

From the other direction, a brougham pulled up the long drive. Carter had returned. Did they have word about Andy or was he perhaps with them? Her heart sped up. Cornelia exited the carriage into Hayes's outstretched arms.

He kissed the top of her head. "Nelly, I love you and Andy. You're the only kin I have. I'm sure Mariah would be happy to have you with us—if she agrees to be my wife." He released her and she looked up into his sincere eyes. Moisture pooled in her own. He wiped them from her face before lightly kissing each cheek.

Only two figures stepped from the carriage. Not her brother. She'd longed to share the good news about the property with Andy and have him home. Since he'd been gone, a part of her was missing.

Mariah scampered down and rushed to Hayes side. He pecked her cheek before she turned to Cornelia and grasped her hands.

A crease deepened between Mariah's eyes. "I fear you are going to lose your brother if you don't get him out of that hospital. We need to talk."

"Mariah!" Carter barked at the woman as he came beside them. Carter angled in toward her and rubbed her hands with vigor. "Mariah misspeaks."

Hayes' forehead wrinkled and he excused himself, heading toward Mr. Squires.

"I do not misspeak. What I say is God's own truth—if you leave Andrew with that Captain Sehler, he will take him under his wing and the boy will never return home. Surely you want your son—I mean your brother—to be with you?" Tears spilled from Mariah's eyes.

"Please hush, Mariah." Carter leaned his head against Cornelia's. His warm breath tickled her cheeks. "Andrew is fine. I will explain Mariah's outburst later." His low reassuring voice calmed her and she placed her hands in his, comfort flowing into her.

Mariah whirled away from them. "I see how things are. Just disregard what I have to say. What would a... spinster know of such things?" She harrumphed. "Let me assure you, I do know of what I speak. You need to get that boy home before it is too late." Mariah's voice broke off on a sob as she ran off, her skirts in hand.

Hayes, who was explaining to the groomsman about what he wanted done with the bay horse that night, turned and pinned Carter with his gaze. "What did you say to upset her so?"

"Not a thing."

Sighing loudly, the big man tore off after her. "Mariah, wait up."

Carter sighed and leaned in closer, resting his arm around Cornelia's shoulders. He began to rub her neck, where all the encounter's tension resided. It felt wonderful. She closed her eyes. What had Mariah meant?

"Why might Andy not come home?" As she spoke, Carter slowed his massage. She didn't want him to stop, but he did.

He made an odd sound in the back of his throat. "Nell, my former captain has been visiting some of Dr. Quinlain's patients at his hospital."

"And? This is a good thing, right? I would hope it would encourage the men there. Especially the veterans." *Like yourself.* Would his former captain endorse her methods for spurring Carter's recovery? She didn't want him so improved that he returned to the Navy. But she didn't want the British sailing up the James River, either.

With a well-muscled shoulder pressed against her own, Carter felt solid, secure. She breathed in his scent of spice and evergreens. Not a hint of ocean breeze. *Lord, don't take him away again.*

Chapter Twenty-Four

Her mind adrift in the "what ifs" of new possibilities, Cornelia viewed the Dogwood Plantation dining room in a different light, literally—nearing day's end, as sunshine filtered through tall windows. Not a mournful goodbye to the day, but an invitation to a new beginning. She could build on her own land if she and Hayes sold a portion of their mutual property. Wouldn't it be lovely, though, if the land could be kept in the family?

Carter readied a chair for her at the table. "Thank you."

"Happy to oblige." His voice was low, for her ears only, his side-whiskers brushing her cheek sending a shiver through her.

From the silver chest atop the mahogany server to the portraits lining the walls were items of worth. Some of her joy departed—without her brother, what would the property matter?

In her heart, she felt assurance from the Lord. She'd been holding on too tight to her brother—Andy belonged to God, and He was more than capable of taking care of him.

Hayes regarded her across the heavily laden table. Hayes may view Andy and herself similarly. He'd lost his wife and son and likely couldn't bear to lose them, too.

"Nelly—you all right?"

She nodded.

Mariah smiled sweetly at Hayes, whose eyes couldn't have been any more calf-like. She touched his dinner jacket sleeve. "Would you say the prayer?"

Beside her, Carter's elbow jutted toward her.

Her cousin's cheeks reddened. "Let's bow our heads. Lord, for what you have given us let us be truly thankful. In Jesus's name, Amen."

Grateful—yes she was, and humbled. But oh how she longed to have her brother home.

Carter's hand surreptitiously slid behind her shoulder, as he paused to sip his coffee. She shrugged but his heavy lidded eyes dared her to push away from him.

Across the wide table, covered with platters of chicken and biscuits, Blue Willow china bowls full of all manner of vegetables, Mariah picked at her food. Macy had told Cornelia that Mariah became ill if she ate much at all, since she'd gone through a long time of deprivation.

Over a spoonful of mashed potatoes and gravy, Hayes grinned. "We've had a wonderful day, haven't we, Nelly?"

Other than my brother not coming home?

Heat rose in her cheeks. "I haven't told Carter our good news." His knee smacked against hers and she pushed into her seatback.

"What good news is that?" He exchanged a wide-eyed glance between her and Hayes.

"I'll share that with you after dinner." She cast Hayes a cautioning glance. "When we walk the dogs."

Mariah turned toward Hayes. "Would you walk with me, a bit, too, to see the ponies?"

Carter chuckled. "I suspect the only time you'll see them at the stables is when it's dark outside."

"Your nephews sure love 'em." Hayes grinned at Carter and then fixed his gaze upon Mariah. "I'd be happy to walk with you anywhere, sweet Mariah."

Cornelia resisted the urge to roll her eyes. Pressing his shoulder against hers, Carter plucked the half-eaten biscuit left on her plate and transferred it to his mouth.

"What kind of manners are those?" Forcing her features to remain immobile, she stifled a smile.

He laughed. "My own."

He dug into the last of his potatoes and gravy. With a crooked grin, he dipped his silver spoon into the last little mound on her plate.

Holding his gaze, she held her breath. Why did such an innocent action feel so decidedly intimate? Carter raised her potatoes to his mouth. He closed his eyes, his features suggesting that he savored Mama Jo's cooking perhaps a little too much. She needed her fan. And she needed to straighten Carter out a bit.

"Is it really true? The doctor said my brother will come home soon?"

"Within the week." Carter patted his mouth with a napkin. She'd like to be the cloth that had stroked his lips.

"I need to go to Richmond—check on some things." Wouldn't Andy be pleased to know about the land? "I want to be the one bringing my brother home."

His nod was almost imperceptible.

Hayes scooted his chair back a bit from the table. "Do you know the Rousch family? Small shipping outfit between here and Williamsburg?"

"I do. Commercial transportation."

"That's right."

Hayes and Carter continued to banter about the Rousch men, whether or not they might be privateers, and how sea-worthy their vessels were. Cornelia tuned them out as the house servants began to clear the emptied plates away.

Hayes must have finally taken notice that Mariah and Cornelia had been excluded, because he sat up straight and clapped his hands. "I'm sorry, ladies, I got carried away."

Carter rose and offered Cornelia his hand. "Shall we ride out to walk the dogs?"

Ride on horseback with him again? The intensity of his gaze told her that was exactly his meaning. Heart pounding, she stood.

"Isn't that rather presumptuous?"

"Yes." He raised her hand and kissed each knuckle.

She shivered in pleasure, unable to pull away.

Carter lowered her hand. "But in fact, I had asked Squires to bring the carriage out front."

Hayes assisted Mariah with her chair and the two departed, arm-in-arm.

"Come. Let's see if the horses are out front."

"Carter?"

"Yes?"

"I have a lot to tell you on this drive."

"Uncle Carter?" Edward stood arrow-straight in the dining room entryway. His nephews had taken their meal in the keeping room, with the servants, that night. "Might I have a word?" The boy's words chilled him despite the stifling heat.

Standing behind Nell, Carter wiped his forehead and closed his eyes as a welcome breeze flowed through the open window. "Do you require privacy?"

The boy's eyes darted to Nell. She looked every bit the lady tonight in the delicate gown that emphasized her lithe form.

"No. I need to speak with you about the crops."

Nell squeezed his arm and her blue eyes urged him to be silent. "They're ruined, aren't they?

"Yes, ma'am."

A lump formed in Carter's throat. "Cash crops?"

"All, sir."

The blasted humidity was fogging his vision. No crops for the household to eat, no cash crops, and no money with which to purchase food, the price of which would be dear if other farms suffered.

Nell crooked a finger at the youth. "Come here, Eddie." She slipped her hand into Carter's. Edward joined them and took her other hand. When she bowed her head, he followed suit.

"Lord, we love you. We trust you. We know you will provide for our needs and for people who live hereabouts. You say You will never leave us nor will you forsake us. Thank You for Your help in our time of need. In Jesus's name, Amen."

For what was she thanking God? A beatific smile spread across her lovely face. "Eddie, come with us—I have a wonderful idea for a way to put those good oxen of yours to use."

Every acre had been planted, despite the agrarian's advice to allow some to remain fallow.

Edward cocked his head. "Do you wish to turn the crops under in this heat?"

"No. I want to clear some land."

Carter glanced between Edward and Nell. "What land?"

"Mine." Her smiled wobbled. "Hayes, Andy's and mine."

"Are you daft?" He closed his eyes not wishing to see the pain his comment would bring. "I'm sorry but the land by your cabin..." He ran his thumb across her hand, which he'd not released. She pulled free.

"Come with me before I change my mind. Shall we?" She strode from the room, Edward following like one of her dogs.

Carter followed the two out and down the steps.

Three large hounds shot from beneath the gardenia bushes, stirring the heady scent. At the drive's perimeter, a light carriage moved forward.

"Tonnie, Lafe, and Lex need exercise." Nell gave each a signal to wait. "They can follow us."

Carter was too tired to argue with his old friend. If she had a way to help, he'd not allow pride's last vestiges to prevent her.

Edward beamed up at him. "I'll be your chaperone."

Wouldn't be too many years before the boy would be courting as well. "And I shall be Miss Gill's humble servant. Direct my course, s'il vous plait."

"Maybe instead of French we should use your other language." She grimaced. "Do I have to use nautical terms then? Starboard and leeward?"

He chuckled. "No, a simple left or right will suffice."

"Take me to the beautiful place we stopped at, when the dogwoods were in bloom." Her face transformed into a picture of serenity.

Squires arrived. He stepped down and assisted Nell into the buggy. Edward scrambled into the small seat behind her. Carter joined them, taking the reins. "Do you mean by the river?"

A smile tugged at her lips. "Where the stone house is."

"Nell, we shouldn't continue trespassing on that land." He'd not told her, but it was one place his father had absolutely forbidden him to go— which made the spot all the more enticing as a child. Still, he should have obeyed his father.

208

"We shan't be. It's mine."

"Yours?"

"Belonged to the Pleasants, before my grandmother married my grandfather. Now to me and Andy and Hayes."

No wonder Father didn't want me down there. Grandfather had absolutely despised the woman whose loss had been his gain—and who would torment him with taunts about how he truly gained his wealth. As a child, Carter had believed her to be a demented liar, but Lee had confirmed that much of what she'd said had been true.

He inhaled deeply, ready to share. "On the way, I need to tell you about my reasons for what I've done with my life."

When they returned, over an hour later, Eddie gave Cornelia a quick peck, his little mouth cool on her cheek. He ran to the kitchen for his evening cocoa.

"Come directly back, Edward. No dawdling." Carter was sounding positively like a father.

She'd nestled against him as they rode back and to her, he felt like a husband should. Cornelia preceded him up the steps and into the house, rubbing her arms at the loss of his.

Once inside, he stepped close to her, wrapping his arm around her waist. "I want…"

Macy entered the hallway and halted, a plate in her hands, the heap covered with a napkin. Carter eased away from Cornelia's side. "Can I help you?"

"I is…" The young woman's eyes beseeched Cornelia for help.

Before she could say anything, Carter beckoned her friend forward. The scent of chicken and something bready wafted toward her.

Carter lifted the cloth. "The boys have instructions—no food in their quarters."

Cornelia's neck stiffened. He could certainly be intimidating. "Carter, I don't believe that's for the children."

Macy's wrapped head nodded almost imperceptibly. "It be for Missy Mariah."

Carter snorted. "Missy Mariah? Leave the platter with me. Tell her to come downstairs and eat at the dining table like a civilized person."

Macy blinked, curtseyed, and then flew up the stairs.

Exhaling loudly, Carter stared down at a roasted chicken thigh and leg, two biscuits, beans, a slab of white cake, and a dollop of *Crème Anglaise* smothered the plate—their dinner meal, which Mariah had picked at.

Cornelia schooled her face to try disguise her understanding.

"Do you know the meaning of this?" He glowered at her. "Why is Mariah ordering food brought to her room?"

She crossed her arms across her chest. "You're not going to bully me into telling you."

"It's wasteful and you know it. She couldn't possibly consume this amount of food in one sitting."

If Mariah failed to keep her agreement and slipped back into her secretive ways then... "Carter, did she eat at all in Richmond?"

He sucked in a breath through his open mouth, his eyebrows knit together. "I'm not sure. She had an errand. And she didn't join me for breakfast this morning. When she met me at the coffee shop, she said she wasn't hungry."

Macy's worn leather soles scuffed on the stair treads. "She comin' Master Carter."

Cornelia took his hand. "Carter, she probably didn't eat all day, not wishing to trouble you. And she ate little at dinner."

He scowled. "Perhaps."

Mariah's heels clicked on the stairs. When she spied Cornelia, she cast her eyes down as though in apology. But the Carolina belle raised them in defiance at Carter. "Might I not partake of some nourishment in a convenient location? Such as in my room? I am exhausted."

Carter's lip twitched. "You sound like a petulant child instead of a grown woman."

Mariah's riding pelisse had been removed. Her high-waisted gown was cinched tight. Absent was the roundedness in her bosom. No padding. Catching Cornelia's eye, she turned slowly in a circle. "You wouldn't want me wasting away now—would you?"

"Egad, haven't you eaten like a bird at our meals, Mariah. This must stop." Carter grabbed her shoulders. "Look at you. Since you've been here, you barely eat. We're sorry for your losses, for all of our losses, but you must eat at regular intervals throughout the day."

Descending down the stairs with a quick step, Hayes stopped, Bible in hand. "Why don't you eat down here, dumplin'?"

Jaw dropping open, Cornelia tried to manage a comment. Her cousin—upstairs with Mariah? Oh, no, how would Carter react?

Mariah's face flushed. "Yes, you're right, Hayes. As you have been about so many things."

First glancing at Cornelia, Hayes slowly directed his attention from her to Carter and to Macy. "We were finishin' our Bible study and Mariah got hungry. No sin in that, is there?"

Cornelia squeezed Carter's arm. "I need to speak with Macy."

As her friend swept by on her way to the dining room, Cornelia tried to catch up with her. Macy shook her head. "Um hum, Missy. You and Mister Carter and Missy Mariah and Mister Hayes—you be speakin' out both sides of your mouth."

Shame washed over Cornelia. She pressed a cool hand to her cheek. Had she misled Carter into believing he could take liberties with her? He'd made no promises, unlike Daniel.

"Macy, I'm sorry. I'm not setting a good example."

The beautiful servant turned and narrowed her eyes. "I be married and gone before you two be sayin' I love you."

Macy's taunt slapped her ears. Carter hadn't said he loved her. She followed her friend outside and onto the walkway. All manner of insects communicated—their sounds loud in the evening air.

"We need to talk."

"Is that what you be doin' with Mr. Carter? Talkin'?"

They stopped and Macy faced her.

Cornelia was in love with Carter. "I..." She wanted to marry him. But she couldn't ask. And he hadn't. "Until tonight I didn't know how much he sacrificed for me."

"You mean 'bout his Papa not givin' him nothin' cause of you?"

Cornelia blinked at her.

"You been lettin' him take liberties like you told me not to let my man do?"

"No."

"Um hum, I see you. He got his arms all tight around you."

Cornelia rubbed her arms, chilled despite the warm evening. "We did nothing wrong."

"I ain't done nothin' wrong with my beau. But I gonna feel those big arms of his 'round me. And I be givin' him one big kiss on his handsome face." Macy closed her eyes and smiled. "Um hum. I am." Cornelia couldn't stop her giggle. She pulled Macy to the bench. "Sit with me for a minute. Tell me about your..." Beau?

"My man be handsome and strong. He look at me like I the most beautiful woman on earth." Macy beamed.

"But you need permission to marry." Sad, but true.

Macy shook her ginger curls. "I know." She scratched her head, a rip sounding as her garment tore beneath her underarm. "Not this one, too."

"I won't tell about your sweetheart, Macy." Not that Carter would do anything about it other than yammer at Macy. "We need to get proper clothes before you wed. Let me purchase pretty fabric when I get Andy. We'll stitch up a few outfits."

"All right." Macy probed where her skin could be seen through the tear. "I ain't the only one doin' without, though, Missy."

Cornelia swallowed her concern.

A family group passed by on the way to the kitchen. She didn't recognize them and they were adequately attired, with blue skirts for the woman and both daughters and brown pants for the man that appeared new.

Macy leaned in. "They be from Mister Davis's house. That be one of Missy Mariah's families she didn't want separated."

How must the others at Dogwood feel to have their clothing be almost threadbare?

"Hayes brought them there?"

"He paid when Mr. Lee couldn't help Missy Mariah no more with buyin' her people."

Why had Hayes done so?

"They be free men now." The beautiful woman's chin raised higher. "One day I be free, too. Soon."

"I pray so, Macy." Cornelia pulled her into a hug but perceived her friend's back becoming rigid. "Tell me how I can help."

"You can't. You just pray for me."

Chapter Twenty-Five

Cornelia was done waiting for Carter to accompany her to Richmond to drag her brother home where he belonged. And Hayes was too besotted with Mariah to venture more than an arm's length away from the woman. So Cornelia set out in the wagon to retrieve her brother with her tiniest pup, Minnie, nestled in an old quilt at her feet. Humidity hung in the air and clung to her. The lightweight linen dress Cornelia wore, one of Anne's, would keep her cool—as would the breeze from the river.

Minnie slept the long drive, until they neared Richmond. Then she poked her head from the covers.

The capital building, with its great columns, stood grand before them, welcoming her back. As the horses pulled the wagon in a slow walk, she took her fill of the proud structure. The edifice resembled pictures from the Greek architecture books in the Williams' family library. President Madison had gifted Lee with several volumes.

Dolley Madison's dresses, stuffed beneath her seat, were sent via Hayes to be altered to fit either Mariah or herself. Cornelia hoped the rich material could be lengthened to accommodate her height. She envisioned Carter dressed in his naval uniform and she in Lady Madison's cream and gold gown—repeating their vows before the minister, with President and Mrs. James Madison looking on.

Hayes confided that the President's rheumatism troubled him sorely. He said Maryland farmers had been attacked by the British. She shuddered. If only the war would come to an end. Around Richmond, more men peppered the streets—wounded veterans.

Drays and carriages rolled by, laden with packages. Minnie stirred at Cornelia's feet and barked. If Cornelia found a buyer for the tiny hound, she could pay for material to purchase Macy's clothing and for alterations to Mrs. Madison's short dresses without having to touch her savings. Even if she failed in finding a purchaser, she wouldn't return empty handed— she'd have Andy.

With relief at spying an empty spot, she directed the horses into the slot. She could secure the wagon beneath two shady magnolias. A water trough stood nearby. After getting down, Cornelia straightened her shoulders and dusted off her skirt. Minnie snuffled.

With a good stretch into the wagon, Cornelia patted Minnie's silky head and ensured the dog was secured in the wagon. The pup would keep people away from the carriage. Mischief had been reported in Richmond, of young men finding it sporting to hack a piece of wood from the spokes. *Not on pup's watch.*

Cornelia made her way toward the mercantile. The grit of sand beneath her shoes confirmed the brick walkway's newness. It had been built only a few months before Pa died and she'd been called home from her work at the school. She'd not have time, this visit, to stop at the school.

In front of Kitterings' Mercantile, floorboards stood propped against its bricked exterior. A workman examined the roof shingles then glanced her way as Cornelia approached the door. Two large glass windows glittered in the sun, the scent of vinegar water attesting to their cleanliness.

A bell tinkled as Cornelia opened, then closed, the heavy door behind her. Several men, dressed in ill-fitting suits, examined bolts of patterned cloth.

Bent over ciphering sheets, a red-haired young man straightened as she approached the counter. "May I help you?"

Help. God had been her ever present help. Why then, did she feel compelled to trade the tiny pup instead of using her funds to purchase the cloth? *Fear. Lack of trust.* Doing things her own way.

215

Behind her the doorbell tinkled and hot air wafted forward.

"Miss?"

Cornelia recollected her purpose. "I need to purchase cloth and notions to make two dresses."

Limpid gray eyes continued to fix on her face. She set her cumbersome reticule on the counter, ready to negotiate. Her action caused his ink pot to jump and the young man grasped it.

Her stomach clenched. She was making a mess of things.

"Kelly?" Behind the clerk, a paunch preceded a man through the curtains. Thinning hair was brushed across his pate.

"What's this?" The heavyset man waved a sheet of paper covered in spidery script.

The young man blinked rapidly. "Why that's our order, Mr. Kittering."

"This isn't what I ordered." The owner's jowls quivered. "Look here."

Cornelia sensed someone staring at her. There had been several gentlemen in the store when she'd arrived.

The clerk's and Cornelia's eyes followed as the proprietor laid the sheet down on the countertop and jabbed a thick finger halfway down the page. "I told you four bolts of tan osnaburg not nine."

Exactly what the field workers needed. Five extra bolts would give the plantation enough material for many pairs of pants for the field hands. But while it would make serviceable work clothes for Macy, Cornelia didn't want her friend's dresses to be of cloth associated with slaves. If she understood Macy, her "beau" didn't intend for her to be enslaved any longer. An ache formed in her chest. Macy had been her closest friend the past few years. She blinked back her tears.

The clerk narrowed his myopic eyes on the page. "That says four."

Kittering lifted the sheet up. "Your loopy four reads like a nine. I can't blame Mrs. Blythe for filling this order with nine bolts. It arrived from Chesapeake this morning. Now I am stuck with all that extra yardage."

Cornelia's mouth started working before she could stop it. "I could use the cloth." Just because she was a landowner didn't mean she now had money nor was she responsible for the field workers. She pressed her eyes shut for an instant. Money from the Puppy Day sale was deposited in the

Charles City Bank. But she hadn't intended to touch it, and she didn't yet know what Andy's hospital bill might be.

Kittering's face lit like a whale oil lamp. "Might you now? And what's your name?"

From behind her, two heavy footsteps sounded as a man moved forward, the scent of pines and smoked meat accompanying him.

"Miss Cornelia Gill." Daniel's sonorous voice startled her.

She pivoted. "What are you doing here?"

Dressed in buckskins, his broad leather hat was slung low. "Buying supplies for my return."

He was leaving finally? *Good.* Cornelia turned to face the shopkeeper.

"You're Gill's daughter—the Dogwood Plantation manager? We haven't seen your father in months, since we built this new store and moved to this side of town."

Pa was gone. Cornelia tried to find her voice, but shreds of muslin seemed to fill her throat.

"Her father died of the fever this spring." Daniel slipped his large hand tentatively towards hers, but stopped when she moved hers away.

"I'm sorry. Such a good man." The store owner tapped the clerk on his shoulder. "Go tell Mrs. Kittering to bring us out a kettle of tea. Tell her Mr. Gill's daughter is here. And Kelly, bring a tray of shortbreads and cream and sugar, too."

Kelly scowled.

When the clerk left, Kittering winked at her. "He's a good worker, if in a bit of a dudgeon today."

Cornelia dare not comment upon the worker's mood. With Daniel nearby, she was fighting the same irritation.

"Your father was a good man. As I recall, you work for the Academy, don't you?"

"Not any longer. I had to return to take care of my brother."

Kittering shook his head. "You two children were his pride and joy."

Tears threatened. Cornelia needed to lighten the mood. "Even more so than his dogs?"

Kittering's eyes widened. Then he barked out a laugh. "I'm sure of that. But what you said reminds me that he once promised Mrs. Kittering a little companion in exchange for some goods for you two children."

"Is that so?"

"Aye." He rubbed his chin. "She misses our children, who've grown and left us. Your father thought a pup might cheer her up."

Would Minnie be just the thing? "I may have a little dog she'd like."

His eyes twinkled as he gazed at Cornelia. "If you do, then I have a proposition for you."

Two cups of tea and three cookies later, an agreement was reached. Mrs. Kittering and Cornelia headed outside. Daniel Scott sauntered ahead, arms full of fabric bolts. She shouldn't have allowed him to assist. But neither Kelly nor Mr. Kittering offered to carry the heavy bolts. Daniel had scooped them up before she could protest.

Mrs. Kittering laughed. "He's a handsome one. And he fancies you."

A niggling worry formed in Cornelia's belly. Daniel's own purchases were left piled high on the counter. "With all the goods he bought, you'd think he already had a wife hidden away."

The woman's salt-and-pepper eyebrows rose into two inverted "V's". "Mayhaps."

Cornelia exhaled. *Let's hope so.* Minnie yipped as they approached.

Daniel strode around and dropped the long bolts of cloth into the wagon bed with a "thunk." She winced. He could have been gentler. She reached for the puppy.

"Here's our little gal—the runt of the litter but sweetest of all of my Pa's dogs."

As she handed Minnie down to Mrs. Kittering, the hound barked and then immediately nuzzled into the woman's neck. The matron shook her head, her tight curls bobbing against the pink skin of her face. "Oh my."

"Minnie, stop."

The woman clasped the small bundle more tightly and the pup stilled. "And you say she's a good little watchdog, aye?"

Cornelia smiled. "She is."

Mrs. Kittering giggled like a young girl when Minnie licked her chin. "Oh, Minnie, you are so sweet, yes you are."

One more pup gone. Cornelia took a deep breath. "Please thank Mr. Kittering again for me, for the discount and the exchange of Minnie for so much yardage."

"Glad to. We're so sorry about your father." The matron hugged her. For an instant the old longing for Ma welled up, almost spilling over.

Mrs. Kittering released her and departed, leaving her with Daniel. His perusal unnerved her.

Cheeks hot, Cornelia glanced to the wagon-bed. "Thank you, Daniel. I appreciate your help." She turned away from him. What form of gratitude he might expect?

Daniel wiped his hands together as he joined her in two long strides. She wished Carter had accompanied her.

"Are your errands complete? If so, I am staying at the inn across the street."

"Not with your grandparents?"

He pointed to a two-story building, its creamy columns supporting a portico over the entrance to the neat establishment. She blinked. Was he being improper? She flexed her fingers to prepare them for a quick slap across his face if need be. But his facial expression, exactly like Andy's when he'd tell her he was "starvin' to death" melted some of her reserve.

"They serve a fine beef roast at the midday. I hoped you might join me." His stomach growled loudly.

She'd never eaten in such an establishment while she'd lived in Richmond.

"I..." She swallowed. "I need to get my brother." And had been in such a hurry she'd failed to pack a lunch.

"You brother is here? I haven't seen the boy." A muscle in his lean jaw flexed. "Where is he?"

"At Dr. Quinlain's hospital."

Aristocratic features pulled in concern. "I'm so sorry. I didn't know." He looked like he wanted to say more, but he rubbed his thumb against his tawny pants.

"We feared we might lose him." Cornelia pulled at her collar.

"Is Andy well now?"

Daniel knew what it was like to lose someone. Both of his parents, who'd established a successful business in Louisville, Kentucky, had died, leaving the two boys to return to their grandparents. And Daniel had lost his wife and child, too.

She sighed. "Well enough for me to take him home." Andy was coming back with her whether the doctor liked it or not.

"Surely he'd not begrudge you a fortifying meal before you take to the road again?" Daniel's broad chest expanded, causing the fringe on his leather jacket to flutter.

He'd been so helpful. And this was a public place. And praise God, Daniel be gone soon.

"As long as they're prompt." And he had no expectations beyond a meal together.

"Thus far." Daniel held out his arm for her and Cornelia reluctantly took it, feeling the corded muscles beneath the soft deerskin.

She patted her pouch, doubting her decision. When he opened the door in to the building, though, the rich scent of beef and fresh bread tempted her senses. Persons who owned property, people who had means—they visited such establishments. And she was the owner, with Andy and Hayes, of the beautiful river property.

Cornelia lifted her chin. They stepped inside. Her heart beat harder in her chest.

What will the price be?

Clutching her reticule, the diners' ruckus echoed around her in the long narrow room. She took a step backward, squarely onto the shoe of the gentleman who'd entered behind her.

"Excuse me."

"This way." Daniel guided her through the dining room. He nodded at a young woman pouring ale into tankards. Tables sized for couples clustered adjacent the windows. He stopped at one and yanked a round-backed chair out for her.

"Thank you." She should go. Leave. Now. Ignoring the warning, she sat. Just this once, she'd take lunch in a public eatery.

Movement outside the window drew her eye to a queue of boys. All dressed identically and moved as a unit, following a silver haired man. The buildings sign proclaimed "St. George's School for Boys."

Strong quince water cologne wafted from their server as she paused before them. "Would you like coffee?"

Cold gray eyes met hers. "Yes, please."

"Dark ale for me." Daniel surveyed the pretty face under the serving wench's cap.

"Very good, sir."

Carter would never have been so bold.

Tilting his dark head, Daniel's mouth formed a tight smile. "Do you know anything about the school?"

"No. Why?"

He stared past her. "No reason." His features remained impassive.

The servant returned and placed Cornelia's coffee before her, then angled her body more toward Daniel, bending low as she set his ale before him.

Daniel's patrician features tightened. "Even in summer the few boys left behind are regimented. A boy accustomed to freedom wouldn't be content there."

She'd loved school life but she'd still returned home for a brief respite in the summer. "If they are used to routine, then…"

Rapping his knuckled on the table, Daniel gazed out the window. "Perhaps."

"Who would keep their child at school in summer?" None of the girls at the Academy had remained behind.

"Someone failing in their duties as parent." His lip curled in disgust. "Wouldn't you agree?"

When she didn't reply, Daniel tossed back the contents of his ale then wiped his mouth with his sleeve. Gone was the blue blood of Virginia and in his place was the Kentucky woodsman. "I'd never leave my boy in a place like that. Not when I could give him a fine home elsewhere. I'd spend the summer teaching things like honor, pride, and the ability to protect himself and his kin from predators."

Their server returned. Plates of fragrant beef, potatoes, and carrots covered the tray. "Nice change from all the shellfish I've been served lately. Though I'll miss all the crabmeat when I go." Daniel winked up at the server and pressed a coin into her wide palm. "Thank you, miss."

"Miss? Not Rachel today?" The woman's accent held a bit of Irish brogue.

Daniel ran his tongue over his narrow lips. "Wouldn't be proper to address you by your Christian name."

She glared at him. "Pardon me, sir."

Daniel cleared his throat. "I'll pay now. We'll not trouble you further."

Relieved that he was able to pay for the meal for them, yet concerned about the interchange between Daniel and the servant, Cornelia fixed her gaze on the street. Her neck stiffened at the sight of a familiar dark head. If she was correct, that was Mariah Wenham entering the boys' school. Either that or someone with an identical wig and petite form.

"Well sir, best wishes in finding yourself a proper wife." The woman's cold voice was filled with suppressed rage.

"Thank you, Miss."

Daniel's hooded eyes covered whatever he was thinking.

The woman stomped off, pulling her stained apron loose as she went. The other diners' voices buzzed around them. She pressed her feet against the plank floor.

"Imagine how surprised I am that you remain unmarried."

"Oh?" Was he now about to insult her for being of the age when she was about to be put on the shelf?

Daniel shoveled a forkful of potatoes into his mouth.

Cornelia cut the beef into smaller pieces first before she took a bite. Savory and tasty.

"I never pictured you married to any of Charles City's young men, though."

Anger pricked her spine and she sat up straighter. "No?" She cut her carrots and brought one to her lips. It was tender, sweet.

"You were always so different. I figured you'd never be the kind of lady they'd want."

Invisible fingers gripped her neck and pinched hard. That was the lie she'd always believed—that no one would want her for herself. She set her fork down and stared at the man across from her.

Daniel's handsome features reflected contentment. "Which is why I wondered if you might be more suited to life on the frontier. You're such a strong woman."

Once, not very long ago, Cornelia would have found this a high compliment. Not now. "So I'm not refined enough to secure a husband hereabouts?"

Daniel's wide eyes reflected understanding. "I'm sorry. I meant that my desire to marry you and take you to Kentucky was due to your strength." A slow grin crossed his face. "As well as your beauty."

Cornelia bit her lower lip. She needed to get her brother. "I've received several offers of marriage."

Granted, that wasn't exactly true. There was Hayes, who hadn't actually asked the words. And a number of men had teased that they'd marry her just to get first crack at choice of the litter on Puppy Day.

"Of course." Daniel raised his hands in conciliation. "I hoped you'd reconsidered my proposal from many years ago. You might find my situation attractive even if you don't find me so." His teasing tone left no doubt he considered himself to be as appealing as, or more so, than his home in Kentucky.

She'd never met so presumptuous a man in her life. And while he was older, his words were similar to those previously spoken. He had no more social graces or understanding of women's feelings than Andy's hounds did.

Another server strode by. Cornelia tilted her head in the woman's direction. "You might find another willing female who catches your eye before you leave."

"Clever and direct. I love the combination." Daniel speared a chunk of beef from her plate. "I always found you amusing. Another trait I prize."

The notion of being bound to a man such as Daniel made her shiver. She'd rather change places with Macy. *Oh no, I didn't get Macy's pretty cloth like I planned.*

Daniel methodically ate from her plate. She'd lost her appetite anyway.

She pushed from the table and rose. "Thank you again, for your assistance. And for the meal."

He withdrew his fork from the potato and set the utensil down on his plate before he stood.

"Might I accompany you to the hospital?" Daniel's strong grip on her arm suggested that he intended to go with her.

"I..." Why not? She swallowed. Cornelia didn't wish to confront the doctor on her own. "All right."

Cornelia gritted her teeth. She wouldn't have to endure his company much longer. And with Daniel's size and presence, perhaps Dr. Quinlain would not deny her request to bring Andy home. She ducked ahead of Daniel, stepping quickly through the narrow aisle between the tables of diners, a few staring openly at his unconventional clothing. Finally, she reached the foyer.

He took her hand and turned her toward him, studying her with an intensity that caused the back of her neck to prickle. He pointed toward the stairs. "I'd like to freshen up. Care to join me?"

Chapter Twenty-Six

The sensation of something solid, becoming known in her consciousness, dropped with a thud into her gut, much like the bolts of cloth Daniel had so cavalierly tossed in the wagon-bed.

Between clenched teeth she hissed, "If you believe for one moment that I would accompany you to your room, you're more foolish than I imagined." And more crass.

Daniel raised his hands, a half grin forming on his face. "A woman like you, who speaks her mind and acts as she wants—"

"You thought wrong!" As he had those many years ago. It hadn't been her. The ill behavior stemmed from one person alone.

"You wanted me to touch you."

Daniel Scott's words had the smell of smoke on them, much like the wood burning as lunches cooked for the taverns. Only his words were like lies from the very pit. Accusations she'd heard in her own mind before. *You'll never find a good husband. No man would want a woman like you. It is useless thinking you could ever be a lady.*

She wanted to scream. Cornelia spun on her heels and exited through the door, face burning.

"Cornelia!"

Ignoring Daniel's shout, she dodged carts and manure as she crossed the street. With a quick glance back, she viewed Daniel being pulled inside the inn by the woman who had first served them. Disgusting man.

She looked up to see Mariah descending the school's steps.

"Cornelia, I'm glad I found you." Mariah's breathless voice was barely audible, her cheeks flushed pink, as she reached her. "Do you have the dresses with you?"

"Lady Madison's dresses?" She frowned.

Mariah gripped Cornelia's arm. "Might I have a few things put into your wagon later?"

"Yes, but—"

Releasing her, Mariah's lips thinned. "I don't have time to explain. I need you to come with me to Madame Favret's."

Before she could give assent, the tiny woman dragged Cornelia down the walkway toward the wagon.

"I saw you with Daniel." Mariah's tiny hands flew about her neck, straightening her banded collar of pearls. "What did he want?"

Cornelia face's heated. Mariah pressed a fan into Cornelia's hand then helped her wave it.

"Stay away from him. He's no good. Never has been." Mariah hissed her words. "He's just like my fa…" The petite beauty clamped her mouth shut. "It doesn't matter. But I need you to do me several favors today. First, I need those dresses."

"All right." An arrow of disappointment shot through her. "Do you require all?"

Mariah frowned. "No, just one for today and the other to be altered if need be."

"Hayes said they might all fit you, but…" She wasn't accustomed to having fine things, like Mariah was. But just for once, couldn't she have clothing that was truly beautiful? She'd failed to negotiate a price that would include fabric for a dress for Macy. Her friend needed something new and serviceable, not threadbare. Still, she knew Macy wouldn't begrudge her the decision to obtain enough cloth for the field workers.

Cornelia took a deep breath—she'd claim one dress to adapt for Macy. She could add osnaburg to the petticoat's top to lengthen it. "I need one."

"Certainly."

They stopped by the wagon and Mariah hugged Cornelia, surprising her.

"God bless you for your help today." Dimples formed in the woman's cheeks.

The southern belle was changing. Perhaps she and Hayes could be happy together.

Cornelia yanked the bulky container from beneath the bench seat. She passed it to the smaller woman to hold for a moment while she checked the horses.

"Here, I'll take that." Cornelia accepted the bag and the two women linked arms and hastened toward the dressmaker's shop. Further away from the hospital. And Andy.

As they entered the oyster shell tabby building, Mariah waved at a dark-haired woman affixing paste flowers to a frilly hat. The shopkeeper beamed. The two women exchanged rapid French.

The proprietress rose and minced toward a high dark-stained counter. *"Oui, certainement."*

Mariah brought the bag to a corner, where streams of rose silk spilled from the ceiling to the floor into a puddle. She eased behind the material, which acted as a dressing area shield.

The Frenchwoman's smile couldn't have been tighter. "Mademoiselle, would you like to sit while you wait on Madame Wenham?"

"Thank you." She lowered herself onto the bench indicated.

The white-washed interior held rows of shelves and pegs. Several day dresses and accessories were displayed in the window. Hats, ribbons, and sashes of all colors, shapes, and sizes arrayed the back wall. She took her fill, ogling each accessory and article while Madame Favret went to provide assistance. How had the obviously new French silks made it past the blockades? *Privateers.* She recalled Hayes and Carter's discussion over dinner.

In a short while, Mariah yanked the curtain aside from the corner where she had changed into one of Dolley's dresses. She emerged, the creamy moiré silk, edged with gold, transforming her into a dark-haired, albeit bewigged, angel. It wouldn't be Cornelia donning this gown for her wedding day—the raiment suited Mariah perfectly.

Cornelia rose and took Mariah's hands. "You look beautiful."

"Inside is what counts." Tears formed in the woman's eyes, and she wiped them away.

Had those words truly come from Mariah's lips? *God is good. He can heal the sick and wash away all our sins.* A cased clock chimed eleven.

Cornelia exhaled the breath she didn't realize she had held. "I should go get my brother. I've put it off too long."

"Nonsense. Let me show you what Hayes and I want you to have."

Hayes and she?

Mariah's eyes danced in delight. "Quick as a flash. Then you go argue with Andy's doctor."

"There won't be any discussion. He's coming home."

Mariah turned toward the store's proprietress. "Madame Favret, could you retrieve that special dress?"

"Certainement."

Mariah grinned like a child. "Hayes asked for a simple dress to be made up for you for your work at Dogwood. We used one of Anne's for the sizing." Sadness accompanied her last words. Mariah, too, was mourning the loss of a loved one.

"*Voila.*" The Frenchwoman lifted a daffodil yellow garment, edged in brown velvet and held it over her outstretched arms. Long enough for someone as tall as Cornelia, or for that matter, Macy. "Mademoiselle—your dress."

Although intended for Cornelia, the gown would enhance Macy's cinnamon hair and green eyes.

"Your beau will find you a vision."

Mariah adjusted the sash slung beneath the high bodice. "Its simplicity enhances a woman's natural beauty."

Praise God. Macy could have that dress, which would be much more practical than the one belonging to the president's wife. And it would be already made.

Behind them the doorbells rattled loudly. Daniel Scott's form dominated the doorframe. His determined look, set on his refined features, contrasted boldly with his earlier brutish behavior.

The frontiersman fixed his gaze upon Mariah. "Miss Wenham." He emphasized the first word of his salutation.

The color that had earlier tinged her cheeks faded to gardenia's pallor.

"What brings you to Richmond, Mister Scott?" Mariah's voice turned all sugar sweetness. Once again, she was the South Carolina belle, but her eyes flashed daggers.

"Skulking around Dogwood. And following me around Richmond, too," Cornelia muttered under her breath.

Mariah's tinkling laugh indicated that she'd caught some of Cornelia's words. "Last I heard you'd departed hastily for Kentucky with your very young bride."

Red splotches appeared on Daniel's prominent cheekbones.

Mariah's tight smile and the flick of her wrist to open her fan warned of her rising anger

Daniel made a strangled noise. "Miss Wenham, I put my wife and son in the grave. I have many regrets but she is not one."

The brash confidence left his face. Mariah snapped her fan closed. "Please accept my condolences."

"'Twas long ago now." His jaw muscles twitched. He tilted his head, a cool look freezing his perfect features. "Perhaps he'd look like one particular boy at the school down the street."

Mariah's knuckles whitened.

The store owner minced toward Daniel. "Monsieur, as touching as this reunion is, we do not allow men in our establishment. I am very sorry."

"If my name was Williams, I bet you'd let me stay in your shop, madam."

The Frenchwoman gasped. "Monsieur. I beg you to leave."

He narrowed his eyes at Cornelia and then Mariah. "Wonder which woman he's buying for? Or is it both?"

Given their earlier altercation, Cornelia's anger had a full head of roiling steam. She directed it at the frontiersman. "Get out Daniel, now."

He spun on his heel and left.

Mariah and Cornelia pushed the boxed gowns under the wagon seat. "There, all set."

"No." Mariah tapped the toe of her shoe. "I need to get my son's belongings."

"Son?" To her knowledge, the woman had never married. Which meant...

The belle's red cheeks and half-lowered eyelids terminated Cornelia's questions.

"I need to bring Coleman to Dogwood. I wouldn't ask this favor if I wasn't desperate. But I'm afraid to leave him here any longer."

"Where is he now?"

"Working at the hospital."

Did Carter know Mariah's plans?

As if reading her thoughts, Mariah leveled her gaze on her. "Carter won't allow Coleman in the main house. Hayes will keep Cole in the South Flanker."

"Hayes?" He must be taking them with him.

"'Twill only be for a few days. We'll be married soon."

"Married?" She felt her eyes widen.

"Yes."

"It had indeed better be very soon if you're going away with him." And her illegitimate son.

"Cornelia, could you keep him with you today until I return, please?"

Perhaps with another boy there she'd not baby her brother too much now that Andy would be coming home. "I will."

"Thank you." Mariah beamed. "I'll have one of the boys put Cole's belongings in the back. And I'll see you tonight."

"Yes, I better get Andy."

"Cole will be there, too. But I'm going to speak to him at the back entrance and tell him to go with you. And if you don't mind, I'd very much appreciate it if you'd pick up both boys in the back rather than on the street. I don't wish for anyone to see my son leaving with you."

Should Cornelia be afraid? It was too late. She'd given her word.

Cornelia fidgeted in the chair outside the doctor's office. If he didn't open the door soon, she was going to just march down the hall and scream until they brought her brother out to her. Mariah's situation, and all the unanswered questions, had her nerves jumping.

The door flew open and a tall boy emerged, his fine features bunching together. When he spoke, a sweet, high voice trilled, rather than that of the older youth he appeared. "I'll bring him straightaway, Dr. Quinlain." He cast Cornelia an inquisitive look then ran the hallway's length.

A smiling man exited the office and adjusted his cravat. "Miss Gill, I presume, by the looks of you."

What had Carter said about her looks? Or perhaps because Andy resembled her. "Yes, Cornelia Gill."

He assisted her up. "Dr. Lawrence Quinlain. Pleased to meet you." He gestured toward his office and she entered, catching a whiff of faint lemon verbena. "You're taking Captain Sehler's prodigy away?"

She stiffened, recalling Mariah's warning about the Sehlers wanting to spirit Andy away from her. "Andy has a good long while before he'd be ready for naval duty." If ever.

"True enough." He laughed. "Come in."

Inside the office, books were stacked floor to ceiling on one wall. She slid into the black-leather chair seat and arranged her skirts around her. "It's time for my brother to come home."

"Yes, he is fully recovered. Thankfully it was not yellow fever. Let me find my paperwork then." He sat behind his desk and pulled open a center drawer.

Everything seemed to involve paperwork. Since this was what she did for a living, she wondered what exactly he would hand her. A bill? A release form of some kind?

"I took the liberty of preparing an agreement between us." He held up a thin sheet of paper.

"For?"

He averted his gaze. "I didn't want there to be any misunderstanding about the bill. I'll consider it completely covered by the agreement Lieutenant Williams offered."

Exactly what had Carter agreed to do? "Sir, what was the cost for the hospitalization?"

Dr. Quinlain slid the paper across his desk toward her. She touched the bottom of the page where a heavy black line had been scrawled and the amount due indicated.

She moistened her lips. Sufficient money was in the bank to cover the expense. She'd not jeopardize her future earnings. And she'd not count on Carter to manage her and Andy's expenses.

The doctor's features twitched in uncertainty. "I wanted you to not worry about the hospitalization fees. When I told Lieutenant Williams, he suggested I accept one of your puppies as payment."

Carter had made an agreement without even asking her. Without checking. And this had been weeks earlier, and he'd said nothing. Although she had been shocked by what folks would pay for one of her father's trained purebred dogs, apparently Carter had no idea—for the bill was far less than they could have gotten for one of the remaining hounds. She exhaled slowly, her mouth dry. Spying the carafe of water, with its overturned glass set atop, Cornelia pointed. Quinlain must have understood, for he stood, poured liquid into the vessel and handed it to her.

He cocked his head. "Miss Gill, I expected you to be overjoyed with this arrangement."

Her hand shook and she held the glass with both hands. A lady would be gracious. A lady would be refined. She'd show no irritation. She'd certainly not discuss the monetary difference. Cornelia took a sip, closed her eyes, and savored the water's sweetness.

"Thank you, Dr. Quinlain. Your kindness is appreciated. I'm at a loss for words to express my feelings." There, that was the truth.

"I'm not a hunter myself, but my boy needs a pet. One he can take hunting with him on occasion. But mainly he needs a well-trained, obedient dog who will keep him company should I be called back into service soon." A fleeting expression of sorrow altered the doctor's visage.

"Thank you, Dr. Quinlain, for serving our country. And I pray your son will be very pleased with his new dog." Happiness again reflected on the man's face.

Footsteps echoed outside the open door. "Sissy!" Andy called as he flew across the office.

Tears clouded her vision. She'd been so afraid he'd die, like Ma and Pa had. "Andy." She stood and whispered his name into his hair and pulled him close, her tears dropping into his hair. She clutched him as he tried to pull free.

"I can't wait to come home. And Cole's mother said he could come with us."

What bag of worms had just been unloosed?

Chapter Twenty-Seven

The trio passed the three-mile marker at the curve, and Cornelia flicked the reins. Only a few miles more to go.

"Andy, when we get home, I'm first going to speak with Carter." Every time she was apart from him and returned, it felt like coming home—but today she arrived home with a full head of steam. Although she felt sorry for the doctor, she'd also lost money for herself and mainly for Andy. But as an independent woman, it truly galled her that Carter could have struck such an arrangement without her approval.

"Yes, Sissy, we'll do what we need to do."

The two boys' heads swiveled toward each other.

"Might Andy be able to show me around, Miss Gill?"

Her breath caught in her throat. "Oh, Andy, I need to tell you…" Her thoughts on the drive had been caught up with Mariah, Daniel, and what she was going to say to Carter when she got ahold of him. "Hayes, our cousin…"

"I know who he is, Miss Gill." Cole beamed at her.

"Yes, but you see, we…" Cornelia directed the horses to turn onto the road that would take them to Pleasant Shores.

"What are you doin', Sis?"

"This is the perimeter of our land." Cornelia transferred the reins into one hand.

"No, it ain't."

She bit her lip, wasn't going to correct him. "Grandmama Lucia's family owned this land but she wouldn't live on it—not after Grandpa gambled it away." Hadn't even allowed her own daughter and granddaughter to go onto the property. And it could have done them so much good had they leased it or sold it. Her entire memory of her grandmother had been tainted by the new revelations. Moisture dampened her cheeks.

"Why you cryin', Sissy?"

She shook her head as she slowly exhaled. "Our lives could have been different had it not been for poor choices our grandparents made."

"So we coulda lived here?"

"It's like I imagine heaven—so beautiful." Cole pointed to the magnolias and gardenias, their scent intense as the wagon creaked along the path. "Cooler here, too, than on the road."

She pointed to the abandoned stone house. "Andy, that's where Grandmama Lucia's family, The Pleasants, lived."

Her brother's face puckered. "It's ours?"

"Hayes' and ours."

"Why didn't you attend St. George's School, if you own all this?" Cole's gentle voice and wide eyes suggested no criticism. They took the turn that paralleled the James River. Cole sighed. "If I lived here, I'd never want to leave."

Precisely. She imagined a beautiful home set there. An odd sensation stirred though her as she pictured something akin to the Dogwood Flankers.

"Thanks, Sissy, for showin' us." Andy squeezed her arm and laid his head against her shoulder for a moment.

"Thank God you're home, Andy, and that the Lord provides for our needs." She blinked back the wetness in her eyes.

Cole rocked back and forth in his seat. "I'm glad Mother let me come."

Mariah hadn't allowed—rather she'd begged the favor. Mariah, a mother. And to this boy who someone claimed was Lee's son. Was Daniel this child's father? Was the legal issue he'd returned to Virginia to address related to Coleman?

235

"Your…" The word came with difficulty. "…mother follows behind us by about an hour."

They rode past Dogwood Plantation's empty fields—nothing to harvest. Some of the women could stitch new clothing while they waited for Pleasant Shores' fields to be readied.

Baying carried from the kennels.

Andy stood. "Hurray! I'm home. The hounds smell me."

"Sit down, brother."

Coleman covered his mouth as he laughed. "Might you release us by the dogs, Miss Gill?"

"Please, Sis, can you?"

"If you both keep your bottoms on the seat until we get there."

"Yes'm," they chorused.

Cornelia quick-stepped across the forecourt from the carriage house. Soon she mounted the house steps. Inside the foyer, she paused to catch her breath.

Nemi crossed from the holding room, arms stacked with trays. "A letter for you, Missy Gill, on the post stand."

"Thank you. Do you know where Carter is?" She tilted her head back and stared up at the engineering marvel of the flying buttress staircase, willing him to appear.

"Not my business." The sulky woman departed. If Cornelia were enslaved, she'd be recalcitrant, too.

Cornelia marched to the stand and pulled the top envelope free. Another missive from Sally Danner. In a childish pique, Cornelia tossed it to the floor. Carter could pick it up. Just like he could fix the mess he'd caused by agreeing to give the good doctor one of her trained hounds. Not that he would have had any idea what the bill might have been.

A blue-tinged envelope, addressed to her, was next in the stack. She cracked the seal and opened it. Scanning the letter, she realized it was from the Sargeants. They'd been unable to attend Puppy Day and Mrs. Sargeant had been ill since. Would Cornelia have a pup left? *Yes.* She'd sell her last trained pup to them for what it was worth, more than enough to cover the hospital bill twice over.

Noisy footfalls descending accompanied Carter on the stairs. "You're back." Carter touched the pin in his neckcloth and rearranged the points of his collar as he approached her.

She glared at him. "How could you?"

His dark eyebrows rose. "Explain."

Pausing but a second, he took two steps toward her and attempted to take her hands, but she swatted his away.

"How could you promise the doctor a hound without asking me?" She caught his scent of spice and leather. His snug pants were tucked inside two-tone riding boots. Cornelia's pulse quickened.

"I…" A lock of hair fell across his brow.

She resisted the urge to touch the stray wave.

Carter's face grew sheepish. "I'm sorry. But I imagine I saved you a large fee."

Did he really have no idea? As he inched ever closer toward her, she backed away, raising her palm. "Do you not realize my father and Andy have spent years raising, breeding, and training the best hounds in the country?" Pride commanded her tongue.

"I do."

"Time during which you gambled away your Navy pay or your brother wouldn't have had to sponsor you through school."

A muscle jerked in Carter's cheek and he slowly rolled his lips together, a sign of either a coming explosion or admission of defeat.

A little thrill went through her at her victory. She frowned, recollecting Grandmama's admonition—don't ever trust a gambling man. Never. But she loved him. Cornelia shook her head.

Carter reached for her but she backed toward the door. He'd lied to her. "Why didn't you tell me about Mariah and her child?"

"I felt that was her news to share."

She swallowed as he took two more determined steps toward her. "You're not limping."

"No." He snatched the letter from her hand and scanned it.

"If you're looking for one from your lover, it's on the floor." Cornelia moved her skirts aside then pressed her dusty boot atop the envelope, marking it with a print. "Right there."

Carter tilted his chin toward her. "Why do you call her that?"

237

I don't know. Because I am jealous.

He sighed. "Sally Danner's latest ploy is to send me letters insisting my father's will stipulated both Lee and I share the inheritance. Which she believes firmly puts Dogwood in my possession."

Cornelia grabbed her invitation from the Sargeants back from him. "Well, I'm going to dine at the Sargeants, where I will discuss the price of my last trained foxhound. I pray they shall be generous, especially since you've managed to make a promise that resulted in us losing money."

"I'm sorry, Nell."

He'd have given his inheritance to save Andy. But he'd lost his portion when he'd informed his father of his plans to marry Nell. Carter shoved his sweat-drenched hair from his brow. After getting this close to Nell again, he'd not lose her.

Eyes glittering like two hard sapphires in her face, she poked his chest. "You gambled. And lost."

Rage rose within him only to be squashed by a peace pressing through him in waves. "Never expected you to be so unforgiving. So uncharitable. So unlike the God you speak of." The One whose arms he'd finally returned to.

Her eyes searched his face, darting about as though to decipher a message he didn't wish to hide.

"I hoped to gain your acceptance, again. Instead, God is the One who receives me as I am. Something you seem unable to do."

Nell squeezed the letter from the Sargeants so hard, it crinkled. "I suppose you have extended that same charity toward Mariah. Yet you refused her son permission to stay." She lifted her chin.

Carter squared his shoulders. "I don't judge Mariah. Keeping the boy here is different."

"His name is Coleman. And he needs a safe home."

"Quite, but not here." How would he manage the many questions his nephews were sure to have?

"You speak of Christian love yet you separate him from his mother? His cousins?"

"It's not that simple, Nell." The responsibility of raising these boys into worthy men rested heavily upon his shoulders.

"Yes, it is." She stuck her index finger in his face.

He grasped her hand, didn't want to argue like this. "I can't bring him here."

Icy blue eyes frosted him. "He's with Andy at the kennels as we speak."

"Here? Now? How could you?" He repeated her own words back.

She spun away, shoving her invitation into her pocket.

"Nell, please, think of my situation." But her stormy face suggested she didn't care how he felt or what he thought.

Daniel, the Sargeant's former son-in-law, was likely behind the request. Had she even considered that possibility? "Don't go. Let's talk about this."

"I'm done talking." She barreled out the door.

Cornelia almost knocked Macy over. Already self-recrimination for arguing with Carter assailed Cornelia, but she was so angry she swept it aside. "Macy, I have something for you. Can you come to the cabin later?"

"Ain't you stayin' up here now?"

"No. Not anymore." Not ever again. But she still needed the job so there would be fences to mend later.

"All right. Do ya need some dinner fixin's?"

"Yes, thank you—enough for three." Because the boy's uncle wouldn't have him stay at the Great House.

"Mr. Davis comin'?"

She couldn't talk with Hayes about it. Mariah had her promise. She was to speak with him first. "No, and please don't say anything to him. Tell him Andy and I want time alone at the cabin tonight."

"He ain't around right now anyway."

"Where is he?"

"He got business with some of them schoonermen down south of us, near Williamsburg."

"I see." Was Hayes yet rounding up vessels to protect them? "Mariah should be here shortly."

"That's good." Her friend's green eyes shone the same color as the dark magnolia leaves behind her. "I got somethin' I want to tell her. You, too, when I bring your victuals down." Macy's pretty face shone.

"Happy news, I hope."

"The best."

Cornelia nodded and turned. Her own happy news, God's provision of the Pleasant land, evaporated like rain on hot August days. All the joy gone up like steam from the heat of her anger.

Lord, help me forgive Carter. Help him know his heart. Thank you, Lord that he has found his way back to you. Don't let me be a further stumbling block to him. Help him be free to start the life You have planned for him. Amen.

Andy and Coleman finished their meager meal and helped Cornelia clean up. Afterwards, the duo washed up again and performed other chores before they'd played several rounds of checkers. Mariah still hadn't arrived nor had Macy.

"Can we play your dulcimer, Sis?"

She assented and the two took turns, each laughing at how awful the other one sounded.

"Sounds like a chicken bein' tortured, Cole." Andy cackled at his own joke.

As she compared the two boys' sizes, Cornelia decided to give up her bigger bed to them.

"Miss Gill, I'm ever so grateful for your hospitality." In the dying sunlight flickering through the window, Cornelia gasped as something of young Daniel appeared in Cole's face. She covered her mouth, embarrassed by her reaction. It wasn't Cole's fault if Daniel was his sire. But perhaps it was a trick of the light. He did also resemble Anne and Mariah's father, whose image hung at the Great House, a great deal.

She sat by the window and darned socks while the two boys settled at the table, playing cards in hand. Before long, fatigue threatened. She yawned. Two heads began to sink as the boys finished another game of Whist.

"Bedtime, boys."

When the duo didn't move, she shooed them like chickens. Both giggled and ran past her toward the bed. She laughed and went to tuck them in for the night.

"I love you, Andy. I've missed you." Chains snapped free on her heart. She hugged him close.

Her brother held her there. "I missed ya, too." He didn't have to say the unspoken words—she knew he loved her, too.

She covered the boys with Grandmama's special quilt, the one Cornelia been saving for a wedding that would never be. She kissed Andy on his forehead.

When Coleman watched with wide eyes, she laid a hand on his dark locks and the other on Andy's lighter ones. "Lord, bless these boys. Give them peace. Heal them, Lord, of any illness or..."

Heartache.

"...heartache, Lord. In Jesus's precious name, Amen."

When she opened her eyes, Cole's yearning glance met hers.

I should kiss him, too.

"Cole, how about a kiss goodnight for you?"

His smile, as he sat up, affirmed the gentle nudge God had given her. She leaned over Andy, and pressed her lips to Cole's brow. He smelled of fresh hay, sunshine, and puppies.

She exhaled and left the room, taking her worries with her to the front porch, to rock away.

The setting sun was a giant red apple in the sky. Fruit soon would be collected from the crabapple trees around the old stone house. If something in the cabin was causing Andy's breathing problems, as Dr. Quinlain suggested, might they repair the Stone House and live there? What kind of money would it take to repair the house—particularly the chimney, window, and doors?

With the Pleasant house farther from the Great House, she wouldn't have to see Sally Danner. No, make that Sally Williams, prancing about on the lawn. Hot tears pricked her eyes as she recalled how she'd treated Carter.

He had no business selling their dog. What if her brother became ill again? Tomorrow she'd visit the Sargeants and pray for their generosity, for Andy's sake.

Chapter Twenty-Eight

Re-reading the invitation from the Sargeants the next morning fanned the embers of Cornelia's anger. After feeding and walking the dogs, she collected and cooked eggs for the boys and left them to clean up. She headed up to speak with Hayes.

Upon arrival at the Flanker, Mariah beamed—one arm firmly clasped in Hayes' and the other hand clutching her broad-brimmed straw hat. Adorned in a cotton print dress, her appearance was reminiscent of Grandmama Lucia—particularly the peacock-and-floral patterned skirt Mariah wore.

"How's Cole?" Mariah's tense smile quivered.

Hayes cleared his throat. "You goin' visitin' today, Nelly? Carter said you were mighty angry with him."

"Still am." Cornelia crossed her arms. She'd rather stay with Andy. But she'd already sent her response, and the couple would expect her for dinner.

"Mariah and I want to spend time with all the boys today." Hayes squeezed the petite woman's hand.

Cornelia blinked. God worked in wondrous ways. If her cousin accepted Mariah, who had squandered her entire fortune and born a child outside of wedlock, couldn't Cornelia forgive Carter his wastrel ways following his injury? He'd spent only his own income not that of anyone else. And if Lee chose to pay for Carter's schooling, so be it.

Her heart ached that Carter hadn't commanded Sally to stop sending messages. Her stomach clenched. "I'm off to get ready."

"Might be a storm brewin'—if Carter is right."

Cornelia scanned the sky. Birds twittered, some songbirds trilling in the bushes nearby. Gardenia blooms lent their scent as the sun rose over the brick buildings in the quadrant.

"Maybe. Maybe not."

"Want Mr. Squires to take you in my carriage?"

"'Tis a short distance." She'd had the perverse notion of riding horseback. "Only a dinner invitation."

One of Hayes's free men carried a battered leather bag up the stairs. Why was Mariah's case being toted into the Flanker?

Red splotches formed atop Hayes' high cheekbones. "Best for Coleman and his ma to stay here."

Macy emerged from the laundry, five yards away, and moved to join them, rubbing her hands against her apron. "We washed all the osnaburg cloth, Missy. Gonna dry it good before we cut cloth into pants for the menfolk."

Hayes exchanged a glance between the two.

"I sold little Minnie, or rather swapped her, for yardage of osnaburg at the mercantile."

"Liked that little runt." He rubbed his chin.

"I know." She avoided his accusing eyes. "Me, too, but she took right to her new owner."

One of the Wenham freed slave families exited the kitchen, on the other side of the quadrant. If Cornelia hadn't known who they were, she'd have assumed they were poor farmers from the countryside.

Her friend followed Cornelia's gaze. "If'n only all folks could be glad with changes."

"Macy, would ya run yonder and ask my man to take Nelly to the Sargeants?"

"You askin' or tellin'?" Fine features tightened further with each defiant word.

Prickles raced up Cornelia's back. Lighter-skinned than herself or Mariah, Macy was a slave nonetheless. Cornelia held her breath.

"Darlin', if it was up to me, everythin' ya did would be your free choice."

"I got work to do." Macy's features pulled in tightly, like a child about to cry. Head held high, her friend strode toward the Great House, her posture making her look more the lady of the house than Cornelia and Mariah combined.

Seated at the Sargeant's long mahogany table, its Chippendale chairs gleaming, unease crept over Cornelia. Outside the wind kicked up, tossing bits of tree branches and errant leaves into the full banked wall of windows.

"Obadiah, serve Miss Gill some crab bisque."

The server, white gloved hands steady, lifted the silver ladle and poured a generous portion into the monogrammed gold and white china bowl. Back home in the cabin, how many nights had she, Pa, and Andy eaten squirrel stew from Ma's chipped mug?

"Thank you."

Edythe Sargeant's eyebrows rose in question. "I'm not sure what has detained Chase."

"Chase Scott?" The delicious soup almost didn't make it beyond her lips. Cornelia forced herself to swallow.

Mason Sargeant scowled. "It's the storm brewing, you fool woman—can't you see?"

The matron tittered and raised her teacup as though to hide her face. Poor woman—no lady should be treated in that manner.

Outside, trees bent to and fro in the rising wind.

"He was our daughter's..." The man's wide brow, plastered with salt-and-pepper curls in the Napoleonic style, furrowed, "brother-in-law, Daniel's brother Chase," Mrs. Sargeant supplied.

"Yes—Reverend Scott's youngest grandson. He's the one who wants a pup for his brother to take back to Kentucky."

Cornelia's appetite fled. Her last dog to go with Daniel? She swallowed hard.

"Hopefully he'll depart very soon." Edythe Sargeant's angry tone left no doubt as to her opinion of Daniel.

At Mr. Sargeant's glare, the matron lowered her eyes to her soup. "We didn't approve of the marriage but what was done was done."

When had Daniel spent any time with their daughter? She a few years younger than Cornelia.

"Forgive me." Lord, do forgive my nosiness. "But until recently, I didn't realize Daniel had married one of your daughters." Grace had been young. Seeing their cheeks redden, Cornelia hastily added, "And I'm so very sorry for your loss. I just learned of her death..." And of their grandchild's demise as well.

Clearing his throat, Mr. Sargeant waved the slave away who was refilling his water goblet. He set his napkin on the table and rose to go to the windows.

"We had only the one child." The woman's voice barely carried to where Cornelia sat.

Cornelia shouldn't have inquired. "I'm very sorry. Please forgive my questions."

Mason Sargeant closed the interior shutters. His broad face relaxed an instant later as he sat down again. "That's better."

"Chase doesn't want his brother to return to Kentucky empty-handed." Edythe Sargeant lifted her eyes to Cornelia's. "That's why he wants us to get a dog for Daniel."

"Humph, wish he'd gone there without our girl. Then she'd be alive right now. Like Miss Gill here." Candlelight illuminated the moisture in Mr. Sargeant's eyes. He grazed his nose with his jacket sleeve. "She was but thirteen-years-old when she ran off with him."

Cornelia flinched as a larger piece of debris hit the window closest to her. "Oh."

Patting her husband's hand, Mrs. Sargeant's eyes fixed on Cornelia, silently begging her to ignore the private moment. Cornelia stared down at her lap, at the blue silk of Anne's dress beneath the fine linen napkin. Daniel had stolen her concept of herself for over a decade, but no more. And he'd taken much more from this couple. The bisque curdled in her stomach. These people's daughter had been only thirteen. And Daniel had to have taken her to Kentucky within days of Cornelia refusing him. What had transpired? She'd probably never know.

More limbs thumped against the house.

She wished she were at home in the cabin. Had Andy pulled the shutters closed on their one window? Had he secured the door? Made sure the kennels had been boarded over for the night? The image of the massive live oaks outside, limbs swaying in the wind, quashed her desire to leave.

"Perhaps we should hurry dinner, my dear, and remove ourselves to the study?" Edythe Sargeant's lined face added more furrows as the skies outside grayed and a gust of wind howled.

"Obadiah, instruct the kitchen to deliver the courses now."

At the stricken look on the servant's face, Cornelia spoke up. "Excuse me, Mr. Sargeant, but they might not be ready—if the house slaves..." She'd never called Macy that, but it was what she was. "...were told to serve them in a certain order." That much she did know from having sat in Mama Jo's kitchen during many a festivity at the Great House.

Mason Sargeant's face reddened at her remark. "Obadiah," he snapped, "instruct Cook to send anything ready."

"Yessir."

Perhaps it was best if Cornelia kept her comments to herself. No longer hungry and interested only in maintaining some sense of decorum, she tried one of Mariah's maneuvers, fixing a pleasant smile on her face. "You have a beautiful home and I appreciate your invitation."

She lowered her head over her bowl, pretending to sip her soup.

"What does Daniel need with a purebred hound?" Sargeant slurped his soup. "A frontier dog requires no pedigree."

"And if Daniel is practicing law, why does he need to hunt?" Edythe's plaintive tone begged her husband's approval. Strands of hair fell loose about the woman's neck as she bobbed her head to prove her point.

"Exactly." Mason's gruff voice prodded Cornelia's own doubts.

Edythe's small fingers wrapped around her crystal goblet. "I don't think he's a lawyer at all but a farmer, like Gracie wrote."

"And a poor one at that, from what she said." He harrumphed. "At least his brother has some gumption. Good of Chase to check on us so regularly, too."

246

Beeswax candles lit brightly and flickered in the numerous candelabra in the room. Whale oil lamps illuminated the corners, defining its expansiveness. For the first time in some while, Cornelia felt small. Had this couple's only daughter Grace been intimidated by her blustering father and unsupported by her mother? What would it have been like to have grown up in a home so full of strife?

Outside the hounds of Hades, Daniel's dogs perhaps, chased the wind. The man had once pursued her like prey until Carter, on a return home from school, put him in his place. If Carter hadn't intervened, would she now be dead? She shouldn't have argued with Carter. Shouldn't be here.

"You'll have to stay the night, my dear." Relief seemed to tinge Edythe's words.

Was she glad to not be alone with this man? Mr. Sargeant rarely brought his wife to church—perhaps twice a year.

"Certainly." Mason motioned the slave to serve Cornelia first but she had no appetite.

"Thank you."

Obadiah's dark eyes widened.

"You're welcome, Miss Gill," Edythe answered for Obadiah.

The slave quickly turned to his master. "Sir?"

Mason aimed his thick digits at his plate, and the slave carried the fragrant roast squab to him.

"Your favorite, dear." Edythe's head wavered as though she feared her husband's disapproval.

He beamed at her. "Of course."

Was this how a lady was treated in her own house? The master's wishes considered first before the guest's or the spouse's?

If Cornelia never married, if it never was to be, she had God. And the Lord was sufficient, and she His precious child. She needed to stop chafing beneath His direction, stop insisting on her independent notions, and allow Him to lead.

My yoke is easy, my burden light.

Later, settled in a guest room, Cornelia splashed water onto her face from the china bowl and patted dry. Her frightened face reflected in the mirror above the spindly stand. She grasped the candlestick and went to the high bed. Setting the candle on the sconce shelf, she lifted her chemise

247

and mounted the three steps into the bed, the wind's wail and the pelting rain a cacophony.

Beneath the smooth sheets and under the satin spread, she longed for the pine-scented quilt that Grandmama had stitched with her own hands and the feel of her brother as she hugged him good night and kissed his smooth cheek.

Thank you, Lord, for sparing Andy. Keep him and all those at Dogwood safe.

Carter's face loomed so real in her mind that her chest heated as though he were present. *Forgive my thoughts, Lord, and heal the breech between my old friend and myself. Permanently. Amen.*

Chapter Twenty-Nine

Another nightmare invaded Carter's sleep. The crack of the boom. The fall of the large mast breaking in the storm. The slamming of the wood onto the deck. Men screaming in agony. His intense pain. The blood, the wet, the cold, and the darkness. Carter sat up in his bed, blinking sleep from his eyes. And he heard it again—an explosion and a slight shaking of the house.

"Oh Lord, what is it?"

He half-expected God to answer him as he threw off his bedcovers. Moving to the windows, jagged lightning backlit the drapes, etching a swirl in the fabric. He threw the fabric aside and opened the window, then unlatched the exterior shutters, water dripping from them. A thunder bolt illuminated two massive felled pines and a third tilting toward the Gill home.

Boom!

The tree crashed down atop the cabin. Right where Nell slept. Nausea welled up.

"No! My God, no." He fumbled with lighting the lamp, his hands shaking. *Lord, she's the best thing in my life.* Carter willed his stiff leg to hurry as he stepped into the hall. Edward's head popped out of his door.

"Uncle Carter, a tree fell on the Gills' house."

"I know, I viewed it." *Lord, if you have any mercy at all, let her live.* "I'm going to check on Nell." If somehow she survived, he'd tell her how he felt. He'd sever any communication with Sally.

"She ain't there," Andy's voice called out.

Carter breathed in hope. "How do you know?"

"Sissy would've brung me home if she'd come back. Miss Mariah told me to sleep here. I 'spect Sis slept at the Sargeants' house."

Heart hammering, Carter drew in a slow deep breath. "I pray you're correct."

"We're coming, too." Edward went to the window.

Carter tugged on his pants. "The sun will rise soon." *Thank God.*

Edward swiveled away from the window. "I've got my shoes on. Go get yours, Andy."

"Don't need 'em. I'll go barefoot."

Carter sighed. He didn't need the boys to see if indeed Nell was inside. He shoved into his riding boots, which better supported his leg than his low ones. He needed to hurry.

Stiffness soon eased from his leg as he reached the first landing. Eddie clattered downstairs.

"Hold the rail, boy. We don't need you injuring yourself on this dark stairwell."

"Yessir."

Andy was behind them, a little slower than Carter as they descended. "The others ain't comin'. They're sleepin'—Nemi, too."

Not Macy?

The trio headed to the door, Edward knocking over the mail tray in the process.

"Sorry, oh I forgot to tell you—Mr. Scott called on us today."

Carter unlocked the door and threw it open. Rain pelted his face as they exited. Daniel had nerve showing up at the house. "What did he want?"

They headed down the stairs as a unit, Edward at his right side. "Didn't say."

Dawn came dimly, chasing the storm away. Lightning ceased and torrential rain slowed to a trickle as dark thunderclouds moved northwest.

They strode through the wet grass. Ahead, Eddie darted forward.

"Can you run, Carter?"

"Yes, Lord willing, I'll try."

"I'm willin', too."

Surprise at the ease with which he moved yet concerned for the boy lagging behind him, Carter continued across the field.

When he reached the house, Edward trotted to the back before returning, red faced. "Uncle Carter, there's a woman in there."

Oh God, no. Carter threw himself hard into his run, pain returning in its first jolt in weeks. Still he coursed on. A thirty-foot pine crushed the roof and threatened to divide the cabin, resting as it was upon the door jamb.

"Sissy!" Andy's cry carried through the mist.

Carter ran to the back, where the window had been. He heard sobbing from within. The concave roof leaned in precipitously.

"Andy—muster all the help you can at the stables." The building was closer and wouldn't tax the boy's newfound health. "Edward, run to the slave quarters and get help."

The boy took off like a cannon ball.

Carter bent to retrieve a thick limb to use on the window. 'Twas a staff. No—an Indian war club. He swallowed. Few men in these parts owned one. He swung it against the window, breaking the glass.

"Nell? Can you hear me?"

Cries carried more clearly now. He pulled off his shirt and wrapped it around his hand. Pulling the old panes free, he then turned his head away as he smashed the wooden casings that held the mullioned window together. With a leap, he thrust inside the cabin, the creaking sound of the tottering roof cautioning him.

"Hold on. I've come for you."

Dank mildew odor from the broken walls caused him to cough. He edged toward the bed, aware of the give in the ancient pine floor beneath his feet.

"I's hurt." Macy's pitiful voice broke his heart.

"Macy?" What was she doing in there?

She didn't answer. How could he move her? "How bad are your injuries?" He had to help her. A stifled sob repeated. Something tangled in

251

his feet as he stepped closer, and he lifted his boots free from what appeared to be a yellow gown on the floor.

Carter bent over the bed, dawn's light revealing blood on the patchwork quilt, but there were no gashes on her face nor arms.

The woman drew the covers up around her neck and turned from him. "Don't touch me," she hissed.

What was she doing here?

"We have to get you out before the cabin caves in."

"I needs my dress."

Had someone harmed her? Defiled her? "I'll wrap the quilt around you." He leaned toward her but she shook her head hard.

He grabbed the gown and passed it to her. "Can you get up? Can you pull that on?"

Rotating with difficulty toward him, Macy's eyes begged him to let her clothe herself. Tears dripped to the floor as she nodded.

"Hurry, Macy." He turned his back to her. "Come to the window and I'll help you get free."

Cornelia maneuvered the cart around debris in the road, mist cloaking her. A pack of hounds and horsemen could have trampled the woods, brush, and grass that lined either side of the roadway. Sun reflected from puddles in the road, belying the storm's ferocity.

Dread tugged at the back of Cornelia's consciousness as she neared home and turned onto the long narrow drive to the cabin. Those big pines. What havoc had they wreaked? They should have been cut, but Grandmama liked having them around the cabin.

A pack of hounds yelped. One lone dog split from those clustered near the Dogwood horse barn in the distance. Tonnie headed toward her as fast as his legs allowed. Hayes emerged from the shadows and waved to her.

She turned her attention toward the cabin. Where there should have been three tall spikes, there were none. She lowered her gaze to the fields and bushes. All three pines were down—one smack dab in the middle of her house. Cornelia fought the bile rising in her throat. Tree limbs, splintered as though a giant snapped them in his hands, impeded her progress down the lane. She secured the horse and buggy as Tonnie reached her.

Yipping, he halted. She motioned him to her. "Good boy." She stroked his silky fur and allowed him to nuzzle her hand. "Nothing there for you, boy."

She lifted her skirts and the two ran, the rich scent of earth greeting her nostrils as the wet grass in the field soaked through her shoes. She kicked the encumbrance off.

A boy pulled a chest between the garden and the crushed cabin and sat. "Andy?" *Thank you, Lord.*

"Sissy, the house is gone." He rose and ran toward her. Tonnie charged at him, and her brother allowed the hound to knock him down to the ground, where he licked him with abandon. She couldn't help laughing even as tears of relief from pent-up anxiety fled her eyes.

Andy leaned up on his elbows in the muddy grass. "I got my treasures out, Sis—my figures that Pa whittled for my chess set."

Besides her brother, what were her earthly treasures? Grandmama's quilts, the few letters her mother had written to her father, the sketch of their great-grandfather? They didn't matter—only that her brother was well.

Sniffing, she dropped to her knees and pulled Andy to her, stroking the back of his head. "You weren't out here, were you?"

The cabin creaked behind him. He pulled free. "Nah—I slept with Eddie."

Thank you, Lord.

"But Macy came out here with someone."

"What?" She froze.

"She'll be all right, Carter carried her yonder to Mama Jo."

"Macy was inside our cabin?" Her stomach squeezed. What had she been doing there? A miracle her friend wasn't killed.

Birdsong and chatter indicated some of God's creatures benefited from the storm. Worms and water would be plentiful. She now had no home. Independence had flown off with the geese heading south. By arguing with Carter, had she placed a barrier between them?

Carter exited through the space where the window had been, his back bare, arms full of quilts. Her heart gave a little flip. He set the stack atop a wooden bench near Andy.

"Thanks, Carter. I knew Sissy'd want those."

Her face heated as Carter closed the distance between them. He needed a shirt on. "Nell, thank God you weren't here."

Strong arms crushed her to his warm chest, matted with dark hair that pressed against her cheek. A strange sensation of longing sped through her, down to her bare toes.

"My home is gone." Her voice squeaked and her lips trembled.

He pulled back and touched his thumb to her lower lip.

"My love," his husky voice held a promise, his breath sweet, "if I had a home, I…"

He leaned his head against hers, the sound of her heart hammering in her ears, closing out all other sounds. The permanence she'd prayed for—was this God's answer? Could two people without a house between them make a home together some day? She sucked in in a shaky breath.

Her home was with him, wherever he was. Conviction brought more tears. The creaking she heard behind her was of the chains being broken on the chest where she'd buried all her fears.

Eddie appeared behind his uncle's back. "We'll put you and Andy up, Miss Cornelia, don't you worry."

Carter wiped tears from beneath her eyes. Warmth spread through her. He kissed her cheek where wetness lingered then pulled her back into his strong arms, his mouth moving to her ear. "There's no coming about with the ship after this. We'll both seek port together, somewhere."

His masculine scent filled her senses. She loved him. With all her being, she needed this man. Forever.

Managing a laugh, she pulled back to look into his handsome face. "Am I a recruit? Or are you officially courting me?"

A grin covered his flushed face. "I am."

Riotous emotions fought to be unleashed. "Well then, could you please make sure my family Bible, beneath my bed, gets brought out?"

Once, when they were younger, she'd shown him the spot in the Bible for family names. She recalled how she'd pointed to the spot where she'd told him their names should be.

254

The center of his eyes deepened to obsidian. If the boys weren't nearby, he'd likely have kissed her. Her lips tingled.

"Indeed, Miss Gill." He brought his index finger to his lips, his touch warm against her cool hand. "'Tis my heart's desire is to enter my name in that fine tome."

Was that his proposal? Cornelia's heart beat faster, a slight dizziness overtaking her. She'd strive to be a lady worthy of him.

"Carter, might I ask for a wedding gift?" But would her request be within Carter's power to grant?

Chapter Thirty

Heat radiated up in waves as Carter trotted his brown mare into what passed for a town. They still hadn't gotten a straight answer from Macy as to what had occurred at the Gill's cabin. Regardless, he rode into Charles City to implement his plan and fulfill a promise to obtain her freedom.

Sweat trickled down his face in rivulets. He'd managed the entire jaunt with minor leg discomfort. As he slowed the horse to a walk, mosquitoes swarmed. No amount of shrugging or swatting away would shake them. He dismounted, removed his hat and waved away the insects feasting on his flesh. He tied Bess to the hitching rail.

"Williams, welcome," James Barrett, the attorney, hailed him from outside the mercantile. Exactly who Carter sought out. Hope stirred.

"Mr. Barrett, I've come to speak with you." Carter waved gnats away and stepped closer to the lawyer.

"About clerking under me?" Barrett squared his broad shoulders. "I was beginning to think I'd have to come out to Dogwood and beg you to do so."

Carter's senses launched to sea.

The country lawyer chuckled. "Don't stand there gape-mouthed, come to my office and we'll discuss the terms before my next appointment arrives."

Carter had not seriously considered clerking until he'd completed his studies. But if God offered this choice, who was Carter to turn Him down?

"You understand I haven't completed my studies, sir?"

"Nor had my clerk, Richard Lightfoot, but he's off to the Navy."

Where I'd yet be if not for my injury.

Several women passing by on the walkway greeted the attorney cordially.

"Ladies?" Barrett removed his hat. When they were alone, the attorney returned his attention to Carter. "Lightfoot left me high and dry. He and Chase Scott, who was supposed to clerk once he'd finished interning with Jackson Forrester." He fixed his blue-gray eyes on Carter as they moved further down the walk. "You've heard about all those terrible goings on—correct? Forrester was your father's attorney."

"No, I hadn't." Carter blew out a breath. "What happened?"

"Forrester is dead."

Dead? "What?"

He glanced at a wagon rolling by, heading toward the court house. "Murdered," Barrett's deep voice dropped even lower.

Dear God. "I just met with him not long ago."

"Forrester received notice of investigation into his legal malfeasance."

Was a will, in which Lee acknowledged Coleman as son, somewhere in Forrester's office? Scandal could ruin Carter's opportunities. Never mind that it wasn't true. A lump formed in his throat.

Would Barrett take him on if the Williams' name was put into ill repute? Within another ten paces they arrived at the lawyer's office. The small lobby overflowed with Italian art that contrasted with the rustic cotton rug adorning the wide-planked oak floor. Law books mingled with tomes on philosophy and art, both sandwiched between heavy marble busts of Aristotle, Plato, and other scholars.

"Hard to believe Forrester, so educated, blackmailed his clients for so long without a challenge."

"What did he do?"

The tall man waved toward an arched door. "He forged signatures. Didn't file documents in court. Would produce several wills and bribe someone disinherited to get what he wanted from them. And he's suspected of starting the fire in Yorktown that burned the courthouse."

"Who brought charges?"

Carter followed the robust man into the office and closed the curved door behind them.

A well-appointed room was fragranced by clusters of crimson roses set into a creamy alcove. \

"Professor Danner, your mentor, for one." Barrett gestured to a narrow high-backed settee, then seated himself behind the desk. "He has a copy of a will he consulted with your father about."

Carter took the seat indicated, his heart heavy. "Sir, I have known for some time of my disinheritance. 'Tis nothing Forrester could have gained from altering."

Barrett's fingers formed a steeple in front of him. "Not sure he did. Danner told me you were the heir unless you engaged in certain stipulated behaviors. You're a bachelor, correct?"

His head throbbed. "For now. I intend to marry soon."

"The woman's not a descendant of Lucia Pleasant, though?"

Nell's grandmother?

"She had only one child, who had two children. There is one female descendant—the manager's daughter at Dogwood Plantation."

Carter head was spinning. "Pardon me, but you quite overwhelm me. I don't understand…" Why hadn't Professor Danner told him? Why hadn't Lee? Was Carter indeed still an heir? If so, how could he give up Nell? He wouldn't.

"Forgive my abruptness, Carter. You came here seeking legal counsel—is that correct?"

"I have the right to make decisions about Dogwood, correct?" If he were heir, he could do so regardless. To obtain Macy's freedom would legally be considered disposing of an asset. The use of those words was vile. Bitter regret filled his mouth. "I wish to bring about what I believe my father and brother intended, but failed to do." And didn't wish upon his conscience. Nell requested her friend's freedom as a wedding present—which had been his own desire. "To free our slave, Macy, and send her North."

"Have you given this decision full consideration?"

"Indeed, for some time." Carter leaned forward, explaining his concerns and wishes. The senior attorney advised him.

258

"And that's how it would work," Barrett concluded.

"I see. Thank you."

"Now, how about my own agenda?"

"Certainly. I would love to hear what you propose."

Scarcely minutes seemed to have passed as Barrett made his offer, the clock chiming the hour as though in agreement.

Barrett rose. "Consider my proposition. I'll handle your request, as well, and send papers out to Dogwood."

"Thank you." Carter shook his head slightly, awed by God's provision. Now to speak to Edward and Macy and to make arrangements.

Heavy footsteps rumbled through the outer office.

Barrett crossed the room. "My client, I believe."

At his approach, the office door vibrated as the newcomer pounded. Barrett swung the door open.

Hayes Davis, fist raised, stared, eyes wide. "The British burned our capital!"

Muscles in Carter's neck knotted tighter than the silk band tied around it. "Richmond?" That close? "Dear God, no."

"The capital of our country, men. My friend, Madison's, home has been burned."

The flowers in Barrett's wallpaper closed in on Carter. In the alcove, the features on the statuette of the huntress, Diana, became sharper. He and Barrett stared at the newcomer.

"Yes, indeed, America's government has been attacked." Hayes slapped the attorney on his arm.

"I didn't think it would come to this." Barrett's deep voice snapped Carter back to attention.

He had to ensure Nell's and the boys' safety.

Hayes rocked back on his heels. "I need settlin' a few things before I go. Gotta do what I can to help James."

Madison and he were on a first name basis?

When Barrett simply stared, Hayes added, "And Dolley, of course. But I've my own items to attend to first."

"Come in and sit, Mr. Davis."

Carter wiped the moisture from his brow. His issues seemed trivial now. Not to Macy, of course. He touched Hayes' sleeve. "How can I help? Did anyone say what is needed?" The siren of the sea called to him.

Hazel eyes perused his face. "Get the word out and seek more men to enlist. Round up and body with a sea-worthy vessel, too."

Carter could make the militia circuit if he paced himself. "I'll take River Road." On land. But the whole while he'd glimpse the beckoning waves.

"Good. We'll talk tonight back at Dogwood."

The heat and the ride had consumed Carter's energy but the news billowed his sails.

Barrett's knuckles bulged around the top of his chair. "There's a shortage of lead for bullets. Anyone who can spare lead implements needs to bring what they have to town. A manufacturer in Maryland—"

"Maryland ain't good." Hayes rubbed his jaw. "Best keep it local in Virginia. Supply the militias from here. James, President Madison that is, has my free men and a passel of horses I sent. I can get the shot there, too, if we have the balls made up."

The Henry family. "The uncle of a former classmate owns a munitions works in Richmond. I'll make sure I stop at his home."

"Do that."

Carter pulled the door closed, his hands trembling. *Oh God, please strengthen me and my country now.*

Cornelia still hadn't spoken to Macy about what had happened to her at the cabin. She found Andy in the dining area of the Guest House. "Where's Macy?"

"Don't know. Think Mama Jo is still tendin' her."

Was she hurt so badly? Carter hadn't said so. "Did you send her down to the cabin for something the other day, Andy?"

"Nah." He swiped an apple from the bowl. Munching, he eyed her then set the fruit down.

"What is it?"

"I don't miss the cabin." Andy gazed at the papered walls punctuated by gilded mirrors and sconces. "Breathe better here."

"The logs were rotting. Could be what made you sick. Water had accumulated under the house."

"We gonna live here in the Guest House?"

"We can for now."

"Eddie and I can stay after you two get married—when there ain't no guests."

She laughed. "I don't think so." And Carter was courting her but he'd not yet asked her to wed him.

"Aw, come on, Sis."

She wanted to find her injured friend. "I'm going to bring Macy here. I'll put her in the room facing the river." Her reality had altered—her cabin gone. Because she and Carter were courting, she would stay in the North Flanker Guest House with Andy until they wed.

There was nothing to deter them now, was there?

"What are you doing here, Daniel?" Mariah's strained voice carried through the wall of the guest room chamber where Cornelia tended Macy.

Her friend's eyes opened wide as Cornelia's heart began to hammer.

"Time to settle our accounts, Mariah. Old ones—long overdue."

Macy pushed Cornelia's hands from the covers as she sat up. "Mister Daniel be here."

Cornelia's throat constricted. Where was Cole? Blood pounded in Cornelia's ears.

Tinkling laughter carried through the thin wall as Mariah responded. "Why, whatever can you mean?"

Something heavy thumped on the floor, causing Cornelia to jerk. She edged toward the door. *Oh God, what am I to do?*

Wait. Be patient. Macy pulled her new day dress on.

"I'm here for my son. Our son." Daniel's volume increased.

Outside, the dogs barked. They'd lost their kennel and had been kept in the stable. *Please don't let that be the boys bringing the pack up here right now.*

"My son? You imagine he belongs to you?" Mariah's cool voice rose.

Macy slipped her feet into a pair of shoes. What was her friend doing?

"He's not Lees'." He punctuated his comment with a grunt.

261

Glancing around the room, Cornelia sought a weapon to use against Daniel. Nothing. Macy pulled several thick ginger curls free, framing her face. It couldn't be—was Daniel her beau?

"What happened between us ended long ago, Daniel."

"We can make up for lost time. Come to Kentucky with me and Cole. Be the mother to him that you should have been all these years, Mariah."

There was a pause but she couldn't hear Mariah's response.

"I'd take good care of you both."

Macy's lips parted. The young woman opened the door to the hall.

If Daniel was Macy's lover, yet he now begged Mariah to come with him, what kind of mess was that? Her friend's face revealed only stony resolve.

Cornelia trailed Macy out of the room.

"Coleman and I shall remain in the Commonwealth of Virginia—with my husband, who will be his adopted father. We were married this week." Mariah's voice, while clearer, wavered.

Stiffening at this declaration, Cornelia bumped shoulders with Macy as they stood in the dining room doorway. Daniel's eyes narrowed at Macy, then Cornelia, who punished the handful of her skirt she'd gathered.

When Daniel returned his gaze to her, Mariah tipped her chin up. "I prefer for you to address me as Mrs. Davis, not in such familiar terms."

"Familiar? A little too late to be discussing familiar." Daniel rose from the chair adjacent the South Carolina belle. "You've no right to keep my boy from me." Handsome features dissolved in sorrow, reminding Cornelia of the lonely boy he once was.

Macy fled, flinging the house door wide open. Was she afraid of Daniel?

"He's not your boy. He's mine," Mariah hissed.

As Daniel charged from the room, he knocked the chair over, breaking its back. Cornelia flinched and drew away so that he wouldn't ram into her.

A muscle in Daniel's jaw jumped. "We'll see about that," he muttered under his breath.

Cornelia hurried to Mariah and took hold of her trembling hands.

262

Once the door was slammed shut, a hall mirror fell—shattering into a million pieces.

Chapter Thirty-One

Dust flew as Hayes and his stallion galloped past Cornelia into the courtyard. Workers, clustered around the crowded greens, ceased their tasks to watch. Her cousin dismounted his horse, wrapped the reins around the hitching post, and wiped dust from his face.

With the dogs and the younger boys trailing, Cornelia hastened toward him.

"British attacked our nation's capital!" Hayes' shout carried. Even slaves at the laundry building could have heard him. All eyes on him, a hush settled over the yard.

Birdsong, the rustling of tree leaves, and a horse's whinny defied the silence. From the Flanker steps, Lazarus Freeman's boots clattered forward toward Hayes.

"Round up all my folks right quick." Hayes gestured around the rectangle.

"Yessir." The Orange County freedman set off toward a cluster of men from Pleasanton.

Mariah emerged from inside the Flanker, hands clutched together. She joined Hayes, who was indeed her husband now. They had wed earlier that week in a ceremony witnessed by Madame Favret and the headmaster of Cole's school—without so much as a by-your-leave to the Gills nor the Williamses.

"Cornelia, let's find the older boys and tell them." Mariah's flushed face belied the ease in her words.

After locating Eddie, Andy, and Cole, the two women gathered on a quilt, beneath the huge swamp oak. They fanned Albert and Lloyd, sleeping, and sipped cool apple cider, brought by Nemi earlier.

Crouched nearby, Andy stroked Lafe's head while Eddie and Cole chased Lex and Tonnie.

Crackling tension permeated Cornelia's body. She attempted to lighten the mood. "Almost like a picnic."

Mariah arched her eyebrows. "I assure you, my dear—this is no picnic."

Cornelia scarce could draw a full breath since Hayes's pronouncement. What might happen if the British continued on?

Within the hour, Hayes assembled the freedmen. "Those willin' to help, I've got a ship comin' within the next several days. Mr. Rousch offered to help. You'd supply the Americans."

"Serve with the navy?" called a tall man, crumpling his worn hat in his hands.

"No—privateers."

The James River, dotted by only a few watercraft, lay forbidding at the end of the lawn. *How must the citizens of Washington City feel to be invaded?* She stroked Albert's tousled hair and waved the fan more vigorously over the sleeping toddler.

A long dark arm shot up.

"John?"

"You be speakin' of piratin'?"

Hayes straightened and cracked his knuckles. "Some folks call privateers pirates—

I don't."

"Who gonna guarantee our pay?" Another man called out.

Hayes mashed his hat brim lower. "I will."

Mariah gasped.

"Turns out this is one thing I can do to support our cause. Friends from Orange County think I can do more by stayin' here. I'll send 'em what they need to fight off the British invaders."

A shard of sunlight glinted on the James River, taunting her. Would Carter return to his mistress, the sea? God couldn't be that cruel to take Carter from her now. Could He?

Such exhaustion hadn't overcome Carter since his Navy days. He'd ridden hard all day as he alerted families along River Road and asked for volunteers to combat the invaders. Leg pain overwhelmed him. He must stop. His mettle had been tested and was lacking.

Nathan Henry's home nestled beneath a circle of tamarinds. His mother would surely offer shelter. A kind woman, Mrs. Henry's brother-in-laws included Reverend Henry, from Carter's home church, who was a "dove", and the artillery owner in Richmond—a "hawk". With their country, their commonwealth, under attack it was time for all to come together as Americans and assert their independence for one final time and bring this war to an end.

Carter directed his horse toward the house. Outside, Nancy Henry, a handsome woman with fading auburn hair, swept dirt from her porch steps. "Welcome, Carter. We haven't seen you in a while."

"Too long, ma'am."

She set her broom aside then wiped her hands on her apron. "Come on in." She turned and entered the house. He followed her inside.

"Nathan home, ma'am?"

With a sigh she gestured to the parlor. "So you've come to recruit my son? He was helping at his uncle's artillery works but they've not the lead to continue."

God, what shall we do? No lead, no ammunition. And fields overrun with invaders. *My life is not my own. Lord, I release it fully to you—the One who created all. Oh God, Lord of my life, help us now.* Sweat ran in rivulets down his neck, absorbed by his neck cloth. Carter fumbled with it, untying the knot.

The lead roof at Dogwood. The gentle whisper stirred him to his core.

If they sold it, the military could make more ammunition and defend themselves. And bring needed cash to support his nephews. *Thank you, Lord.* How could he have been so blind and not seen before now?

Lean not on your own understanding.

Carter's lips trembled. "Ma'am, I need to get word to your brother. The lead in the roof on our Great House…" Pain ripped through his leg. He stifled his cry.

The woman's smile faltered. "Come sit." She ushered him to a chair in a small parlor. Mrs. Henry lit a lamp.

He lowered himself into the wingback chair. "Thank you."

"Let me get Nate." Plump hands folded together. "Young Bradley rode out earlier today. They talked a long time."

Carter took a slow breath. "I'd like to speak with them both."

"Nate's putting the animals in for the night. But I'll call him." She fluffed a pillow for Carter. "Time for supper. 'Twill be ready soon. And you must stay the night."

"If it is no trouble." He exhaled in relief at the offer.

Mrs. Henry dragged a footstool close and placed Carter's foot upon it. "'Tis too late to be meandering down these roads—lest you break your neck."

"Yes, ma'am. Thank you."

Boots clomped up the short hallway and ceased. "Carter, good to see you. Here to recruit me, eh?"

"Ah, 'tis true." Carter smiled as his stout friend entered the sitting room.

"Mother?"

"He's staying the night, dear."

"Thank you, Mum."

The matron gently squeezed Carter's arm. "Were you trying to say you wish to sell your lead roof? I can advise my brother."

"Yes, ma'am."

Giving her son a pointed look, Mrs. Henry sighed. "Would keep you busy here, son, instead of running off with the militia like your brother." She wiped a tear from her eye then left.

Nathan sat across from Carter and leaned forward. "Gads—forgot about your lead roof or I'd have bothered you for it long before now."

"Hadn't occurred to me until tonight." When he'd given God command of his heart.

His friend tapped his fingers on his thighs. "It's a sorry mess about Forrester's death but I hear many shall benefit. And it's glad I am—he stole my grandmother's estate from her."

"Truly?" He'd heard Forrester bought the Richmond property when Nathan's grandfather died.

"My grandmother was so distressed at the time, that she allowed Forrester to buy her home—lock, stock, and barrel. At a pittance of what it could have brought if the estate had been sold fairly, what with all the new building going on around near there."

"How did he manage that?"

"Forrester was Grandfather's attorney. When my grandfather died, Forrester told my grandmother he would 'help' her by taking it off her hands quickly. She came to live with us. When she found out what the property could have brought, Grandmother was heartbroken."

"That's despicable."

"Did you hear about Forrester's murder weapon?" Nathan's eyes widened. "A hunting knife. Old Reverend Scott's eldest grandson owned it—had his name on it. The priest claimed it'd been stolen—along with Reverend Scott's Indian war club."

Carter's leg spasmed and he doubled over.

"Are you all right?" Nathan made to rise but Carter gestured him to remain seated.

Daniel's knife had killed Forrester. And the club had been abandoned outside Nell's cabin. "The Scott family—had Forrester mishandled something for them?"

Nathan scratched his chin. "Chase's parents died long ago. I don't think Chase would have accepted Professor Danner's internship with Forrester if so."

Chase must have seen Lee's second will at Forrester's office. He likely told Daniel about Lee acknowledging Coleman as son. He cleared his throat. "I'll be clerking with James Barrett."

"Congratulations. Let's hope we can throw the Brits out first."

"And I'll be getting married." Though not till after the war was over.

Lamplight flickered across features that twitched in disbelief. "You're marrying? Not Sally?"

"No. I'll wed Cornelia Gill."

"The gal who came to the college and got you? The estate manager's daughter?" Nathan's mouth relaxed.

"Yes." He checked for censure in his friend's eyes and found none. "Nell and I shall wed."

He laughed. "I declare—you and Chase Scott are alike."

"How so?"

"He says he's marrying Sally."

On what would Chase support her? "His grandfather approved?" Reverend Scott had urged both boys to earn a living.

"Seems Chase's brother Daniel told Reverend Scott that he never plans to return to Virginia. Told him to name Chase full heir. At least that's what Chase claims—doesn't make sense to me, though."

Carter would be glad to see Daniel gone. Good riddance. Yet he was sorry the Scott brothers' parents had died when they were young. Their father had been the Scotts only child. Carter now raised his parentless nephews. *Dear God, help me do this job right.*

Had the investigators seen the two codicils yet? "Has anyone said what they found in Forrester's records?"

His friend averted his eyes for a moment. "Your father's will and your brother's were found atop his desk."

"I asked Mr. Barrett to send for them only this morning." It seemed a week ago.

"There were ashes in the fireplace."

"Too hot out for a fire." What had he burned?

Nathan returned his gaze. "Exactly."

He could hear his heart beating in his ears. Which one had burned?

Nathan's mobile features stilled. "I didn't want to say anything. Truth be told there is no way I believed the allegations. Carter—you're a suspect in the killing."

"What?" He tapped his fingertips on the table.

"You said your Father disinherited you."

"Yes."

"He hadn't. So why did you say that?"

"My father did cut me off—said I couldn't wed Cornelia." And Lee had never corrected that perception that Carter had been left out of the

269

will. He'd longed to make his sweetheart his wife then but not half as much as now.

"Did you ever see the will?"

"No. But Professor Danner asked me something that made me think he'd advised my father on it." Sally. Her father. They both saw something indicating Carter was to have received half the estate. That had to be it. And Barrett had indicated the same. Carter ran his tongue over his parched lips.

Wide, old-fashioned skirts swished against the doorframe as Nancy Henry appeared. "Time to wash up and have dinner. Nate—show Carter where the basin and towels are."

After a hearty meal of beef, cabbage, and carrots and a dense Irish bread, Carter's head drooped. Thank God Nathan hadn't brought up Forrester's death during dinner. He'd have enjoyed it more if his gut wasn't tied in the tightest sailor's knot he'd ever known.

Mrs. Henry removed their plates. "Show him to Michael's room. He's probably to Norfolk by now to sign up with your uncle's regiment. Pray the good Lord protects him."

Carter needed God's help, too. "Thank you for your kindness. I'll set off for home at sun rise."

"Come on." Nate escorted him down a narrow hall, candlelight flickering. "You can sleep in my brother's bed."

"Good thing you don't believe I'm a murderer."

Nathan's face bunched in disbelief, then he shook his head. "Don't fret about your horse. She's put up for the night." He lit the candle inside the sparsely furnished room. "Not as fancy as Dogwood but clean and dry."

"Thank you. I'm grateful for your hospitality."

He longed to tell Nell what he knew. But 'twas better to remain here the night. Truth be told, when she was sleeping so close by at the house, the nights had been almost unbearable—knowing only a short distance separated them.

Nathan clapped him on the shoulder. "Shall you marry before you join us?"

"It depends upon Nell's wishes." She wouldn't believe he'd murdered Forrester.

270

"If you've claim to half of Dogwood, I imagine it would be quickly." Nathan laughed.

Not humorous. His father sought to control Carter even now. "No son of mine shall wed a Pleasant." The will must contain the stipulation. Roger Williams didn't direct Carter's path. Not then and not now.

"Let's hope so. Good night." Nathan nodded and departed the room.

Years earlier, Carter accepted his father's disinheritance. Barrett's comments implied Father's decisions were impacted by old Mrs. Pleasant. The irascible old woman had tormented his father. Whenever she'd escaped her daughter's oversight, Mrs. Pleasant snuck up to the Great House to harass Father. It hadn't been Father's fault that he owned Dogwood. Nor was it Nell's responsibility for her grandmother's bizarre behavior. He finally sank into sleep, reliving the hurt his father had inflicted.

In the middle of the night, he awoke to crushing pain in his leg. Reenlistment—null, void. Was that God's will? Carter couldn't leave his nephews, regardless. If he perished, their devastation would be complete—Nell's as well.

Mariah looked skittish as a cat crossing a hot brick walk when Cornelia left her at the South Flanker. Both of their nerves were stretched taut. The Williams boys had run around like the banshees in her Scottish grandmother's tales. Grandmama Lucia had brought the phantoms to life—made the supernatural beings seem so real. Cornelia shivered. English and Scottish soldiers were her specters. Her grandmother's, too, during the revolution.

Evening crept closer. After checking with Mariah, Cornelia located Cole. The new bride's son and Andy cavorted with Lex, Lafe, and Tonnie. "Cole, your mother granted permission—you can stay with Andy and me tonight."

As Andy chased Cole, he called out, "Sis said we could share a room downstairs."

It wasn't her place to be granting permissions, but Carter hadn't returned. Her cousin warned that Carter might not get back that evening.

271

Where was he now? He shouldn't have pushed himself so hard—not with his bad leg only recently improved.

Nemi strolled by, a basket of linens in her arms. Muscles twitched around her mouth as though she longed to share a secret. The slave continued on to the main house, eyes now downcast. Would Carter's nephews mind the woman? Doubtful, but Macy was to stay with Cornelia until she fully recuperated.

Soon the sun nestled low, yet Andy and Coleman continued to gambol about like spring lambs. All Cornelia desired was sleep. She went inside, lit the candelabra, and sat in the parlor where she commenced to wind the yarn Hayes had given her. She hadn't knit anything since Pa had died.

Macy arrived, a bag tucked under her arm. "I's hopin' we can talk."

About what happened? "All right." She pointed to the settee.

"Those boys be wild. They ain't gonna sleep tonight." Macy clucked her tongue.

Cornelia laughed in agreement. She looked up from the rosy yarn when Macy sighed audibly.

"I wants to talk about Mariah and Daniel." She wrung her hands. "I knowed him when I be a child. 'Fore they brung me here."

"Are you feeling well enough for this?" If Daniel had harmed her, she didn't want Macy caused undue distress.

In the bright beeswax candlelit, her friend's luminous eyes glowed like Anne's emerald earrings. "I think I be all right."

As a child, Macy came to Virginia with Anne. Macy spent most of her time under the watchful eye of Mama Jo and up at the Great House.

"You know Carter and I both grew up with Daniel." Cornelia pulled the strands hard and tight around the ball.

"He a might older'n you, but younger than Missy Mariah." Macy rocked back and forth, on the velvet-upholstered bench, her hands wrapped across her stomach.

"True."

"I don't know that you gonna be all right hearing what I got to say."

"About Daniel?"

"And other things."

"Tell me."

"He always nice to me."

Cornelia's neck muscles tightened. "When?"

"When I young and he call on our father."

Their father. Cornelia wound the yarn in a crisscross pattern.

"We sisters—same father, Master Wenham. He a bad, bad man." Macy's arms trembled, causing her sleeves to flutter. "But Daniel like him. He don't know what kind of man he be."

Macy continued rocking and stared at the floor. "Missy Mariah—she like Daniel. He a fine young man, she use to say."

Knowing eyes pierced hers. Cornelia ceased winding. "But she was engaged to Lee."

Shaking her head, Macy laughed. "He not man enough for her, she say. She try and get him drunk and…"

Heat stole into Cornelia's cheeks. "I think I know, go on…"

"She screamin' and carryin' on when Mr. Lee say he ain't gonna marry her. Daniel say he marry her." She opened her eyes wide. "He ain't but seventeen-years-old and no prospects."

"Was he in love with her?"

"No. I think he like to help people. I don't know. He talk about you, too, all the time to her. Cornelia Gill—I knowed your name long before I come here."

She crushed the ball of yarn in her hands as Macy spoke. "He say his grandpappy tell Lee's papa you might end up just like your grandmamma Lucia—crazy as a loon. Old Reverend Scott tell them boys no man in his right mind marry that crazy lady's granddaughter who keep botherin' Mr. Roger so bad."

A wave of dizziness threatened to topple Cornelia over. Reverend Scott had said those things to Carter's father? It was hard to imagine the elderly priest being so heartless.

Macy continued, heedless of Cornelia's distress. "Sometime Daniel go to Mariah's room—for what she call 'lessons for wooing a woman.' I didn't know what that mean back then. I watch the hall and make sure no one comin'." Macy let out a long sigh. "I think he be lonely, and he want to make you love him when he come home. He don't care what his grandpap say."

273

Had Daniel thought no one would want Cornelia and that he would rescue her from spinsterhood? He'd once been such a good and gentle boy.

Candlelight flickered in the mirrors on all four walls. "Missy Mariah 'fraid she gots a baby. That why she do what she do."

The shards from the fractured looking glass had been swept up earlier. What kind of mess had Mariah Wenham made? How many people's lives might be shattered by her behavior?

"I blame our father. Master Wenham—not Missy Mariah."

"Why?" Had he been such a harsh father that she wanted out of her house whatever it took? Cornelia knew of several other women who had done so. And their lives ruined.

The entry door banged as it slammed into the wall. Macy flinched.

"Sorry," Andy called out. "We're goin' up to look at the full moon from the top floor."

Shoes clattered as the two boys chased each other up the stairs to the second floor. Her spell of dizziness failed to subside. She didn't think she could continue this conversation with Macy. Didn't want to hear any more.

Macy took the ball of yarn from her. "I can make 'em mind. Ya need to sleep, too. Who know when Mr. Carter gonna show up again."

She wanted to awake refreshed. "Yes."

"Get to sleep early, I be watchin' the boys. Tomorry get yourself beautified before he see you." Macy's tiny smile encouraged.

"Maybe so."

Macy grabbed her bag of belongings. "I gonna put this in where I was earlier."

"Fine. Thank you." She'd sleep better knowing another adult was present.

When the boys returned downstairs, she allowed them three rounds of checkers. Her eyes fought to stay open.

Macy returned, feet bare, dressed in a cotton wrap. Her friend wrung her hands as though squeezing the last bit of water from a rag. "I's got to get them boys settled down for the night. Gonna put Cole in with me."

The last time Andy stayed the night with Eddie, Carter had to send him to another room to sleep. "That might be best."

"And Missy." Macy's chin trembled. "Don't you worry 'bout nothin'—you take care of yourself in the mornin', and Cole and I'll help with the dogs."

"I'd appreciate that. If you're up to the task."

Tears welled in Macy's eyes. "You been a good friend to me."

Compassion filled Cornelia. She hugged her. "Thank you."

Macy wiped her tears away.

"Sissy!" Andy's yell preceded him into the room.

She cringed. "What?"

"Cole's tired but I want to stay up." His nose crinkled in defiance.

"Macy is going to watch over Cole tonight."

"Aw, we were gonna sleep together and get up and tend the dogs in the mornin'."

Macy shook her head, her eyes hard. "Me and Cole gonna get up at the crack of dawn and take care of 'em. You and your sister sleepin' in."

Cornelia was too fatigued to take exception to Macy's demanding words.

"I ain't goin' to bed." Andy crossed his arms over his chest. "I'm too keyed up."

Sighing, Cornelia gestured for her brother to follow her. "You need to calm down. We'll put you upstairs tonight. I'm going to play my dulcimer for you up there where we won't bother anybody."

"Would ya, Sis?" His eyes yearned.

Coleman stretched. "I'll go wash."

"Get your nightclothes on, too." Cornelia smiled at him.

The boy headed off down the hall.

"You gots a long night ahead of you, I'm thinkin'." Macy chuckled.

And Carter, what about him? Her arms ached, wanting to hold him close. If only she had time to soak in bathwater sprinkled with rose petals from Ma's rosebush—to cleanse herself of rising fears. Would the tides of the James River carry him away—perhaps permanently this time?

Chapter Thirty-Two

Nightmares assaulted Carter with ferocity. Throughout the night, metal balls whizzed past, cannon balls flew, and sheets of lead threatened to cut off his head as they shot through the air toward him. He rose before dawn, dressed, and headed toward the barn. Mounting his horse, he hastened home. Would there be a warrant for his arrest when he arrived?

Last night interminable miles separated the homes. Now, the distance passed quickly.

Dogwood Plantation's somber roof, visible above the treeline, never appeared more inviting.

The lead roof.

Lead that would make bullets to save Americans from the invaders.

Lead that would bring money to refill their coffers.

His sails loosened, a stiff wind kicking up, ready to take him on course. He'd wed Nell posthaste.

"Where is everyone, Hicks?" Carter patted the mare before he released her to the competent man.

"Wondering myself, sir. Took the dogs out early but they've not returned."

Carter checked his pocket watch. "Perhaps the boys took them for a long walk."

"Just Macy and the new boy—Cole."

"Macy?" She'd been recuperating when he left. *Odd.*

"Yes sir, they came up to the stables before daybreak." Hicks rubbed his chin.

"Where are the others? Have you seen my nephews or Miss Gill?" Niggling worry crept in.

"Hectic day yesterday for everybody."

Carter slacked a hip to ease his painful leg. "Not surprising after the news."

Hicks shoved his hat back. "Lamps burned late at both houses. Kept an eye out because they were right agitated after Daniel Scott left."

Fear gnawed at his gut like a rat taken aboard ship while on shore. "He was here?"

Hicks wiped his hands on a rag. "Yesterday afternoon. Haven't seen him since."

Prepare.

He didn't see nor hear any horses other than those used to pull the carriages. "Hicks, are the horses stabled?"

"No sir, they're out in the field."

"Bring them in!" His voice held the urgency he'd hoped to convey. Sweat broke out on his entire body.

Scrambling toward the North Flanker, he viewed no sign that occupants stirred. Once inside, he inhaled the aroma of coffee. He entered the dining room where Nemi filled Nell's cup with the dark liquid.

"Praise God—you're home."

He closed the distance between them and resisted the impulse to pull his love into his arms. "Nell, is everyone accounted for?"

Nemi paused as she set a fragrant plate of sweet rolls mid-table before Cornelia.

His stomach growled. "Nemi, did you remain with my nephews last evening?"

"Yessir." Thick fingers plucked at her apron. "They be sleepin' when I left the house."

"Very good." He slid into the chair next to Nell, taking her hands in his. "I need to know where everyone is."

"Why?"

277

"Hicks said the dogs are gone and Macy and Cole not returned." His leg muscles burned.

"They should be back. Macy watched Cole last night—here." She wadded the napkin on her lap.

"Why?" Irritation rose within him.

"So Mariah and Hayes could have some privacy."

Kindled fear grew to low flame. "They could have slept at the Great House—with the other boys."

"Yes, but…" Nell stared at her hands as though she'd find an answer there. "Cole and Macy were supposed to walk the dogs this morning."

"Neither has before. Why today?"

"So Andy and I could sleep in." Her eyes pleaded forgiveness.

Carter rose and stroked the bristle on his cheeks. War was at their doorstep. Mariah's son and Macy missing.

"Sissy!" Andrew's voice preceded him down the hallway. "Tonnie and Lex are barkin' outside my window. And Macy and Cole ain't with 'em and they ain't in the other room."

Her face wan, Nell pushed away from the table.

Carter wrapped his arm around her. "Andy, run and see if they're with Hayes and Mariah."

The rug beneath Cornelia's feet could have been pulled out beneath her. She held onto Carter to keep her equilibrium. Nemi lingered by the sideboard, glancing surreptitiously at them.

Andy sucked his lips in and made a smacking sound. "I can't go over there."

Heat raced across her cheeks. "He's right. They're newly married—I told him not to disturb them."

"Married?" He'd catch flies if he kept his mouth open.

"Yes." A fact she'd still not absorbed.

He fisted his hands. "She'd want to know if her son is gone." He turned to Andy. "Go get her."

The boy shot past and out the door.

Carter lifted the curls from her neck and wove his fingers through them. "What did Daniel want yesterday?"

Nemi would see. Carter needed to stop. But with his lips so close— she wanted to kiss him. "Daniel spoke with Mariah. He was furious. He wanted to take Cole to Kentucky—claimed he was his son. When she said no, and told him she'd married Hayes, he stomped off."

A serving spoon clattered from the serving table to the floor. Nemi bent to retrieve it.

Her beloved leaned his head against hers. "What does this have to do with Macy?"

She should have shared her fears earlier. "Daniel may be Macy's beau." Cornelia rubbed her arms.

Carter called to the servant, "Nemi, what do you know about Macy and Daniel Scott?"

She shook her head. "Don't know nothin' 'bout Mr. Daniel. But Macy—she say she goin' away. She a foolish girl, runnin' away."

"Did she say when?"

"No, sir."

Nemi's comments splashed awareness. Cornelia's closest friend hadn't told her about the plans she'd made. Yet Macy had confided in Nemi. "Carter, did you meet with Mr. Barrett?"

"I did." Too late.

In a short while, Hayes followed Andy into the dining room where a map of Virginia and Kentucky lay atop the table. "My wife'll be here shortly. We're believin' Daniel grabbed Cole and Macy."

"And our dogs." Andy rubbed his nose. "Not all of 'em, but most."

Carter pored over the map. "Daniel's hunting knife was used to kill Jackson Forrester."

Murdered by Daniel? Bile rose in her throat. "Do you think he did it?"

"Reverend Scott told the sheriff that the knife, as well as the war club…" He pointed to the ugly staff propped in the corner. "…were stolen."

"Or did his grandfather say that to protect him?"

They had to save Macy and Cole from Daniel. "Daniel bought a lot of supplies for his return trip. I feel certain he'd have taken a wagon. Wouldn't that slow him?"

Hayes, who'd been staring dumbstruck, met her eyes. "Maybe not— depends on whether he made this plan sudden-like."

Carter grimaced then sat.

"Are you all right?" Would Daniel harm Hayes and Carter? Her stomach clenched

Sweat moistened Carter's brow. "This shall pass."

His choice of words fired an arrow of fear into her heart.

Andy waved his arm. "Looky here." He tapped on two routes crossing the river.

Tugging on his collar, Carter glanced at Hayes. "Only one could handle a fully loaded wagon."

Moving closer, Hayes cocked his head. "Dependin' on his horses and weight of his load…" He tapped his foot. "With our fastest mounts we could overtake them with a difference of half or greater. Better stop yammerin' and get movin'."

Andy slapped a hand on his forehead. "I bet Daniel took those pups when Cole and Macy brung 'em out this mornin'."

Must be why she offered to do so.

"Hicks told me he saw them before daybreak." Carter's eyebrows rose. "So they have a four hour lead on us."

Hayes stomped his feet. "Sounds right."

Cornelia did the calculation. "Then you could be gone for, what, eight hours or more?" It would be closing in on dark.

Carter met her gaze. "I'd like to send Andy to the sheriff. In case we don't return."

Before terror gripped her, she sent up her prayer, *Lord let them return unharmed.*

Her brother nodded. "You'd gain time if'n you take the old Indian paths here." He rapidly pointed out a spot on the map. "He can't get a wagon through there." Andy touched another location.

"Ho, the house!" a rider's voice carried through the open window. A horse whinnied. Andy ran outside.

Through the window, she saw Andy accept a packet from the man.

"Thank you. Go by the kitchen and get ya some tea and biscuits before you go."

Her brother behaved as though he owned the place. If she weren't so distressed, she might laugh. Andy returned and tossed two envelopes on the table. "For you, Carter."

Carter bent, retrieved a knife from his boot, and slit the missives open. He scanned the first and shoved it aside. "My father's will." Upon perusing the second, the corner of his lips tugged upward. "Macy's freedom papers."

But her friend was gone.

Carter grabbed his jacket from the back of the chair and slipped the second document inside his waist coat. He regarded her. "Cornelia, we may not make it back tonight."

Boots clacked up the stairs then ceased as someone knocked on the door. "Enter," Carter called out.

A groomsman appeared in the doorway. "Three fresh horses ready, sir."

"Andy, make sure you verify the sheriff knows our route."

"If'n he don't, I'll show him."

Cornelia sucked in a breath. "Come back and tell me if you go with him, do you hear me?"

Andy saluted her.

Carter cleared his throat. "As officer, I take exception—this man has his marching orders. No need to further encumber him."

She sighed. He was right.

Mariah arrived, slippers shushing against the wood floor. Swollen eyes downcast, she stood there, clutching her arms until Hayes swallowed her up with one of his arms wrapping around her petite frame. "Don't worry little darlin', we're gonna get our boy back."

Cornelia maneuvered around to Carter, and he pulled her close. She smelled fear in his sweat—and pain. "Can you do this?"

"I must."

She swallowed. "What do we tell the sheriff? I don't want Macy harmed but I don't want her forced back here. Cole is another matter. What if Daniel tries to harm any of you?"

"We'll take arms."

Guns.

"I'm hopin' we won't have to use weapons, darlin', but we better take 'em with us."

Cornelia cleared her throat. "Macy may have gone freely."

Fire shone in Mariah's eyes. "Unlike my son."

Cornelia exchanged glances with Carter. He squeezed her hand. They were thinking the same thing. What if the boy had chosen to go with his father?

"Please get my son back." Mariah's tears were soon wiped against Haye's shirt front as he pulled her into a bear hug.

"We'll have our boy back soon and then we'll all get situated up in Orange County. You'll see, my angel."

Had there been a more unlikely angel? But hadn't this woman helped Cornelia and Carter come together? And brought life back to her cousin? Cornelia went to her and took Mariah's hand. "We'll go pray."

"He ain't too hard to track on that main path." Hayes took a swig from his canteen. "But we're makin' good time on these old trails."

Carter wasn't worried about time as much as he was about facing the end of a rifle. On board a ship he couldn't see the faces of the men firing at him. Nor did he know them. "Daniel used to boast that he could shoot the nose off a squirrel from one hundred feet."

Hayes cackled. "Not if he don't see the squirrel he can't."

The two men rode on through the musty woods. "Do you think we made a mistake?"

"Lettin' Andy go by himself to the sheriff? I don't think so." Hayes offered his canteen. "Want some?"

Carter accepted and drank before passing it back. "Up here we ride along the river trail. It's pretty straightforward. You have to watch for low lying tree branches."

"And snakes. But Daniel's the only snake I'm worried about."

Cornelia and Mariah knelt on the soft rug beside the woman's bed and prayed. "Father God, keep them safe."

"Yes, Lord." Mariah shifted on her knees.

"Bring them home." *If that is Your will.* Might it not be God's will for Macy to live free somewhere?

"Please, God, bring my boy home." Mariah sniffed.

"Bring peace and guidance, in Jesus's name, Amen." Cornelia wrapped her arm around Mariah's shoulder.

"I finally find a good father for him and look what happens." She pulled away. "God is punishing me, isn't He?"

"No, Mariah, this is Daniel Scott making himself God. Taking things into his own hands."

"Do you think so?"

"I believe so." Cornelia hugged Mariah.

Mariah sniffed. "I used to tell people that I was Mrs. Williams. It was a lie. I was so ashamed."

"It's like Hayes told you—Jesus's blood washes all our sins away."

"You'll soon be Mrs. Williams."

If Carter didn't get himself killed by Daniel Scott. With the two men together, surely Daniel couldn't attack both.

Chapter Thirty-Three

They'd finally located the miscreant and all he'd taken with him. Carter's sweat-soaked shirt clung to his back, the cool inland air now chilling him. He shivered.

Stationed by a fresh water creek with his loaded wagon, Macy alongside him, Daniel waved his rifle at Carter and Hayes. "Stay back or you'll regret it."

Cole's head popped from the wagon covering.

Glancing at the rider adjacent him, Carter saw a tic begin near Hayes' eye.   Macy was young. And desperate.

"Did you leave of your own accord?" Carter called out to Macy. He leaned into the saddle horn as his leg cramped.

Macy's eyes darted about. "He gonna give me a chance."

Hayes and his mount moved toward the wagon. "You plannin' on marryin' her?"

"I'd have married Mariah. I'm an honorable man." Daniel's shouts flew off into the woods, finding no echo in the glen.

Honorable? Carter almost laughed.

Wind rustled through the tall pines and wafted a pleasant scent—incongruous with the wickedness taking place.

Tilting his head back, Hayes appeared unconcerned, but his hands fisted around the reins. "So you say—but you offered to marry Nelly, too."

Hot fury burned inside Carter. "You wished to have husbandly privileges before any wedding from what I saw."

Scarlet spread up Daniel's neck to his hairline. "A woman likes to know a man finds her appealing."

Carter coughed. "Is that what you call it?" His knuckles itched. He'd love to punch him off the wagon seat. *My ways are not your ways.* Shaking his shoulders, Carter sensed constraint as sure as a ship moored by chains.

Macy squirmed. "It be true—he offer to marry Missy Mariah. Long time ago. But she don't tell him 'bout no baby." Daniel looked away.

Carter urged his horse closer. He'd not let Hayes sacrifice himself if this man fired.

Daniel whirled and aimed at him. "I'm not your enemy. I just want to protect what's mine."

Chilling fear, erased by peace, swirled through him. God's palpable presence eased his turmoil.

Cole jumped from the wagon, followed by a half dozen hounds.

"Come here." Hayes motioned to Coleman, but the boy froze.

Lord, thy will shall prevail.

Daniel relaxed his grip on his gun.

"The boys weren't taking care of the dogs. They were riding ponies and frolicking. Nor Cornelia who was up working in the South Flanker, like her pa used to do. And Hayes—you didn't spend much time with them, either, chasing after Mariah like a..."

Carter heard Hayes' sharp intake of breath as the horse breeder slid his hand to his rifle.

"I want to go to my mother, sir." The boy's sweet voice touched Carter. No way would he allow Daniel Scott to remove the child from Virginia.

The Kentuckian smirked. "You got your father, boy. Your mother never took care of you anyhow. Not like I will."

Hayes's horse inched closer to Daniel. "You heard the boy, Daniel. Cole belongs with his ma and me."

Urging his horse forward, Carter's legs trembled.

"Who are you to my boy?" Daniel spat into the dirt. "Nothing."

"I married his ma, unlike you. Runnin' off with this child and young woman."

Daniel leveled the gun at Hayes, who directed his attention to Macy. "You pondered this?"

Highly doubtful. "Lower your weapon. 'Tis not right for the boy to see. And we shall do likewise."

Cole squirmed. "Mr. Davis is my new father."

The gun shook slightly in Daniel's hands. "I could keep him safer in Kentucky if the British get this far."

Carter inched forward on his mount. "You're grasping for straws and you know it."

Hayes jerked his head toward Carter. "You shoot me and Carter shoots you. I'm not afraid of dying. Carter'll take my new son home. Mariah'll have my money. They'll live just fine. And I'll be with my Lord in heaven."

Was this the Hayes he knew?

"Sir, I protest. I am no coward. If Daniel murders me, might you shoot only his firing arm? And assure me you shall care for the boys? I trust you'd foster Andy and take Nell to your home." Carter motioned, surreptitiously for Coleman to move away from the wagon.

Birds chirped and flew overhead. Smaller creatures rustled in the brush nearby as the men stared at each other. From the corner of his eye, he saw the boy move further away from the adults.

Carter unclenched his teeth. "You hurt Macy, didn't you? That was you in the cabin."

Macy's pretty, tear-streaked face was not that of a bride about to begin a life together with the man she loved. He prayed he never saw such tension in Nell's face.

Hooded eyes surveyed him. "I'd never hurt a woman. Not deliberately."

Carter grimaced in disbelief. "I want to show you something, Daniel."

"Go ahead—slow."

"I found this by the Gill cabin." Carter seized and displayed the war club, his heart hammering. He tossed it to the ground between them. If

Daniel showed the guilt he expected, Carter needed to be ready to fire. To die. Slipping his hands into place, he prayed his pained leg would hold.

Macy raised a hand to her mouth.

Daniel's nose crinkled as though he smelled something unpleasant. But he looked innocent as a new naval recruit. "Looks like my grandfather's memento from the war."

"Macy, was it Daniel who came to the cabin?"

"No!"

Carter blew out an exhalation. "So it wasn't Daniel who harmed you?"

"She just told you." Daniel looked on her with pity but didn't release his hold on the long rifle.

Carter cleared his throat. "Did you kill Jackson Forrester?"

"The attorney? Dead?" He straightened. "Of course not. You crazy?"

"Did you know your grandfather's club was stolen?"

"No. He told Chase he could have it. My brother always had his eye on my knife, too."

Carter's skin crawled with recognition.

Chase Scott.

Chase.

The visits to the Henrys. And Nell said he'd been visiting with the Sargeants and asked for a dog for Daniel. Chase had interned with Forrester. It was Chase who had recently come up to their house not Daniel. Carter sank into the saddle.

He caught Macy's watery eyes. She shook her head at him as if begging for his silence.

Daniel looked from Carter to Hayes, who had removed his hat and was gazing up through the tree bower to the sky. With a sigh, Daniel set his gun in his lap. "Hayes, you know what it's like to lose a wife. And child."

The big man raised his head, eyes damp. "Yes."

"I lost my wife and son. Then I get word from my brother, Chase, that I have another boy. He's so sure, Chase begged me to come back. I'd been out of my mind with grief. But when I saw Cole—I knew it was true."

Carter couldn't argue with that. Cole, who'd continued wandering away, greatly resembled Daniel at that age. But the boy also reminded him of Mr. Wenham, whose portrait hung outside Anne and Lee's bedroom.

"And if you look at it this way—Mariah's father told me she was dead to me. So finding out I had my boy…"

Hayes sat upright, intent.

Daniel continued, "Can you imagine if you found out your child hadn't died? Wouldn't you do the same? Especially if you found out he was thrown in a boarding school. Saw his mother only twice a year?"

If it were Carter, he'd do the same thing with one exception. "If I was in your situation, I hope I'd do what was best for everyone."

"Missy Mariah don't think you the daddy." Macy glanced at Cole, who was out of earshot.

Daniel shook his head dismissively.

"Cole, he look like our…" She crossed her arms and hung her head.

Hayes threw out a hand. "Don't say anythin', Macy, please. I know all 'bout what happened with Mariah. What would've happened to you to, if she'd not sent ya with Anne."

The metallic taste of horror filled Carter's mouth. There was an evil reason that Cole closely resembled his grandfather.

Revulsion wrote itself across Daniel's face but was quickly erased by resolve. "I say he's my son." But his features twitched in disagreement.

"Chase tell Daniel 'bout Forrester. That lawyer brag to Chase that he gonna get me for hisself. He gots papers he say Mr. Lee sign. But he don't sign 'em—Forrester do."

"Forged them?"

"Chase, he…" Macy's tears overflowed.

Daniel put an arm around her shoulder. "Don't cry. You're coming with me to Kentucky. I'll take care of you."

Carter slowly reached into his jacket. "I've got a legal release for Macy."

Her eyes lit. "My freedom?"

"Yes. You can go North. You can stay in Virginia if you wish, but I don't advise it. You don't have to go with Daniel to be free, Macy."

Daniel's knuckles whitened.

288

"I beg Daniel to take me—after Mariah tell him she won't go. I wait for him when he leave the guest house. I ask, and he say yes." She squeezed Daniel's hand. "He good to me."

Hayes wrinkled his nose. "Did he say he'd take ya if'n ya brought Cole to him? Was it like that?"

Macy's lips trembled. "Mariah never be 'round that boy 'till she lost all her money. Daniel be a good man. I know it in my heart. He just wanta help people."

Carter prayed she was right. It was her decision. She was free, as he and Nell wished.

"You let the boy come back with us and we don't send anyone after you and Macy. I have two men about to join us within the hour. If I give them the word—they'll pursue you." Daniel didn't need to know that one of the "men" was Nell's brother.

Defeat and doubt painted Daniel's features as he gazed at Coleman.

Hayes dismounted. He began speaking in low tones, smacking his lips, then whistled. All the mother dogs and pups, surrounded him. All but Lafayette. Playfully, he patted each dog and made more sounds of approval. Cole moved forward, too.

"Ya see how it is, don't ya, Daniel?" Hayes' eyebrows rose high. Lafe panted and shook but stayed by Daniel.

"I believe I do." Daniel laid his rifle across his lap and took up his reins again. He sniffed and stared at Coleman. "Son, don't ever say I didn't try to do right by you because I did. I'd claim you any day. You're a fine boy. You'll always be welcome wherever I am and I'd be proud to be your father."

He took Macy's hand in his and kissed it gently, bringing a tentative smile to her lips. "Wherever we are."

The man's voice broke, surprising Carter. Maybe there was hope for the Kentuckian after all.

My hope I give to all. Are you not a sinner saved by grace? Have not all sinned and fallen short?

Chapter Thirty-Four

It was only midday but to Cornelia a week could have passed since the men and Andy departed. She rocked with Mariah at the North Flanker, doing handiwork to keep busy. Mariah periodically escaped to her room and sobbed. She returned later, her eyes swollen and puffy. Maybe Grandmama's quilt would comfort her.

The house servant brought a basket of linens inside. A quilt corner peeked from beneath the pile. The woman trudged toward the back rooms.

"Nemi, bring me that quilt you washed for me, please." Cornelia was starting to sound rather bossy, and she didn't like it. But if Mariah didn't calm soon, she didn't know what she would do.

"Drink the rest of the chamomile tea that Mama Jo sent over." Cornelia held the teacup out but Mariah averted her gaze.

The tearful woman leaned her head back, staring up at the ceiling. "What if Daniel murdered Forrester? What's to stop him from killing Hayes?"

And Carter. Cornelia shoved the cup and saucer into Mariah's hands, the light brew sloshing over the side. "Let's pray."

Mariah clutched the tea and bent her head over it, tears dropping into the china dish.

Cornelia blinked back her own tears. "Lord, bring our loved ones home." She swallowed. "And give Daniel and...whoever You chose to go with him, safe passage home. Amen."

With one hand balancing the tea and plate, Mariah dabbed at her eyes with a napkin.

Nemi returned, her arms full of the quilt. She bunched it then searched for something. The woman knelt by Cornelia and showed her a brownish stain. "This here wouldn't wash out no matter what they did in the laundry."

"Did...was..." She bit her lower lip. "Macy?"

Dark eyes dared meet hers. "No, Missy. She tell me she havin' her monthly and that stop him from botherin' her." She fished in her apron pocket and produced a calling card.

Cornelia lifted it. *Chase Scott.* "Thank you." She displayed the card to Mariah.

Nemi didn't respond to the dismissal but rubbed the front of her apron. "That be who she sneakin' 'round with. He lie to her. I knows him and I try tellin' her but she don't listen."

Mariah sniffed. "Not Daniel. Which is a good thing."

With a shake of her shoulders, Cornelia threw off the yoke that had pulled so hard this day. Carter implied that whoever had the war club likely killed Forrester, and he suspected it was Daniel. But if it was Chase, perhaps their concerns were not as grave. Hope blossomed.

The servant took Mariah's dishes and carried them from the house, along with the basket. And some of Cornelia's load of worry.

Sweat dripped down Carter's collar. Pain, almost as severe as his initial injury, might unseat him. Ahead, the sheriff had taken Cole onto his horse, Andrew and Cole having ridden together the last hour. Hayes directed his stallion back. The animal snorted. Carter's mare, and he, needed a rest.

"Let me tell them to go on ahead. I'll ride alongside you."

"I need a respite."

"Gonna send the sheriff back with Cole and Andy, right quick. That'll ease Mariah's mind. And Nelly's. Thinkin' we better give them dogs a break."

"T'would be best." His leg injury hadn't fully healed. Had he ruined his chance of recovering its full use?

"Sissy!" Andy's shout brought tears to Cornelia's eyes. She rose from the bench and ran toward the drive.

Behind her brother rode the Charles City sheriff and Cole.

No Carter.

No Hayes.

She bit her lip. But her brother was beaming ear to ear.

"Carter and Hayes and the dogs is behind us!"

She didn't care how Andy said it—his news was good.

Later, when Andy had finally bathed and gone to bed after a visit with the boys, Cornelia sat at the table and read and re-read Roger Williams' will. If Carter married a descendant of her grandmother, he would lose his half of Dogwood Plantation. At present, Carter was owner of at least half of Dogwood Plantation. But not if he married her.

Andy's soft snuffling carried down the hallway. Cornelia awaited, pooled in candle and lamp light. Lex and Tonnie, asleep at her feet, shook and rose. The clock chimed another hour. Outside, darkened skies closed in. The hounds' nails clattered on the wood floor as the dogs scrambled to the door. Horse hooves had never sounded as beautiful as they did that moment. Nor the glorious baying outside. She rose, covering her mouth.

They were home. Chills ran up and down her arms, and she hugged herself tight as she ran out to meet them.

"Whoa, there." Hayes dismounted first.

"We put Mariah to bed," she called out. "Had to give her an herbal tonic for her nerves, earlier."

Cornelia lifted the lamp, revealing Carter's face. The bottom half, covered in two days dark growth of beard, gave him a pirate's appearance. Perspiration matted dark hair to his head. Collar open, his shirt front was soaked.

As Carter slumped over the horse, she called for Hayes. She took hold of the reins with one hand and reached for her love with the other.

Hayes rushed to them. "What's wrong?" Her cousin gently pushed her aside and pulled Carter from the mare.

The dogs encircled them. "Lex, Tonnie—behave!"

Hayes muttered something to the hounds and they clustered on the lawn then sat. "Gonna get him to the bench." He lifted Carter and carried him the few yards.

"Get my cane," Carter rasped, as he leaned back into the seat and closed his eyes. "In the hall by the post stand."

Cornelia pressed her hand to his forehead, and he covered it with his. "I'm not ill. 'Tis my leg. And it won't be better in the morning—so don't say it."

She rolled her lips together to stifle a sob. She'd make a willow bark tea with chamomile and put a generous portion of honey in it. What would make him buck up? She straightened her shoulders. "Well, I guess I can't marry you then."

He opened one eye and stared at her with a frown. "You don't say?"

"I'm an heiress now. Got a lot of land. Waterfront, too. And Mariah said she and Hayes would give me their third as a wedding gift."

With the lamp held between them, she could see the flecks of gold in his eyes as both fixed her with their gaze. Then he pressed them closed as a shudder passed through him.

She set the lamp down, wrapped an arm around him, and kissed his bristled cheek. "Carter, we're going to get you something to help your pain."

Where could he sleep? They couldn't take him upstairs to the Great House.

Hayes returned with the cane. "I'm gonna help ya get to the Guest House."

Cornelia lifted the lamp so Hayes could see she meant what she said. "He's staying in the North Flanker tonight. With Andy and me."

"All right."

Her jaw slacked. Her cousin had given her no fuss.

"Long as Carter, here..." He squeezed his arm. "Picks up a marriage license tomorry."

"I shall."

"But Carter, I read the will."

Carter stood, leaning heavily on the cane. "I know what it says." He threw an arm around Hayes' shoulder.

She shouldn't have suggested he stay with them rather than in his own room. "It wouldn't be fair to you to let this legacy go."

The two men slowly made for the north building. Wringing her hands, the loss of Carter's inheritance weighed heavy. *Thy will Lord, not mine.*

Cornelia scarce could sleep, worried about Carter and whether he was in pain. She and Hayes had cleaned him up, clothed him in an old nightshirt, and gotten the medicinal tea down him—despite his protests. Not a peep had she heard from him.

Kneeling beside her bed, she prayed. *Dear Lord, give Carter healing, as You will it. Give me rest. Thank you God, oh thank you Lord, for bringing them home safely. And be with Macy and Daniel. In Jesus's name, Amen.* Back in bed, Cornelia finally drifted off to sleep.

Barking and licking woke her from a wonderful dream—she was walking down the church aisle, Ma and Pa and Grandmama smiling and nodding approval. As she got there Hayes opened his arms to her but was pulled away by a laughing Mariah. At the altar, a man with dark straggly hair had his back to her. He turned and—

She opened her eyes. Thin rays of sun shone through the curtains. A scruffy stubble-faced man smiled down at her. Carter leaned on his cane and closed his eyes in pain. "We need to talk."

Too late for that. Any household slaves already knew he'd slept in the house. The marriage would have to take place.

"Come out to the parlor."

"You're making me nervous."

"Put a robe on." He tossed the wrap hanging from a hook.

Quickly putting it on, she went to the hall. Carter limped terribly. God had not removed his infirmity. *Not yet.*

Once he'd lowered himself to the seat, he gestured her to him and she sat. His firm hand squeezed hers gently. "How do you feel about marrying a poor man?"

Perched on the brocade settee's edge, she arranged her robe. "You ask ridiculous questions."

"Answer me."

She turned to face him, but cast her eyes downward. "Depends upon who the poor man is."

Carter stroked her jawline. She shivered.

"No land of his own, no income of his own at present."

He lowered his head and kissed her cheek, his whiskers tickling her.

His father was not going to control Carter, nor would his painful injury. If Nell accepted him, she took him as he was. Long ago, he'd accustomed himself to the notion that his father disinherited him. So be it. If she was willing, Nell would be his wife. He'd not compromise her reputation. And he'd given his word.

Her soft breath whiffled against his hair, arousing his senses.

"Nell—this man has children to raise." Moving his lips to her tender neck, he lingered there, her rosewater scent of innocence intoxicating him. "And they come with him—four boys, his nephews." She shuddered as he pressed his lips to her warm flesh again. She'd be his wife. He pulled away to take in her reaction.

"A widower?" Her voice held a tease.

"No." But craving marriage with this beauty before he burst. "Never married."

"A poor man, single, but with children to raise?" Her hands trembled as he covered them with his own and brought them together.

He'd need control his feelings. At least until they were properly married. Which would be soon. He grinned.

"Exactly."

Nell pulled her hands free and placed them on his bristled cheeks. He gazed into the sea depths of her eyes. He could sail with her forever.

"Sounds wonderful."

His home port was in sight.

"He may have a permanent injury. One God hasn't seen fit to completely remove." As if in agreement, his leg ached.

"Does he believe that God will help him overcome his infirmities and get him through whatever else comes his way?"

"He does."

"Very good, but does this man have somewhere he could house me and my brother?" Nell cocked her head.

He made an expression of mock annoyance. "I don't think Edward will kick us out."

She giggled like the girl she once was. "Especially since you're his guardian until he comes of age."

"I suppose you'd have to continue managing the plantation, too." The woman he loved would be right by his side.

Nell cocked her head at him. "I expect so."

"And after the war is over—"

"Won by America," she interrupted.

"Indeed. Once we've sent the Brits back home, this former naval officer will pursue God's plans for his legal and political career."

"I'm not sure I'd like to be a politician's wife." She frowned but her tone was playful.

"Is that so?" He shifted weight, pressing against Nell.

He wrapped her inside his arms. Her warmth, the fit of her against his chest, the scent of her roses, all anchored him firmly to this woman. He held her tight. He rubbed the back of her neck and pulled the pins free from her hair. Releasing the golden cloud, he stroked the silken mass of curls that trailed down her back.

"Would you wed a man such as I described?" he whispered in her ear and brushed his lips against her neck, certain he felt her pulse beating rapidly there.

"I would."

His kiss was the most marvelous thing that had ever happened to her. Cornelia knew she shouldn't cling to Carter but his warm lips on hers caused her to feel that she would melt into a puddle of butter and honey on the floor at any moment. She forced herself to release him at the same time as he pulled back.

Both laughed.

"I must be a politician already." He rubbed her arm, sending chills down to her hands. "To get you to accept that deal."

Tremors coursed through her like the rapids in Richmond. "I have to tell the boys."

"I'll let Andy know." His lips were only a fraction away from hers. She sensed the heat of his face, his mouth. And then he covered her lips with his again and Cornelia wrapped her arms around his neck, uncaring who might think her unladylike. She never wanted this moment to end.

Chapter Thirty-Five

"Sir, I believe this is yours." Carter offered the war club to Reverend Scott.

The elderly gentleman indicated for Carter and Nell to sit. He rubbed his chin. "I presume you're not here for advice on child-rearing? Not from someone who did his best yet still failed."

Nell's blue eyes questioned him. "Sir, we came to ask if you would perform our wedding—but I would love to hear your thoughts."

Carter knew they needed to make plans for his future and to guide him—together. "Please, Reverend Scott."

The Revolutionary war veteran accepted his club, fingering the smooth wood. "I doubt you will enjoy, but I shall tell you. I had but one son and loved him dearly." He glanced out the window, moisture glistening in his eyes. "And he died too young—before his own parents. Leaving my wife and me to raise our grandsons."

"Yes, sir." Carter wished he could say something complimentary about Chase or Daniel, but with the recent revelations, all positives fled.

"Daniel changed after Charleston—due to no fault of yours." Nell lifted a thin envelope from her reticule.

A servant carried in what smelled like strong black tea and cinnamon rolls—Carter's favorite. She set them on a table nearby and then systematically presented them to each, beginning with Reverend Scott and finally ending with Carter. The first bite was perfection. Nell cast him a scolding glance as she continued.

She rose and presented the retired priest with the letter. "Don't blame yourself. Things happen that we have no control over."

The clergyman ran a hand over his face, momentarily covering his mouth. "I always thought Daniel the most troubled—so sensitive. Destroyed really, by his parents' deaths and by what amounted to having their home and business stolen from them by their parents' advisor in Kentucky."

"But you were so good to him." Nell's tight smile encouraged.

"We tried too hard, I think. But Chase was younger—we thought too young to understand the impact. And we thought we'd simply raise him as if he were our own son—that such an attempt would overcome his losses. We were wrong."

Cornelia lifted the strong tea to her mouth, wishing she'd asked for more sugar. She feared Reverend Scott's comments would hit too close to home with her.

"So when our quiet grandson, the compliant one, wanted to study law, we encouraged him—never questioning his motives. Till it was too late."

Andy and his desire to scout, to track, and travel—had she questioned him? No. "And you wish you had?"

Carter pressed a fingertip to his chin. "I'm not sure it would have made any difference. Chase kept his thoughts close to his vest. He'd have lied to you."

"Poor Daniel—I constantly peppered him with questions about his behavior. And he'd tell me."

Cornelia sipped her tea. "Andy is a talker." But he was changing. "For now, anyway."

The retired priest shook his head. "I may not have wanted to hear that Daniel intended to gain custody of his son. To marry the mother and take her back to Kentucky with him, but I listened." He smiled wryly. "I knew it couldn't be you."

Carter raised an eyebrow to her as he consumed a huge bite of roll.

She wasn't sure how she could eat her own without making a mess but her fiancé seemed unconcerned. "Carter only recently learned that Lee believed himself to be the father of Mariah's son."

"Chase is responsible for Daniel discovering that." Reverend Scott lifted the flap of the letter. "I fear Chase decided to take God's judgment into his own hands. I believe he sought revenge for what happened with his parents. And he thought your family chased his brother off, Carter. Jealousy for what the Williams's had, and what he didn't, ate Chase up—and I didn't even know." He raised his handkerchief to his nose.

Would Chase pay for what they all suspected he had done? He was unaccounted for after the battle.

"He attended law school, cozied up to Professor Danner—until you got there, Carter. Of which he was not too happy. Intended to marry Sally."

"With him missing, sir, and possibly..." Carter pressed his lips together.

"Perhaps we should not speak ill of him, Reverend Scott." Cornelia didn't want to hear any more. Not right now. She wanted to move on with her life. "But I would like to point out that Daniel's letter..." She pointed to the missive he held. "Gives us hope."

Reverend Scott lowered his spectacles on his nose. "He gave his heart over to the Lord." He looked up, tears glistening in his eyes. Raising the letter, he smiled. "Thank you for this."

The three sat in silence, sipping their tea.

"Now, what was it you said you'd come here for?"

Despite the negative comments the priest made to Carter's father, Cornelia understood. The reverend's wife, and his mother, both suffered from bouts of extreme sadness—his mother having even been hospitalized in Williamsburg for her madness.

"I'm sorry, Miss Gill, for speaking ill of you to Roger. I feared your grandmother's odd behavior might manifest itself in you. I was wrong." He rubbed his chin. "But I cannot change what is past."

"No." Cornelia smiled at him. "But you can perform the wedding ceremony—if you are willing."

1815

"This war is finally over!" Carter raised the newsprint so Cornelia could view it from the chair across from him in the Great House parlor.

"Praise God." She inhaled the scent of the dried flowers Nemi had brought into the room earlier.

He stood and moved closer, and then kissed her on the cheek. "And we've enough funds from the roof that all of the boys shall be able to attend boarding school." His quick wink assured her that he was jesting.

Cornelia patted his face, warm beneath her hand. He leaned in to kiss her lips.

"Uncle Carter?" Lloyd rose from where he assembled blocks into castle walls. "Aunt Cornelia said she'd keep teaching us."

"True." Cornelia gestured the child toward her and gave him a quick squeeze as Carter returned to his chair, chuckling. "Go play and don't let your uncle tease you."

From his seat on the divan with Mariah, Hayes handed her a sheet of paper covered with names. One pair stood out—President and First Lady Madison.

"Hayes, can you be serious for one moment?"

Coleman rose from the floor and looked over her shoulder. "I liked meeting them. They're the best neighbors. He's nice—even if he is the president."

"They're my friends." He patted Mariah's hand. "Our friends."

Cornelia had imagined it but had never believed such an honor was possible. "I'm already nervous—"

"Just normal people like us." Hayes's lop-side grinned suggested he knew better.

About to argue, she instead clamped her lips shut.

Mariah's pointed glance silenced Hayes, too. "Carter—this rightfully belongs to you."

He returned to Cornelia's side and knelt beside the chair as Mariah offered him a tiny box. Fleeting sadness bunched his features together, but then departed.

"I don't recognize it, Hayes."

He handed it to her. "I believe this is for you."

Cornelia accepted the gift, the dark wood smooth.

"Open it." Mariah's excitement urged her on.

Inside, nestled in cotton, lay a rosegold ring, a deep purplish-blue stone set within the raised cabochon setting. Glittering diamonds trailed down each side. She'd never seen anything so beautiful. This was a fine lady's ring. She sucked in a breath.

Carter lifted it free. "'Twas my grandmother's ring." His firm hand wrapped around hers as the band slipped easily over her knuckle.

Mariah rolled her handkerchief in her hand. "Lee gave it to me when he proposed."

"I'm glad you gave it back finally, darlin'." Hayes squeezed Mariah's hand.

"I am, too, husband." Mariah gave him a peck on his cheek.

Hayes blushed. "Great-grandma Pleasant's diamond circlet will look pretty atop that glittery ring, Nelly."

Cornelia had watched her cousin polish her great-great-grandmama's gorgeous diamond band the night before. "Hayes, you should have given it to Mariah."

Mariah twisted the simple gold band on her finger.

Hayes raised his wife's hand to his lips and kissed it. "No. She wanted you to have it."

Mariah dipped her chin in agreement.

"Where has it been all these years?"

"My ma gave it to me when I married. Cried and said Great-grandma Pleasant would have been happy I'd made something of myself."

Mariah covered her unladylike snort. "Marrying a wealthy only child."

Rosy cheeks glowed above his newly grown beard. "I worked hard."

"I know you must have." His wife patted his arm. "Like you did on those invitations."

Cornelia reviewed the list. The rolls she'd consumed at lunch converted to lead and sank into her gut. "Over a hundred people? We've a simple service planned in the parlor. What were you thinking?"

"Do it up right." He chuckled. "Grandma Pleasant has finally gotten her wish."

Glancing up, she read a bit of seriousness in his hazel eyes. "Homecoming celebration."

Anne Williams's uncomfortable wedding gown stole Cornelia's focus as she perched on the edge of the guest room bed. Beneath the gown were the satin pantaloons Hayes purchased from a French privateer. She'd think about how comfortable those felt instead of how restricted the dress made her movements.

Dogs' nails clattered over the wood hallway outside her door. "Sissy, get out here," Andy called through the door, "or Hayes says he'll take the hinges off the door and carry you over."

"Coming in a minute." Mariah was to meet her in the keeping room for last minute attention. At least Cornelia hadn't had to sit for hours having her hair curled. Nemi had stuck a dozen pins in her scalp, securing her wayward curls.

Footsteps moved away from the door, but Tonnie's wheezy panting announced he'd remained behind. She sighed and went to the door. "Don't mess up my dress."

He wagged his tail and followed her to the window. She peeked through the window blind slats. Couples streamed into the Great House. All of the boys lined the south walkway. Were they guarding her? Keeping her from running away? Beneath her window, musicians gathered. She laughed then sat back on the bed.

She buried her face in her hands. Outside, violinists tuned their instruments, the noise like a screech of metal. "I'm not ready for this, Tonnie. What if I'm a terrible wife? What if I can't make Carter happy? What if—"

Tonnie yipped.

Carter stood in the doorway, key in hand. "What if your husband fails to please you? What if he can't convince his bride to attend the ceremony?" He limped toward her, a wide grin forming.

"How'd you get in?"

He held up the key. "Came through the back way." He kissed her forehead. "Come on. Let's get this bit of business over with. Shall we?"

Mopping his brow, Carter marveled that he'd convinced his quivering bride to go with Hayes and Mariah to the keeping room. He resisted the urge to rearrange the curls tickling his forehead and paused in the hallway. In the oval mirror reflected a bent, stressed man—his cravat askew. Carter straightened both his neckcloth and his spine.

Now on to the parlor. Fresh lemon oil mingled with the scent of late roses. Carter smiled, nodding at each of the many guests, as he crossed to where Reverend Scott waited. The elderly man would remain seated until the actual ceremony.

Nathan Henry and his mother chatted with James and Elisabeth Barrett. All of the furniture, save for the priest's chair, was removed or shoved against the walls.

Nemi found him, though how she did so, keeping her eyes downcast, stymied him. "Sir, the violins be ready."

"And my bride?"

"Humph."

From the archway, Hayes signaled him. Carter moved closer to Reverend Scott. "I believe we are ready, sir."

"Very good."

Nathan Henry gave Reverend Scott a hand up as violin music carried from the keeping room, now open.

The path left in the middle of the parlor widened for Nell, who reminded him of the marionettes he'd seen in France. She paused and looked down at her feet before wiggling them. What was she doing?

Andy bent and lifted his sister's skirts. He took hold of two heeled satin shoes and carried them to a side table, grinning. Carter exhaled a laugh.

Nell progressed freely now, Mariah arranging the long dress behind her.

He'd waited so long for this moment. Booming a salute, his heart rejoiced that soon his beloved would be his wife—his companion, with God, at the helm of their life together. Both of their hands shook as she placed hers inside his, her fingers cool. The blue gem ring from Carter's family gleamed on her finger.

Beside him, Hayes patted his waistcoat pocket. Then pretended to search it before winking at Carter. "Right here." He whispered loudly enough for the front two rows to have heard. President Madison and his wife laughed, the sound quickly repeating as others followed his example.

Hayes grinned at the guests.

Carter recalled what the man told him earlier. "No matter what goes wrong today, Carter, you'll still be a married man come sundown. Remember that fact and you'll be all right."

Cornelia shivered in front of the mirror, brushing her curls starting from the end. She'd hidden in the alcove of the master bedroom on the third floor of the Great House for nigh on thirty minutes now, embarrassed to come out wearing what Mariah had left for her. A bare-chested man appeared in the mirror, behind her. Carter took the brush from her hand and bent to press a kiss atop her head.

He pressed his warm hand on her bare shoulder then gently brushed each curl. When he set the brush down, Carter leaned his chest against her back. After he straightened, he placed his fingers as the base of her skull and began to massage her neck.

Heavenly.

"Your neck is like stone." He kneaded and pressed his fingers up and down her neck rubbing out knots she hadn't known were there. Her head began to loll back as she relaxed. Carter's fingers slid up through her hair, his fingers wide. She longed for him to continue.

"Have I ever told you how beautiful you are?"

She laughed. "No." Shivers ran down her arms as he stroked them slowly.

"Well, you are."

"Do you tell all your wives that?"

"No," his voice emerged as a husky moan.

Tears filled her eyes. Cornelia stood and turned to him. Carter pulled her into his arms. Safety, love, home—her husband's body pressed against hers offered those things and more. "Never leave me again."

"No, wife. I shan't." With a flurry of kisses, he convinced her, each passionate kiss leaving her more breathless.

Cornelia clung to him. Finally, he was hers and she was his. They would be one in God's sight.

Forever.

THE END

Author's Notes

Authors find inspiration for stories in many different places. Over a decade ago, I was a psychologist and attended a school meeting in Charles City County. While there, I read some of the interesting historical notes from the area such as a severe outbreak of the "flux" during the early nineteenth century which had killed many people. Around the same time, I visited Shirley Plantation, which is also the setting for my novella *Return to Shirley Plantation*. The docent on the tour talked about how one couple had died, leaving young sons, and their uncle(s) were then left to care for them. In the beautiful dining room, a sword was on display that was given in honor of a Carter family hero during the War of 1812 and nearby was an image of a dashing young man—hair styled in the Napoleonic fashion in Regency attire. Those various pieces swirled together to form the kernel of this story.

Yellow fever hit the Philadelphia area very hard about twenty years before this story. Dr. Benjamin Rush, who prominently treated Philadelphians, was a friend of the Carter family. Outbreaks of yellow fever continued on the eastern seaboard since the end of the seventeenth century, often carried by mosquitoes aboard Caribbean ships. Thirty-odd years after this story, Hampton Roads in Virginia lost thousands of people to a yellow fever outbreak. I don't get into the specifics of this illness in the story—if you want the gory details you will have to look elsewhere!

There really was a fire in 1814 that burned the Yorktown, Virginia courthouse. See the York County government's document center online for the timeline and I used this true history to give a twist to the story.

For the Colonial Quills blog, www.colonialquills.org (of which I am a founder), we feature colonial to early American history. Sadly, during research, I did come across real instances of a soldier gambling off his

307

family's property and a stranger showing up to claim the property. As a psychologist, I wondered—what would that do to someone? Could it even drive you mad if you were one of those old Virginians whose families had been prominent property owners for many generations? The grandmother in this story, and her impact, even down to my heroine's generation, was borne of that question.

Dogs, especially foxhounds who could fend off predators, were important to the farmers across the fledgling country, especially in Virginia. Gifts of highly pedigreed dogs from prominent Europeans did happen such as Lafayette's gift of a dog to George Washington. So I had my heroine's family raising later generations of these pups. Noted horse and hound journalist, Glenye Oakford, was invaluable in helping me and I suggest you read some of her wonderful work.

The lead roof at Shirley Plantation was indeed sold during the time of the War of 1812—when lead bullets were sorely needed. Shirley Plantation is still open to the public at this time and has a remarkable history. I strongly recommend visiting and learning more about this, with the most complete American plantation structures and longest-running family-owned farm in our country.

For the character Hayes Davis (and by the way, many characters are names after my ancestors' names) I placed his important horse farm by President Madison's home in Orange County, Virginia. Montpelier is a beautiful place to visit with its own remarkable history.

While I was doing my research on the War of 1812, the term "doves vs. hawks" came up quite a bit in describing the feelings of the Americans trying to make decisions about what to do about the British. These terms first became prominent during that era. We'd not adequately built up our military after the American Revolution, which was also a huge topic of debate prior to the War of 1812.

Inheritance laws for American women were more lenient than in England. Women such as Cornelia's grandmother and her mother could have property left to their daughters. Rights varied state by state, but in Virginia, a single woman could have property in her own name. For more information, "Rights Most Precious Common Law Female Property Rights from Early Modern England to Colonial Virginia" by Amber Kamp is available through Liberty University's Digital Commons Library.

If you've wondered how I understand Carter's leg injury so well, I could barely walk for about five years due to a foot problem. During that time, I had to learn many ways to accommodate my infirmity, including the use of a cane at times. Praise God, I've had much improvement after surgery and other interventions. In Carter's time, the medical treatments I received wouldn't have been available. But I believe God would have gotten him through life!

Acknowledgements

I always want to thank my Father, God, first for it is only the Lord who sustains me and my work. So many people have helped with this story. Thank you to my son, Clark Jeffrey Pagels, who was my "working buddy" as I completed edits on this novel. Much appreciation to my husband, Jeff, for his support.

Glenye Oakford, an expert in foxhounds, was a great help to me in researching hounds from this time period. The staff at Shirley Plantation in Charles City County and in particular Julian Charity, the former historian there, were extremely gracious in assisting me.

Author Kim Taylor was my erstwhile critique partner in the early version of this novel as was author Kathleen L. Maher. Critique partner, author Debbie Lynne Costello, stepped in to help with the current heavily revised version. Diana L. Flowers, Teresa S. Mathews, and Chappy Debbie Mitchell were my initial beta readers years ago when I wrote the first version of this story and Diana also returned to beta read this new version. Much thanks to my current beta readers, also, especially Tina St. Clair Rice who always goes above and beyond, and Melissa Henderson, a multi-published author, who took time out to support my writing ministry. Thank you to Kay Davis Moorhouse, Jennifer Forbes, Sherry Moe, Sally Dennis Davison, and Andrea Stephens who read the final copy of this novel and offered valuable feedback.

Much appreciation to my Pagels' Pals group members and in particular, the *Dogwood Plantation* Promo sub-group members.

Thank you to my editor, Narielle Living, for all her work and encouragement on making this novel shine.

Bio—Carrie Fancett Pagels, Ph.D.

Carrie Fancett Pagels, Ph.D., is a Christian fiction bestselling and award-winning author of over twenty books—tagline, "Hearts Overcoming Through Time". Possessed with an overactive imagination, that wasn't "cured" by twenty-five years as a psychologist, she loves bringing characters to life. Carrie enjoys American history, listening to audiobooks, walking the family's adopted Kelpie, and visiting beautiful places surrounded by water.

Carrie's novel, *My Heart Belongs on Mackinac Island*, won the Maggie Award, and was a Romantic Times Top Pick. Her romance novella, *The Steeplechase*, was a finalist in the prestigious Holt Medallion Awards. Her short story, "The Quilting Contest", was Historical Fiction Winner of Family Fiction's The Story national contest. Her novella, *The Substitute Bride* was a Maggie Award finalist. All three of her Christy Lumber Camp books were long list finalists for Family Fiction's Book of the Year and *The Fruitcake Challenge* was a Selah Award finalist.

Carrie Fancett Pagels' Books

You can find Carrie's books with links to purchase on her website at
www.carriefancettpagels.com/books

You can also sign up for her newsletter through her
Contact page on her website!

If you enjoyed this story, a review posted

is always appreciated!